TANGLED ROOTS

TANGLED ROOTS

Marcia Talley

This first world edition published 2019
in Great Britain and the USA by
SEVERN HOUSE PUBLISHERS LTD of
Eardley House, 4 Uxbridge Street, London W8 7SY.
Trade paperback edition first published
in Great Britain and the USA 2019 by
SEVERN HOUSE PUBLISHERS LTD.

British Library Cataloguing in Publication Data
A CIP catalogue record for this title is available from the British Library.

ISBN-13: 978-0-7278-8882-2 (cased)
ISBN-13: 978-1-78029-600-5 (trade paper)
ISBN-13: 978-1-4483-0217-8 (e-book)

All Severn House titles are printed on acid-free paper.

Severn House Publishers support the Forest Stewardship Council™ [FSC™],
the leading international forest certification organisation.
All our titles that are printed on FSC certified paper carry the FSC logo.

Typeset by Palimpsest Book Production Ltd.,
Falkirk, Stirlingshire, Scotland.
Printed and bound in Great Britain by
TJ International, Padstow, Cornwall.

GENEALOGY (from the Gr. *yènos*, family, and *λογos*, theory), a pedigree or list of ancestors, or the study of family history.

— *Encyclopedia Britannica*, 11th edition, Vol. 11, Cambridge, England, 1910, p. 573.

ACKNOWLEDGMENTS

My research for *Tangled Roots* began with the obvious first step: I spat into a test tube and sent it off for DNA testing. I spent the weeks before the results came in constructing my family tree on a popular genealogy website and soon, like Hannah, found myself sucked, head-first, down a rabbit hole. Now, nearly a year later, I've reconnected with a long-lost cousin (Hello, Ellen!), discovered that a first cousin in fact wasn't, learned how my great-grandmother actually died, confirmed family legend that I'm directly related to John Hart the Signer, and visited a cemetery not far from the King Arthur Flour Company in rural Vermont where generations of my family lie buried. Some of these genealogical adventures inevitably wove themselves into the fabric of this book.

Although writing is a solitary business, it often takes a family to make a novel.

I'm particularly indebted to my Native American friends who listened patiently, answered countless questions and trusted me to get it right. If I failed, it's my fault, not theirs.

Thanks to my sister, Deborah Kelchner, who helped build our family tree and whose passion for genealogy rivals my own.

A shout-out to my long-time friend, Linda Sprenkle, who knows my characters almost as well as I do. You were totally right about Georgina.

And to my friend and colleague, Sujata Massey, for sharing her neighborhood and favorite restaurants.

Kudos to James A. Earl, whose winning bid at an auction to benefit the Annapolis Opera Company earned him the right to appear as an artist in this book. Since Jim *is* an accomplished artist, no acting on his part was required.

I'm grateful to Tim Keane, winner of a character auction benefitting Lyme Elementary School in Lyme, New Hampshire, where my grandchildren go to school. In real life, Tim runs a biotech firm producing antibodies for cancer research. He's moonlighting as an attorney in this book.

For 'tough love' I appreciate my partners in crime Mary Ellen Hughes, Becky Hutchison, Debbi Mack, Sherriel Mattingly, Penny Petersen, Beth

Schmeltzer and Bonnie Settle of the Annapolis Writers' Group who read every word, sometimes more than once.

Hugs to Kate Charles and Deborah Crombie, dearest friends, confidantes and advisors, who keep me grounded. Your 'two-cents' are always worth a hundred bucks.

And, as always, to Vicky Bijur.

ONE

I t started with a phone call. Doesn't it always?

Although my cell phone was resting face down on the patio table within easy reach, vibrating noisily against the glass, I almost didn't pick up. My hands were encased in rubber gloves while I smoothed marine varnish over the sun-bleached teak of our deck chairs. I could tell by the ringtone, however, that Georgina was on the line. I knew from experience that she'd keep dialing my number until I silenced the chimes either by switching the phone into airplane mode or chucking it into the rhododendrons. So, I caved.

I dunked the paintbrush into a yogurt tub filled with paint thinner, peeled off the gloves and used a damp pinky finger to accept the call.

'Hey,' I said as I leaned over the table and stabbed the speaker button. 'What's up?'

I hadn't heard from my baby sister in two or three weeks. It's probably not nice to say, but Georgina usually called only when she wanted something. I braced myself.

'Did you ever send in that DNA test kit I gave you?'

Georgina had been dabbling in genealogy lately, exploring the Alexander family tree. How she found the time between caring for four school-age children and Scott, her high-maintenance, self-employed CPA husband, I couldn't imagine.

'Not yet. Why?'

'I don't know why I even bothered to give it to you, Hannah,' she huffed.

'I'm sorry, sis. It slipped my mind, is all. I'll get to it soon, I promise,' I said as I puzzled over where I'd put the damn packet. At a family picnic a couple of months before, Georgina had given me and our older sister, Ruth, each a test kit. At the time, she'd seemed eager – with Scott egging her on – to join the Daughters of the American Revolution which required tracing our forefathers (and mothers, Ruth had been quick to remind her!) in an unbroken line back to 1776.

'How hard can it be to spit into a tube?' Georgina sighed in exasperation. 'And postage paid?'

'Sorry,' I apologized again. 'Is it important?'

'I don't know,' my sister said, sounding cautious. 'It's just that I think they might have made some sort of mistake when they tested mine.'

'Yeah?'

'The English and Scottish roots I expected,' she continued. 'There was a smattering of Scandinavian and Iberian Peninsula that didn't surprise me, the Vikings and the Romans, you know,' she rattled on, 'but according to Gen-Tree . . .' She paused. 'Are you sitting down?'

'Don't build me a clock, Georgina. Just tell me what time it is!'

'Gen-Tree says I'm twenty-five percent Native American.'

I reached for a chair I hadn't yet painted and sat. How could my fair, green-eyed, red-headed sister, and by extension Ruth and I . . .?

The Alexanders, I knew, emigrated to Virginia from the Scottish Highlands sometime in the mid-eighteenth century, and our mother's family, the Smiths, descended from frugal, Puritan stock, going back – Grandmother Smith always claimed – to 1630 and the Winthrop Fleet. My husband, Paul, used to tease that this explained my propensity to rinse out and reuse Ziploc bags.

'That's nuts,' I said, after catching my breath. 'It's probably a mistake. Got contaminated, or your sample mixed up in the lab with somebody else's.'

'That's what Scott thought,' Georgina said.

'Call them,' I suggested. 'Ask them to re-do it.'

'I did, Hannah, and they're sending me another test kit for free, but it'll take weeks and weeks to get the results! That's why I was hoping you'd sent yours in. I mean, we should be the same, right?'

'As far as I know. Have you checked with Ruth?'

'She flat-out refused to do it. Hutch said he had serious privacy concerns about those testing companies.'

Ruth's husband was an attorney. He always agonized over the fine print.

Frankly, I thought it'd be rather cool to have Native American blood, but I didn't see how that could be possible. Twenty-five percent? I did the math.

If that were the case, one of our four grandparents would have to have been a full-blooded Indian. I'd known my grandparents on both sides – they'd lived well into their eighties. A long-ago Alexander had migrated from Virginia to southern Maryland where he married a sixteen-year-old Catholic girl related to George Calvert, the first Baron Baltimore. I'd forgotten the fellow's name, but the couple prospered, growing tobacco on a Chesapeake County farm not far away from the one now owned by my husband's sister, Connie. She raised cows down there, though, not tobacco.

Stephen and Charlotte Smith had been farmers, too, on a two-hundred-acre spread near Norwich in rural Vermont, now home to a Christmas tree farm run by one of my second cousins. A cemetery not far from the King Arthur Flour Company was chock-full of our relatives. A wedding photograph still sits on my living room mantel: Grandpa Smith, string bean tall, his sandy hair sticking out in tufts from beneath a broad-brimmed hat. Grandma, diminutive, deceptively frail, her peach-colored hair in full bloom around her face.

'Hannah? Are you still there?'

'Sorry,' I said. 'I was just trying to wrap my head around all this. Honestly, I don't recall any one of our grandparents having Native American features, but I'm not sure what I'd be looking for.'

'Maybe Mom or Dad was adopted,' Georgina cut in. 'Or maybe . . .' She paused dramatically. 'Maybe there were shenanigans.'

I laughed out loud. 'Let's wait until our tests come back, OK?'

She giggled. 'OK. Thanks for putting up with me, Hannah.'

Georgina could be a handful, that was certainly true, but it wouldn't help to agree with her. As I watched the varnish in the open paint can start to skim over, I tried to remember where I'd put the darn test kit. Under the bathroom sink?

'Hey!' Georgina was saying when I tuned in again. 'You're

much better with computers than I am, Hannah. How 'bout I
set you up as co-editor on Gen-Tree.com? You can check out
the information I've entered so far. Do a bit of poking around.'

'Sounds like fun,' I said truthfully. I'd seen the ads for Gen-Tree
on television. Click on one ancestry hint – a flapping pennant
icon – then another and another, leading back to – potentially
– Adam and Eve. It could end up being more addictive than
playing Words With Friends. 'Maybe there'll be horse thieves in
the family, or moonshiners,' I mused.

'Then again,' Georgina said, 'they could all be totally boring.
Like accountants.'

After we said goodbye, I capped the paint can, cleaned the
paintbrush with turpentine and trotted upstairs to shower. The
Gen-Tree test kit was, as I suspected, under the bathroom sink.
After I dried myself off, I put on a fresh top and a clean pair of
shorts, grabbed the kit and padded barefoot down to our basement
office. I sat down at the computer. While I waited for it to power
up, I opened up the packet and read the instructions.

Activate the fifteen-digit code. Check.

Agree that I can't sue the company for DNA results I didn't
like. OK.

Receive emails from our business partners? I don't think so.

Health reports? You bet.

I also agreed, in spite of the vagueness of the wording, to
allow my DNA to be used for projects to 'better understand the
human species'. Why not, I reasoned. It's the closest I'll probably get to doing scientific research.

When I got to the section about DNA matching, I called
Georgina back.

'When you sent in your sample, did you sign up for the DNA
matching service?' I asked.

'Gosh, no. Scott had a fit when I mentioned it. He even made
me check the box instructing them to destroy my sample after
they tested it.' She paused, then said slyly, 'But that wouldn't
prevent *you* from signing up for it.'

'Of course not,' I said as I checked the box that would allow
Gen-Tree to match me up, DNA-wise, with potential relatives
in their database, unsurprised to hear that Scott had kicked up
a fuss. My brother-in-law left claw marks on the road as his

family dragged him into the digital age. He used email in his work now, but still didn't 'do' Facebook or Twitter and had only reluctantly allowed his children to join the scary new world of social media.

Recently, a serial killer had been tracked down by matching DNA left at a crime scene to distant cousins registered in GEDcom, a public genealogy database. I hadn't murdered anyone recently, so adding my DNA to the pool didn't seem a particularly risky decision.

You were instructed to wait an hour without eating, drinking or smoking before taking the test. I figured the meatloaf sandwich I'd had for lunch was long off my breath, so I obediently spit – and spit and spit and spit – into the tube they provided. When the spit reached a black line, I screwed down a cap containing a blue liquid preservative and shook it for the required five seconds. That done, I slid the tube into a little bag, and the bag into a small, postage-paid box.

Ten minutes later, I intercepted the mailman as he strolled from house to house down Prince George Street. I traded the box for a packet of bills and advertising flyers. 'Take good care of that,' I said.

He scrutinized the mailing label. 'There's a lot of this going around.'

I grinned. 'We could compare notes. Maybe we'll turn out to be fifth cousins.'

'My wife found out she has a German half-sister,' the mailman commented as he tucked my precious cargo into a side pocket on his pouch. 'Seems Daddy was a naughty boy while stationed with the Air Force in Ramstein. It's a good thing he's already dead, or Mary's mother would have killed him.'

'I doubt there'll be any surprises,' I said with a smile. 'My family's so conventional they could have starred in a fifties sitcom sponsored by Walt Disney.'

'Well, good luck,' he said, touching the brim on his cap.

'Thanks,' I said over my shoulder as I returned to the house.

According to Gen-Tree.com, it would be at least six weeks before my test results would be ready. In the meantime, I decided to sit down, roll up my sleeves and see what I could discover by exploring their database.

TWO

I spent the remainder of the afternoon in the basement office, fleshing out the Alexander family tree started online by my sister, Georgina. I was new to genealogical research, but I immediately ran into what must be every genealogist's nightmare: a relative bearing the last name of Smith.

We had a Zebulon in the family woodpile, and a great-grandfather married to a woman named Azubah, but otherwise ordinary Johns, Marys, Sarahs and Abrahams appeared in biblical abundance throughout New England, and Mother herself was just plain Lois Mary.

As I explored the Gen-Tree database further, half the population of Vermont seemed to be Smiths, including Joseph Smith, of magic spectacles, golden tablets and Angel Moroni fame. The founder of Mormonism turned out to be, when I clicked down to it, my sixth cousin several times removed, depending on how one calculates those things.

As far as Smiths in my direct line were concerned, however, the closest Native American connection I could find happened on July 18, 1694 during King William's War. On that day, several hundred Abenaki Indians led by two French priests, massacred nearly everyone in my ancestors' village on the Oyster River near present-day Durham, New Hampshire. 'Just think,' I said to Paul, who had been hovering behind me for twenty minutes, kibitzing, insisting that I open intriguing Family Story documents and read them. 'If eight-year-old Mary hadn't scooted out the back door and hid in the woods while her family was being scalped, I wouldn't be here today.'

'Thank you, Mary,' Paul breathed close to my cheek.

Dad's family, the Alexanders, descended from sturdy, Scottish stock. Our dad was a George from a long line of Georges who were fairly easy to track through successive US censuses, not having moved around a lot during the previous three hundred years.

'If you're going to keep interrupting,' I said while typing, adding a trio of siblings to the Alexander line, 'do something useful, like massage my shoulders.'

'Have you run up your grandmother's line on your father's side?' he asked, applying gentle kneading pressure to my aching muscles.

'Not yet,' I said, leaning back gratefully and surrendering to his magic fingers. 'Right now I'm trying to clean up the mess Georgina's made. She's got one of our great-great-grandmothers married to herself and two of the poor woman's children born years before her marriage, which would probably have been a big no-no back in 1820.' I corrected the spousal connection, then clicked off through the database in search of Sam and Maud Alexander's marriage record.

Working on Gen-Tree was as addictive as playing the quarter slots at Atlantic City. I'd just be thinking of quitting and then . . . I'd click on one more pennant. And then, well, OK, maybe one more. Before long, I had followed a promising hint and found myself back in Vermont with the Smiths.

My third great-grandmother on my mother's side, Helen Smith, was one of thirteen children. Four of the poor woman's ten children perished in a typhoid epidemic in 1856 while still in their teens. 'I. Can't. Even,' I muttered, as I linked to a photo of a weather-worn tombstone for sixteen-year-old Abigail that someone had posted on FindAGrave.com.

'That's why they had big families,' Paul offered, not so helpfully.

'Some simply can't manage it,' I said, indicating an icon of a sorrowful angel. Back in 1876, baby Richard lived for six hours, and his mother died the following day.

I'd lost a baby sister, Mary Rose, to crib death, and even after all these years, the memory still stung. 'Vermont keeps terrific records,' I said, moving on quickly before I could tear up, 'but some other states, not so much.' Baby Richard's father had remarried, but I lost track of him after the 1880 census. The entire US census for 1890 had been destroyed in a fire at the Commerce Department in Washington, DC, and by the time the 1900 census rolled around the guy had disappeared.

'What are you looking for, exactly?' my husband wanted to know. 'I can't see how tracking this dead boy's father is going to get you any further along on the Native American question.'

I clicked on my own icon – my senior yearbook picture from Oberlin College, the one where I was rocking the Dorothy Hamill wedge – and displayed my immediate family tree. My parents, four grandparents and eight great-grandparents lined up in rows of tidy boxes. 'If I am one-quarter Native American, it stands to reason that it happened in this generation here,' I said, indicating the row of boxes representing my grandparents.

Although my mother had died fairly young of congestive heart disease following decades of smoking, the four grands had lived long and happy lives, until – as one death certificate had put it – 'a surfeit of years' had carried each of them away. Earlier, I had uploaded family portraits of each of them. 'Nobody looks the least bit Native American,' I pointed out.

Paul leaned closer to the screen, adjusted his reading glasses to better study the images. 'I'd have to agree.'

'I wish I could ask Mom some questions,' I told him.

'You can't assume it's on your mom's side of the tree,' Paul said. 'Could be your dad. He's still alive and kicking. Why don't you ask him if he remembers anything?'

'I plan to,' I said, 'but he's been away. When I talked to Neelie the other day, she mentioned he's off in Florida tweaking some component on a SpaceX guidance system.'

Cornelia 'Neelie' Gibbs was my father's long-time girlfriend. Why they hadn't tied the knot, I couldn't say, although I suspect it had something to do with the retirement benefits from Neelie's late husband which, I gathered, had set her up for life as long as she didn't remarry. It didn't trouble me that Daddy was 'living in sin' with Neelie, but it had been an issue for Georgina's husband, Scott Cardinale. A 'recovering Catholic', he dragged his family off every Sunday to an evangelical mega-church just outside the Baltimore beltway, where he served as Treasurer, taught Sunday School, and led a Wednesday night Bible study class. 'I called Dad's cell and left a message for him to call,' I said. 'But I didn't say exactly why.'

Paul pulled up a chair and sat down next to me. 'Meanwhile, since you don't have your test back, and just for the sake of argument, let's assume that Georgina's results are accurate.'

'OK.'

'First scenario. Your DNA is relentlessly North European and Georgina's adopted.'

'Impossible. I remember when she was born. Mom was so pregnant she couldn't fit behind the wheel of a car.'

He held up two fingers. 'Second scenario. Your dad's in the Navy, on active duty. Maybe your mom had an affair while he was deployed?'

I punched him in the arm. 'Shut your mouth! That is totally out of the question.' I thought for a moment. 'Besides, when Mom got pregnant with Georgina, we were living in San Diego. Dad had a desk job at the Naval Sea Systems Command, doing . . .' I paused to think. 'Developing something that had to do with landing planes on aircraft carriers.'

Paul shuddered. 'Those guys are gods.'

I had to agree. Anyone who could land a plane at full throttle on a moving target no larger than a football field in the middle of the ocean deserved respect.

'So, one of these,' Paul said, indicating my grandparents, 'is full-blooded Native American.'

'So it would seem.'

'Or, perhaps two of them were half Indian?'

I shot daggers. 'You can be exasperating sometimes, you know that, darling?'

'Or one-eighth and three-eighths,' he continued with a grin. 'Or, three-sixteenths and five-sixteenths, or . . .'

'That's enough for today,' I said, cutting him off before he could lob more fractions my way. I logged off the website and shut down the computer.

Paul rose from his chair and rested a hand on my shoulder. 'Maybe Georgina's test was wrong and all this is for nothing.'

'Oh, not for nothing,' I said. 'Aren't you the least bit curious to know why a Vermont death certificate lists great-great-great-grandmother Smith's death at age eighty-three as "suicide by hanging"?'

'The one with thirteen kids?'

'Ten,' I corrected.

'I rest my case.'

'Go away,' I said. 'Isn't it your turn to cook dinner?'

For our thirty-fifth wedding anniversary, our daughter Emily had given us a three-month subscription to a popular meal delivery service. Turns out, Paul enjoyed the service more than expected, throwing himself into meal preparation like, well, a mathematician. His small dice of green peppers – precisely six by six by six millimeters – had to be independently verified using a specially-marked cutting board he'd bought for himself from a company called Obsessive Chef.

It was agonizing to watch.

'Besides,' I said, 'how else would I know that I'm related to Lovey Bean, whose descendent, Leon Leonwood Bean, founded L.L. Bean?'

'Think that will get you a free pair of duck boots?'

I put a hand flat on his back and shoved him out the door ahead of me. 'A gal can dream.'

THREE

Not long after Paul and I had crawled into bed, Dad returned my phone call. 'Did I wake you up?' he asked to my groggy hello.

'No, no,' I said while squinting at the bedside clock. 10:42. I propped myself up on one elbow. 'I had to get up anyway. The phone was ringing.'

Dad chuckled, deep and gravelly. 'Sorry to be calling so late, but I was out to dinner with some of the team.'

I heard ice clink against glass – my father's nightly tonic and lime ritual. 'Papa Vito's,' he said, adding in his best Valley Girl accent, 'the cheese bread is to die for. I may never have to eat again.'

'Where *are* you, exactly?' I asked.

'If I told you, sweetheart, I'd have to kill you.'

'Seriously, Dad!' I really wasn't in the mood for jokes.

'Florida.' The ice clinked again.

'Neelie said it had something to do with SpaceX,' I said.

'Tangentially,' he said. 'What goes up must come down, at least that's the idea. Sideways spoils everyone's day.'

'When do you get back?'

'Back' would be to the two-bedroom condo he shared with Cornelia Gibbs at Calvert Colony, an upscale retirement community that sprawled grandly along the banks of the Chesapeake Bay just outside of Annapolis. It was adjacent to Paradiso, the day spa owned by our daughter, Emily, and her husband, Daniel Shemansky, or Dante as he preferred to be called. Just plain Dante, like Elvis, Madonna or Cher. The spa had been a dream of my son-in-law ever since he dropped out of Haverford College a year before graduation and eloped with our daughter. Somewhere I had a photo of the happy couple posing in front of a wedding chapel in Las Vegas. Not an auspicious start to a life-long relationship that now included three adorable children.

'Next week,' Daddy was saying. 'Neelie's signed us up for a Road Scholar trip to Cuba. Thirteen days of birdwatching.'

'I didn't know you were interested in birds.'

'I'm not, but Neelie's passionate about her feathered friends. According to the brochure, there are twenty-five avian species unique to Cuba. She hopes to add some of them to her life list.'

Tramping around all day in hot, humid, tropical rainforests didn't appeal to me one bit, and I said so. 'I'd rather hang out with artists and musicians in Havana.'

'What? And miss the opportunity to spot a rare Gundlach's hawk?'

'Tragic,' I said.

Next to me, Paul stirred, opened an eye and said, 'What's going on?'

I flapped a hand at him and whispered, 'Sorry. Just talking to Dad. Go back to sleep.'

After another sip of his drink, Dad said, 'It's wonderful to hear your voice, Hannah, but I got the impression from your message that there was something on your mind.'

I scooted up in bed and rearranged the pillow between my back and the headboard. 'I wanted to give you a heads-up on something. And also pick your brain.'

'Sounds ominous. Do I need to add some gin to my tonic?'

This was a joke, and I knew it. Dad was a recovered alcoholic. He'd earned his ten-year medallion from Alcoholics Anonymous and was proud of his hard-won sobriety. And so were we.

'You know those DNA test kits Georgina handed out a while back?' I asked.

'If you're calling to nag me about sending it in . . .'

'No, it's not that,' I said, gathering my nerve, stalling for time, 'but, uh, did you?'

'Did I what? Take the test?'

'Yeah.'

'Forgot all about it, sweetheart.'

That didn't surprise me. He'd accepted the test kit from Georgina reluctantly. She'd flounced off in a snit after he referred to the commercial testing company she'd chosen as 'recreational DNA'. He'd made no secret of his disdain for the industry either, lumping it together with pseudosciences like aromatherapy and homeopathy. I thought he was overreacting.

I forged on. 'You know the fine print, where they warn you to be prepared for identity-disrupting surprises?'

'Uh huh,' he said cautiously. 'Cut to the chase, Hannah.'

'Georgina's test just came back. According to Gen-Tree DNA, she's one-quarter Native American.'

A long, low whistle came down the line, then silence.

'That means that either you or Mom—'

He cut me off. 'I know what it means. And it's nonsense.'

I explained that Georgina had demanded a re-do from the company and was still waiting for results. I told him I'd sent my test kit in, too.

'So the jury's still out,' he said.

'Yes, but . . .'

'But, what?'

'I've done a good bit of reading since Georgina called with the news, and Gen-Tree's quality control is convincingly solid. Because each company uses a different database, results may vary from one DNA company to another, even between identical twins, but specimen contamination and out-and-out mix-ups are rare.' I paused to take a breath. 'I'm proceeding on the assumption that Georgina's test results are accurate.'

Daddy let the remark pass. 'Did the test identify a specific tribe of Native Americans?'

'The science is confusing, Dad, at least to me. Apparently they can link you to one of five broad mitochondrial DNA haplogroups but they're unable to pinpoint a particular tribe or even a particular combination of tribes,' I told him. 'The database is too small. I read while I was poking around that forty-four percent of Native Americans belong to haplogroup A.'

'What was Georgina's haplogroup, do you know?'

I confessed that I didn't. 'I'm waiting to see how my test results turn out before digging any deeper. I don't intend to become the world's foremost authority on Native American mitochondrial haplogroups unless I have to.'

'When will you know?' Dad asked.

'I waved goodbye to my saliva this morning,' I said, 'so five or six weeks. I hope the suspense doesn't kill me.'

After a moment, Dad said quietly, 'Hannah?'

'What?'

'I don't want you to lose any sleep over this. It doesn't change who I am or who your mother was.'

I puffed air into the phone. 'I know that!'

'There's nothing you can do to change the past,' he added gently.

'I know that, too,' I said, but there was something in his voice – was it a hint of apology? – that made me think Dad knew more about our family tree than he was admitting.

After we said goodbye, I lay flat on my back staring at the ceiling, listening to Paul's gentle snoring. Shadowy leaves hopscotched over the striped wallpaper, cast by a full moon shining through the branches of a tulip poplar just outside our bedroom windows.

I closed my eyes, slowed my breathing and concentrated on repeating the mantra I'd been given – *hirim, hirim, hirim* – but my thoughts kept drifting.

DNA. Fractions.

All along, I'd been focusing on one of my grandparents. But as Paul had pointed out before dinner, there were other mathematical possibilities. Despite everything I believed I knew about her, had my mother been unfaithful?

FOUR

'In the nucleus of every cell,' I read aloud to Coco, 'there are twenty-three pairs of chromosomes. Twenty-two of these matched pairs are called autosomes, while the twenty-third pair – either X or Y – determines your sex.'

My daughter's chocolate-colored Labradoodle cocked a shaggy brow and considered this information with eyes of liquid gold. Her tongue lolled as if to say, 'And dogs have *thirty-nine* pairs of chromosomes, did you know that, Hannah? Neener, neener, neener!'

'Smarty pants.' I patted the dog's head and continued reading.

Autosomal DNA is inherited equally from both parents – I remembered that from college biology – and includes contributions from previous generations in ever lessening fractional degrees: your grandparents, great-grandparents, great-great-grandparents and so on. It's a genetic snapshot of what makes you uniquely you. By comparing the bits we have in common with our mutual predecessors, Gen-Tree's DNA test can match us up with relatives, both known and unknown.

The frustrating part at this early stage of the process was the realization that the test couldn't pinpoint exactly where on Georgina's family tree that the Native American match occurred. No wonder she had encouraged everyone in the family to get tested; it would help narrow down the field.

But Mom was no longer with us, Dad seemed reluctant and Ruth openly hostile, having told Georgina to ask her again when someone developed a test that could tell who you were in a previous life. It seemed to me that good, old-fashioned research might be the way to go.

I'd spent a significant portion of my professional life commuting from Annapolis to Washington, DC, getting my ticket punched along the way until I made it to the top – a high-paying job at Whitworth and Sullivan as head of archives and records. All was going well until a quality management team somewhere on the tenth floor began throwing darts at the accounting firm's organizational chart and twenty-five percent of middle-level management, including yours truly, found ourselves tossed out on K Street, dazed and blinking, clutching our dress-for-success briefcases.

Frankly, I had mixed feelings about being RIFd. I'd been recovering nicely from a mastectomy and chemo-from-hell, thinking that there was nothing like a cancer diagnosis to give me the permission I needed to ditch the punishing long-distance commute and seek part-time work closer to home. With the decision out of my hands, I registered with a local agency and worked on and off as a temp in libraries, insurance agencies and even for Spa Paradiso when I could spare the time. Paul was a tenured professor, so we didn't really need the money, but no sense allowing my brain to grow rusty.

Fast forward. Me, sitting in our basement office, refreshing my research skills by reviewing census records for 1920 and 1930 that placed my grandparents firmly in Vermont and southern Maryland, respectively. Although Indian tribes inhabited both states during English colonization, they had either been forced onto reservations further west or been assimilated into local populations by the time my grandparents were born.

Genealogical research should come with a warning. I linked to a photograph of my grandfather Smith's tombstone in Tunbridge Village Cemetery in Vermont. It was like getting sucked, head first, down a rabbit hole into a parallel universe entirely populated with dead people.

For several days, I worked on expanding our tree, adding supporting documents – birth and death certificates, city directory listings, high school and college yearbook photos – until the tree looked fleshed out and attractive when displayed on the screen, but I was no closer to an answer. Eventually, when Gen-Tree ran out of hints and I'd exhausted the search engines of the historic newspaper databases, I had a brainstorm and decided to call my father again.

'What happened to the storage boxes that were in the attic when you and Mom lived in Providence?' I asked, naming the upscale community on the Severn River where my parents had lived before Mom's final illness. I hadn't thought about those gray Tupperware tubs in years. The last time I'd pawed through one of them I was looking for *Tiger Tales*, my high school yearbook, when I volunteered for the reunion committee. Mother had saved everything – ancient report cards for my sisters and me, school pictures, immunization records, juvenile artwork and essays. There were boxes containing nothing but loose photographs, I recalled, and at least two dozen fully-loaded Carousel slide trays.

'Aren't you putting the cart before the horse?' Dad wondered.

'Maybe,' I admitted, 'but it occurred to me that somebody ought to sort through all that stuff. Organize it. And who better than I?'

Daddy laughed. 'You planning to digitize it, Hannah?'

'Maybe,' I said. I'd actually given some thought to digitization of the family archives, but in my saner moments, worried I'd be exchanging one obsolete form of technology for another. I had a five-and-a-half-inch floppy disk reader somewhere in the basement, for example. One never knew when you'd need to find that letter you wrote back in 1982 that was pure genius, although the *New York Times* foolishly failed to print it.

'Remember our family trip to the Outer Banks?' Dad asked.

'How could I forget?' I said, wondering why he'd segued in that direction. Our first day at the condo, ten-year-old Georgina had scattered complimentary peanuts from American Airlines on the deck and we'd spent days fighting off scavenging seagulls.

'How many pictures of seagulls does one need?' Dad asked.

I laughed. 'Point well taken. Someone needs to do a proper culling. I'm not sure I'm up to wading through boxes of gap-toothed photos of myself with untamed curls and ineffectual hair bows.'

'Times three,' he said, meaning Ruth, Georgina and me. After a moment, he added, 'When we moved, I put most of what didn't sell at the garage sale in a self-storage facility on Route 2, near the South River, along with the big chest freezer and your grandmother Smith's bedroom furniture. Pop-pop's roll top desk is down there too,' he added. 'There's a complete inventory back at the condo if that will help.'

'Since I don't know exactly what I'm looking for, *anything* might help,' I said.

Since my father hoped to wrap up his business in a couple of days, I agreed to wait until he returned to Annapolis and could lay hands on the inventory, rather than send Neelie off on a wild goose chase through Daddy's records. Besides, I might be hearing back from Gen-Tree any day. If Georgina's results turned out to be a fluke, I'd have spent days spinning my wheels for nothing.

Except a perfectly gorgeous online family tree.

FIVE

our weeks later, my feet were soaking in warm, sudsy water at Spa Paradiso while Wally Jessop worked wonders on my nails. I'd just set the chair's remote to gentle massage and melted into the buttery leather when my cell phone dinged.

Wally's emery board paused its see-sawing motion. If he'd had any eyebrows, he would have raised them. 'You need to get that?'

Even if my phone hadn't been stuffed in the handbag hanging from a decorative wall peg more than six feet away, I knew Wally too well to bother. 'It's only an email,' I told Wally. 'It can wait.' I waggled my fingers. 'Besides, it would be criminal to ruin my manicure.'

'You got that right.' Eyebrowless Wally of the gleaming scalp and multiple piercings flashed a smile that let me know I'd made a wise decision. One of Dante's original hires, Wally was a card-carrying perfectionist. It was rumored he used a thermometer to make sure the water in the pedi-spa was maintained at a perfect 143 degrees. I had no reason to doubt it.

'What color?' he asked a few minutes later. His voice seemed to drift in from a long way off.

'Hmmm?' I managed.

'What color rings your chimes today?'

Earlier that morning I'd had one of Garnelle's famous, deep-tissue massages and I still felt like a boneless chicken. Before sitting down for my mani-pedi, I'd half-heartedly selected two bottles of polish – My Solar Clock is Ticking, an in-your-face red, and a rosy pink shade called Aurora Berry-alis – but I still couldn't make up my mind. 'Surprise me, Wally.'

So he did.

Turn On the Northern Lights is a deep, dark purple. After I'd lived with it for a while, Wally assured me, I'd adore it as much as he did.

I'd arranged to meet my daughter for lunch in the spa cafe. Emily was late, as usual, so I ordered iced tea with extra lemon for both of us and decided to kill time by checking my email.

As I expected, there was a lot to delete. Junk mail from political candidates I'd never vote for in a million years. Invitations from sexy Asian women simply dying for a date. A notice that our Volvo was due for its sixty-thousand-mile check-up. My purple-nailed index finger was swiping messages into oblivion so quickly that I nearly missed it: a notice from Gen-Tree.com that my DNA test results were ready.

I pressed the iPhone to my chest, closed my eyes and tried to steady my breathing.

Emily found me like that. She pulled out a chair but stopped short of sitting down in it. 'Mom? Are you all right?'

I lay the phone down on the marble-topped table, carefully avoiding a puddle caused by an errant ice cube. 'Of course,' I assured her, stalling for time. I had no idea with whom Georgina had shared information about her initial test results, but until the results were confirmed, I had seen no reason to discuss them with anyone other than Paul and my father.

Emily sat down, looking relieved. 'Order the fish taco,' she advised. 'It's today's special, and François is a genius with the *baja* sauce.' She flipped her single blond plait over her shoulder and squinted across the table at me. 'There's something on your mind, I can tell.'

I took a deep breath and let it out slowly. 'I had my DNA tested at Gen-Tree.com, and the results are in.'

Emily flashed a grin. 'Quick! Somebody call *The Washington Post*!'

Our eyes locked. I scowled. Emily's grin vanished.

'I don't want to be alone when I open up the results,' I said at last.

Her eyebrows disappeared under a fringe of professionally trimmed bangs. 'Why? You can't be worried about skeletons in the family closet . . .' She paused and frowned. 'Can you?' She leaned across the table and lowered her voice. 'Honestly, Mom, nobody gives a shit about that sort of thing these days.'

I was saved from providing an answer by Chef François, who materialized at our table dressed in full chef regalia. He'd come a long way since Haverford College days where the name on his transcript read Frank Lesperance. François dipped his head in deference to Emily, then turned to me. 'Welcome, Mrs Ives. It's been a while since we've seen you.'

'I'd show up every day, if I could,' I told him truthfully. 'Honestly, I don't know where the summer's gone. You commission the Firsties in May and ship them off into the Fleet, and before you know it, here comes July and the Plebes are being sworn in. Paul and I haven't even had time to squeeze in a mini-vacation.'

'You need a Spa-cation,' he suggested, 'and what better place . . .?'

'I'm working on it,' I said, displaying my freshly manicured nails, 'but Paul has an aversion to hot tubs. Just had a massage, though. Garnelle's hands should be insured by Lloyds of London.'

We chatted a bit about his family – a pregnant wife and young son – and after he left with our order for fish tacos, Emily said, looking serious, 'You're not worried about the test turning up some weird genetic disease, are you?'

This made me laugh. 'No, no, not that. I didn't pay extra for that sort of test.'

'Well, that's a relief.' Emily opened a pink packet of sweetener and stirred it into her iced tea. After she'd taken a sip, I explained about Georgina's earlier test results.

'Wow, just wow!' Emily flopped back in her chair, almost as if I'd punched her. 'That would mean . . .'

'Exactly.'

'So you've taken the test, too.'

I tapped my iPhone. 'And the results are in.'

Emily waved our server over. 'Will you bring our lunch to my office, please?' She stood, picked up her glass of tea and indicated that I should do the same. 'Follow me, Mom.'

A few minutes later, I was seated at my daughter's desk in an ergonomically-correct chair, my feet planted firmly on an ergonomically-correct adjustable foot rest, powering up her environmentally-friendly, twenty-seven-inch iMac. After the Gen-Tree website appeared, I logged on and clicked the pull-down DNA menu, waiting impatiently for the 5K retina screen to refresh.

A world map appeared, centered on the Atlantic Ocean. Colorful blobs indicated the geographic origins of my ancestors.

And there it was.

56% England and Wales.
25% Native American.
15% Ireland.
4% Norway.

I didn't realize I'd been holding my breath until I let it out. 'Well, that's it, then.'

Emily laid a hand on my shoulder. 'Freaking awesome!'

'I'd say so.'

'That means I'm one-eighth Native American.'

'Presumably.'

'And the kids . . .'

'One-sixteenth.'

'What side did it come from, Mom?' Emily asked, her blue eyes wide. 'Your mom's or your dad's?'

'I don't know,' I told her, 'and neither does my father. I've been building our family tree on the Gen-Tree website, but I'm no closer to an answer than I was when Georgina first told me about it.'

'Wait till I tell Dante,' Emily hooted. 'He'll be totally psyched.'

'And I'd better telephone Georgina,' I said.

My call to Georgina was unexpectedly short.

'Shit,' she spat when she learned of my results. Hers had not yet come in.

'What's the big deal?' I asked.

'They warn you,' she said, 'right on the damn website. But did I listen? Nooooh!'

'What are you talking about, Georgina?'

'They said the test might contradict prior assumptions and lead to distress.' She paused, then yelled into the phone so loudly I had to pull the device away from my ear. 'Well, I'm distressed! Dammit!'

'But, Georgina, you just said you knew it was a possibility when you sent in your first sample, when you gave them permission to analyze it.'

'I can't deal with this right now, Hannah.'

'OK,' I said, 'but when *would* be a good time to talk about it?'

'I'll let you know.'

And the connection went dead.

I stuck my tongue out at the screen. Georgina was treating me like a telephone solicitor for an Ocean City timeshare, and I didn't appreciate it.

Feeling thoroughly put out, I called and left a message for my father, then went home to wait for Paul.

SIX

Around nine o'clock that evening, Dad returned my call. They'd had unexpected delays on his top-secret project, so he was still being held captive in Florida.

I waded right in. 'I'm twenty-five percent Native American,' I told him. 'No doubt about it at all.'

'Well, that's settled then,' he said.

'I don't think it settles anything at all,' I whined. 'I'm dying to figure out where the DNA came from.'

'I can solve part of the mystery,' my father said. 'After we talked, I drove out to Sam's Club and bought a test kit from

23 and Me. I'd planned to call you tonight anyway, because my results are in.' He paused so long I could hear him breathing.

'Don't you *dare* keep me in suspense,' I said. 'You're as maddening as one of those makeover shows on HGTV. "We've decided to . . ." then they cut to the ads before saying whether they'll Love It or List It.'

'It has to be on your mother's side,' he said, taking pity. 'I'm English, Welsh and Irish, with a bit of Norwegian thrown in. Nothing unexpected.'

I let the significance of his results sink in. One massive branch of the family tree – the Alexanders – had instantly been eliminated from the DNA equation.

'That's cut my work in half,' I said with relief. 'Now I'll just have to explore further up the Smith family tree.'

'Why?' he asked.

'Why?' Daddy's question had me stumped.

'What difference can something that happened almost a century ago make to you or to us now?'

'Don't you want to know?' I asked, hardly believing what I was hearing. My dad was a scientist, an engineer. He dealt with facts.

'Not particularly.'

'How could it hurt?' I reasoned. 'Everyone directly involved is already dead.'

On the other end of the line, I could hear his television tuned to the *Rachel Maddow Show*. It was a while before my father spoke again. 'Be careful what you wish for, Hannah. You might just get it. Old Chinese proverb.'

'Ha!' I scoffed in a good-natured way. 'Sounds more like the inside of a fortune cookie.'

'Georgina can be fragile,' Dad said. 'Be careful with her.'

'Kid gloves,' I said. 'I won't cause any trouble.'

One day, I'll learn to keep my big mouth shut.

SEVEN

was on my hands and knees weeding the herb garden when my back pocket trembled. I stripped off my gloves, wiped my sweaty hands on my jeans and checked the phone.

U home?

It was a text from Julie, my niece, Georgina's seventeen-going on eighteen-year-old daughter.

Sup? I texted back.

Can U come up?

'Up' would be Baltimore's Roland Park neighborhood, to Scott and Georgina Cardinale's lovingly restored Craftsman near the end of Colorado Avenue.

Ask your mom?

Just U & me.

??

I'm grounded for life.

I located the Edvard Munch 'scream' emoji and hit send.

Sucks, she replied.

So I show up, casual like?

I wasn't sure what was on my niece's mind, but I was a good listener. When she was fourteen, Julie had been drugged and assaulted on a cruise ship. Her parents had been overprotective ever since; Scott was particularly inflexible. I didn't know what crime had merited a life-long grounding but it wouldn't be the first time Scott had made a federal case out of a parking ticket.

Besides – if she didn't cut me dead – it would be an opportunity to discuss our DNA test results with Georgina. Dad had telephoned her about it, too, I knew, but I hadn't talked with my sister since.

However, our older sister Ruth had embraced her new-found heritage. Being part Native American had flipped her 'no way' to a 'hell, yes' now that *her* actual DNA wasn't drifting around the Webosphere. She'd beamed like a celestial body when I told her about it at lunch over Irish tomato-whiskey soup and crab cakes at Galway Bay. Ruth owned Mother Earth, a funky shop on Main Street in downtown Annapolis where she sold a variety of New Age gizmos. After we hugged goodbye on the sidewalk outside the popular restaurant, she probably rushed straight back to Mother Earth, where I pictured her combing through catalogs looking for kachina dolls, orca spirit boxes and beaded mandalas to add to the dreamcatchers already in her inventory.

The day I decided to drive to Baltimore, the traffic was mercifully light. I merged off 295 onto the MLK expressway and zipped around Camden Yards in record time. Fifteen minutes later, I turned the Volvo around in the cul-de-sac at the bottom of Colorado Avenue and found a parking spot not far from the Cardinales' home, heading uphill.

Georgina stood in her front yard, attached to a pair of ear buds, attacking the hawthorn hedge with clippers of medieval proportions. Her long hair – gleaming in the sun like buttered sweet potatoes – was twisted into a knot high on her head and secured with a turquoise claw. If the ragged results of her hedge trimming efforts were any indication, Georgina's work was less a matter of hedge containment and more an act of anger management.

I stood on the sidewalk and watched the clippings fly, waiting for her to notice me.

Two minutes later, she did. She dropped the clippers, yanked out the ear buds and frowned.

'Sorry,' I said. 'Did I catch you at a bad time? If it were me, I'd welcome any interruption from trimming the hedge.'

'No, you surprised me, is all. Why didn't you tell me you were coming?'

'I'm meeting a friend for lunch at Jimmy's,' I lied. 'It's restaurant week and they're offering a twenty-dollar prix-fixe special.' I shrugged. 'So, thought I'd pop in for a minute.'

'Oh,' she said, wiping sweat off her brow with the back of her hand, looking worried.

'You OK?' I asked.

'Of course I am, Hannah. What would make you think I wasn't?'

'It's just that when I called the other day, you hung up on me.'

'I can't talk about it,' Georgina said, cutting me off again.

She glanced around the yard, almost as if she was afraid of being overheard. There was nobody within earshot, at least as far as I could see, but she lowered her voice anyway. 'Scott wants me to forget the whole thing.'

This surprised me. 'Wasn't Scott the one who insisted you send the test in to begin with? To verify your Revolutionary roots?'

Georgina flushed. I didn't think it had anything to do with the August heat. 'It accomplished that all right,' she said. 'I'm cross-matched straight back to old Enoch somebody-or-other who was a Minuteman at Lexington and Concord. Scott's already filled out the paperwork for the DAR and sent it in.'

'Then what's the big deal, Georgina?'

'Scott won't admit it, but I think he's worried about his stupid men's club. They have a couple of Jewish members, I know, but if you're black, brown, yellow or red, forget about applying.'

I knew about the Cosmopolitan Forum, a league of local businessmen so far to the right on the political spectrum that they made the Tea Party look like flaming liberals. The smear ads the forum had sponsored during the previous presidential campaign made me cringe. As a result of this affiliation, family visits could turn ugly in an instant, so I tended to avoid my brother-in-law whenever possible. I hadn't seen him since last Easter dinner where . . . well, rifts in the family might be more easily repaired than my vintage Imari earthenware platter. More than once, I wondered why my sister stayed with the pompous jerk, particularly now that the children were older. There had to be more to a marriage than financial security and, as Georgina had once confided, fantastic sex.

Tears glistened in my sister's eyes.

'Talk to me, Georgina,' I urged.

She drew a deep, shuddering breath. 'He yelled at me, Hannah. He called me a squaw!' She spread her arms wide. 'Honestly, do I look like an Indian to you? *Do* I?'

It's a good thing Scott was nowhere in the vicinity or I would have slapped him six ways into Sunday. What century did he think we were living in? Georgina began to sob.

I gathered my sister into a hug, stroking her back, soothing her like a child. A half-dozen anti-Scott remarks perched on the tip of my tongue, but I knew from past experience that if

I let fly, Georgina would bristle and begin making excuses for her husband, so I held back.

She didn't disappoint. 'A lot of Scott's business is driven by social contacts,' she whimpered into my shoulder. 'He can't afford to lose clients because of me.'

I took Georgina by the shoulders and held her at arm's length. 'Have you looked at yourself in a mirror lately?'

'That's my point, Hannah! I don't look like an Indian, so why would I want to *be* an Indian?'

I could think of several reasons, although I hadn't dug into the matter too deeply. Tribal membership might mean a share in casino profits, oil and gas revenues, free health care, college scholarships. As far as tribal membership was concerned, the more Indian blood you have the better, but you'd have to be descended from a federally recognized tribe and be able to prove it. Short of divorce, it seemed certain Georgina had no interest in pursuing the tribal membership route, so I let the subject drop.

'Is Julie here?' I asked. 'How about Colin and the twins?' I quickly added Julie's siblings to cover for my niece. 'I haven't seen them in ages.'

Using the hem of her T-shirt, Georgina dried her cheeks. 'Sean and Dylan are at swim club today, keeping an eye on Colin. Julie's around somewhere.' She managed a smile. 'In the meantime, I'd kill for a glass of iced tea. I just brewed a fresh pitcher. Interested?'

I smiled back. 'With extra lemon?'

She nodded.

'Sold.'

EIGHT

Georgina and I were perched on stools at her kitchen island discussing their vacation plans – a week at Bethany Beach, Delaware at the end of the month – when Julie breezed in. 'Aunt Hannah! Gosh, what a surprise!'

I sent Julie a glance that said: *Chill. Don't overplay your hand, missy.*

Julie opened the fridge, eased a Coke out of the door dispenser and popped the top. She made a beeline for a vacant stool, sipping noisily along the way.

'I'm meeting a friend for lunch,' I told her. 'Just popped in.'

'Uh huh,' Julie said, feigning boredom. 'How long can you stay?'

I checked the wall clock, a Route 66 gas pump reproduction that echoed Georgina's retro 1920s décor. If I manufactured a late lunch, I'd have a better chance of getting Julie alone. 'We're meeting at one,' I said.

Georgina refreshed our tea from a frosty, ice-filled pitcher, then went on to brag about how the twins would be starting grad school at Johns Hopkins in the fall. 'The acceptance rate is only ten percent,' she boasted. 'Even with three point eight GPAs, it was by no means a sure thing.' She leaned sideways and lowered her voice, as if sharing a confidence. 'And they won $10,000 scholarships. Each!'

'Big deal,' Julie snorted. 'It still costs the earth. I hope food stamps are still around when we need them.'

Georgina's glare would have stopped a charging rhino in its tracks. 'Don't you have something you're supposed to be doing, young lady?'

Julie slid off her stool, Coke in hand. 'I'm supposed to be memorizing the Maryland driver's manual. It's pretty lame.'

'Are you taking drivers ed this summer?' I asked.

'Nah. Took it at school last year, but you have to get in sixty practice hours. Dad's been my coach.'

I'd rather learn to drive from Jabba the Hutt, but thinking about Julie's need to clock in some practice hours gave me an idea. 'Would you like to take me for a drive, Julie?'

Julie beamed, bouncing on her toes. 'I'd *love* to! Mom? It's OK, isn't it?'

'I don't know . . .' Georgina began.

'Please?' Julie was channeling *Les Miz* starving orphan full-on.

'I'm sure Hannah has better things to do, Julie.'

'No, I'd like that.' I smiled and turned to my niece. 'I'm not taking my life in my hands, am I?'

Julie giggled. 'I've had *almost* sixty hours of driving experience, Aunt Hannah. You can check out my practice log if you
don't believe me. Dad says I might be able to take the driving
test next week.'

'Julie is . . .' Georgina began, then paused. I suspected she
had started to mention something about Julie's restriction, but
thought better of airing the family's dirty linen. Instead, she
flapped a hand. 'It's fine, Julie. Just don't make your aunt late
for her lunch.'

We agreed to take my Volvo. As I settled into the passenger
seat and strapped in, Julie took her place behind the wheel.
'Ahhhh,' she sighed, running her hand affectionately over the
gear shift knob. 'Automatic transmission. I think I'm in love.'

After she adjusted the seat and fastened her seatbelt, I handed
over the keys.

'Dad's making me learn to drive stick,' she said, slotting the
key into the ignition. 'That's the way he learned, so he expects
me to suffer, too.'

'Builds character,' I suggested. 'Plus, what'll you do if there's
an emergency and the only vehicle available is equipped with
standard transmission?'

She looked at me, wide-eyed. 'That's exactly what my mom
says!'

'That's because our mom said it to us when we learned to
drive stick.'

Julie released the parking brake and eased the car forward.
'Do you have any idea how hard it is to up shift on this stupid
hill with a clutch?'

When we got to the top of Colorado, Julie turned right on
Roland Avenue and demonstrated her parallel parking skills in
front of Eddie's Supermarket. 'Well done!' I said, genuinely
impressed.

She accepted the compliment with a self-satisfied grin, then
turned off the engine.

I wasted no time. 'Now, tell me. Why are you under house
arrest?'

'I hacked into my mother's laptop,' she confessed.

'No wonder you're in trouble,' I said.

'It was super easy,' Julie said, as if that made it OK.

Before I could comment, she said, 'I know about the DNA test, Aunt Hannah. About being part American Indian.'

'Ah, I see.'

'Even if I hadn't seen it with my own eyes, I'd have to be deaf not to. Dad was yelling so loud that they probably heard him on Mars.' She turned sideways in her seat and looked directly at me. 'I don't get him, I really don't. This is twenty-first-century Maryland, for heaven's sake, not the wild, wild west.'

'How do you feel about it, Julie?' I asked, reaching across the center console to squeeze her hand.

'I think it's awesome, don't you?'

'I do, but I don't see how it's going to make any difference in my day-to-day life. It's just an interesting fact that I know about myself.'

'But only if you decide that's how it's going to be, Aunt Hannah. Being one-eighth Native American may not sound like a lot, but it's more indigenous blood than most people have in them. I think it means I have a responsibility to my people.'

Her people? According to Gen-Tree, I was four percent Norwegian, but I wasn't stocking up on pickled herring, lutefisk and krumkake. Then again, I was a generation older than Julie and far more jaded.

We sat quietly for a moment, watching shoppers pass in and out of the popular grocery, carrying bags laden with Eddie's signature Gourmet to Go.

'The DNA isn't able to link you to any particular tribe,' I reminded her gently.

'I know that,' she said. 'That's why I need your help.'

Somewhere in the recesses of my brain a brass band was tuning up, ready to launch into 'Ya Got Trouble (Right Here in River City)'. You'd think I'd heed it. But, no.

Genuinely curious, I waded right in. 'In what way?'

'When I hacked Mom's account, I noticed some DNA matches. Second and third cousins. That's pretty close, isn't it?'

I agreed that it was. But something was puzzling me. 'Your mom told me she hadn't signed up for the genetic matching.'

'Then she lied.'

'Julie!'

'Well, maybe that was the truth second test around, but not the first. Dad was printing out data for that DAR form he was filling out when he caught me snooping. It's all gone now, of course. He deleted the Gen-Tree account.'

Of course he did. Typical Scott.

'I still can't believe you hacked your mom's account,' I said. 'Wasn't it password protected?'

'Of course it was password protected, Aunt Hannah!' she said as if I were a particularly slow and difficult child. 'But Mom's passwords are easy to guess. Besides, she keeps a list of her accounts on her computer saved under the file name "Passwords1". Yeah, stick a one on the end. That'll really throw hackers off.'

I had to laugh.

Maybe she took my laughter for assent. 'So, you'll help me?'

'That depends,' I said.

'It's really important to me,' she said.

'OK,' I said. Then, 'Maybe,' I clarified. 'But you have to promise that you'll quit hacking your mom's computer.'

Julie rolled her eyes, sighed theatrically, then nodded. 'I promise.'

'So,' I said after several beats of silence. 'What's the deal?'

'Can you keep a secret?'

'As long as you haven't murdered anyone, yes.'

'I sent in my own test kit.'

I sat back in surprise, wondering where she'd gotten the money to pay for it. Scott and Georgina were fairly well off, but Julie didn't work a part-time job, and I didn't think she could afford ninety-nine-dollar DNA test kits on her weekly allowance, even with a twenty-percent-off coupon.

'Aunt Ruth gave me hers,' Julie explained, as if reading my mind.

'Don't you have to swear that you're eighteen years of age or older?' I asked, having read the fine print on the test kit I sent in.

'So, call the cops,' she said. After a moment, she reverted to a more reasonable tone. 'I'm seventeen and ten-twelfths, Aunt

Hannah. Close enough, it seems to me. Besides, I'll turn eighteen by the time the test comes back.'

Based on my Gen-Tree turnaround experience, that was certainly true.

'So, what do you want *me* to do?' I asked.

'Be there for me, serve as a resource, help me out if I need it.' She took a deep breath. 'Dad's confiscated my laptop until further notice, so I may not be able to manage this on my own. I can't count on my parents to help, I just *can't*!'

I thought carefully before answering. 'Julie, you can always talk to me. I don't guarantee that you'll like what I have to say, but we're family. I'll always have your back.'

It was lunchtime. Customers were starting to double park in front of the market, jealously eyeing our parking space. 'Aunt Hannah?' Julie said as she fired up the Volvo and pulled out into the street.

'What?'

'Thanks.' Then, a few seconds later, as if the previous discussion hadn't even taken place, 'I'll bet I can guess your password.'

'Go for it,' I said as she swung wide right and headed down Deepdene Road.

'123456?' she suggested.

'Nope.'

'Admin?'

'I'm not that stupid!'

'Letmein?'

'Ha ha, but no.'

'How about Cocodoodle?'

I swiveled in my seat. 'Julie! You *are* a witch!'

Then it was my niece's turn to laugh. 'Not today!'

'Then how did you guess . . .' I began.

She brought the car to a jerky halt at the corner of Summit and Colorado, leaned forward and looked both ways before easing the car into the intersection and turning left. 'Last time I visited, you had it written on a Post-it stuck to your monitor.'

With the engine still running, Julie set the parking brake and climbed out of the car. I walked around and took her place in the driver's seat. As my niece stood on the sidewalk, smiling and waving goodbye, I made a mental note to change my password the minute I got home. Family or not, I wasn't sure the little minx could be one hundred percent trusted.

NINE

Following sage advice I read on the Internet, I created a new system password that earned a 'highly secure' rating from Doctor Google. 'Make up a phrase you can easily remember,' Google advised, 'like "Christopher Columbus discovered America in 1492", then use the first letter of each word plus the number as your password.'

Now that I seemed to be closely related to Native American people, I decided to give old Christopher Columbus, a latecomer to the New World if there ever was one, a pass. After considerable thought, I decided on: Sacajawea guided Lewis and Clark across the Rocky Mountains to the Pacific Ocean in 1805.

Sglacatrmttpoi1805, I typed a few minutes later, testing it out.

While I was at it, still feeling cyber-vulnerable, I reset the security questions on my bank and credit card accounts.

Credit card companies seem to have a thing for pets and grandmas. 'Mother's maiden name' and 'city of your birth' were popular, too, information readily available in public records such as the ones I'd been scrolling through recently on Gen-Tree. 'High school attended' and 'name of favorite movie' were equally risky, easily figured out by any hacker – like my renegade niece – with access to my Facebook friends or Twitter feeds.

Where were you on New Year's 2000? my bank, BB&T wanted to know. The question got points for being un-guessable, but it gave me the heebie-jeebies. On December 31, 1999 I'd been racing around Annapolis during gala First Night celebrations, trying to stop a maniac from shooting my daughter. I didn't think that was any of BB&T's business and scrolled on.

Who was your least favorite boss? That was easy. *Fran,* I started to type, then paused. What if there were a massive data breach like what happened at Yahoo? Would it help Fran to learn that she was universally despised? I tried again.

Where do you want to retire? BB&T asked. Maybe it would be safer to lie. *On Mars*, I wrote, smiling, hoping I'd remember if ever called upon to provide the correct answer.

BB&T's security questions were less quotidian than most, but I was thinking that if companies were truly serious about protecting their clients, how about asking *What Monopoly game piece is your older sister's favorite?* or *Who did your maternal grandfather vote for in the 1964 presidential election?*

Better yet, what could be more private than our sex lives? *What was the make, model and year of the car in which you first lost your virginity?* for example.

I'll never tell.

Several weeks later, I decided to tackle the online accounts I had with Amazon, eBay, Home Depot, Best Buy and numerous department store chains. I was giggling to myself and filling in the usual 'boyfriend' and 'first grade teacher' – Ron and Mrs Grieg, respectively – for Macy's when Julie telephoned, two days after she turned eighteen. Scott and Georgina had celebrated this milestone in their daughter's life by taking the immediate family not to Bethany Beach as planned, but on a week-long holiday to Disney World in Orlando, Florida. Julie suspected the trip was more about ten-year-old Colin than her but confessed to having a good time anyway.

'I passed my driver's test,' she announced breezily.

'I had every confidence you would,' I said. 'Congratulations.'

'Now I can drive down to see you.' She paused for a moment. 'If they let me have the keys to the Subaru.'

Was Julie speaking figuratively, I wondered, or fishing for an invitation?

'I thought you were under house arrest,' I said.

Julie laughed. 'I babysat Colin the whole week. Went with him on all the rides that made Mom barf, so Dad sawed off the leg irons.'

I chuckled at the image. 'You can come visit me any time, Julie, but call first to make sure I'll be home.'

'How about tomorrow?' she asked before I could draw breath.

'I'd like that,' I said. 'Want me to arrange a spa day?'

'That would be awesome, Aunt Hannah, but I don't think I'll
have time for that.' She paused. 'There's something serious I
want to talk to you about.'

'Can you give me a clue?'

She ignored the question. 'Ten o'clock OK?'

I said that it was.

'Cool,' she said, and the line went dead.

Using the house key I'd given Georgina in case of emergency,
Julie let herself in the front door a little after ten the following
morning. 'Aunt Hannah!'

'I'm in the kitchen,' I called.

Julie breezed into the room, slipped a backpack off her
shoulder and let it drop to the floor. She made a beeline for
the fridge and helped herself to a cold Coke. 'Do you mind?'
she asked as she ripped off the metal tab.

'Too late for minding,' I said with a laugh.

Ignoring the Coke for a moment, Julie took a deep, exaggerated breath. 'God, it smells good in here!'

'I'm baking chocolate chip cookies,' I said, reaching for an
oven mitt. 'This is the last batch.' I pointed to the cookies
already cooling on racks on the counter, then opened the oven
door. 'Help yourself.'

Using her free hand, Julie stacked three cookies on top of
one another, then carried them over to the kitchen table. After
I'd turned off the oven and racked up the remaining cookies, I
poured myself a cup of coffee, grabbed a warm cookie and
joined her.

'So,' I said, getting straight to the point. 'What's on your
mind?'

Julie pressed her hands, palms down, on the tablecloth. 'I've
decided to take a gap year.'

This announcement surprised me. Julie had seemed excited
about starting her freshman year at Towson University in the
fall. She'd even gone to Target with Georgina, shopping for the
mini-fridge and microwave oven every college student seemed
to require these days, as well as stocking up on cartons of ramen
noodles.

'What about Towson?' I asked.

'Everybody's taking gap years,' she said. 'Even Malia Obama.'

Presidential daughters aside, I doubted that *everyone* was delaying college by a year to go off on some extra-curricular, horizon-expanding adventure, but decided not to challenge her.

'Towson's totally cool with it,' she added.

'How about your parents?' I asked, thinking that Scott was rarely totally cool about anything that didn't fit in exactly with his plans.

'Even they know I'm not a mental giant like Sean or Dylan,' she said with a ladylike snort.

'So instead of hitting the books at Towson, what *will* you do?'

'I'm not really sure,' she admitted. 'That's why I wanted to talk to you. *Before* I talk to my parents.'

Swell, I thought.

'Look,' she said, leaning closer across the table. 'I'm in my prime! When else will I have no job, no significant other, no kids to hold me back? The answer is never!'

I simply stared, letting the truth of what she said soak in, but Julie was just warming up. 'I can travel to new places, make new friends! I want to volunteer somewhere, Aunt Hannah. Make my life count for something!'

'I don't want to dampen your enthusiasm, Julie,' I said with a smile, 'but becoming a global citizen might require a bit of money.'

She dismissed my concern with a flick of her hand. 'I know that! That's why I'm looking at VISTA. It's kind of a domestic Peace Corps. They give you a modest living allowance.' She paused. 'And health care.'

'Don't you have to be a college grad for VISTA?' I asked.

She shook her head. 'According to their website, you have to be at least seventeen.'

I felt Julie's eyes on my back as I carried my coffee mug over to the sink, rinsed it out and inverted it over a peg in the dishwasher.

'You think I'm crazy, don't you, Aunt Hannah?'

I turned to face her. 'I don't think you're crazy at all, Julie.

But I know your parents fairly well, and I suggest you do your research very thoroughly before springing this idea on them. Is there a guidance counselor at Poly you can talk to?' I asked.

Baltimore Polytechnic Institute, located at the corner of Falls Road and Cold Spring Lane, was one of Baltimore's highly-ranked magnet schools, specializing in STEM: science, technology, engineering and mathematics. Julie's grades at Poly, while not stellar, had been solid.

'I emailed for an appointment this morning,' she said. 'So stay tuned.'

I assured her that I would.

'Oh!' Julie said, suddenly leaping to her feet and retrieving her backpack. After unzipping the front pouch and rummaging inside, she produced what looked like a novelty key chain. She held it in front of me where it tick-tocked like a pendulum: a miniature Yoda from *Star Wars*. 'Here,' she said, handing it over. 'I almost forgot.'

'Cute,' I said, 'But what is it?'

'A flash drive,' Julie said. 'You pop off his head.'

I wrapped my fingers around the tiny Jedi Master.

'I thought it might help,' she said in what turned out to be the understatement of the year.

I looked up. 'Help with what?'

'It's my raw DNA data. I downloaded it at the public library when my test results finally came in.' She shouldered her backpack and turned toward the door. 'But don't tell Dad. He'll go ballistic.'

I squeezed Yoda a bit tighter.

'Take good care of it,' Julie said. 'Dad's got this crazy hang-up.'

'So I gathered,' I said. 'I'll try to upload it this afternoon.'

'Do or do not,' Julie quoted. 'There is no try.'

'Funny girl,' I said. 'Did you keep a copy?'

Julie shot me a dismissive blink that made me feel like an idiot.

I was quick to catch on. '*Duh*, right?'

Julie tapped her forehead with an index finger. 'But I deleted my Gen-Tree account. Just in case Dad asks me . . .' She paused. 'He can always tell when I'm lying. Best not to take chances.'

TEN

After a hasty lunch – cream of mushroom soup and a peanut butter sandwich – and with Yoda curled in my hot little hand, I traipsed downstairs to our basement office and powered up the computer.

For everything to work properly, I'd need to set up an account separate from my own to hold Julie's data. And if Scott were as All-Wise-and-All-Knowing as his daughter feared, I'd need to protect her identity. After some thought, I chose her initials and birth year: JLC2000 and linked the account to a Gmail address I sometimes used for Internet purchases. Then I uploaded Julie's test kit data.

Julie would also need a family tree. I'd already built an extensive one for the Alexander-Smith side of the family. Fortunately, the Church of Jesus Christ of the Latter Day Saints had developed GEDCOM – GENeaological Data COMmunication files – that enabled one to share genealogical data from one software program to another. Creating a family tree for Julie was as simple as down-loading the Alexander-Smith GEDCOM from my account and uploading it to hers, then linking Julie's individual family tree record to her test kit. While Julie's DNA was out there, I kept her family tree strictly private. If anyone should inquire about possible matches, they'd have to go through me.

It would take a few hours, I knew, for Gen-Tree to verify, process and crunch the new data, so I spent the afternoon reorganizing our bedroom closet, making a pile of gently used clothing I intended to donate to Purple Heart.

My head was deep in the closet, my hand reaching for a pair of prehistoric brown and green plaid trousers when Paul, home early from the Academy, breezed into the bedroom.

'Don't you dare throw those away!' he barked.

I dropped the hanger and pressed a hand to my chest. 'And don't you dare sneak up on me like that! You scared me half to death.'

'Those are my lucky pants,' he explained.

'You weren't even born when these pants were popular,' I said.

'Don't be silly.' He stooped, picked up the hanger and smoothed the trousers gently over it. 'I rocked that plaid in the seventies.'

'I'll bet they don't even fit,' I said.

Paul checked the label inside the waistband and flashed a sheepish grin. 'You're right, but I'd hate to see them go. I shot a hole in one at Oakmont while wearing those pants.'

'You don't even play golf anymore, darling.'

'There is that,' he admitted.

'And you gave your golf clubs to Dennis a couple of years ago,' I reminded him.

'I wonder if he's using them?' Paul mused as if contemplating a quick snatch-back from his sister Connie's husband.

I gave him the evil eye.

'OK, you win,' Paul said, tossing his lucky trousers onto the donation pile. 'But if the Ravens don't advance to the Super Bowl this season, it will be all your fault.'

'I'll try to live with the shame,' I said.

Paul sat down on the edge of the bed and unlaced his shoes. 'So, what did young Julie want?'

I explained about the gap year.

'Oh, oh,' he said. 'That spells trouble.'

'I'm not so sure,' I said. 'While I was strolling down memory lane in the closet just now, it occurred to me that Scott might be strapped for cash. Sean and Dylan are starting graduate school in the fall, and Georgina mentioned that Colin was transferring to Friends. Tuition at Friends is almost twenty-eight thousand. I looked it up.'

'For a fifth-grader?' Paul whistled. 'And we thought putting Emily through Bryn Mawr College was a financial stretch.'

'I don't think Scott would want to deny Julie a college education,' I said, 'but Towson runs about twenty-two thousand. Scholarships and loans go only so far. He might welcome a year's respite.'

Paul stretched out on the bed, propped his hands behind his head and eyed me speculatively. 'Interesting that he seems to have no trouble shelling out for the boys.'

'Don't get me started!' I said, and quickly changed the subject before I could launch into a fruitless, anti-Scott rant. 'Julie brought me another surprise.'

'Oh?'

I told him about Yoda and Julie's test kit. 'I'm waiting for her kit to process now.'

'What do you hope to learn from Julie's test results that you don't already know from your own?' he asked.

I flashed him a toothy grin. 'That Scott is mostly Hispanic or Asian? That would be positively delicious.'

Paul laughed out loud. 'You have an evil mind, Hannah Ives.'

'Thank you,' I said.

As it turned out, Scott was in no danger of being blackballed from his snooty club. Based on the DNA he'd handed down to his daughter, Scott's pedigree was as Italian as his name, Cardinale, would suggest. And Julie's Native American ancestry was also confirmed.

I texted Julie with the news:

Italy	30%
England/Wales	28%
Native American	13%
Ireland	10%
Greece	10%
Sicily	7%
Norway	2%

A few minutes later my niece got back to me with a thumb's-up icon, followed immediately by a smiley with its mouth zipped shut.

I replied with a heart and the 'speak-no-evil' monkey, then returned to my research.

I logged on to my family tree, rather than Julie's, reasoning that I was one generation closer to my grandparents than she. Because I'd linked both of our data to the DNA matching service, I was ridiculously relieved to see that the first thing that popped up when I clicked on 'DNA Matches' was that Julie and I were 'Close Family'.

I had no first cousins that I knew of. My mother had been an only child and my father's only brother had died childless. But the list of possible second, third and fourth cousins that followed Julie's listing made me gasp. I scrolled through the list, looking for familiar names, but most people, like Julie, were identified by cryptic screen names.

Concentrate, Hannah. Think.

Charlotte Drew Smith was my grandmother. In order to share Charlotte with me, a person would have to match at the first cousin level. But no first cousins were listed. That didn't mean that no first cousins existed, just that they weren't part of the Gen-Tree database.

A second cousin, then, with a shared great-grandparent.

I began a methodical search down the list of possible second cousins, clicking on each entry and examining our relationship. If the person were linked to a family tree, Gen-Tree's 'Shared Match' function made the task simple. I eliminated several Alexander and Collinson cousins on my father's side that way.

If no family tree had been linked to a person's DNA results – maddeningly often – or if that person's family tree was set to 'private', the only option was email.

So I emailed potential matches, keeping it short and simple.

> *Hello, cousin! My name is Hannah Ives. According to Gen-Tree, we share a common ancestor. Would you be willing to give me access to your family tree so I can learn how we are related? I'd be happy to share my tree with you, too.*

Around four-thirty, Paul came downstairs to check on me, carrying two glasses of chilled Pinot Grigio. 'How are you doing?'

I accepted the glass, clinked his in a toast and took a grateful sip. 'Relatives are multiplying like guinea pigs left to their own devices with unlimited access to sugar.' I took another sip and gestured at the monitor with my wine glass. 'When a three-times great-grandmother has ten children, the cousins that accumulate at the bottom of the family tree can number in the thousands.'

'What's that?' Paul asked suddenly, leaning in so close I could tell he'd eaten an Italian sub for lunch.

'What's what?' I asked.

'That.' He tapped the monitor where a miniature pennant was flapping over the box labeled Paul Everett Ives.

'It's a hint for you,' I explained, moving the mouse until an arrow hovered over the pennant. 'I thought I'd checked out all the hints yesterday, but it looks like we've got a few new ones.'

When I clicked the mouse a single suggestion appeared. 'This looks interesting,' I said, clicking again. A page from a high school yearbook materialized on the screen. Several dozen fresh-scrubbed youths, dressed in band uniforms, sat in a semicircle holding their instruments. I adjusted my reading glasses and squinted at the screen until I could read the list of names underneath the picture. 'I didn't know you played the trumpet in high school!' I said.

'Very badly,' Paul said with a grin.

'I'm saving *this* record for posterity,' I said as I added the entry to my husband's Gen-Tree profile.

A second flapping pennant caught my eye, this time for my grandfather, Stephen Axford Smith. Holding my breath, I clicked. According to the state of Vermont, a Congregationalist minister in Randolph had joined Stephen Smith and Charlotte Drew in holy matrimony on October 15, 1932. I added the record to my grandfather's profile, linked it to my grandmother's, then flopped back in the chair. 'Whoa!' I muttered, as the significance of the date sank in.

'When was your mother born?' Paul asked, although I suspected the question was rhetorical. Paul knew very well when my mother was born.

'May 25, 1933,' I reminded him.

I didn't need to count on my fingers to figure that out.

When her great-granddaughter Chloe was born, tipping the scales at ten pounds, my mother, citing herself, had quipped that hefty babies ran in our family. If these genealogical records were correct, Lois Mary Smith, my mother, had been a nine-pound-fourteen ounce, seven-month preemie.

ELEVEN

B ehind my eyelids it was summertime. The honk of a car
horn, the slap of a screen door and Grandma Smith – all
flowered aprons, broad smiles and damp, cinnamon-
ginger hugs – waiting for me on the stoop. Now it seemed
disrespectful to be counting backwards on my fingertips, trying
to determine exactly when my mother had been conceived. A
full-term pregnancy was, what, approximately forty weeks?
Back in high school biology class, persnickety, prune-faced Mrs
Garfield had glossed over human gestation periods.

According to Professor Google, the average length of human
gestation is two-hundred-and-eighty days from the first day of
the woman's last menstrual period. I sagged in my chair; like
I'd know when that was for Charlotte.

Somebody should invent a reverse conception calculator, I
thought as I typed in the terms on the Google search bar. To
my surprise, a website named babyMed had, saving me from
having to count backwards on my fingers. When I plugged my
mother's birth date into their online calculator, it estimated that
she had been conceived on September 1, 1932 and that
Grandmother's last period had begun on the eighteenth of
August. Only four percent of babies are born on their estimated
delivery day, the website cautioned, but for my purposes, early
September was close enough.

Where had Charlotte Drew, just turned twenty, been living
in September of 1932? In Vermont, I presumed. When she
married Stephen Smith there the following month, she would
have missed only one period. Had she even known she was
pregnant?

There had been Indian tribes in New England for centuries
before the colonists came. By the 1600s most had moved west,
into Canada, or had been assimilated. Every school child knew
that. According to Wikipedia, though, remnants of the Abenaki,
Mohican and Pennacook tribes were scattered throughout the

state of Vermont to this day, but none of these groups were federally recognized. Was a young man from one of those tribes our Native American connection?

With renewed determination, I launched the Gen-Tree website and pulled up my grandmother's record. No pennants were waving to attract my attention to a new fact. I stared at Charlotte's image for a long time, as if willing her to explain everything to me. I'd uploaded several family pictures to her gallery, but for her icon, I'd chosen the photo from her wedding day. The bright blue eyes, the plump lips, the rosy glow – had Charlotte been the quintessential radiant bride, or simply a pregnant one?

I slapped my own cheek. *Behave yourself, Hannah!* The two were not mutually exclusive.

Since Gen-Tree had no suggestions for me, I decided to do a deep dive into early twentieth-century US census records. Using the Advanced Search option, I selected Charlotte's father, my great-grandfather Josiah Drew, and requested the 1920 census for Vermont. I found the Drews almost immediately living in South Royalton on Chelsea Street. Josiah, head of family with Jane, his wife, and Charlotte, age eight. A son, Adam, was also listed, age five.

Using the same search criteria, I requested the 1930 census. Josiah and his son Adam, now fifteen years old, were still living on Chelsea Street, but Charlotte – who would have been eighteen at the time – was not listed. Neither was Jane.

The question of what happened to Jane was answered easily enough. Under 'marital status', Josiah was listed as 'W' – a widower. Sometime between 1920 and 1930, then, Jane had passed away. I made a note to search for her death certificate.

But what had happened to Charlotte?

Using my grandmother's full name, I did a broader search across the whole US census for 1930. I spent the better part of an hour scrolling through more than seven hundred results spanning the continent from sea to shining sea. I eliminated the Charlotte L. in Nashville (too old), the one in Kansas (dead) and the one in Cleveland who was only a Drew by marriage. Several dozen others seemed promising, but none turned out to be a positive match for my grandmother.

I sat back in my chair, feeling defeated.

What next?

Small town newspapers, I'd found, were a treasure trove of information and, thanks to digitization, almost as easy to read as if strewn across my coffee table. In the halcyon days before Facebook, Twitter and Instagram took over our lives, newspapers reported on town meetings, social events, and land sales; on births, deaths and weddings. You learned who was visiting whom, both in and out of town, and why. Whose sheep had escaped and were roaming freely on the green. Umbrellas lost and pocket watches found. Police reports and personal notices often revealed facts about our ancestors that they'd rather have been kept shrouded in mystery.

As it turns out, my subscription to Newspapers.com would have been cheap at twice the price. Among the dozens of historic newspapers in rural Vermont, I found the announcement for Charlotte's wedding, titled Smith-Drew, fairly easily. It had taken place on a day when frocks with 'pep' were two dollars ninety-eight at J.C. Penney, a pound of Maxwell House coffee cost thirty-three cents, Miss America smoked Lucky Strike (It's toasted!) and Rinso was so easy on the hands.

I shot from my chair and yelled upstairs for my husband. 'Paul! Come see what I found!'

His voice, drifting down from the living room, was muffled. 'I'm watching the game! Can it wait?'

'No, dammit!' I grabbed my laptop and trundled up to join him.

According to the *Bethel Gazette* for Thursday, October 20, 1932:

> *All the brilliant tints of autumn in branches of the changing foliage adorned the residence of Mr and Mrs H.H. Westerly for the wedding of their niece, Miss Charlotte Louise Drew of South Royalton, Vermont who was united in marriage Saturday morning to Stephen Henry Smith of Randolph, in the presence of sixteen relatives and intimate friends of the contracting parties.*

At eleven o'clock the bride and groom descended the stairway and entered the parlors, attended by the maid of honor, Miss Ida James of South Royalton and the best man, Charles Keane of Baltimore, a friend of the groom.

Very lovely was the bride in her wedding gown of white crepe de chine with lace and pearl trimmings. For orna-ments she wore a watch, the gift of the groom, and a pearl necklace that had once belonged to her mother, and she carried a beautiful shower bouquet of white carnations. The maid of honor was prettily gowned in pink messaline. Among others in attendance were the groom's mother, Mrs Jacob Smith of Randolph, and the bride's grandparents, Mr and Mrs Asa Drew of South Royalton, the former having reached the age of eighty the 29th of August and the latter attaining to fourscore the 29th of September, and being now in the 59th year of their married life.

After the service came an elegant wedding breakfast in a dining room decorated in pink and green with spruce, sweetpeas and asters.

I sat in the living room with my laptop on my knees, reading the article to Paul in the plummy tones of an old-time radio announcer. I glanced up from the screen to see if he was paying attention. 'Small town newspapers are gems. This is like the Rosetta Stone.'

Paul was half listening to me and half watching the Yankees get trounced by the Orioles on ESPN. 'In what way?'

'In addition to the birthdays of my Drew great-great-grandparents, I can also calculate the year of their marriage.'

Paul silently pumped his fist, not to recognize my brilliance but as Mancini homered to center.

I ignored him. 'Also, reading between the lines here, Charlotte's mother and father must have passed away by October of 'thirty-two. Stephen's father, too, or they all would have been attending the wedding.'

Paul leaned closer to the television, sending positive *mojo* to Nunez who had just stepped up to the plate. 'Uh huh.'

'And I picked up a couple of relatives I never knew about.'
Paul risked a glance my way. 'You did? Who?'

'An aunt and uncle I've never heard of, the Westerlys. I
wonder if she's a Drew or a Smith?'

'I thought you said her name was Westerly.'

'*Mr* H.H. is the Westerly,' I explained. 'Before her marriage,
Mrs H.H. must have been either a Drew or a Smith if Charlotte
is her niece.' I paused. 'My guess is Mrs H.H. is standing in
for her late sister, Jane.' I sighed. 'Back in the day, a woman
lost her identity upon marriage, at least as far as the social
columns in newspapers were concerned. I'll have to do some
digging through the census files for Mrs H.H.'s first name.'

Paul leapt to his feet as Nunez singled to center, sending
Joseph sliding into third. 'Yes! That's what I'm talking about!'

'You're hopeless,' I said. With two players on base, getting
my husband's undivided attention was mission impossible.

While I jotted down some dates on the back of an old *New
Yorker* magazine, Joseph managed to score on an infield single
by Valera, giving the Orioles a safe six-point lead and Paul
permission to go for a beer. At the door to the dining room he
turned and said, probably as an afterthought, 'You want anything?'

'Maybe later,' I said, glancing up from my notes. 'There's
more to the article, if you're interested.'

'The anticipation is killing me,' he said.

I reached behind me for a pillow and tossed it at his head.
'You haven't heard one word I've said!'

Laughing, Paul batted the pillow away. 'Oh, yes I have.'

I gave him a hard side-eye.

'There's one thing I really have to know,' he said.

I set my laptop to one side and looked up. 'Yes?'

'What's messaline?'

When Paul returned to the game carrying his beer and a steaming
bag of microwave popcorn, I described the fabric to him.
'Messaline's a lightweight silk, with a textured finish, like twill.
I don't think they make it any more.'

I helped myself to a fistful of popcorn. 'There's more to the
article,' I said, chewing thoughtfully.

'Read on, Macduff,' Paul said.

'Very punny, Mr Shakespeare.' I reached for the laptop. 'There's more about fabrics, you'll be pleased to hear,' I said, paging forward and continuing to read where I'd left off.

The bride having donned a traveling gown of green broad-cloth with a hat to match, Mr and Mrs Smith left in a cloudburst of confetti for Boston and after November 1st will be at home on the Smith family farm in Randolph. The bride was last year studying nursing in Pierre, South Dakota. For the past month she has been staying with relatives in South Royalton.

'South Dakota?' I nearly fell off my chair. All that time spent trolling through the census files and the answer was in the newspaper all along. 'What's in South Dakota?'

'A school of nursing, I presume,' Paul said.

'But why go all the way to South Dakota to attend nursing school?'

'Maybe she got a scholarship,' Paul suggested. 'Money could have been an issue. Didn't you say her parents were dead?'

'According to the census, her mother died sometime before 1930, but her father was still alive then. There could be another reason he didn't attend the wedding.' I made a note to check the 1940 census to see if Josiah and his son Adam still appeared, chiding myself for not doing it earlier.

TWELVE

Pierre, South Dakota, has a population of 14,000, according to the Pierre Chamber of Commerce. The state capital was described as a friendly community whose 'tree-lined streets, historic downtown and lush green parks give way to rolling hills and steep bluffs as the county spreads east into the state's expansive plains'.

But that was today.

Back in the thirties, it must have been the wild, wild west, and only George Washington's carved granite head would have greeted tourists visiting Mount Rushmore. Pierre, then as now, was located in the heart of Sioux Indian territory, not far from the Lower Brule and Rosebud Indian Reservations.

I had to be on the right track.

Armed with the information I'd learned from the *Bethel Gazette*, I called up the 1930 US census data. This time, I limited the search to 'South Dakota' and 'Charlotte Drew'. When I studied the search results, I saw immediately why I'd missed Charlotte in my earlier, much broader attempt to find her. When the census taker knocked at the door back in April of 1930, whoever answered his questions had given Grandmother's name as 'Lottie'.

I'd never known my grandmother to use that nickname. Grandfather always called her 'Buttercup' after the heroine in his favorite Gilbert and Sullivan operetta, *H.M.S. Pinafore.* 'Lottie' was definitely my grandmother though – the age was correct, as was her place of birth, Vermont. In 1930, Lottie Drew had been living with seven other 'boarders' at a house on North Huron Avenue. Her occupation: student.

The census also answered another question – how Charlotte happened to find herself in South Dakota.

Another boarder in the house on North Huron was Charles Keene, her future husband's good friend, the one he'd chosen for best man at his wedding. Charles's occupation? Doctor. One other doctor, two nurses, a stenographer and a drayman also shared the house, which was headed by Bertha Lumley, age fifty-one. With all that medical horsepower close at hand, where better to be struck by a car in Pierre, South Dakota, I mused, than the middle of North Huron Avenue?

If proximity were any guarantee, Charles Keene was a likely candidate for my biological grandfather. I imagined a smart, ambitious Native American lad, the first of his family to attend medical school, returning home to care for his people after completing training at a university back East.

A search of online yearbooks put the kibosh on that theory. Charles Jameson Keene had been a graduate of Johns Hopkins University, class of 1926, transferring from Middlebury College in Vermont in 1922, majoring in Pre-Med. His picture in the

Hullabaloo for that year showed a blond, blue-eyed poster child for a Finnish health spa, his curls marcelled into a swirl on top of his head, like a cone from a soft-serve ice cream machine. Chuck also ran track his first two years and had been a member of the Musical Club.

I'd peppered my research with periodic updates to Paul, who finally gave up on the ball game, switched off the television and perched on the ottoman next to my feet.

'"Chuck" had some great loves,' I read aloud from the yearbook entry, 'but not for girls. They are for vases, flowers and paintings, in fact for anything old and interesting.'

'I'm old and interesting.' I studied my husband over the tops of my reading glasses. 'He would have loved me.'

Paul snorted. 'Sounds like your good friend Chuck might have been gay.'

I gave him a soft kick in the thigh.

Chuck's craving for old things was illustrated by the mention that he'd recently purchased a second-hand flivver and, reportedly, broken all speed records in Towson over the summer. 'However,' the entry continued, 'it is hard to imagine Chuck dissecting a "stiff" or, worse still, performing an operation on an honest to goodness human being.'

'Joy riding around town in an old Model T Ford?' I said. 'I think I would have loved this dude.'

Doctors and nurses had to be working somewhere nearby, I reasoned. Almost reluctantly, I clicked away from Chuck's colorful yearbook entry and brought up Google. A search for hospitals in present-day Pierre came up with only one, now owned by Avera, a health care conglomerate with more than 300 locations in South Dakota, North Dakota, Nebraska, Minnesota and Iowa. Before it became part of a sprawling, for-profit enterprise, though, the hospital had been simply called St Mary's.

I navigated to the Avera St Mary's website and clicked on the 'history' tab. Back in 1882, I read, a doctor named D.W. Robinson who planned to practice medicine out in California, found himself stranded at the end of the railroad line in Pierre. Out of funds, he began to support himself by caring for patients in the old Park Hotel there, operating on kitchen tables, ironing boards and even the floors.

In 1899, ten years after South Dakota became a state, five Benedictine Sisters took over the old Park Hotel. It had been deserted for several years by then, the only guests being animals and birds, and was so filthy from critters and river sand that the Sisters couldn't even determine the color of the woodwork. Their intention was to clean it up for use as a school, but the city fathers convinced them that health care was an even greater need than a school. The Sisters immediately changed their plans, opening a hospital and a training school for nurses. Mary Woods was the first white baby born in the hospital on December 9, 1899 and the first operation was performed a little more than a month later on a proper operating table donated by the afore-mentioned Dr Robinson.

The enterprise thrived. By the time Charlotte and Charles arrived in Pierre nearly thirty years later, the hospital had been accredited and a new facility was being built with one hundred beds.

'No wonder they needed doctors and nurses,' Paul said. 'They were expanding.'

I smiled. 'Imagine how a staunch Congregationalist like Charlotte must have chafed under the yoke of the Benedictine Brides of Christ. I'm old enough to remember when John F. Kennedy, a Catholic, was running for president. "We can't have a mackerel snapper occupying the White House!" Grandmother would rant. "He'll answer to the Pope, not the American people!" What she'd say about the far-right religious wingnuts who seem to be calling the shots in politics these days I can only imagine.'

It seemed clear that an invitation from Charles Keene had drawn Charlotte to a professional training opportunity in South Dakota, almost two thousand miles from her home. I wondered if she had grown homesick out on the Great Plains, so far away from the lush, Green Mountain state.

Nowadays Charlotte would have texted: School sux. Send $$. Had she written letters to her father and little brother back home?

A hundred years before her great-great-grandchildren's every move would be chronicled on Facebook and Instagram, had Charlotte kept a diary?

A search of the storage facility mentioned by my father just moved closer to the top of my To-Do list.

'Do you know what happened to Charles after he attended your grandparents' wedding?' Paul asked.

'Not yet, but stay tuned.'

A search of Fold3, the military database, turned up Charles's World War Two draft registration card. According to the Cuyahoga County draft board, Charles was working as a surgeon in Cleveland, Ohio, had blond hair and blue eyes, was five foot ten inches tall, weighed one hundred and eighty pounds and had a slight scar on his forehead. 'After the attack on Pearl Harbor in December of 1941,' I reported, 'Charles shows up on Navy muster rolls as a Lieutenant in the Medical Corps. He must have been deployed somewhere in the Pacific theater.'

'How do you know that?'

'He's got a fleet post office address in San Francisco,' I said. 'If they'd shipped him out to Europe, it would be FPO New York.'

Paul squeezed my big toe. 'I'm going for more wine. Refill?'

'You bet,' I said, handing over my empty glass.

While Paul was fetching the wine, I logged on to the newspaper database and searched Ohio newspapers for Charles's name. A short obituary in the *Cleveland Plain Dealer* provided chilling details: Lieutenant Charles Keene had been killed in action on Tarawa, November 23, 1943, when the field hospital where he was operating was hit by enemy fire.

On FindAGrave.com, I found an image of Chuck's tombstone at Greenmount Cemetery in Burlington, Vermont. I stared at it for a long time, thinking about my grandmother's friend, feeling desperately sad that his, and so many other young lives, had been cut short by war. I didn't realize until tears dripped onto my keyboard that I'd started to cry.

Paul appeared at my elbow, holding a glass of wine in each hand. 'What's wrong, sweetie?'

'He died,' I sniffed.

Paul's eyebrows shot up. 'Who died?'

'Charles Keene, my grandfather's best man.'

Paul set the wine glasses down on the end table. 'Hannah, he would almost certainly be dead by now anyway.'

'I know, but I wish I had known him, is all. He was only thirty-eight years old when he was killed.'

Paul sat on the ottoman, looked into my face and swiped an errant tear away with his thumb. 'You're very good at this, you know.'

I swallowed hard. 'Good at what? Weeping at the drop of a hat?'

'Research.'

'Just shut up and get me a tissue,' I snuffled.

'How about a pizza?' Paul asked when he returned. 'I don't think either of us feels like cooking.'

I snatched a tissue from the box he held out to me and blew my nose. 'With mushrooms?'

'With whatever toppings you want.'

'I don't want to go out. Let's have it delivered.'

Paul picked up the wine glasses and handed one to me. 'Your wish is my command.'

We clinked the rims of our glasses together and sipped.

'You know,' he mused after a few moments of companionable silence. 'When you finish with this family project, maybe you can find Amelia Earhart.'

THIRTEEN

I had plenty of research pending on my To-Do list before charging off on fruitless searches for Amelia Earhart – or Jimmy Hoffa or D.B. Cooper, for that matter.

After checking my email for responses to my DNA matches – nothing heard – I went looking for information on my maternal great-grandmother, Jane Drew, and her son, Adam, the great uncle I never knew.

Fortunately, the state of Vermont keeps meticulous vital records. Since 1779, town clerks were required by law to record all marriages, births and deaths. Most of this data appears on handwritten index cards, images of which can be found online.

When my great-grandmother married Josiah Drew in 1910, her maiden name was listed as Jane Gillette, daughter of William Gillette and Susanna Cook of Rutland, Vermont. Jane's age at the time was nineteen, so I calculated she had been born around 1891, which was confirmed by another card recording the birth of a daughter named Jane to a William and Susanna Gillette on October 18, 1891.

Jane and Josiah's daughter Charlotte blessed the happy couple in 1912. Before Charlotte's brother, Adam, came along in 1917, there had been another child, a boy named Josiah Drew after his father, but the lad died in the winter of 1915 when the poor thing was only three months old. No cause of death was recorded.

Jane's death, however, was fully documented. She passed away on December 22, 1926 of rheumatic heart disease, a complication, according to the doctor who signed her death certificate, of infantile scarlet fever.

If only penicillin had been discovered earlier, I mused sadly as I updated my family tree with this new information.

But what had happened to Charlotte's brother, my great uncle Adam Drew? After crawling around my databases for an hour, I gradually drew a picture of his life. Adam had graduated from Dartmouth College in 1938 with a degree in engineering. While in college, he rowed crew and sang in the glee club. When 1940 rolled around, he was living with his widowed father, Josiah, in Rutland, Vermont and working as a mechanic, although the census didn't say where. He'd enlisted in the Navy in October 1942, where he served as a MoMM2c. Motor Machinist's Mate Second Class Drew had shipped out to Europe on a destroyer, the USS *Gleaves*, which had been named, I was fascinated to find out, after an 1877 Naval Academy graduate who invented ways to improve the accuracy of torpedoes.

Adam Drew had survived the war – he was granted an honorable discharge in 1945 – but after that, his online record turned grim. In 1947, two days after his thirtieth birthday, Adam committed suicide by shooting himself in the head with a revolver. The *Rutland Evening Dispatch* carried the story in blunt, no-nonsense terms:

*On Monday, during the forenoon, Mr Drew purchased a
revolver. Returning to his father's house, he seated himself
at a table and wrote a brief note, wherein he stated that
people were talking falsely about him, etc., and then,
without rising from his chair, placed the muzzle of the
revolver to his right temple and fired. The ball passed
through his head, killing him instantly. Temporary aber-
ration of mind is assigned as the cause of the fatal act.*

Swell. Like red hair, did mental illness run in the Drew family?
More likely, I chided myself, young Adam had been suffering
from post-traumatic stress disorder, which was called shell
shock back then. If this kept up, I'd either have to start taking
anti-depressants or give up genealogical research altogether.

Hoping to uncover uplifting news, I went in search of the
mysterious Mrs H.H. Westerly, the woman who had hosted my
grandmother Charlotte's wedding. What facts I discovered did
nothing to lighten my dark mood.

According to her obituary in the *Bethel Gazette*, Mrs H.H.
turned out to be my grandfather's younger sister, Mina Smith.
I'd never known my great aunt Mina; like Charles Keene,
she'd died in the early years of the Second World War, or so
I'd been told. According to family lore, she'd taken a train
to Boston for dental surgery and never returned, succumbing
in 'Beantown' to a fatal reaction, perhaps an overdose of
anesthesia.

I created a record for Mina and connected it to her husband
Howard Harrison Westerly. When the screen refreshed, a pennant
on Mina's icon began flapping, and when I clicked on the
pennant, there it was: an image of Mina's death certificate from
the state of Massachusetts. My eyes were first drawn, as they
always were these days, to 'cause of death'.

Ovarian tumor?

Damn! I flopped back in my chair. Years back when I was
diagnosed with breast cancer, I'd claimed with confidence, when
interviewed by the doctor, that there was no history of cancer
in my family. None. And yet, there it was, typed out in black
and white on an official Massachusetts death certificate: the Big
C, a diagnosis too embarrassing to talk about back then.

I felt like everything I thought I knew about my family was tumbling like dominoes.

What next?

Unlike Adam, who was single when he died, Mina left Howard with four youngsters to raise. He'd remarried within a year and moved to Denver where, according to the census for 1940, he worked as a mining engineer. At that point, we'd lost track of that branch of the family. I figured that some of the cousins I'd recently matched may well have descended from Mina's line. But in spite of the emails I'd sent out, no one had responded. I was beginning to grow impatient.

The first nibble came a week later in the form of an email alerting me to a message waiting in my Gen-Tree account. I was at Whole Foods picking out some pork chops for dinner, but as soon as I got home, I stuffed the groceries in the fridge, bag and all, then rushed downstairs and turned on the computer.

Dear Hannah Ives, the message began. *My name is Nicholas Ohanzee Johnson, born in 1996 on the Pine Ridge Indian Reservation in South Dakota. I am Ogala Lakota, and I may be the connection you are looking for. Please write back and tell me more.*

When my hands had stopped shaking, I emailed Nicholas back, telling him what I knew about my grandmother, Charlotte Drew, concluding with:

Although our Native American ancestry came as a complete surprise, we are delighted to learn of it and hope you can help us fill in the blanks in our grandmother's early life. She was living in Pierre studying to become a nurse and would have come into contact with your family sometime between 1929 and 1932. Do you know where Charlotte might fit into your family tree?

Hoping to speed up the conversation, I added my private email address and hit send.

I'll ask my Great-Great-Aunt Wasula, Nicholas replied almost at once. *She might know. She just turned 102 but has a Wikipedia-like memory. Back to you soon.*

But I didn't hear any more from Nicholas for a maddening three days. I lit candles at St Catherine's Church for great-great-aunt Wasula's continuing good health, praying she hadn't

suddenly passed away, taking all that valuable knowledge along
with her.

In the meantime, I met up with a group of like-minded
political activists at a real estate office on Old Solomon's Island
Road. Fueled by coffee and donuts, we manned the telephone
banks and hand-addressed postcards (the personal touch!) to
everyone in our precinct, urging them to vote in November.

In my spare time, I read up on the Pine Ridge Reservation.
Located in the southwest corner of South Dakota on a border
it shared with Nebraska, the reservation was about the size
of the state of Connecticut and was, according to Wikipedia,
the eighth largest Indian reservation in the United States.
Several years before, Pine Ridge had been in the news when
tribal members joined with other Native American activists
on the Standing Rock Indian Reservation to protest the 1,172-
mile Dakota Access crude oil pipeline that runs through North
and South Dakota, Iowa and Illinois and has a capacity to
move 500,000 barrels of oil per day. The pipeline cuts across
huge swaths of native ancestral land. 'It's like constructing
a pipeline through Arlington Cemetery or under St Patrick's
Cathedral,' a lawyer for one of the tribes stated. And where
the pipeline crosses the Missouri River, it becomes a real
threat to the drinking water supply.

In truth, the Lakota Sioux had been 'troublemakers' ever
since Custer made his Last Stand at the Little Big Horn in
1876. That same year, perhaps in retaliation for Custer's defeat,
the US Congress decided to open up the Black Hills to development, putting 7.7 million acres of Indian land on sale to
homesteaders and private interests. In 1889, what remained
of the Great Sioux reservation was divided into five separate
reservations, one of which was Pine Ridge.

Needless to say, none of this set well with the Sioux. Nerves
were on edge, and when US troops descended upon Wounded
Knee in order to relieve the restive Lakota of their rifles, a
scuffle with a tribesman named Black Coyote – who refused
to give up his rifle because he'd paid a lot of money for it –
resulted in a massacre. At least one-hundred-and-fifty men,
women and children were murdered, and fifty-one more
wounded.

Almost ninety years later, in 1973, Wounded Knee was back in the news, receiving widespread media coverage as American Indian Movement (AIM) and Ogala Lakota activists – petitioning for restoration of treaty rights – staged a seventy-one-day stand-off with US law enforcement that resulted in gunfire and several deaths. The stand-off ended, but the violence continued. In 1975, an armed confrontation between AIM activists and the FBI resulted in the Pine Ridge Shootout and the death of one activist and two FBI agents.

Nowadays on the Pine Ridge Reservation, eighty percent of the residents are unemployed; forty-nine percent live below the federal poverty line; the infant mortality rate is five times the national average; obesity, diabetes and heart disease are epidemic; and 4.5 million cans of beer are sold annually in White Clay, Nebraska, just over the border from Pine Ridge. That's 12,500 cans of beer a day. The reservation itself is dry.

Golly. Why would anyone voluntarily live in such a place? Did Nicholas live on the reservation now, I wondered, or had he escaped to a better life?

'When are you going to tell your sisters about Nicholas?' Paul asked me as we were eating dinner several days later.

'When all the facts are in, I think. I don't want to confuse things. Ruth is pretty solid, but I'm worried about Georgina. One minute she's nagging us to take the DNA tests, the next, forget about it, so sorry I asked.' I gnawed thoughtfully on a raw carrot. 'Scott's got something to do with Georgina's crazy about-face, you can bet on that.'

'Julie certainly seemed keen,' Paul remarked.

'Emily, too,' I said. 'But Emily's less likely than Julie to go off half-cocked.'

'Half-cocked?'

'Oh, like painting her face, braiding feathers into her hair, hopping on a bus to South Dakota and spending her gap year on the reservation.'

Paul laughed, then his face grew serious. 'From how you describe it, the reservation could use all the help it can get.'

'I know. Maybe there's something we can do.' I lay my fork down on my empty plate. 'But, dammit! Why doesn't Nicholas get back in touch? I don't even know him and he's already driving me crazy!'

'That proves he's family,' Paul said.

FOURTEEN

As if to illustrate a cosmic connection between us, I received an email from Nicholas the following morning, time stamped 20:18, sent exactly when Paul and I had been finishing dinner.

'Hi, cousin! Can we FaceTime?'

Taking this as a sign he had information to share, I emailed back, 'Of course! Name a time.'

At seven p.m. EDT, with Paul hovering behind me, I powered up the computer, launched the FaceTime app and waited for Nicholas to call.

In preparation for the session, I'd washed and coaxed my unruly curls into submission with a generous squirt of styling mousse, then fluffed them out around my face in a casual, beach-blown way. Lipstick and a judicious application of eyeliner kept me from looking like a washed-out hag, or so I hoped. No use scaring the kid.

The computer began to ring.

Suddenly nervous, I looked back at Paul who smiled, nodded encouragingly and said, 'What are you waiting for?'

I clicked *Accept*, and in less than a second Nicholas's image filled my screen.

'Hi, cousin,' he said.

'Hi,' I said back, feeling tongue-tied and stupid.

Nicholas's strong brows arched over dark eyes set handsomely into a round face. His straight nose and full lips would have looked right at home on a Roman statue. He wore his jet-black hair trimmed close on the sides and long on top, swept back in an iconic quiff. A tendril had escaped whatever hair product he used to tame it, dangling fetchingly over one eye. As I pondered what to say next, a young woman swam into view behind him, as stunningly beautiful as he was handsome. Her blue-black hair was parted on the side and cascaded loosely over her shoulders. She waggled her fingers at the camera.

'Hi,' she said.

'This is my sister, Mai. We're twins.'

'Twins run in the family,' I said. At least on my side of the continent, the ice had been broken.

I was going to introduce Paul, but he scooted his chair aside and waved me off, letting me know that this was my show, not his.

'I won't keep you in suspense,' Nicholas said. 'I talked to my aunt, and she remembers your grandmother. She says Lottie was one of the nurses who came with the doctor to treat patients on the rez.'

I pressed a hand to my chest in a futile attempt to slow my racing heart. 'Does your aunt know how we might be related?'

'Auntie had two brothers, Matoskah and Tahatan, although your grandmother might have known them by their English names, Joseph and Henry. Tahatan, Henry, was our great-grandfather.

'They were cowboys,' Nicholas continued. 'Both of them died before I was born, so I never knew them.'

Cowboys? I must have looked puzzled because Nicholas went on to explain that Joseph and Henry had been Lakota cowboys active on the rodeo circuit.

'Does your aunt Wasula think Henry was my grandfather?' I asked.

'It's hard to know what Auntie thinks, Hannah. When I explained about the DNA, she listened quietly, but she stared out the window the whole time I was talking to her. She didn't say anything for two whole days, so I thought maybe she didn't believe me, but then she called me into her room. She wants to talk to you.' He paused. 'Annapolis is near Washington, DC, right?'

Although I couldn't figure out why he was asking, I agreed that it was. 'About thirty miles.'

'It's total coincidence, but next week we're coming to Washington for the big Native Lives Matter March. I'm hoping we'll be able to meet you then. Will you be home?'

'I will, and I'd like that very much,' I said. 'I'll come to your hotel. Where will you be staying?'

Nicholas laughed. 'Not in a hotel. Dad's driving us down in the RV. We plan to stay for a week or two at a campground in College Park, Maryland. Cherry Hill. Perhaps you know it?'

'I do,' I said.

Situated in a tree-lined park just north of Interstate 495, Cherry Hill was one of the Washington area's premier campgrounds, offering cottages, cabins, tents and hookups for a gazillion RVs. They had a restaurant, swimming pools, hot tubs, a dog park and recently had gone even more upmarket by adding yurts for glamping.

'Cherry Hill's not far from IKEA,' I added. 'Unless I leave my credit cards at home, I can get into a lot of trouble at IKEA.'

Nicholas chuckled. 'Tell me about it. That's how I furnished my dorm room.'

'Where do you go to college?'

'Went,' Nicholas corrected. 'I graduated from Marquette last spring with a major in Finance. Mai and I were luckier than most. Dad's a security officer at Prairie Wind Casino, so the tuition for Red Cloud High wasn't a stretch. I got a full ride at Marquette, and Mai . . .' He paused and looked over his shoulder. 'Here I am hogging the computer, you tell her, Mai.'

Mai gave her brother a friendly swat on the head and leaned into the camera. 'I went to Creighton in Omaha. It's a Jesuit-run school, too, just like Red Cloud was, and Marquette.'

'What was your major, Mai?'

'Marketing. Nicholas and I, both of us, are working at the casino, at least for now. I'm a floor attendant in the Bingo hall. The pay sucks, but I'm getting experience. Nicholas's a slot technician, but he won't be happy until they put him in charge of the auditing department.'

Nicholas grinned at his sister. 'Mai's helping out with the casino website, too. She's aiming for something in the promotions department, but if that doesn't work out, I think she'll move on.'

'You mentioned your father . . .' I began.

'Everybody calls him Sam, but his Indian name is Chaska

which means "Eldest Son". My mother's name is Wachapi. Star.'

Nicholas grabbed a piece of paper and held it up, closer to the camera. From the boxes and lines hand-drawn on the page, I could tell it was a family tree, but Nicholas's writing was too small to read. 'It's complicated, so I've drawn a family tree.'

'Is your family tree online?' I asked. 'It might be easier for me to see it that way.'

'We didn't upload our tree,' he said. 'Just the DNA. Dad was reluctant even to do that, but one of his sisters needs a bone marrow transplant and nobody on the rez is a match.'

I quickly volunteered to be tested, then asked, 'What issues did your father have with the DNA testing?'

'It's the fear of appropriation,' Nicholas explained. 'Historically, our land, artifacts and even our ancestors' remains have been taken away, shared and studied. That was beginning to happen with our DNA, too.'

This was ringing a bell. 'Ah, I remember reading an article in the *New York Times* about a Grand Canyon tribe who successfully sued Arizona State for using their genetic samples to conduct research outside the purpose of the original study.'

'The Havasupai, yes. They settled for seven-hundred-thousand dollars, I think.'

'Could you scan that page and email it to me, Nicholas?'

'Sure. Or I can bring it when we come.'

'I'd like to study it ahead of time, if you don't mind. It might answer a few questions.'

'No problem. I'll take care of it as soon as we hang up.'

'When do you think you'll arrive?' I asked.

'Hard to say, but we're aiming for Thursday, weather and traffic permitting.' He paused. 'Tell you what. I'll text you after we get settled so we can set up a time to get together. Aunt Wasula goes to bed crazy early, so it'll probably be in the morning.'

'Your aunt's coming, too? Didn't you tell me she's one hundred and two?'

Nicholas laughed. 'Try telling Auntie *not* to do anything. She lives in an oil and gas area and there's oil flares and pipelines everywhere. She had two horses drop dead from the fumes.

They just started kicking, then keeled over. I'll be pushing her wheelchair, but she'll be carrying the "Keep Calm and Frack Off" sign.'

I had to laugh. 'I can't wait to meet her.'

FIFTEEN

Nicholas was as good as his word. Half an hour later I had the Johnson family tree in hand.

While I waited impatiently for Thursday to roll around, I spent time getting acquainted with the ancestors on his, and probably my, family tree. If my suspicions were correct and I had descended from either Joseph or Henry Johnson, my maternal great-grandparents would have been John Otaktay (Kills Many) and his wife, Mary Ehawee (Laughing Maid).

In addition to the family tree, Nicholas had included a helpful note:

Hannah: Sometime before their son Joseph was born in 1911, Otaktay and Ehawee chose the last name, Johnson, as their surname. To facilitate land transfers after the Dawes Act of 1887, the purpose of which was to break up the reservations, assimilate the Indians and turn them into land-owning farmers, the Commissioner of Indian Affairs in 1890 ordered that all Indians living on reservations be given an English Christian name. They would retain their surname but translate it into English and shorten it, if necessary. Thus Otaktay officially became John Kills Many. The Indian agent was not happy with Kills Many, my Aunt Wasula says. He gave her father a choice between Washington, Adams, Jefferson or Monroe, but Otakay picked Johnson, naming himself after the agent. There must be a story behind that! – N.

I didn't know how large the Johnson's RV was and I didn't want to overwhelm the family with newfound relatives, but I didn't want to meet them alone, either. Paul sensibly suggested I give right of first refusal to blood relations, but Ruth and her husband were on a Viking river cruise to the Baltic and Georgina was avoiding the topic like small pox.

I called Emily and invited her to join me, but she demurred. 'You should take Julie,' Emily advised. 'Her mom's the one who started the whole thing, and Julie's totally into it. She'll never forgive you if you don't.'

'I'm not sure her father would approve,' I said.

'What's the worst that will happen?' Emily said. 'Scott will never speak to you again? Sounds like a win-win to me.'

'Don't be naughty, Emily.'

'It's my job, Mom.'

'Thanks,' I said with a laugh.

'And Mom?'

'What?'

'Take pictures.'

'If I don't ask, they can't say no,' Julie said when she presented herself at my house on Thursday morning. She'd driven herself there in the Cardinale family Subaru. 'We're shopping,' she said. 'You're buying me a suitcase.'

'What happens when you come home without one?' I asked.

Julie tossed her car keys on my kitchen counter, shrugged and said, 'I couldn't find one I liked? I'm notoriously picky.'

Remembering the words of Admiral Grace Hopper – *It is often easier to ask for forgiveness than to ask for permission* – and against my better judgment, I went along with Julie's plan.

From the moment we hit Route 50 outside Annapolis to the time we merged with the Washington beltway, Julie chattered non-stop. I'd told her about my FaceTime session with Nicholas and Mai, emphasizing their academic achievements, hoping they'd serve as a shining example to someone who was about to step off into a gap year of the Great Unknown. Sadly, I'd miscalculated. Julie seemed more interested in hearing about their casino jobs. 'I wonder how much training you need to be a blackjack dealer?' she mused.

I handed her the Johnson family tree. 'Shut up and read,' I said.

Fifteen minutes later, we took exit twenty-five toward College Park and followed Cherry Hill Road as it wound back north, passing under the beltway.

'There it is!' Julie bounced in her seat, the family tree forgotten. 'There's the sign!'

I swung the wheel left onto Jayrose Drive and entered the park.

'The Johnsons are expecting us,' I told the guard at the security gate. 'Site number four-seventeen.'

'You can park over there,' he said, gesturing to his right. 'Near the bus station. It's a short walk from there.' He handed me a map of the campground. Site 417 on Crater Lake Vista was circled in pencil. I passed the map to Julie and thanked him as the turnstile rose up to let us pass.

I'm no expert on recreational vehicles, so when Nicholas told me to look for an Allegro 31 motor home, I had to look it up on the Internet. The RV was bigger than I expected from the online photograph. It was the size of a school bus, with maroon, silver and black Nike-style swooshes painted along the side. A hand painted wooden sign hung from a hook on the door: *Cikala Inipi*. I wondered if that was Lakota for "Welcome".

I'd texted Nicholas from the parking lot, so he and Mai were expecting us, sitting outside the RV in canvas lawn chairs under a green and white striped canopy. When we ambled around the corner, they leapt to their feet, arms outstretched in welcome.

Julie lunged forward, hugging her newfound cousins as if she had known them all her life. 'I'm so excited!' she said, as if we couldn't guess.

I extended my hand. 'I'm so pleased to meet you, Nicholas.'

'Please,' he said while handing me off to Mai. 'We're family. Call me Nick.'

'Father!' Mai called out. 'They're here.'

Their father, I saw now, was crouched at the rear of the RV, his head deep into one of the undercarriage compartments. As I watched, he hauled out a barbeque grill, set it on the ground, unfolded his six-foot-something-inch frame and stood.

Cousin Samuel 'Eldest Son' Johnson was about my age. He wore a black T-shirt belted into slim-fitting jeans, and a pair of expensive, handcrafted leather boots. His black hair was worn long, fastened at the nape of his neck with a loop of braided leather. He whipped a yellow bandana out of his back pocket, used it to wipe sweat off his forehead, returned the bandana to his pocket, then stepped forward to greet us.

'Welcome,' he said, taking my hand in both of his.

'Nick has explained Lakota names to me,' I said. 'But it's still a bit confusing. Shall I call you Chaska, Eldest Son, or Samuel?'

He smiled, revealing a row of dazzling, slightly crooked teeth. 'Sam will do fine. Let's go inside where it's cool.'

Sam held the door open while Julie and I stepped into the RV.

I couldn't stifle a gasp.

The inside of their motor home was larger than some New York City apartments. We found ourselves in a bright, living room-dining room-kitchen area, fully carpeted and beautifully furnished with rich, buttery leather upholstery. In the cab to my right, the driver and passenger seats, equally plush, sat before a dashboard cluttered, at least to my mind, with screens, knobs and buttons like the bridge of the Starship Enterprise.

'It's roomier than it looks from the outside,' I commented as I eased sideways into a kitchen equipped with stainless steel appliances, including a full-size refrigerator, more up-to-date than any in my kitchen at home.

'We have two slides,' Sam explained, indicating the bedroom where the foot of a queen-sized bed covered with a Navajo quilt was just visible. 'Once we get parked and leveled, the bedroom and the living-dining room areas pop out.'

'Do you live in the RV year round?' Julie asked. She seemed to be admiring the flat-screen television built into the wall. Underneath the television, incredibly, was a gas log fireplace. I must have been ogling the fireplace because Sam smiled and said, 'It gets cold in South Dakota.'

Turning to Julie, he said, 'My wife and I live on a farm near Oglala. Aunt Wasula still lives in the house my father and I grew up in. Nick and Mai have moved in with her temporarily.'

Julie glanced around the living area, her brow slightly furrowed. 'But where do you all *sleep*?'

I'd been curious about that, too.

If Sam found the question rude, he gave no indication of it. 'Mai shares the queen bed with her aunt, I sleep on the pull-out sofa and Nick . . . wait, I'll show you.' Sam strolled into the cab, released a couple of pins, reached overhead and pushed a button. A bunk bed began to emerge from the ceiling over the cab. He let the bed descend about a foot before sending it back up where it came from. 'The seats fold back at night,' he explained, 'so the bed can be fully deployed.'

I was beginning to wonder whether Aunt Wasula had actually made the trip when a door next to the television slid open and a stooped, elderly woman emerged from what I assumed was the bathroom. This had to be Wasula.

Her hair, still predominately black but evenly streaked with gray, was parted in the middle and had been freshly-braided. It hung over her shoulders in double plaits almost to her waist. She wore an ankle-length, cotton skirt splashed with flowers, and in spite of the August heat, a red cardigan buttoned over a yellow blouse. As she shuffled toward us, the smallest pair of Birkenstock sandals I'd ever seen on an adult peeked out from beneath her skirt.

Sam took his aunt gently by the arm and steered her toward a seat on the L-shaped sofa. 'T'unwín-la, this is Hannah and her niece Julie, the cousins I told you about.'

Wasula beamed, accentuating her already deeply-creased smile lines. She nodded, saying nothing but looking incredibly wise. Once seated, hands folded in her lap, she commanded the room. I found it hard to look away.

There was a bit of friendly chatter while Mai directed everyone to a seat, and then – silence – as one by one we noticed that Wasula had raised her hand.

Something extraordinary was about to happen.

'I have many names,' she began. 'The Indian name given to me by my parents, their first gift to me, is Wasula. Wasula means Hair Storm, because I was born with a full head of black curls.' She stroked one of her braids and smiled wistfully.

'My Christian name is Miriam,' she continued, 'given to me by the missionaries after the sister of the great prophet Moses. Since I left the day school, I have not used that name, but if

I ever want to travel abroad it will be the name on my passport.

'Chaska Eldest Son – Samuel – calls me T'unwín-la, father's sister.'

She leaned back and closed her eyes, her small frame seeming to melt into the cushion. For one long minute, Wasula said nothing and I thought she might have dozed off, but then she opened her eyes and looked directly at me.

'Before me, Hannah, came my two brothers. They were named Matoska and Tahatan, born two years apart. From the time Tahatan learned to walk, the boys competed over everything. Who could shoot the arrow the farthest, whose sled reached the bottom of the hill first, whose horse was faster, who got to eat the last piece of molasses bread.' She leaned forward. 'But when it came to races, it was Matoska's horse that usually won.'

Wasula's dark eyes flashed. She turned her head toward Julie who sat rigid with attention in one of the dinette chairs. 'The Lakota are the best horseback riders in the world. Did you know that, Julie? My brothers were cowboys. Horses were all they knew. Raising them, training them, riding them, raising and selling cattle. They worked the rodeo circuit, too, using their Indian names, White Bear and Hawk. Roping, branding, bronco riding, steer wrestling – there was no competition my brothers could pass up. And for Hawk it was always a good day when he bested his older brother.

'Lakota cowboys were like rock stars,' she continued, inclining her head toward me. 'When our father, Otaktay, was a young man, some Lakota left their farms and joined Buffalo Bill's Wild West Show, travelling all the way to England to perform for Queen Victoria.' Wasula took a deep breath. 'It must have been a spectacle. Father's friend, a Lakota named Blue Horse was one of the performers. They billed him as chief of the Shoshones.'

'All Indians looked alike,' Nick interjected.

Wasula smiled indulgently. 'The English had never seen anything like the Wild West Show. Crowds thronged the streets to catch a glimpse of the cavalcade. Blue Horse told me that they travelled with eight hundred performers, nearly two hundred horses, eighteen buffalo, ten elk, five Texas longhorns and two deer.'

'They re-enacted Custer's Last Stand only ten years after it occurred,' Sam added. 'Remarkable, while reprehensible. It goes without saying that the Indians were portrayed as savages. Attacking wagon trains, stage coaches and settler's cabins until Wild Bill Cody and his troops rode triumphantly into the scene.'

Wasula smiled. 'It was a little bit more low-key in my day. We had the annual Pine Ridge Sioux Rodeo to look forward to, of course. It was a big tourist attraction. And cowboys like my brothers often left the reservation to compete in tournaments in other cities.'

As I waited for her story to continue, hardly daring to breathe, Wasula paused and closed her eyes. Were long-ago events scrolling past her eyelids? After a moment she raised a hand, as if reading my mind. 'You will want to know how our families met.'

'My grandmother was a nurse,' I said. 'I'm guessing it was in that capacity.'

'You are right. About once a month, there was a doctor from Pierre, I do not recall his name, who would drive to our clinic in an old Model T. Sometimes there would be another doctor with him, too, but he always brought a nurse.

'Matoska, White Bear, had gotten into a disagreement with a Brahma bull and the bull won. Just broken fingers, I was told, but Nurse Lottie helped the doctor patch White Bear up. The next month, White Bear reported for a checkup, and the next month, too, even though his hand had healed.

'After that, whenever the Model T was spotted coming down the road he'd show up at the clinic, offering to help out around the place. I was only thirteen, but even I knew it wasn't the doctor White Bear wanted to see.

'When Hawk informed Mother about his brother's interest in the nurse, I think he expected Mother to forbid such a relationship, but that didn't happen. Everybody respected Lottie. Besides, it wasn't all that unusual for a Lakota man to marry a white woman. Our day school teacher came from Chicago and married a Lakota. They had two children together.

'I do not know if Lottie returned White Bear's affection. She smiled and was kind to everyone. She brought flour for the women, tobacco for the men, books and candy for the children. They honored her with the Indian name, Mika, which means Clever Raccoon.' Wasula circled an eye with her index finger. 'Lottie wore round eyeglasses with tinted lenses. The children had never seen sunglasses before.'

I remembered those eyeglasses. Grandmother had kept them in a beaded case on her dresser, next to a bottle of Shalimar perfume.

'Julie?' Wasula patted the empty spot on the sofa next to her. When Julie joined her, Wasula turned and took both of my niece's hands in her gnarled ones. After a moment, she reached up to touch Julie's cheek. 'You look very much like her, Granddaughter.'

I choked back a sob.

'After White Bear died,' Wasula continued, still holding one of Julie's hands, 'Lottie never came again. I was fourteen then, and heartbroken. Lottie would bring me lipstick. She taught me how to French braid my hair. She gave me movie magazines.'

She grinned mischievously. 'I was obsessed with Claudette Colbert. I confessed to Lottie that I wanted Claudette's eyebrows, so the next time she came, Lottie brought tweezers and showed me how to use them. The clinic had closed, but the doctor had to wait while she finished doing my Hollywood makeover.' Wasula laughed. 'I didn't care that the older girls made fun of my war paint.' She lowered her voice. 'I think they were jealous.'

'Tell me how White Bear died,' I said. 'He was so young!'

'They said he was trampled to death by a horse,' Wasula said matter-of-factly. 'Father found him in the horse trailer, slumped against the wooden slats. They loaded him into a wagon and drove him to the hospital in Pierre, but he died two days later.'

'Massive head and internal injuries,' Sam supplied. 'Liver, spleen, intestines.'

Wasula's face clouded. 'Wakinyan could *not* have done that.'

'Wakinyan?' I asked.

Sam answered for his aunt. 'White Bear's horse, Thunder Spirit.'

'White Bear raised him from a colt,' Wasula said. Her eyes, unwavering, caught mine. 'I do not know who beat my brother to death, but it was not his horse.'

SIXTEEN

Wasula sagged, her eyes closed. I glanced over to Mai with alarm.

'She's just exhausted,' Mai said with a smile. 'It's been a long and interesting morning. Stuff I never knew.' Mai gently stroked Wasula's arm. 'Nap time, T'unwín-la.'

While Mai was helping her aunt get settled in the bedroom, we relocated to the patio where Sam had arranged a half-dozen canvas chairs in a semi-circle under the shade of a sugar maple tree.

'What does the sign mean, Nick?' Julie asked as we were taking our seats.

'Cikala Inipi?'

Julie nodded.

'Mai's idea. It means Little Lodge.'

'Nick carved the sign when he was in high school,' Sam added. 'It used to hang in our old Airstream trailer.' After a moment he pointed toward an Igloo picnic cooler and said, 'I've got cold beer and soft drinks in the cooler. Can I get anyone anything?'

I'd never developed a taste for beer, besides, I was driving. 'Coke for me, please, if you have one.'

As we were making our selections, Mai emerged from the RV carrying a box of sugar cookies.

Julie selected a cookie to go along with her Coke, then turned her green eyes on Nick. 'Can I ask you something, like, personal?'

Nick seemed to flush. 'Sure.'

'I don't want to step on any toes, so I'm wondering what, um, the indigenous people of the Americas prefer to be called. Indians? Native Americans?'

'Speaking for our tribe,' Nick said, 'we use the term LDN Peoples – Lakota, Dakota and Nakota.'

'I'll bet that has some people scratching their heads,' Julie

said. 'Trying to figure it out, I mean, like LGBTQ or
something.'

Sam laughed out loud. 'Tell me about it!'

'Julie probably mean Indians in general,' Nick offered.

Julie nodded.

'"Indian" is the term we've known for generations. The term
Native American is relatively new. Like African-American, it
arose in the sixties and seventies out of political-correctness
concerns of the civil rights era.'

'Not too long ago somebody took a survey and asked Indians
that same question,' Mai cut in. 'Fifty percent said they preferred
American Indian, thirty-seven liked Native American and the
rest had no preference.'

'So Indian is good?'

'It's good.'

I angled my chair so that it faced into the sun and adjusted
my sunglasses, hoping to make my Vitamin D quotient for the
week. 'Tell me about the Native Lives Matter March,' I said.
'Is it about police brutality? I read in the *New York Times* or
somewhere that Native Americans are being killed by police at
a higher rate even than African-Americans and are three times
more likely to be killed by police than white people.'

Nick rested his beer can on his knee. 'Organizers are taking
a page from the Black Lives Matter movement, sure, but the
fact of the matter is that you can't have a legitimate conversation about racism, about institutionalized racism in particular,
or about white supremacy without inviting native peoples to the
table. At Pine Ridge, though, we're focused much more broadly.
Lack of housing is our number one concern.'

'Then there's poverty, unemployment, struggles with substance
abuse,' Sam added, gesturing with his beer can. 'It's all related.'

Mai's face grew serious. 'Two of my friends from high school
committed suicide last year. There were twenty-three youth
suicides in 2015. It's an epidemic.'

'I'm so sorry, Mai,' I said.

But Mai was just getting wound up. 'This country gives away
billions and *billions* in foreign aid to countries most people
have never even heard of. Our nation was built on two horrors.'
She ticked them off on her fingers. 'One. The genocide of

indigenous peoples and, two, the enslavement of Africans . . .'
She paused. 'We want politicians to listen to us. They just *have*
to do better!'

Considering the current occupants of Capitol Hill, there was
vast room for improvement.

Julie plunked her empty soda can down on a folding end
table. 'OK, you talked me into it. I'm coming to the march.
Where do I sign up?'

I shot a warning glance her way, but if Julie noticed, she
ignored it.

Nick and Mai exchanged glances, then Nick turned to Julie
and grinned. 'We're assembling at Judiciary Square at ten. The
first stop is the Government Accountability Office at 4th and G.'

Mai shot from her chair. 'I'll get you a printout,' and
disappeared into the RV.

'GAO?' I asked. 'The waste, fraud and abuse agency? What
does GAO have to do with Indian affairs?'

'That's where the Bureau of Land Management has their
offices.'

'Ah,' I said, thinking pipelines and fracking.

'Then we march down 7th Street to the FBI, and from there,
on to the White House. We'll end up at the park in front of the
Department of Interior, at 18th and E. That's where the Bureau
of Indian Affairs hangs out.'

I'd worked in Washington, DC for years and was familiar
with the route. 'That's a long walk,' I said. 'I hope the weather
cooperates.'

'According to Alexa this morning, it's supposed to be sunny.'

'Here's the information.' Mai was back.

She handed me two sheets of paper. One was a black and
white map of the parade route, the other a list of instructions:
*So You're Going to Join a Protest March: Health and Safety
Tips*. My eyes scanned the list. I'd need to have $100 in my
pocket, in case I was arrested, and leave my contact lenses at
home because of tear gas. Swell.

Maybe it was the ominous advice about writing the telephone
number of your lawyer on your arm in Magic Marker that made
me turn to Julie and say, 'Julie, you will absolutely have to ask
your parents for permission to do this.'

'Why? I'm eighteen.'

'But you're living at home,' I said reasonably. 'Unless you're planning to move out, they still get to call the shots.'

She scowled. 'Can I tell them you'll be coming with me?'

Mai and Nicholas stared at me expectantly.

I looked at Julie. Her face wore that obstinate you-know-I'm-going-to-do-it-anyway look I'd seen hundreds of times before on my own daughter Emily. Somebody had to watch out for the kid. 'How can I refuse?' I said.

SEVENTEEN

6:30 a.m. I had just begun to enjoy my first cup of coffee when Julie texted with a last-minute change of plans. Rather than driving herself down to Annapolis, she would be catching a Baltimore Light Rail train at Cold Spring Lane. Could I pick her up at the BWI airport station?

An hour and a half later, I cruised past the International Air Terminal and pulled into the 'no standing' zone in front of the light rail station, but the platform was practically empty. A uniformed guard scowled and waved me away, forcing me to exit the airport and circle around. When I pulled into the station again, I was relieved to see that the guard had moved on. As my car idled, I checked my iPhone to see if Julie had left a text message.

Someone rapped on my car window. Thinking it was the guard back to scold me for the second time, I dropped the phone onto the passenger seat, shifted into drive and prepared to pull away.

But it wasn't the guard. Julie's Baltimore Poly T-shirt filled the passenger side window. I popped the lock. She opened the door, tossed her book bag on the floor and slid into the passenger seat.

'What have you done to your hair?' I gasped, although the answer was perfectly obvious. Julie had dyed her hair flat, shoe-polish black and arranged it in a single braid, the end wrapped with a yellow and red woven band. No wonder I'd missed seeing her on the platform.

'I'm embracing my heritage,' she explained.

'But . . .' I began.

'My parents hate it, too,' Julie said, as if reading my mind. 'Dad had an absolute fit. That's why I'm car-less again.'

'Seatbelt,' I said, and waited until my niece was strapped in before driving away. 'It's not your best look.'

'It'll wash out,' she said. 'Eventually.'

'I always wanted red hair,' I confessed as I merged onto US 1 heading south toward DC. 'You and your mother seem to have cornered the red hair market in our family. You should show more respect for such a gift.'

Our older sister, Ruth, had been fair-haired as a girl but had gone prematurely white, courtesy (I always felt) of her first marriage to the womanizing Eric Gannon. My curls were the same mousy brown they'd always been, although these days streaked with more gray.

'So, who do you think your grandfather was?' Julie asked, wisely steering the conversation in another direction. 'If what Aunt Wasula told us is true, it has to be either White Bear or Hawk.'

'It certainly seems so,' I said. 'She may be one hundred and two, but memory-wise she's still playing with a full deck of cards.'

'I'm hoping it's White Bear,' Julie said. 'He seemed, I don't know, nicer? Always helping out at the clinic and stuff.'

'Your great-grandmother was very attractive,' I said. 'I'm not surprised he hung around.'

'Wasula believes that White Bear was murdered, doesn't she?'

'It certainly looks that way,' I said.

'Two juniors got suspended from Poly last year for fighting in the restroom,' Julie said. It seemed like a non sequitur until she added, 'One didn't like that the other was taking Maryanne Grayson to see *Despicable Me 3*. What anyone sees in that stuck-up little bitch is beyond me.'

I shot a scowl sideways.

'Tramp?' Julie amended.

'How about floozy,' I suggested with a grin. After a minute

I added, more soberly, 'You may be right. Lovers' triangles sometimes end in tragedy. Think about Julius Caesar, Marc Anthony and Cleopatra.'

'Or John Mayer, Taylor Swift and Katy Perry,' she said.

I had no idea who Julie was talking about: two generations separated by a common language.

By the time we pulled into the Greenbelt Metro parking lot (only two dollars all day Saturday!) Julie had concluded that White Bear and Charlotte had been romantically involved and someone had killed him in a jealous rage. Julie's alternate theory, in which Charlotte, the attractive visiting nurse, had been raped and gallant White Bear had had a confrontation over it, was put on the back-burner. 'Nobody wants to be the product of rape,' Julie said reasonably. 'So until evidence surfaces to the contrary, I'm going with the first story.'

'You read too many romance novels,' I teased as Julie and I headed for the ticket machines. 'Ever heard of Occam's Razor?'

Julie slotted a ten-dollar bill into the machine and topped up her SmarTrip card. 'Help me out, Aunt Hannah.'

'*Entia non sunt multiplicanda praeter necessitatem,*' I quoted. 'All things being equal, the simplest explanation is usually the correct one.'

'You mean White Bear's horse got spooked and trampled him to death?'

'It could have been that simple,' I said as we passed through the turnstiles.

From two steps above me on the escalator, Julie looked back and said, 'I like my theory better.'

My niece and I rode the Green Line into the city and got off at Gallery Place where we flowed in the direction of the escalator, joining an ever-increasing river of high-spirited, poster-carrying protesters. In such close quarters, I was thankful that Nick and Mai had volunteered to bring the protest signs. I had no idea what mine would say but prayed it wouldn't embarrass me if in the future I lost my mind and decided to run for political office.

Hoping to avoid the larger crowd that I knew would be assembling at the police memorial at Judiciary Square, I'd suggested we meet the Johnson family on the southwest corner of 5th and F Streets. By the time we got there, however, the crowd was already surging down F, heading for the memorial, carrying us along like trees uprooted in a flash flood. 'Stay close, Julie,' I said as we bobbed on tiptoe, like prairie dogs, scanning the crowd for our new-found family.

'No worries.' Julie leaned against the wall of a fire station, eased her cell phone out of her back pocket, woke it up and tapped the Find My Friend app. 'Almost here,' she announced, turning the screen so I could see the map. Nick's icon was moving east along H Street, rapidly closing the distance between us. 'They must have gotten off at Metro Center,' she said, her thumbs darting about the keyboard as she sent her cousin a text.

While being jostled right and left, Julie and I had a hard time staying put, but eventually we spotted the real Nick rounding the corner at 5th and G. Nick was skillfully steering the wheel-chair with Wasula in it through the crowd which parted before them like the Red Sea.

Julie waved both arms overhead and shouted, 'Over here!'

As he drew closer, Nick caught sight of her, his face puzzled. 'Don't ask,' Julie said, gently shoving him aside and taking charge of Wasula's wheelchair. 'Yesterday I thought it was a good idea.'

Mai giggled and linked her arm through Julie's. 'Whatever,' she said. 'Dye or rinse?'

'Rinse,' Julie said. 'I wasn't *that* brave!'

'Shall we wait for your father?' I asked, thinking that Sam had somehow gotten lost in the crowd.

'Worst luck.' Nick frowned. 'The air con in the RV's conked out. He's waiting for the repairman. If it weren't so hot . . .' His voice trailed off.

'C'mon, Nick!' his sister said.

Wasula, I noticed, was in charge of the picket signs, stowed as they were in a bag hung over the back of her wheelchair. She was dressed in the same outfit she'd been wearing when I first met her but had swapped the cardigan for a multi-colored shawl that matched the beaded circle earrings that dangled from her ears. Wasula's green ball cap made me smile: MAKE AMERICA NATIVE AGAIN.

Nick did the honors, handing me a handmade sign that said, 'INDIGENOUS RESISTANCE SINCE 1492.'

'I like it,' I said. 'Very much.'

'Dibs on this one!' Julie said, grabbing another of the signs he'd fanned out in front of him. She waved it in a few practice arcs over her head: TWEET NATIVE AMERICANS WITH RESPECT.

Carrying a sign that said, HONOR THE TREATIES, Mai charged ahead leading Julie, Wasula and the wheelchair. We followed close behind. Soon our family cluster became engulfed by a crowd that pitched and heaved, amoeba-like, along the entire length of the street between the General Accountability Office and the Pension Building.

At ten o'clock precisely, a Native American I took to be the leader of the demonstration mounted the steps in front of the soulless, block-like building and took charge. Dressed in a fringed white leather jacket and wearing a magnificent feathered headdress, he aimed a bullhorn at the protestors.

'Irresponsible decision . . .' the bullhorn spit and crackled. 'Future generations . . .'

'What's he saying?' I shouted into Julie's ear.

'Who knows?' she shouted back. 'Isn't this fun?'

'Suffer the consequences . . .' the spokesman continued. 'Risking natural resources . . .'

Wasula tugged on Nick's arm. 'Isn't anyone from the Corps of Engineers going to come out and speak to us?'

'It's Saturday, T'unwín-la. They're probably at home, grilling burgers in the back yard.'

'Cowards,' she muttered. 'We're here. They should be, too.'

'Who's the guy with the bullhorn?' I asked Nick.

'Spotted Dog,' he said, 'One of our sub-chiefs.'

'Water is life, water is life, water is life!' Spotted Dog chanted into the bullhorn.

As he no doubt intended, the protestors picked up the cry: 'Water is life, water is life, water is life!' as we followed Spotted Dog west, marching to the hypnotic beat of a half-dozen native drums and waving tribal flags and protest signs.

At 7th Street the exuberantly noisy crowd flowed south, heading for the crumbling J. Edgar Hoover Building where the

FBI still had its headquarters. I warned our group well away from the building, recently swathed in construction netting to keep chunks of it from falling on the heads of passersby.

A Native American girl I took to be around ten climbed up on one of the concrete planters and, borrowing a protest song from the early days of the civil rights movement, launched into 'We Shall Overcome' in a clear, high soprano. Several thousand voices strong, we joined in while continuing west on Pennsylvania Avenue. Spotted Dog stopped short in front of what used to be the old Post Office Building, now converted into the controversial Trump International Hotel.

The singing gradually died. Boos and catcalls ensued. No surprise. Donald J. Trump was the president who had signed an executive order, reversing an earlier Obama administration stay, that allowed construction of the Dakota Access Pipeline under Lake Oahe to resume. 500,000 barrels of crude oil per day now flowed under the reservation's main water supply.

'Too bad it's not dark,' I said. 'There's a renegade multimedia artist who sometimes shows up with a projector to beam messages over the entrance, like "Emoluments Welcome: Pay Bribes Here".'

Mai's eyes widened. 'Doesn't he get arrested?'

'I don't think the guy's breaking any laws,' I said. 'He's got the projector hooked up to his laptop on a rolling battery-powered cart, and he's not blocking the sidewalk or anything.'

'It's totally hysterical,' said Julie. 'Remember when Trump was calling Africa and Haiti shithole countries?'

Nick, who had been releasing the brake on his aunt's wheelchair preparing to move on, looked up with interest. 'Yeah?'

'The guy projected "This place is a shithole" over the door.'

Nick and Mai laughed.

I wasn't sure Wasula was following our conversation until she gave a big thumbs up.

As we marched up Pennsylvania Avenue in the direction of the White House, I took over wheelchair duties, while Nick, Mai and Julie ambled slightly ahead, their protest signs and three dark heads – Julie's dye job still had the ability to shock – bobbing along together. Every once in a while Nick would glance back, presumably to make sure he hadn't lost the geezers.

The heat was intense and it was only eleven o'clock. I was grateful for my hat, but my nose stung; I wore no sunscreen because, according to Mai's brochure, it would cause tear gas to stick to your skin.

At the street corner by the Willard Hotel, we were confronted by a band of anti-protesters, carrying signs: THE ONLY GOOD INDIAN IS A DEAD INDIAN and GO BACK TO THE REZ.

'I wondered how long it would take before the likes of them showed up,' Wasula grumbled.

The ragtag band – about ten in number – danced at the periphery of our march, just out of fist-fight range. The police presence, I noticed, had increased, too. Uniformed officers – DC Metro by their insignia – lined both sides of the street. As we spilled into Lafayette Square Park, those officers were supplemented by US Park Police, some wearing green Day-Glo vests over their summer uniforms.

Even before the terrorist attacks of 9/11, cars had been banned from the block in front of 1600 Pennsylvania Avenue – heavy, steel crowd-control barricades and strategically-placed concrete bollards made sure of that. I was busy positioning Wasula next to one of the bollards and as far as possible from a row of ripening porta-potties, when the anti-protestors made their move. Whooping like back lot Indians in a Grade B western, they began to taunt the marchers by twirling 'scalps' in the air. One of the scalps – a long, blond fright wig no doubt dug out of a Halloween costume box – brushed Julie's face. Julie started, touched her cheek in surprise, then lunged in the jerk's direction.

I gasped. Before I could let go of the wheelchair and sprint after her, Nick grabbed Julie from behind by both arms and drew her back out of harm's way.

As the youngsters rejoined us, I mouthed a silent thank you. At least someone in this crazy family group was level-headed.

'Is the president in residence?' Mai asked, shouting over the counterfeit war cries intensifying behind us.

'It's Saturday,' her brother snorted. 'What do you think?'

A woman standing next to Nick and holding a miniature helium-filled Trump Baby balloon by a string had apparently overheard. 'He's at one of his goddamn golf clubs, don't you think? Attending to urgent business.'

'Hah!' Wasula muttered.

Soon, the anti-protestors' taunts were drowned out by native drums and rhythmic chanting as half a dozen Lakota teens, dressed in shirts and trousers decorated, not with feathers, but fringe, began swaying from side to side in time to the beat.

'Grass dance,' Wasula explained.

'It celebrates our relationship with Mother Earth,' Mai added.

The anti-protesters were still whooping it up, but they were soon outnumbered by a group of Japanese tourists, iPhones held aloft to capture the dancers or fastened at the end of selfie sticks in order to put themselves in the scene.

'God, it's hot,' Mai said. 'You'd think Mother Earth could send us a breeze.'

'Water?' I dug a few bottles out of the compact cooler stowed under Wasula's wheelchair and offered them around.

I untied the lightweight jacket I hadn't needed from around my waist, spread it out on the warm pavement and sat down, cross-legged, to sip my water. Protected by Wasula on one side and a wall of marchers on the other, I closed my eyes, hypno-tized by the warmth of the sun and the rhythmic pulsing of the drums.

I was dozing, blissed-out, when a familiar chant muscled its way in, so out of place that my eyes flew open. 'Hell no, we won't go!' it began, transporting me instantly back to my Oberlin days and to campus demonstrations against the war in Vietnam.

'Hell no, we won't go!' echoed down the corridor of years. 'Hell no, we won't go!'

We'd made life hell for the Army recruiters visiting campus. In the excitement of that moment, I'd helped overturn one of their cars. With the guy still in it.

But, why were they chanting it here, and now?

Sweat dripped down my neck and trickled between my breasts. I took a generous swig of water, shook my head in an attempt to clear my vision. Wasula's wheelchair was gone.

I struggled to my feet and looked around. I seemed to have lost my family. The crowd roared and surged forward, moving closer to the iron fence that separated us from the White House grounds.

'Hell no, we won't go!'

Sirens pierced the air. An ambulance, I wondered? Had someone been injured?

More sirens. The Park Police who had been standing off, closed in, wearing helmets and carrying batons.

'What's happening?' I asked the woman holding the Trump Baby balloon.

'They're ordering us to disperse!' she shouted.

Two policemen appeared in front of us. 'Move along, now,' one of them said. 'Time to go.'

Move along? Our next stop, according to Nick, was the US Department of the Interior, just two blocks further west. I aimed myself in that direction and, to my great relief, caught sight of Julie less than ten feet ahead, walking backwards, waving her arms to attract my attention.

'Here,' the balloon lady said, thrusting her arm in my direction. 'Hold this for me a minute, would you, while I text my husband?'

I grabbed the string and followed after Julie with Trump Baby bobbing over my head.

'MAGA, MAGA, MAGA,' somebody hissed in my ear. I turned to see who it was. A gap-toothed anti-protestor wearing a red *Make America Great Again* ball cap had infiltrated our ranks. He snarled and made a grab for the balloon. Instinctively, I jerked my arm away and watched in dismay as Trump Baby floated off, drifting over the bronze, outstretched arm of Major General Comte Jean de Rochambeau.

'Sonofabitch!' Balloon Lady yelled, looking directly at me. 'I paid twelve bucks for that!'

I shrugged and pointed an I'm-not-guilty finger at Mr Make America Great Again who was doubled over, laughing like a demented hyena. Balloon Lady got the picture immediately. She balled up her fist and let the guy have it.

'Bitch!' he yelled, clutching his upper arm.

She grabbed his MAGA cap by the bill, cocked her arm and sent the hat sailing, like a Frisbee, into the park. 'Now we're even!'

He lunged, sandwiching me between them as they flailed away. I dropped to my knees in self-defense, covering my head with my arms. A boot missed its intended mark and landed hard against my thigh. I'd have a world-class bruise there in the morning.

Seconds later, when I dared to look up, I was relieved to see a Park Police officer looming over me. Before I could thank her for breaking up the fight, she said, 'Stand up. You're under arrest. You have the right . . .'

As she rattled off the familiar litany, I glanced around in bewilderment. Balloon Lady and Mr MAGA Hat had vanished.

'But . . .' I started to protest, but then wisely clammed up.

Rules, remember the rules. *Don't argue with the police*, we'd been instructed. *Do exactly as you are told.*

'Yes, ma'am,' I said as I staggered to my feet, rubbing the sore spot on my thigh. 'May I ask with what I'm being charged?'

My impeccable grammar didn't impress her in the least. 'Failure to obey,' she grumped as she secured my hands behind my back with plastic zip-tie cuffs. With a gentle but firm hand grasping my upper arm, she began to lead me away.

Piercing in its urgency over the roar of the crowd was Julie's voice, 'Hey! Hey! Where are you taking her?'

EIGHTEEN

'Where' turned out to be a white police minibus parked on 15th Street near the Willard Hotel. The arresting officer escorted me to the door and after the driver opened up, waited until I climbed inside. 'Sit anywhere,' she said rather pleasantly.

I slid into a window seat behind the driver and struggled to get comfortable, an impossible task with hands tied behind your back. Meanwhile, my cell phone vibrated frantically in my back pocket. When I didn't answer after three attempts, it began to ping. Once I got my hands on it again, I knew I'd find a zillion frantic text messages from Julie.

I rested my head against the window and closed my eyes. I could still hear the distant chanting and the drums as the protestors moved on without me. Where were Julie, Nick, Mai and Wasula now?

When I opened my eyes again, the minibus – which I estimated could accommodate sixteen people – was nearly full. I was impressed with my fellow passengers – seven women and five men, so far – a veritable United Nations of gender, race and ethnic diversity that, unlike a great many things these days, made me proud to be an American.

Moments before the door was shut and secured, a fair-skinned woman, her dark blond dreadlocks semi-contained by a bandana, plopped down in the seat next to me.

'Hey,' she said.

'Where are they taking us?' I whispered.

She grinned. 'First time?'

Not counting the terrifying weekend I once spent in Baltimore as a guest of the US Marshalls, I said, 'Yes.'

The woman, who I took to be in her mid-thirties, twisted in her seat. Her lips moved in what I guessed was a silent head count. When she turned back around she said, 'Good thing we're fourteen.'

'Why's that?'

'If it was just you and me, less than ten or eleven anyway, they'd take us to the Central Cell Block for processing.' I felt her shiver. 'That hellhole ought to be on the black list of Amnesty International.'

'Good to know,' I said. 'I'm Hannah, by the way.'

'Katherine Emily Tuckerman hyphen Dutton,' she said, 'but you can call me Kit.'

Kit's last name rang a bell. 'Tuckerman-Dutton, as in Tuckerman-Dutton Development Corporation?'

'My grandfather,' she said.

Tuckerman-Dutton had been responsible for the revitalization of countless Baltimore neighborhoods following the deadly race riots of 1968. I whistled softly. 'I'm impressed.'

Kit shrugged a richly-tattooed shoulder. 'I'm somewhat of a disappointment to my family, as you probably guessed.'

'So, where *are* we going?' I asked after a bit.

'It's the DC police motor pool. A big parking garage, anyway. Down in southwest.'

'You sound like you've done this before?'

She nodded. 'Three times, maybe four.'

'So, why should I be glad I'm not going to get intimately familiar with the inside of the Central District Cell Block?' I asked.

'Ever been to the pound?' Kit asked.

'Stray dogs, you mean?'

'Like that. Stainless steel cages, inside and out, so you can hose them out, I suppose. Can in the middle . . .'

'Can?' I cut in.

'Toilet.'

'Ah.'

'Last time I had to stay overnight. Didn't sleep a wink. Spent the whole night stomping roaches.'

Now it was my turn to shiver. 'Gross.'

'Tell me about it! And the bologna sandwiches . . .' She imitated a cat coughing up a hairball.

I had to laugh.

Twenty minutes later I was relieved to see that Kit had been correct about our destination. According to the street signs I read through my window, we were somewhere in southwest DC – K and Half Streets, SW, I would learn later, at the Capitol Police's Vehicle Maintenance facility, directly across the street from DC's Motor Vehicle Inspection Station.

The minibus idled for several minutes on Half Street waiting for an intimidating black garage door to roll up. Once the bus was safely secured inside the building, we were invited to disembark. Still handicapped by handcuffs, we followed one of the officers, like obedient ducklings, into a large, empty room where we were ordered to line up against a stark white wall.

Despite Kit's nonchalance, I began to hyperventilate. Breathe in, Hannah. Breathe out. In . . . and . . . out.

'Feels like a firing squad, doesn't it?' Kit quipped.

I exhaled, shook the tension out of my shoulders and said, 'Maybe the white paint makes it easier to clean the blood off the walls?'

'Ha!' Kit said. Then quickly added, 'It usually doesn't take too long, unless somebody's cranky.'

After cooling our heels for ten minutes or so, I was beginning to worry that Captain McCrankypants was definitely in charge when two officers showed up to relieve us of our handcuffs.

Shortly thereafter, a woman in uniform appeared, identified herself as Sergeant Susan Wilson and read aloud from a laminated card. We were, all of us, being charged under 18DCMR 2000.2 with Failure to Obey a Lawful Order, a misdemeanor. Apparently we hadn't moved along quickly enough when ordered to do so by the police.

I wanted to wave my hand and shout, not guilty! If a lawful order had been given, I surely hadn't heard it, but then I'd been caught in the middle of a feral squabble over a Trump Baby balloon and a MAGA hat and hadn't been paying proper attention. Recently uploaded YouTube videos with Japanese subtitles might even acquit me in a court of law.

'You will be booked, fingerprinted, photographed and searched,' Sergeant Wilson continued.

I sucked in breath, let it out slowly. Not for the first time, I flashed back to the nightmare of being arrested by the FBI for the murder of Jennifer Goodall. The charges had been dismissed, of course, but yet I worried. Were my fingerprints still in the database? When they fingerprinted me here today, would lights flash and an alarm whoop-whoop-whoop until burly, grim-faced officers charged in to cart me away?

When I tuned in again, Sergeant Wilson was explaining how I could end my case immediately – hallelujah! – by paying a $100 fine. Should I decide to take the 'Post and Forfeit' option, she said, in two years' time if I kept my nose clean, the arrest would be sealed.

'If you want to go to court . . .' Wilson continued.

I glanced sideways at Kit, who frowned and shook her head.

I relaxed, grateful for the advice. My lawyer's phone number was inked on my forearm, but I was glad I wouldn't have to use it. Murray had already earned enough gray hairs – and money – on my account.

'Why go to the trouble of arresting us in the first place?'

I whispered to Kit after Sergeant Wilson finished addressing the troops.

'Gets us off the street, I guess, not to mention lining the government's pockets with cash.' She waved an arm, taking us all in. 'This sting is worth thirteen-hundred dollars. Imagine how much they netted after the march against the Trump administration's immigration policy.'

I'd followed that particular protest with interest. According to the *Washington Post*, over five hundred protestors had been arrested that day. I did the math. 'I see what you mean,' I said. 'Enough to buy a new police cruiser, you think?'

Kit nodded, her dreadlocks bobbing. 'Post and forfeit. It's the only way to go.'

Take my advice: always listen to a pro.

A massive bit of paperwork and two crisp fifty-dollar bills later, I was released to the corner of Half Street and K with only vague instructions on how to find my own way home to Annapolis.

Although I certainly hadn't planned it that way, according to Google Maps, I was only six blocks from the Navy Yard-Ballpark Metro station on the Green Line. If I caught the Metro, it would take about thirty-five minutes to be reunited with my Volvo.

But first, I'd need to check in with Julie.

I began scrolling through her messages:

OMG! Where are you? They won't tell us ANYTHING!!

Who do you want me to call? I won't call anyone UNLESS YOU TELL ME TO!

Don't worry, it's OK. I'm going home with Nick and Mai!

I sighed with relief and had started to text back, 'Stay put. I'll pick you up soon,' when the phone began to ring. 'Julie?' I said.

'Not Julie. It's Nick. Where are you?'

'I'll explain when I see you, but the short story is I paid a fine and the police let me go. I should be able to pick up Julie in about an hour.'

'Didn't she text you? Julie's not here.'

I swallowed my rising panic. 'But Julie said . . .'

'Oh, she *was* here,' Nick said, 'but she got an upsetting call from her mother, so we put her in an Uber and sent her home.'

'Upsetting? In what way upsetting?'

'She seemed worried, is all. And since we didn't know how long you'd be in police custody, we thought it best to get her home.'

'Thank you, Nick. That was exactly the right call. How much do I owe you for the Uber? That ride must have been expensive.'

'Forget about it,' he said. 'Are you sure you're OK?'

Was I? Loitering on a street corner, in an unfamiliar light-industrial neighborhood, in southwest DC, across from a vehicle inspection station and a post office? 'The Metro's nearby,' I reassured him. 'I'm heading there now.'

'Call us if you need anything,' Nick said, sounding sincere.

'How much longer will you be in town?' I asked. 'I'm hoping to introduce you to more of the family.'

'A while. Until we get the air-con fixed, anyway. We'll stay in touch, right?'

'You can count on it, Nick.'

NINETEEN

At first, I thought I'd reached a wrong number. All I heard was heavy breathing.'

'Julie?'

Her response was breathless, garbled.

'Slow down, Julie. I can't understand a word you're saying.'

Julie gulped. 'Dad didn't come home last night!'

Last night seemed an entire lifetime ago. 'I'm sorry, but I'm confused. I thought you said you saw him this morning.'

'No,' Julie whimpered. 'I left home around seven. Dad was still asleep, or so I thought.'

'What does your mother have to say? Surely she would have missed your father before this morning.'

'Colin was being a little asshole yesterday.' Julie sniffed, her voice steadied.

I was about to ask what Colin's behavior had to do with Scott going missing, when Julie continued, 'He bought a thousand dollars' worth of virtual coins on TikTok. Said it was by accident. Mom called to get the money refunded, and Apple was being shitty about it. He is sooo grounded.'

Confiscating Colin's cell phone would be one solution, I thought, and docking his allowance, maybe forever, but it didn't seem like a good time to offer pro tips on parenting. 'Yikes,' I said.

'Mom ended up with a migraine,' Julie rattled on breathlessly. 'She took some Imitrex and crashed early, so I made chicken fingers for dinner.'

Georgina had been plagued by migraines since her late teens. For the past several years she'd been seeing a chronic migraine specialist. Medication and a diet regime had dramatically reduced the number and frequency of her headaches, but the pills, I knew, could knock Georgina out cold. Zoned out on Imitrex, she could sleep through the Zombie Apocalypse.

'When was the last time anyone saw your father, Julie?'

'Mom saw him just before noon yesterday. He had a lunch meeting or something. When he wasn't home by two, she figured the meeting ran over, so she didn't actually miss him until she got up this morning.'

'Can I talk to your mom?'

'She's pretty fuzzy. You know how she gets on the pills.'

'Have you tried calling your dad's cell phone?'

'Of course I did, Aunt Hannah! And it goes straight to voicemail.'

Scott worked from home, in an office carved out of a space in their former attic. If he had a lunch meeting it could have been just about anywhere. 'Did you check his desk calendar?'

'He keeps it on his cell phone,' Julie said.

Of course he did, I thought. The phone that was missing.

'Can you help me, Aunt Hannah? Mom's a mess.'

'I'll be there as soon as I can,' I promised. 'But where are your brothers?'

'At Cape May for a week. One of their friend's parents has a condo on the beach.'

'You need to call them, Julie.'

'Mom won't let me. She says it might be a false alarm. School starts soon and she doesn't want to wreck their vacation. If he's not home by tomorrow . . .' Her voice trailed off.

I sighed. Dealing with Georgina could be exhausting, and not something easily accomplished over the telephone.

'I'll be there as soon as I can,' I repeated.

'I love you,' Julie said, and ended the call.

I made a snap decision: the hell with the Metro. I tapped the Uber app, requested a car then watched the screen as the icon representing Tamara in a Red Ford Taurus inched along Maine Avenue, heading in my direction. While waiting, I called Paul and told him what I was doing. I didn't mention my arrest. That would need to be a steak dinner, home fries and bottle of fine, red wine discussion sometime in the future.

Twenty-two minutes, twenty-seven dollars and a three-dollar tip later, Tamara reunited me with my car in Greenbelt.

In Baltimore, Julie greeted me at her front door, her eyelids red and puffy. She wrapped her arms around me, squeezed tight, and buried her face in the crook of my neck. 'Thank God you're here.'

I reached up to smooth her hair, her ridiculous hair, with my hand. 'Where's your mom?'

'In the kitchen,' Julie said. 'She's telephoning hospitals.'

'Has she called the police?'

Julie nodded. 'She actually went to the station on West Cold Spring. They told her to file a missing persons' report, but when she saw a copy, she freaked.' She lowered her voice. 'They want a description and a picture, you'd expect that, but they also want the name of his dentist.'

I shivered. 'That would freak me out, too.'

'So she's phoning hospitals instead.'

'Let me handle your mother,' I told her. 'Where can I find you later?'

'I'm supposed to be in the basement doing laundry,' she said.

'As good a place as any,' I said. 'Off you go.'

I found my sister perched on a stool at her kitchen counter, a printout lying open in front of her, a cell phone pressed to her ear. 'Well, thanks for checking,' she was saying as I walked in.

'Georgina,' I said.

She glanced up, flicked the pages. 'Do you have any idea how many hospitals there are in Baltimore? I'm only halfway there.'

I crossed the room and wrapped her in a hug. Her body sagged, and she began to sob. 'What could have happened to him?'

I let her cry for a bit, then offered her a paper towel, soaked in cool water and squeezed out. She pressed it to her eyes.

'Has Scott ever . . .' I began, weighing my words carefully. 'Has he ever stayed out all night before?'

'Gosh, no, Hannah. I get where you're going though.' She blew her nose on the towel, then looked up at me. 'But you don't have to stay somewhere overnight to, you know, have an affair.'

Something in my sister's voice made me ask, 'Do you think Scott was cheating on you?'

'I honestly don't know. It's just that he spends a lot of time at the church, and when I ask him about it, he claims he's working on the books.'

'But, he's church treasurer, right? So that makes perfect sense.'

Her green eyes flashed. 'Well, it didn't used to take up so much of his time.'

Filling out the personal income tax forms for the Ives family didn't used to take so much time either, I thought. It's just that our finances, and the tax laws, had grown more complicated over the years.

'Church of the Falls membership has doubled, hasn't it?' I reasoned aloud. 'I imagine Scott's workload has doubled right along with it,' I added, surprising myself by making excuses for Scott.

Georgina's mouth formed an obstinate line. I could tell she wasn't buying that argument. 'His wallet's gone, and so are his car keys, but the car is still in the driveway.'

'Maybe his lunch date picked him up?'

'Colin had a dental appointment yesterday morning, then I took him to Pepe's for pizza. When I came back, Scott had already left for lunch and he'd taken the car. He was meeting somebody at the church, that's all I know.'

'If the car's in the driveway now,' I said reasonably, 'then he must have returned at some point.'

'Well, somebody brought it back.'

Grown men had been known to run away from home before, I thought. Go out for a carton of cigarettes and ten years later they're found living in Arizona with a new wife and two adorable kids. But no matter how many ways I looked at it, Scott didn't seem like the deserting type. He'd stuck with Georgina through some tough times, back when the children were young and she'd come completely unglued. I couldn't see him walking out on her now.

'What about his cell phone?' I asked gently.

'It goes straight to voicemail,' she said. 'He must have it with him, because it's not in the house. I've looked everywhere.'

'Have you tried using Find My iPhone?'

Georgina's eyes widened. 'You can do that?'

'If Scott set it up that way.'

Georgina's face clouded. 'Well, he changed all his passwords after that incident with Little Miss Smarty Pants, so now, because of Julie, I guess we're screwed.'

Knowing my clever niece, I wasn't so sure about that. I walked over to the basement door, opened it and yelled down. 'Julie, can you come up here a minute?'

When her head appeared at the top of the stairs, I asked, 'Do you have access to your father's computer?'

Julie scowled. 'I can't believe you're asking me that, Aunt Hannah. No. He changed his passwords.'

I slumped. 'I was hoping he'd set up Find My iPhone.'

Julie's face brightened. 'Wait a minute!'

Without another word, she bolted through the kitchen, slamming the basement door behind her. I could hear her clump-clump-clumping up the stairs that led to the second floor, followed by a moment of silence, then more clump-clumping up the next flight of stairs to her father's office.

A minute later she reappeared, brandishing an iPad. 'Tah dah!'

Julie pulled out a stool and sat down at the kitchen island next to her mother. 'Dad fixed his computer, Mom, but maybe he forgot about his iPad. He hardly ever uses it.' She opened the black leather case. After several seconds she said, 'Damn! Battery's dead. Where's the charger?'

Georgina pointed to the kitchen counter. Julie hopped off her stool and plugged the device into a cord dangling from an outlet it shared with the toaster. For what seemed like hours, with the clock tick-tick-ticking overhead, we waited for Scott's iPad to revive.

'It's got fingerprint ID,' Julie said when the login screen finally materialized, 'but you can use the access code, too.' She tapped a few numbers, shook her head, backspaced and tried again.

'We're in!' Julie beamed at her mother. 'He's using your anniversary date, Mom.' To me, she confided softly, 'One of his faves.'

Georgina smiled, but blinked back tears.

I watched over Julie's shoulder as the screen refreshed and populated itself with Scott's personal icons. Julie swiped sideways, located the Find My iPhone app – a green radar screen icon – on the third swipe. She tapped the icon, and a map appeared with symbols for each of her father's devices on it: the iMac, the iPad and the iPhone.

Julie turned to her mother, eyes wide. 'Jeesh! His phone's in the backyard, Mom.'

Georgina shot from her chair, heading for the kitchen door.

'Stop!' I caught up with her and grabbed her arm, guiding her gently back to the stool. 'Was Scott working in the yard yesterday, Georgina?'

'He mentioned he might finish clipping the hedge I started, but from the looks of it, he never got around to it.'

'I'll go look for the phone,' Julie said.

'No!' Georgina shouted.

'But . . .'

'Don't argue with me, young lady!'

'I'll go,' I said. I extended my hand, palm up. Julie got the message and handed Scott's iPad over.

'I'm coming with you,' Georgina said.

'Are you sure, Georgina? What if he's . . .'

'Don't you even think that, Hannah.' And with a freezing sit-stay look at Julie, she shot out the door with me following, carrying the iPad.

TWENTY

Once we'd stepped off the flagstone patio, the neatly-manicured Cardinale lawn sloped gently down to the alley that separated the Colorado Avenue backyards from the backyards of the houses on Deepdene. The hedge Georgina had been tending was on the left – scraggly tendrils indicated where she'd left off – and a trampoline popular with the boys sat at the head of the driveway on the right.

Scott's cell phone signal seemed to be emanating from a shed in the back left corner of the yard, one that Paul had helped Scott assemble from a prefab kit purchased at Home Depot. The shed was approximately eight by twelve feet, in a classic farmhouse style, and the door was secured with a keypad combination lock.

Georgina cupped her hands around her eyes and peered into one of the windows that flanked the door. 'I can't see anything.'

'We'll need to go inside, Georgina.'

She turned a worried face in my direction. 'I'm afraid to look.'

'Scott could simply have left his phone in the shed.' I didn't sound convincing, even to myself. I considered the lock, suddenly filled with dread. 'Do you know the combination?'

Georgina nodded, punched in the code, pushed down on the handle and pulled the door open. I reached out to hold her back, but she was too quick for me. She stepped into the shed, froze, and started to scream.

My brother-in-law lay sprawled on the concrete floor, his head resting on a bag of mulch that had been slashed open, spilling its contents.

Before I could stop her, Georgina rushed to her husband's side and knelt in a pile of rich, dark soil.

'Don't touch anything!' I yelled, hoping she could hear me over her own anguished cries.

It was obvious from all the blood and Scott's open, sightless eyes that there was nothing we could do to help him now. I fell to my knees next to my sister and wrapped her in an embrace while she shook with sobs.

'He's dead, isn't he? Isn't he, Hannah? Who . . .?'

I didn't know the who but the how seemed clear. The garden shears I'd seen Georgina working with earlier in the week had been discarded nearby, their blades darkly stained with a substance that had to be blood, and Scott's head . . . I closed my eyes for a moment, swallowing the bile that rose in my throat.

Gathering courage, I felt Scott's neck, hoping for a pulse, but there was none. His skin was cold.

'We need to call the police,' I said, all the while urging my sister to her feet.

'I can't, I can't just leave him alone,' she stammered.

'There's nothing you can do for him, sweetie. C'mon. The sooner the police get here, the sooner they'll find whoever did this to Scott. Our being here will just make their job more difficult.'

I guided my sister reluctantly, step by agonizing step, back across the lawn and into the kitchen.

Julie, obedient for once, still sat on her stool, texting with someone on her iPhone. When she caught sight of our faces, hers crumpled. 'Did you . . .? What? He's . . .'

I reached out my hand. 'I'll need your phone, Julie. Take care of your mother.'

While Julie comforted her mother, I used her phone to dial 9-1-1. 'There's been an accident,' I told the dispatcher. 'I'm afraid he's dead.'

When the paramedics arrived just five minutes later, all three of us were bawling.

TWENTY-ONE

It's wicked to say so, but it's the honest truth. I will not miss Scott.

In the twenty-five years he'd been married to my sister, I could count on the fingers of one hand the number of times we'd actually agreed on anything, other than our mutual fondness for rum raisin ice cream. I had to be there for my little sister, though. Her tortured face, red eyes and swollen lids still haunt my dreams.

Two days after Scott's murder, I let myself in through her mudroom door, set the casserole I was carrying down on the cluttered counter, and wandered into the living room where I found Georgina propped up with pillows on the sofa, staring at the television.

Georgina's hair was swept up and clipped into place with a black, rhinestone-studded claw. Soft tendrils damply framed her face. She wore black slacks and a black scoop-neck pullover. A gold and ruby cross hung from a chain around her neck, resting lightly in her cleavage. I have to say this about my sister: she looked stunning in widow's weeds.

'What are you watching?' I asked, for want of anything cleverer to say.

Georgina picked up the remote and aimed. The TV screen went dark. 'Something on the Nature Channel. Meercats, with cameras strapped to their necks. They're ridiculously cute. I'm trying to cheer myself up.'

I sat down on the sofa next to her. 'What can I do to help?'

The question resulted in an avalanche of fresh tears. I watched in respectful silence as her mascara bled into black smudges under her eyes and left telltale trails down her cheeks.

'I'm sorry, sis,' I said after a bit. 'I didn't intend to upset you.'

She snatched another tissue from a box next to her on the end table, used it to dab at her eyes, then crumpled it up. It joined a heap of used tissues on the carpet next to her feet. She flapped a hand. 'It's OK, really. It comes and goes.' She pressed her palms flat against her knees, took a deep, shuddery breath, then let it out slowly. 'There's just too much to do. I'm overwhelmed.'

'Where are the kids?' I asked.

'Julie's taken Colin to the movies and Dylan . . . Dylan, he's . . .' She grabbed another tissue. 'Dylan's at the funeral home.'

'What about Sean?' I asked after a few seconds had passed and there was no sign of fresh tears.

'Sean's meeting with the lawyers. I can't deal with the financial stuff, Hannah. Stocks, bonds, investment accounts, I'm clueless. Sean's like his dad. A good head for figures.'

After a moment she said, 'I don't know what to do, Hannah! The police took Scott's computer, so we don't have access to any of his important accounts.'

'Maybe Julie . . .' I began.

'Absolutely not!' She stood up so suddenly that it surprised me. 'That little miss has overstepped her bounds, big time.' Her eyes narrowed. 'I thought you'd have a moderating influence on her, Hannah. I didn't expect you to aid and abet.'

It was second nature to object, but I kept my mouth shut. Georgina was speaking the truth.

'Can I get you anything? Coffee, tea . . . sherry?' she asked cheerfully, as if her stinging reprimand had never happened.

'No thanks, I have to drive home, but don't let me stop you.'

I trailed after my sister into the dining room where she poured herself a generous tot of dark liquid from one of the bottles she kept on a silver tray on the buffet. 'Gonzalez Byass Sherry Polo Cortado Anada 1987,' she recited, toasting me with her glass. 'A gift from one of Scott's clients. Only 987 bottles produced.'

I grinned. 'Finest kind.'

'Scott was appreciated by his clients.' She carried the glass to the kitchen, wobbling a bit unsteadily, even in her low-heeled sandals. I suspected this wasn't her first sherry of the day.

'Are there any plans for the funeral?' I asked.

'Plans? Plans?' Georgina shouted. 'Of course I don't have any funeral plans! Nobody expected Scott to die!'

I tried again. 'I just want to help, Georgina!'

Georgina shrugged and sipped her sherry. After a moment she said, 'I'm leaving the funeral up to Dylan. He can slug it out with the church.'

'Slug?' I said.

'Let's just say that the meeting I had with Brother Bob yesterday didn't go well.'

Although I was dying for details, I knew from past experience that now was not the time to press her. 'Why don't I start by putting some of these casseroles in the freezer?' I suggested instead.

'Suit yourself,' she snapped.

I was losing patience. 'I didn't drive all the way up here from Annapolis to have my head bitten off, Georgina.'

'I'm sorry,' she said, sounding genuinely contrite. '"Take a pill, Georgina!" That's what Scott would say.' She turned her back on me and stared out the kitchen window.

I steeled myself. 'Did Scott have a will?'

'What?' She hadn't even been listening.

'A will, Georgina. Did Scott leave a will?'

'Yes,' she said, much more calmly. Maybe the sherry was doing its job. 'We both did. Remember? When I asked if you and Paul would take care of the children if anything happened to us?'

'Of course I do. I just wasn't sure you'd gone forward with it.'

Georgina slid onto a kitchen stool and took another sip of her sherry. 'Oh, yeah. Signed, sealed, advance directive and all that shit. Scott was very thorough.'

At least my brother-in-law hadn't died intestate. What a mess that would have been.

'I feel like I'm living somebody else's life,' Georgina said after a bit. 'Why would anybody want to kill Scott, Hannah?'

'I don't know,' I replied, 'but once the police figure out the why, I'm sure they will quickly get to the who, or vice versa. We'll just have to wait for them to finish their investigation.'

'Hah! What's the Baltimore solve rate? Fifty percent?'

Most of those victims, I knew from reading the *Baltimore Sun*, had been young, male and black; the solve rate for white victims was much higher. But, I knew better than to argue with her. The police had taken Scott's computer and business records,

Georgina had said, so they must be working on the theory that the crime was related to his business, or maybe his crazy club, or maybe both. Scott had been a social guy. There could be a lot of crossover.

Georgina set the wine glass down. It was empty. 'Besides, they're way too busy questioning Julie,' she said.

'But they questioned you and all your children, didn't they?'

'Two times,' Georgina said. She pinged her wine glass with a flick of her fingernail. 'Dear me. It seems to have sprung a leak.'

The police had questioned Julie twice? That was news to me. Then again, of all the Cardinales, Julie's alibi had been the shakiest. The medical examiner estimated that Scott had died on Friday afternoon between two and four o'clock. After his dental appointment, Colin had been back in school, Georgina zonked out on Imitrex, the twins hanging out at the ocean with six friends and a keg, while Julie was home alone. The fact that she'd recently clashed with her father was an open secret, yet I found it impossible to believe that she had bludgeoned her father to death in the afternoon, then calmly cooked up chicken nuggets for her little brother at dinner time.

'Did Scott have any enemies?' I asked, sounding, even to myself, like a standard issue television detective.

Georgina rolled her eyes. 'Are you kidding? Everybody loved Scott. You saw all the cards, flowers, food.' She swept her arm around the kitchen. Her expansive granite countertop was littered with baking dishes, aluminum foil pans and Tupperware canisters, including the blue and white Corning Ware dish that held my own famous turkey tetrazzini. I wondered why I had bothered. It was like carting sand to the beach.

'I don't know what I'm going to do with it all,' Georgina whined. She wrapped a hand around her wine glass and struggled to her feet.

I plopped a bag of somebody's homemade dinner rolls on top of my turkey tetrazzini and headed for the basement door. 'Deep freezing things before they spoil would be a good start.'

'Go for it,' she slurred, and disappeared into the dining room with her wine glass.

TWENTY-TWO

'm ashamed to admit that the first time I set foot in my sister's church, it was to attend Scott Cardinale's funeral.

A lifelong Episcopalian, I preferred small parish churches like St. Catherine's in West Annapolis where my longtime friend, Eva Haberman, served as pastor.

Nothing prepared me for the Church of the Falls, an ultra-modern megalith that sprawled over a forty-acre site just north of the Baltimore beltway. Its spire, a twisted aluminum needle several hundred feet tall, seemed to pierce the sky.

'Jeesh,' said my sister, Ruth, sitting next to me in the back seat. 'It's even bigger than it looks on TV.'

Hutch glanced at his wife's reflection in the rear-view mirror. 'This guy's on TV? Like the "Hour of Power" or something?'

'Not that I know of,' Ruth said. 'I saw a show on PBS about the architect, some Swedish guy with lots of diacritical marks in his name. He's famous.'

I dipped my head, trying to get a better view of the spire out of the car window. 'So famous you forgot who he was?'

Ruth laughed. 'I remember he had a mustache and wore funny-looking square eyeglasses.'

'With a steeple like that,' Paul commented, 'they could broadcast Sunday services to Mars.'

'Maybe that's the plan,' I said.

Hutch steered his BMW off Padonia Road and into a paved lot the size of the satellite parking lot at BWI airport. An elderly gentleman carrying a clipboard and wearing an orange vest and matching ball cap greeted us at the entrance that was controlled by a turnstile sitting in the up position. The funeral home had provided us with a numbered card for our dashboard that said 'Family'. The attendant squinted at the permit, made a checkmark on his clipboard, then directed us to a parking place in a row of spaces marked *Reserved* nearest the sanctuary. 'Sorry for your loss,' he said, almost as an afterthought.

'What flavor is this church?' Hutch wanted to know as we joined a line of mourners in the antiseptic foyer, waiting our turn to file into the sanctuary.

'Evangelical,' I whispered. 'Where any liturgical tendencies come to die of neglect.'

Paul's elbow found my ribs. 'Shhhh.'

'Scott must have been popular,' Ruth mused as we accepted our programs from a young woman dressed entirely in white. Another young woman, identically clad, led us down the center aisle to our seats, our footsteps muffled by the dense blue carpet. With its raked, theater-style seating and overhanging balconies, I estimated the church could seat around a thousand. It was already half full.

Georgina and her children were seated in the left front row. Her glorious Titian hair hung long and loose, as I knew it would, 'the way Scott liked it'. Julie's stark black tresses, pulled back in a high, sleek ponytail, stood in sharp contrast to her mother's and the sandy, Scott-like heads of his three sons.

While the usher waited respectfully, we hugged our family one by one, shedding fresh tears, then slipped into our assigned seats in the row directly behind. A few minutes later, just as a female vocalist launched into a cringe-worthy rendition of something, as best I could determine, entitled 'I Will Rise', Emily, Dante and our three grandchildren arrived to occupy the seats just behind us.

Once at a family dinner, Georgina had given me an earful about music at Church of the Falls. It's fair to say that Georgina, a former church organist at All Hallows Episcopal in Baltimore's upscale Roland Park, was unimpressed.

'Honest to God, it breaks my heart,' she had said as she described a music program being led by a praise team that included a singer and an eight-piece band. 'I don't know where they've stashed the hymnals,' she said. 'They display the lyrics on flat screen Jumbotrons suspended from the ceiling.'

I looked up. Georgina had been right about the Jumbotrons. As the vocalist warbled and swooped her way through the song, its lyrics scrolled by on massive screens at the front of the church, flanking a colorful stained-glass window that depicted Christ's ascension into Heaven. 'Five years ago, a wealthy parishioner donated a brand-new Rogers Infinity pipe organ to the church,' Georgina had reported. 'It's got four keyboards and more than ten thousand pipes. Most organists would kill to play such an instrument. But that was before everybody was bashed over the head with guitars and pan flutes. It's hardly ever used, now.'

The vocalist had wrapped up her last Worthy-is-the-Lamb, when I felt a hand on my shoulder. I turned to see who it was and sprang to my feet. 'Daddy!'

I hugged my father, leaned back and mouthed a silent 'thank you'.

'Wrapped everything up as fast as I could,' Dad whispered. 'Had to put the birdwatching on hold, but Neelie thinks she can reschedule.' He released me, leaned across Paul to grasp Ruth's hand then focused his attention on Georgina, who nudged everyone over a seat to make room for him on the aisle. Dad sat down, slipped his arm around the back of her chair and drew his youngest daughter close. My heart lurched when Georgina rested her head on his shoulder.

Twenty years before, when her children were young and a decade before the happy surprise that was Colin, Georgina's sick fantasies had nearly torn our family apart. Scott had stuck with his wife, shepherding his family through the dark days until her recovery. If he seemed a little overprotective at times, well . . . Looking at my sister now, sitting strong and straight with her children around her, it all seemed worthwhile.

The praise band – guitar, electronic keyboard, flute, violin and drum kit – began to massacre the classic hymn, 'Old Rugged Cross'. In self-defense, I studied the program. The cover featured a color photograph of Scott lifted from the church directory. For his official mugshot as church treasurer, he'd worn a dark-blue suit and a yellow tie, which made him look more like your friendly, neighborhood real estate salesman than a highly-paid certified public accountant.

R.I.P. March 2, 1964 – August 18, 2018 was centered under Scott's picture. I swallowed hard. Just seeing the dates laid out in black and white made my brother-in-law's death seem more real.

As if I didn't need Scott's presence – in the form of cremains – to remind me that this day was no dream. Scott's ashes rested in an urn on a cloth-draped mini-altar centered just below the steps leading up to the chancel. Georgina certainly had good taste, I mused as I admired the ceramic Grecian-style urn. If Scott had been around to make the selection, it might have been a Tardis that launched his soul into time and space like Doctor Who.

I don't know who had written the memorial note – certainly not Georgina, who had told me she simply couldn't deal with it. I suspected one of Scott's two brothers – one older and one younger – who sat across the aisle from us looking shell-shocked, staring straight ahead. Scott had been born, according to the program, into a 'Catholic family of modest means' in Philadelphia, most of whom had predeceased him. I imagined his surviving brothers were having a hard time dealing with the vocalist, microphone in hand, who was roaming the aisle and plowing her breathless way through a tune called – according to the program – 'Just Save a Place for Me'. I felt nothing but relief when she wound it up and Pastor Robert Thomas Selden stepped up to the pulpit.

'My friends,' he began, 'I thank you and the family of Scott Cardinale thanks you for coming here today to celebrate Scott's life. I especially want to recognize . . .'

And the service droned on. And on. And on. As a general rule, Episcopalians discourage eulogies. If multiple speakers are allowed, they are usually limited to two or three minutes each, max. Apparently, no such rules applied at Church of the Falls. By the time two parishioners, a local businessman, three clients, the president of the local Rotary Club and one of Scott's brothers had finished eulogizing Scott, I pretty much felt like shuffling off this mortal coil myself.

My spirits revived when Dylan, the older of the twins by three minutes, stepped up to the pulpit. He stared straight into the congregation and recited, without notes and without fault, the Twenty-Third Psalm: *The Lord is my Shepherd, I shall not want . . .*

As the ancient prayer of comfort continued, Paul's arm snaked around my shoulder and pulled me close as I let the tears flow.

Ruth passed me a tissue from the packet she had half emptied herself.

After Dylan finished, I was astonished to see Julie ease out of her seat and exchange places with her brother in the pulpit. Taking her pitch from a single D from the instrumentalist sitting at the keyboard, my niece sang 'Amazing Grace' *a cappella* in a pure, high soprano voice.

The last note died away into total silence, broken only when a woman across the aisle, obviously overcome, exclaimed, 'The voice of an angel!'

I had no way of knowing whether Scott had gone to heaven or to 'the other place', but if heaven was his destination, I thought as I sobbed, he surely must have heard his daughter sing.

TWENTY-THREE

After the service ended, a white-clad usher escorted family members around a pink marble Baptismal font the size of a Volkswagen and out a side door. We followed the young woman down a long, glassed-in corridor that bisected a meditation labyrinth and a well-manicured courtyard abloom with seasonal flowers – coneflowers, asters and mums.

The corridor terminated at a pair of double doors that opened into a massive fellowship hall; a curtained stage dominated one end and a serious industrial-style kitchen the other. A wall of picture windows framed the neighboring woods like a mural in a budget hotel. Church ladies carrying trays bustled between the kitchen and a line of cloth-covered tables where volunteers busily arranged donations by basic potluck food group: salads, casseroles, breads and desserts with a token section, identified by tent cards, for diners of vegetarian or gluten-free persuasions.

A smartly-dressed woman – whether representing the church or the funeral home, I couldn't say – shook her head and silently tut-tutted, making it clear by gentle nudges that Ruth and I were meant to join Georgina and her four children in a receiving line.

I could think of nothing worse to ask of a grieving widow and her family. By some sort of sisterly telepathy, Ruth and I moved into protective positions flanking our baby sister. While I served as initial greeter, Ruth acted as relief pitcher, keeping well-wishers moving smartly along the line to Scott's two brothers and finally, to his bewildered children.

I was half listening to an over-caffeinated woman who had sung with Scott in the church choir – such a gorgeous tenor voice! – when Emily ushered her family into the room and, rather than joining the lengthening queue, sensibly shooed her ducklings toward the food. My stomach rumbled, no doubt in anticipation of the traditional green bean onion bake. I prayed there'd be some left by the time our ordeal was over.

I greeted choristers, musicians, ushers, flower arrangers, Bible study group members, sound technicians, janitors, cooks, gardeners and day care workers – was there anyone Scott didn't know? – until my hand throbbed. I had pretty much lost the will to live when a familiar face loomed into view. 'Dennis!' I kissed his cheek.

'I'm so glad to see you,' Georgina said, sounding completely sincere. 'It's been a long time.'

Chesapeake County police lieutenant Dennis Rutherford was married to Paul's sister, Connie. Although related to Scott only by marriage, they'd grown to know my sister and her husband well at family gatherings over the years. I was wondering what was keeping Connie when Dennis said, 'Connie sends apologies for not being here. She's got a sick calf.'

'I understand completely,' Georgina said with a wan smile. 'I hope the calf will be OK.'

'The vet's on the way,' Dennis said. 'Some sort of respiratory infection.' He kissed her cheek. 'I won't hold up the line, Georgina, but I hope to catch up with you later.'

'I'd like that, Dennis,' she said.

Dennis was followed by a succession of prosperous-looking businessmen – bankers, lawyers, restauranteurs and real estate developers, who according to whispered asides from Georgina, were members of Scott's 'stupid social club'. I wondered, briefly, why Cosmopolitan Forum members were coming through in a clump but gathered from casual chit-chat as they made their way past my duty station that they'd held some sort of pow-wow in the hallway following the service. As I smiled and greeted one bigshot after the other, I despaired. If everyone who attended the memorial service came through the receiving line, we'd be standing up shaking hands until Christ's Second Coming.

Fortunately, some parishioners were bypassing the queue hoping to get first dibs at the King Ranch chicken casserole or cheesy spaghetti bake. The praise band must have been particularly hungry after their performances because they sidestepped the line waiting to speak to Georgina and made a beeline for the pork sliders.

I was passing an elderly parishioner down the line and thinking I could kill for a pork slider myself when Emily materialized, seemingly out of nowhere. 'I'm probably breaking some sort of church protocol,' she announced, 'but this is silly.' So saying, she took ten-year-old Colin by the hand and snatched him out of the line. 'Let's get you something to eat, young man. After that, you can go outside and play with Timmy.'

I could see through the window that his cousin Timmy, my youngest grandson, was already swinging hand-over-hand from a piece of playground equipment that belonged to the church's day care center. Other youngsters were testing the durability of swings, slides, seesaws, spinners and spring riders. I wished I could join them, but at least thirty more people waited in line. I felt drained.

'Can you fake a faint?' I whispered to Georgina.

'I can do better than that,' she whispered back, and precisely on cue, burst into noisy, snuffling tears. Ruth, feigning concern, escorted Georgina in the direction of a round table near the stage, while I turned to those waiting in line and announced, 'So sorry, but Georgina's exhausted. I'm sure you understand.'

Unfortunately, the rules didn't seem to apply to the pastor and his wife. Five seconds after the receiving line disbanded, Pastor Robert Thomas Selden swanned into the room, aimed himself at my sisters and charged. Under the black robe he'd been wearing when he delivered the homily, Brother Bob wore a dark-blue silk suit, a pale-blue dress shirt and a red tie with a conservative blue stripe. His hair – a deep brown not heretofore seen in nature – was magnificently coifed, but suspiciously immobile. Was that a toupee, I wondered, or did his hair naturally grow that way? I tried not to stare too obviously at his forehead, searching for roots.

Clopping along behind him in sensible, low-heeled pumps was the minister's wife, Tamara, equally well turned out in a dark-navy suit and a white silk blouse. Her hair was styled in a no-nonsense chestnut pageboy that reminded me of my tenth grade Civics teacher. I hated her at once.

Target achieved, Tamara leaned in, her lips brushing Georgina's cheek, and said simply, 'Darling.'

'Georgina,' Brother Bob said, capturing Georgina's hand. 'We're so terribly sorry, uh . . .'

'For your loss,' Tamara said.

'If there's anything Tamara and I can do . . .'

'Please let us know,' his wife concluded.

I was sandwiched between a pair of talking bookends.

Ruth, the coward, took the opportunity to make her escape, heading for the food tables.

'The Women's Bible study group has organized a meal train,' Brother Bob began.

'With all you have on your mind . . .' Tamara continued.

'We don't want you to have to worry about shopping or cooking for a while,' Brother Bob said.

'They started the food deliveries two days ago.' Georgina smiled ruefully. 'Or maybe three. And they left such a helpful calendar saying who is bringing what on each day. My children and I can't thank you enough.'

'God never gives us more than we can handle, Georgina.' Brother Bob continued to pump Georgina's hand.

'You call us if you need any little thing,' his wife said.

Brother Bob leaned in, speaking close to Georgina's ear but loud enough for me to hear, 'What a blessing it is that Scott knew Jesus.'

After the pastor and his wife drifted away, I caught Georgina wiping her hand on her skirt.

Ruth waited until the coast was clear before returning with

a plate of food and a glass of pink lemonade. She set them down on the table and urged Georgina to tuck in. With Georgina in her capable hands, I went off to forage something for myself.

I ran into Julie and her brother Sean at the dessert table. 'I'm not really hungry, but if I'm stuffing myself with lemon bars I won't have to talk to anybody about Daddy,' Julie said, taking a bite.

I added a brownie and a cheesecake square to the chicken salad, green beans and cornbread on my plate. 'You look beautiful, Julie,' I said.

Julie shrugged. 'This dress? It's from my Goth period. Mom loaned me the pearls.'

'You ought to eat something other than sweets, Jules,' Sean scolded.

'You should talk,' she said, pointing out the assortment of desserts piled on her brother's plate.

My niece and nephew followed me back to their mother's table. In the few minutes we'd been gone, Daddy and Dennis Rutherford had also joined her.

'You're a cop,' Sean said to Dennis as he took a seat. 'Do you know what the police are doing to catch the sonofabitch who killed our dad?'

'See that guy over there, in the gray suit?' Still holding his lemonade glass, Dennis extended a finger and pointed. 'Dick Evans. Baltimore City homicide. He's leading the investigation. His partner's over there, next to the salads. Name's Pat Edwards. Wearing the black suit with the pink blouse.' He glanced at me. 'She kinda looks like you, Hannah.'

I followed his finger, squinting hard at the female officer. 'No, she doesn't.'

'Same height, weight, coloring, general build. Wears her hair the same way, too.'

I scowled. 'If I ever show up wearing a pussy bow like that, Dennis Rutherford, you will know that aliens have landed and taken over my body.'

'Hah!' He sipped his lemonade. 'She does, though.'

'Does what?'

'Look like you.'

'Poor thing,' I said.

'Do murderers often attend the funerals of their victims?' I asked after a bit. 'Like they do on TV?'

'That seems dumb,' Sean said. 'I'd sure as hell stay away.'

Dennis considered my nephew as if weighing his words. 'But what if the murderer is expected to be there? His absence would be a giveaway.'

'Do you mean . . .' Sean began.

'Murderers almost always know their victims,' Dennis said. 'That's why they are here.' By the tilt of his head, I knew he meant the Baltimore cops.

Julie said, 'Well, nobody's going to stand up, cackle like a maniac and say, "Ha ha ha! Glad he's dead! I did it!"'

'No,' Dennis said, glancing from Julie to Sean, 'but sometimes we get lucky.'

Dylan chose that moment to approach our table, head down, carrying a plate so heaped with food that he had to keep an eye on it. When he got close he looked up, frowned and veered away. Although two empty chairs remained at our table, he chose to sit down with some of the band members instead.

'Was it something I said?' Dennis asked of no one in particular. 'Has my deodorant failed?'

'What's up with Dylan?' I asked his twin.

Sean swallowed and waved a chicken wing. 'You'll have to ask him.'

'Where's your ever-loving?' Dennis asked me, suddenly shifting gears.

I pointed out Paul and Hutch who had their heads together with Dante over the industrial-sized coffee urn. I suspected by the way his arms wheeled about that Dante was holding forth on Spa Paradiso's latest acquisition: a hydrotherapy whirlpool.

'I'll just have a word,' Dennis said, and walked over to join them.

'Wait up,' Sean called after him. 'I need a cup of coffee.'

'Don't you want to join the boys?' I asked my father.

'Got some business to take care of first,' he said, reaching into his pocket. He pressed a key attached to a US Navy fob into my hand.

'What's that?' Ruth asked.

'Hannah said she wanted to look for something in the storage locker.'

My eyes slid to Julie and back. 'I'm hoping Grandmother Smith left some letters, diaries or something that might help solve the mystery of who our grandfather was.'

'That's a long shot,' Ruth said.

'Thanks, Dad,' I said. 'With all that's happened recently, the storage locker flew straight out of my head.' I slipped the key into my purse. 'Are you giving me carte blanche?'

'Keep the key as long as you need to, sweetheart. I'm glad you're going to sort through it, actually. After your mother died . . .'

I squeezed his arm. 'I know.'

Suddenly he smiled; his blue eyes twinkled. 'Besides, the rental is costing me a fortune. I'll have to clean the unit out eventually.'

A thought occurred to me. 'Are you back now for good, Dad? I'm thinking you might want to come along.'

My father shook his head. 'No can do. I'll trust you girls to take care of it.' He patted my hand. 'And now, I think I'll join the boys for some coffee.'

A few minutes after Daddy wandered off, Georgina said, 'See that woman over near the water cooler, talking to Brother Bob?'

I followed her gaze. 'Talking' didn't describe what I was seeing. 'Arguing' was more like it. Brother Bob stood nose to nose with a forty-something, bottle-blond, Botoxed woman dressed in a form-fitting gray sheath. She had the well-tended veneer I usually associate with third wives of aging billionaires. Brother Bob's face, on the other hand, had taken on a dangerously ruddy hue.

'Who is she?' I asked my sister.

'Judee McDaniel. Joo-dee with two Es, if you please.'

'Yes, but who is she?' I tried again.

'I know who she is,' Julie said. 'Director of the day care center.'

'Julie helps out in day care a couple of times a week,' her mother explained, favoring her daughter with an affectionate smile.

I stared at my niece. 'I didn't know that!'

Julie grinned. 'I try to keep a low profile.'

'What's day care got to do with Scott?' I asked.

'Oh, she's a church member, too,' Georgina said. 'And I don't like the way she manages . . . I mean, managed to sit next to Scott at Bible study. She always had the significance of the scripture reading down cold.' In a phony Southern accent, dripping with syrup, Georgina quoted, '"I've always thought that the book of Deuteronomy is structured as a series of farewell talks by Moses to the Hebrews as they prepare to end their years in the wilderness and claim the Promised Land."' She puffed air out through her lips. 'She probably looked it up on the Internet and practiced reciting in front of a mirror.'

Brother Bob ended whatever discussion he was having with Judee Two-Es by executing an abrupt about-face and stalking away.

'I really didn't think much of it at the time,' Georgina said, her eyes still on Judee, 'but Judee showed up a couple of weeks ago.'

'Showed up?' Julie squeaked. 'You mean at our house?'

Georgina nodded. 'One morning before lunchtime. I almost didn't recognize her. No make-up, and she was dressed in a fancy pink jogging outfit. Even her fricking shoes were pink. Said she'd stopped by to drop off an envelope for Scott from Brother Bob. Now I'm wondering . . .'

'Do you think Scott was having an affair?' Ruth cut in.

'No . . .' She paused. 'But . . .' She let the thought die.

My brother-in-law was smart enough not to be trysting with a woman in his own house, not with his wife likely to pop in at any minute. For a fleeting moment, though, I allowed myself to wonder how soundproofed Scott's third-floor office was.

As if reading my mind, Georgina said, 'If Scott had been having an affair, I would have known, Hannah. I would have known.'

'That's what Hillary Clinton thought, too,' I said.

Georgina suddenly ducked her head and muttered, *sotto voce*, 'Oh, oh, look out. Here she comes.'

Bearing down on us like a heat-seeking missile was Judee McDaniel. Target achieved, she leaned over the table and gushed, 'Georgina, I'm so sorry for your loss.'

'Thank you,' Georgina said in a small, flat voice.

'And you must be Georgina's sisters,' Judee said, glancing from me to Ruth and back to me again.

'Guilty,' I said. 'I'm Hannah and this is Ruth.'

'You girls look so different,' she said. 'If I hadn't seen you sitting together . . .'

'Oh, we're sisters, all right,' Georgina cut in dryly. 'And we have the DNA to prove it.'

Judee gaped like a fish, then plopped down in the empty chair between Julie and her mother. 'I understand you're taking a gap year, Julie. I was wondering if you'd be interested in taking a more active role in the day care center.'

While Julie described her plans, which in no way included the Church of the Falls Day Care Center, I had a chance to compare Georgina and Judee side-by-side. If Scott had preferred this sharp-edged, superannuated Barbie over my sister, he must have had rocks for brains.

Georgina abruptly stood, knocking the edge of the table with her knee, causing the drink cups to teeter. 'I'm done,' she announced. 'Time to go.'

'I'll rally the troops,' I said. 'Ruth? Julie? You ready?'

Both women looked relieved.

Ten minutes later, as we stood on the sidewalk outside the church waiting for Hutch who was driving us home, Georgina said, 'Now that Scott's gone, I'm never going to set foot in this horrible place again.' She linked arms with Sean on one side and Dylan on the other. Julie followed just behind, holding Colin's hand. And the little family walked to the waiting limo.

TWENTY-FOUR

Two days after Scott's funeral, I drove up to Baltimore to check on Georgina. When she didn't answer the doorbell, I walked around the back and let myself in through the mudroom door.

Georgina sat at the kitchen island nursing a cup of coffee,

leafing listlessly through a stack of sympathy cards. She glanced up when I came in, not seeming at all surprised. 'Sorry, Hannah. Was that you ringing the bell just now?'

I confessed that it was.

With a fluid sweep of her hand, she fanned the cards out on the counter like a deck of cards. 'I don't have to answer these, do I?'

'No, sweetheart, you don't.'

I hardly recognized Georgina's kitchen. Empty food containers littered the countertops; dirty plates and bowls teetered precariously in the sink; empty two-liter soda bottles were piled next to the recycling bin rather than in it. It looked like the morning after a New Year's Eve party when everybody slept in.

I opened the dishwasher, preparing to be helpful, but it was already full. I groaned silently. I pulled out the top rack and started putting glasses and cups away, making room for the next load.

'You don't have to do that, Hannah.'

'I know I don't, but your kitchen is usually so spotless. All this mess must be driving you nuts.'

'It's funny, but I just don't care.' She waved a card with a bouquet of lilies on the front. 'I hate lilies,' she said as she slid the card back into the envelope it had come in.

'With Scott not around to nag,' she said after a moment, 'I don't feel a pressing need to alphabetize the spice rack. Yesterday I put the basil away next to the poultry seasoning. It was surprisingly liberating.'

Georgina hopped off her stool and snatched the cereal bowl from my hand. 'I mean it, Hannah. Leave the dishes for the kids.'

'What's been wrong with the children up till now, then?' I asked, indicating the culinary detritus that surrounded us. 'Both arms broken?'

'School's back in session now,' she explained, 'and Julie's in and out interviewing. But they'll get around to it.'

'If you say so, but let me take the trash out, at least.' I peeked into the cabinet under the sink where Georgina kept the trash can hidden and wrinkled my nose. 'It's getting pretty ripe.'

Without waiting for permission, I tied up the reeking bag,

lined the can with a fresh one and began to fill a third bag with empty take-out containers, tinfoil pans, soiled plastic wrap, paper cups and balled up napkins. When the bag was nearly full, I stamped the trash down with my foot and added another couple of tinfoil pans.

'Do you recycle?' I asked my sister, indicating the accumulation of plastic soda bottles.

She picked up two bottles and handed them to me. 'Not today I don't.'

I added the bottles to the bag, pulled the plastic drawstrings and tied a knot. The rest could wait for the kids. Carrying the bags, one in each hand, I left through the mudroom door, heading for the garbage can in the back alley. As I passed the shed where Scott's body had lain for so long, I shuddered. No wonder nobody wanted to take out the trash. I scurried past the shed and escaped into the alley.

Baltimore City provides its residents with large green municipal trash cans on wheels. Using an elbow, I flipped open the top and tossed the bags in, jostling them around a little to make them fit.

Across the back alley, a Deepdene resident was doing the same thing. 'That's nice of you,' the woman said. She was dressed in khaki pants and a freshly pressed white camp shirt.

'I do what I can,' I said.

'Well, it's totally above and beyond the call of duty, I'd say.' She deposited her own, smaller bag into a trash can and let the lid fall with a hollow thud. She stared at me quietly for a while, as if waiting for me to say something, her gray eyes enormous behind thick lenses. 'You're here to collect the tape, I suppose.'

'Tape?' I repeated, thinking I'd misheard.

'From the security camera,' she explained.

Now that she mentioned it, I spotted the eye of a camera installed in the eaves of her house, aimed in our direction. 'Ah, yes,' I said. 'The tape.'

'Gordon installed the system himself,' she said, beaming with pride. 'As I told your partner, something has been getting into our garbage can and we were determined to catch it in the act. I never dreamed . . .' she began, then her face clouded. 'Didn't he tell you?'

Suddenly, the penny dropped. *She looks like you, actually,* Dennis had commented at Scott's funeral. Georgina's neighbor must be mistaking me for Pat Edwards, one of the homicide detectives working on Scott's case.

'It's always better to hear from witnesses directly,' I said, deftly sidestepping her question.

'I was on my hands and knees weeding my roses when I heard loud voices, so I looked up to see what was going on. We keep to ourselves, Gordon and I, and I don't like to stick my nose into other people's business, but after Mr Cardinale was murdered . . .' She paused, pressing a hand to her bosom. 'I saw one of the twins arguing with his father.'

My heart flopped in my chest and I struggled to keep my voice neutral. 'When was this?'

'On the very day the poor man died,' she said, wagging a finger to emphasize her words. 'I'm not sure of the exact time because I wasn't wearing my watch, but I'd just finished giving Gordon his lunch. Gordon has pimento cheese on wholewheat toast and a bowl of tomato soup every day at twelve-fifteen, so it must have been around one o'clock.'

I took a deep breath. My nephews had been one hundred and fifty miles away in Cape May, New Jersey on the day their father died. Or had they?

'Which twin?' I asked, trying to keep my voice steady. 'Sean or Dylan?'

She flapped a hand. '*I* can't tell them apart. But once you have the tape, I'm sure *you* can sort it out. Gordon transferred everything to a CD. Shall I get it for you?'

'No, don't do that, please,' I said, dismissing a totally insane impulse to grab the tape and make it disappear into the murky depths of the Patapsco River. 'An evidence technician will be around to collect it in due time. Chain of custody, you understand.'

'Oh, right, of course.'

'I was just . . .' I waved vaguely in the direction of my sister's house, then smiled. 'Guess I better get on with it.'

'I hope you catch whoever did this,' she said. 'Mr Cardinale was the *nicest* man. It's hard to believe that one of his children . . .' She shook her head.

'The investigation is far from over,' I said, hoping I was speaking the truth.

'Well, until they put that murderer behind bars,' she said, 'I'm sleeping with my doors double locked!'

'Always a good idea in the city,' I advised her over my shoulder as I trudged back to the house. When I got to the patio, I turned. She was still looking at me.

Back in the kitchen, Georgina had switched from coffee to wine. A bottle of Pinot Grigio, glistening with sweat, sat on the counter next to her elbow. Good. She was going to need it.

'When do the twins get home?' I asked.

She shrugged. 'They have different class schedules, but I expect them both for dinner.'

'Julie?'

'Who knows? Why do you ask?'

'We need to have a family meeting,' I said. 'And it needs to involve an attorney. Do you have one?'

'What the *hell* are you talking about, Hannah?'

'I was just talking to your backyard neighbor, and—'

'Claudia Turner?' she interrupted. 'Let me guess. Our dog's gotten into her garbage again.' She reached for the wine bottle and started to refill her glass. 'Buster has been dead for over a year. The woman's a kook.'

'Well, that kook just told the police that she saw one of the twins arguing with his father in the backyard on the day of Scott's murder.'

Georgina's hand began to shake. She set the wine bottle down. 'But that's crazy! Both of the boys were in Cape May that day. You know that. She's making it up.'

'The Turners have a security camera, Georgina. The police have a tape.'

Georgina stared at me, eyes wide and frightened. 'I don't understand.'

'Call your attorney, Georgina. And text the boys. They're needed at home. Now.'

TWENTY-FIVE

That evening, the Church of the Falls meal train ordered Pepe's pizza to be sent over to the Cardinale home. Pepe's pies are eleven on a scale of ten, but the funk I was in, even the Hawaiian Delight tasted like cardboard. I sprinkled hot pepper flakes on my slice. Result? Extra spicy cardboard.

The five of us perched uneasily on high stools around Georgina's kitchen island which was strewn with paper plates, plastic cups and half-eaten pizza. A sixth stool, still empty, was reserved for the family attorney, Tim Keane, one of Scott's Cosmopolitan Forum mates who specialized in tax law. He was running late. Neither was a good sign.

'Might as well get started,' Georgina said, officially bringing the family meeting to order. Skewering the twins with a penetrating, ice-green glare, she said, 'If what Claudia Turner told your aunt is true, the police already have, or are about to have, in their possession, a videotape of one of you arguing with your father in the backyard on the day he was murdered.'

Julie gasped. 'That's bogus! They were in Cape May.' She leaned into the island and addressed her brothers. 'You were in Cape May, right? Tell her, you guys.'

To my astonishment, the twins exchanged uneasy glances.

'OK,' I said, picking up on their body language. 'Which one of you was it?'

After a moment of nerve-wracking silence, Sean finally spoke up. 'We were *both* in Cape May, Aunt Hannah. An entire week, Saturday to Saturday. Sharing a condo. Partying at the beach with a bunch of fraternity brothers. That's what we told the police when they interviewed us last week, and it's the absolute truth.'

'But . . .' Dylan began, only to be interrupted by the jangle of the front door bell.

'Must be Tim,' Georgina said. 'Go let him in, please, Julie.'

Minutes later, Julie returned to the kitchen leading a dark-haired, stylishly-bearded man I guessed to be in his early forties dressed casually in deck shoes, chinos and a navy-blue V-neck sweater. He sported a bow tie spotted with *fleur de lis,* which in spite of the dark mood I was in, made me smile. 'Sorry,' Tim apologized as he joined us at the island. 'Parents night at my kid's school. Skipped out on Nora's study hall. Was the soonest I could manage. Blythe wasn't thrilled but agreed to cover for me.'

'Dylan was about to explain how he and Sean spent beach week,' Georgina said in a small, unsteady voice.

'What does it matter what we did?' Sean said, appealing to the attorney directly. 'What's important is we were in Cape May, New Jersey, not here.'

'Cape May's not that far away,' Tim Keane pointed out. 'You could get here from there in what, two and a half hours? I think we'll need to drill down a bit on your exact whereabouts on the afternoon your father died, don't you?'

'I can tell you what *I* was doing,' Dylan volunteered. 'Around ten, we hosted a kegger on the beach. Beer, barbeque from the Surfing Pig, the works.'

'Who is "we"?' Tim wanted to know.

'Sean, me, some frat brothers. Mike, Duke, Mac, Griff. Jeff was there for a couple of hours, too, but he had to leave early to go to work.'

'These guys have real names, I suppose?' Tim slid a small notebook out of his back pants pocket and extracted a slim, gold pen from its elastic pen loop.

'Sure.' Dylan scooped up his cell phone from the countertop and tapped the screen.

While Tim scribbled rapidly, copying down the twins' fraternity brothers' contact information as Dylan thumbed through the screens, Sean said, 'There were girls, too. But they weren't part of our usual gang, so we can't help much with that.'

Tim looked up. 'So, you were partying on the beach with a bunch of girls.'

'Yup. They just kinda showed up.'

'It's been a while since I graduated from college,' Tim said, 'but isn't the whole point of throwing a kegger on the beach that girls in bikinis will show up?'

'Busted,' Sean said.

Tim didn't smile. 'How long did this beach party go on?'

'Most of the day,' Dylan said. 'I left with Mike around three. A couple of the girls invited us to a poetry slam at The Magic Brain, so we went and hung out there until dinner time. I can't vouch for Sean.'

'Magic Brain?' Tim raised an eyebrow. 'Help me out here.'

'Awesome coffee shop,' Dylan explained. 'The kind of joint that whips up an oat milk iced dirty chai without breaking a sweat.'

'So, what's your story?' Tim asked, turning to Sean.

Sean shifted uncomfortably on his stool.

'He's about to lie,' Julie piped up unexpectedly. 'The tips of his ears are red.'

'Sean!' Georgina shrieked. 'This is important!'

Sean's face flushed the same color as his ears. 'I'm afraid I got wasted, Mom. I remember Dylan leaving the party, but it's hazy after that. There was this girl . . .'

'Says her name was Lacey,' Dylan supplied.

'Lacey, right. She'd remember me, but so would a lot of other people. What do you expect? We were out on the beach. There were a lot of party crashers.'

'Lacey who?' Georgina asked.

Sean shrugged, looking like a lost child. 'I don't know.'

Georgina's eyes narrowed dangerously. 'You don't *know*?'

Before the situation could escalate into full-blown war, Tim moved on. 'When did you last see your brother, Dylan?'

'He was there at noon, for sure, but after that . . .' His voice trailed off. 'As Sean said, the party attracted a lot of people.'

'Dylan! You have to vouch for Sean!' Julie cried.

'You want me to lie, Jules?'

'Of course not, but you *know* Sean didn't kill our dad.'

'All I *know*,' Dylan said, turning to address his twin, 'is that you disappeared from the party around noon and I didn't see you until the next morning when you staggered back to the condo, hungover and stinking of hops.'

'Jesus,' Georgina whispered.

'I'm sorry, Mom. I must have blacked out. I remember playing a couple of rounds of beer pong . . .' Sean rested his head in his hands, wagging it slowly as if still nursing the massive hangover he must have had that day. 'I woke up around ten in a motel room with this girl. She didn't seem in any hurry to leave . . .'

'So. What. Could. You. Do?' Dylan sneered.

Tim held up a cautionary hand, then turned to Sean. 'What motel?'

'Three stories, balconies overlooking the beach. Might have been blue. God, I don't know, Mr Keane! They all look the same!'

'No sign out front? In the lobby?'

Sean shook his head. 'I left out the back, via the beach.'

'If you show up on that surveillance tape, you'll need to beef up that alibi,' Tim warned.

'Wait a minute!' Sean said, his face brightening. 'How was I supposed to get here, huh? Walk? You can check out my car. It never left the parking garage. Check the EasyPass records. Any route you take, there'd be a toll. Interstate 95, the Bay Bridge, the Lewes ferry. All tolls.'

'Good point,' Tim said.

'Are we supposed to know about this security tape?' Georgina asked me, sounding eager to change the subject.

'Of course not,' I said. 'I didn't exactly lie to Mrs Turner, but I didn't correct her when she mistook me for a police officer, either.'

'It could be *anybody* on that tape,' Georgina insisted. 'Scott met lots of clients at the house. And Mrs Turner is blind as a bat.' She turned to me. 'You must have seen her glasses. And she mistook you for a woman at least twenty years younger.'

'Thanks, Georgina,' I said. 'I wonder where I stashed my cane?'

'If the Turner tape has any evidentiary value, and we're just guessing here, I'm sure the police will want to talk to you about it,' Tim said, moving on. 'But let's not jump the gun.'

'Mrs Turner told me her husband installed the security system himself. We can always hope he wasn't very good at it,' I said wryly.

'You need to alibi for each other,' Julie urged her brothers. 'Nobody can tell you apart, so if the tape shows one of you arguing with Dad, there's no way anyone could tell which one of you it was.' She managed a lackluster smile. 'I read that in an Agatha Christie novel once, or maybe it was Mary Higgins Clark.'

I wasn't so sure about that. Sean wore his hair parted on the left, his bangs swept casually to one side, while Dylan preferred a French crop, rocking that tousled, just-climbed-out-of-bed look. If they both opted for crew cuts, however, it would definitely take a family member to tell them apart.

Sean bristled. 'But, Jules! I don't care what's on the tape. I was nowhere near Baltimore when Dad died!'

'I can definitely prove where *I* was,' Dylan cut in. 'Sean needs to be held accountable for his own actions. Getting blind drunk and shacking up with a woman he doesn't even know . . .' He paused. 'What happened to your Virginity Pledge, Sean? Huh?'

Sean recoiled as if he'd been slapped.

'True love waits,' Dylan recited. 'I am making a commitment to myself, my family and my creator that I will abstain from sex before marriage. I will keep my body and my thoughts pure as I trust in God's perfect plan for my life . . .'

'Total bullshit,' Sean growled. He picked up a piece of pizza, considered the cheese congealing on top like a sheet of blistered plastic, frowned and dropped it back on the paper plate.

'"Flee from sexual immorality",' Dylan sputtered, rising from his stool. 'First Corinthians. "Every other sin a person commits is outside the body, but the sexually immoral person sins against his own body".'

'"He that is without sin among you, let him cast the first stone",' Sean shot back. 'John eight seven. Remember Kayla Mills? Senior prom?'

Georgina pressed her palms flat against her ears. 'La, la, la, la, I can't hear you!' she sing-songed.

I snatched my sister's hand away. 'Not listening isn't going to help, Georgina.' I turned my attention away from Georgina long enough to give the evil eye to my nephews. 'And hurling Bible verses at one another like rival evangelicals isn't going to help either, dammit.'

Aunt Hannah's curse seemed to have a sobering effect on the twins.

'I have a rock solid alibi,' Dylan said after a moment of quiet reflection.

'And I don't,' Sean said, finally admitting the truth.

'Unless we can find Lacey,' I said.

'Facebook?' Julie suggested.

'Did anybody take pictures at the beach party?' I asked the twins.

'I imagine so,' Dylan said. 'Everyone has a cell phone.'

'Do either of you have a picture of Lacey?'

'I do!' Sean said, bending over to retrieve his cell phone from the backpack at his feet. 'I can't believe I forgot about that. We took a selfie at Uncle Charlie's Ice Cream.' While Sean brought his cell phone to life, I turned to his brother.

'Did any of your friends – Griff, Duke, whoever – hook up with any of the girls in Lacey's group, Dylan?'

'Maybe. Dunno.'

'Here it is!' Sean said, rotating the screen of his cell phone so we could all see the photo.

The young woman glancing sideways at the camera – lush lips puckered, caught in the act of planting a kiss on my nephew's check – wore her dark blond hair in a tousled, jaw-length bob. The straps of a flowered, halter-style bikini top were tied loosely around her neck. The waffle cone she held out – two scoops of chocolate topped with a rainbow of sprinkles – loomed gigantic-ally in the foreground.

'Lacey's cute,' I observed.

Sean flushed. 'I thought so, too.'

'Email that photo to your pals,' I said.

Sean cradled his cell phone in his left hand. 'What am I supposed to tell them?'

'Don't mention the police, that might scare them off,' Tim suggested. 'Say that you met this girl, Lacey, you really liked her, but because of what happened, yadda yadda, you forgot to get her contact information.'

Head down, Sean's thumbs began to dart over the tiny screen. Suddenly he paused and looked up. 'You actually believe me, don't you, Aunt Hannah?'

'I do.'

'Then who the hell could be on that surveillance tape, arguing with Dad?'

'I don't know, Sean,' I said, 'but if the police take the tape seriously, and if we're allowed to see it, maybe we'll be able to figure it out.'

'That's a lot of ifs,' Georgina said.

'And here's another if for you,' Tim said, rising to his feet. 'If the police come around asking questions about the tape, you're going to need a criminal defense attorney, and that's not me.'

'Bite your tongue,' Georgina said.

Tim scribbled in his notebook, tore the page out and handed it directly to Sean. 'Just in case. Call this number. Ask for Sydney Foster.'

Sean stared at the slip of paper, looking sad and vulnerable. 'But how can I afford—'

'Hush, Sean,' his mother interrupted. 'We'll pay for it somehow.' She slid off her stool. 'Thank you for coming, Tim. I can't tell you how much we appreciate your advice. Let me know how much we owe you.'

Tim waved the request for payment away. 'No charge, Georgina. It's the least I can do for Scott. He sent a lot of business my way. I'm going to miss him, in more ways than one. Scott was one hell of a bocce player.'

Georgina escorted Tim out of the kitchen. When she was out of earshot, Dylan laid a hand on his brother's arm.

'Sorry I lost it back there, bro. Just want you to know that I've got your back. Blood is thicker than water, as they say.'

'Damn right,' Julie said.

TWENTY-SIX

Several days went by. No homicide detectives knocked at the Cardinales' front door and I began to wonder if I'd dreamt up the whole conversation with Claudia Turner. Nobody mentioned it, but the specter of the neighbor's videotape hung over our heads on the slenderest of threads, like the sword of Damocles.

Yet our lives went on.

Through daily text messages, I learned that the twins were throwing themselves into their graduate work at Hopkins – Sean in Economics and Dylan in History – while Julie was busily applying for volunteer positions with AmeriCorps, teaching internships in East Asia, as well as exploring missionary opportunities in poverty-stricken Central American countries sponsored by Church of the Falls. At the moment, she was leaning in favor of an international organization that would send her to teach computer skills to children in the Dominican Republic, but according to Julie's latest Tweet, 'The jury is still out.'

Meanwhile, nobody had been able to track down Lacey.

Nope, sorry. Good-looking chick, though.

Sweet! But no clue.

Good luck, dude. She's hot.

Hey, babe! You can grab me a beer any time!

Is she the ice maiden who came with Brie?

Sadly, Brie had no clue either.

To keep my mind off looming disaster, I threw myself into work on our family tree, an exercise that I'd sadly neglected in the aftermath of Scott's murder. I signed up for GedMatch, the most scientific of the publicly available genetic databases. It had been created in 2010 by a Florida grandpa and a transportation engineer from Texas who had no idea that their little 'side project' would eventually become the go-to destination not only for serious genealogists, but for investigators across the country to solve the coldest of cases.

Nick had recommended the site during a FaceTime chat from a state park in Iowa, one of several stops they'd made on their long drive home. He'd recently contributed his own family data to the database, a consolation prize, he soberly claimed, for having to leave town before they'd had a chance to meet the rest of the cousins. In the heartbreak and confusion following Scott's death, however, it seemed the proper thing to do.

Nick had warned me that GedMatch was barebones and utilitarian. After I uploaded Julie's and my raw data and selected the One-to-Many analysis, I could see what he meant. I was presented with a multi-columned table with cryptic headings that went on for screen after screen after screen. The meaning of kit number, name and email were transparent, but the remaining columns? Something only a rocket scientist could love.

Back in the day, my technical support team at Whitworth and Sullivan had an abbreviation for it: RTFM. As I puzzled over my search results, I decided I'd better Read the F-ing Manual myself.

I watched the YouTube tutorial three times. I downloaded the GedMatch Absolute Beginners Guide and read it from beginning to end.

SNP, IBS, IBD and MRCA? The manual lost me at single nucleotide polymorphisms. And the red, yellow, green and blue bars that compared individual chromosome strands like disk fragmentation charts on my old PC made my eyes roll back in my head.

We had another abbreviation at Whitworth and Sullivan: KISS. Keep it Simple Stupid.

Did I need to know what haplogroup I belonged to? Probably not, but the number of shared centimorgans (cM) seemed key. The more centimorgans you have in common with someone, the closer you are related. Julie's name topped my match list. My niece and I shared approximately 1700 cMs, or about twenty-five percent of our DNA. No surprises there.

The GENerations column was critical, too. Using the One-to-One option, I compared Julie's results with Nicholas's and Mai's. The GEN column for each read four. Roughly translated, according to the tutorial, the cousins' MRCA – most recent common ancestor – was four generations away. Thus they shared a great-great-grandparent. When I compared myself with Nick and Mai, the GEN value was 'three' – my great-grandparent, their great-great-grandparent. Who could that be but John Otaktay 'Kills Many' Johnson? If Hawk had been our most recent common ancestor, the values would have been two for me and three for them, respectively.

Proof positive, at least to me, that White Bear was my biological grandfather, and not his brother, Hawk. My heart beat a little faster just having my suspicions confirmed.

Seeking more information about my new family, I Googled 'American Indian census' and was directed immediately to the website for the National Archives and Records Administration in Washington, DC. The Indian Census Rolls 1885-1940 were archived on six-hundred-and-ninety-two rolls of microfilm, but, sadly, not indexed. Further complicating my research, the pages were displayed sideways, and the view could not be rotated. After half-an-hour's scrolling with my head tipped sideways, I stopped, massaged the crick in my neck and muttered aloud, 'There has to be a better way.'

Fortunately, there was. Google informed me that Ancestry. com, bless their generous hearts, had uploaded the microfilm records from the National Archives and (hallelujah!) indexed them. I logged on to their website.

In 1913, Otaktay, his wife Ehawee and their children Matoska, age two and Tahatan, age zero, lived together on the Pine Ridge reservation. Wasula joined the family in 1916. By 1936, Tahatan had married Kimimela and baby Takoda joined the tight-knit family unit, but Wasula, then around twenty years old, had moved on.

Had Wasula married? I added the question to the list I had for my cousin Nick the next time we had a FaceTime conversation.

Extrapolating from the census information, White Bear had been born around 1911. When, exactly, had he died and, thinking about Wasula's belief that her brother's death had been no accident, more importantly, how?

Finding the 'when' was easy. According to the South Dakota death index, grandfather Joseph White Bear passed away on September 4, 1932. No birth date or cause of death was listed on the digital record, though – a scan of a printout so old it had holes at the sides for feeding the paper through a dot-matrix printer.

Wasula had mentioned that White Bear had been a rodeo star. I wondered if his skills had attracted the attention of any contemporaneous newspapers. If he'd been famous enough, his death would surely not have gone unreported.

Deadwood, South Dakota must have been a happening place in the 1930s. Of eleven South Dakota newspapers publishing between 1920 and 1932, five were located in Deadwood. And Joseph White Bear himself had been a busy boy. Beginning in 1927, his name began popping up in lists of rodeo performers all over the Mount Rushmore State. By 1930, his appearance would be a headliner for the annual Days of '76 Celebration held in Deadwood every August.

The August of 1932 was no exception. According to the *Deadwood Pioneer-Times*, my grandfather had won the champion bucking contest and a purse of $800.

I sat back. $800 would have been a fortune back then. I minimized the newspaper and brought up a new search window. Adjusted for inflation, $800 in 1932 would equal $13,508.16 in today's dollars. White Bear was a rock star, indeed.

From the *Pioneer-Times* several weeks later, though, came this distressing news:

> *Saturday, September 3. Yesterday this newspaper received advices from John Kills Many in Pine Ridge stating that his son Joseph White Bear, who was injured recently in a rodeo accident at Rosebud when a bucking horse fell on him, had suffered similar injuries in a rodeo performance at White River. Reports first received in Pine Ridge stating that he had been fatally injured later proved to be exaggerated. His son resumed participation in different rodeos in that section. Riding again on Wednesday of this week a bucking horse again fell with him and he sustained injuries from which recovery is quite doubtful. He is at St Mary's hospital in an extremely critical condition from a fracture to the skull. Many friends and acquaintances in this section of the Hills will regret to learn of his misfortune.*

Although I paged forward looking for it, there was no formal announcement of his death or any funeral.

The newspaper's account of White Bear's accident didn't dovetail with the story Wasula had been told, that he'd been trampled to death by his horse in its stall. Had she been intentionally misinformed, or had the *Pioneer-Times*? Being fatally trampled by one's own horse would have been an ignominious way for a rodeo star to die. Had John Kills Many invented a rodeo accident in order to salvage his son's reputation? Or had he invented the story to cover up his murder, as Wasula clearly believed?

When Nick called several days later, his hair sticking out in spikes as if he'd just stepped out of the shower, I told him what I had found out about his great-great-uncle, my grandfather. 'He died on September 4th,' I said. 'According to the newspaper, it was a rodeo accident.'

Nick's dark eyes flashed. 'He didn't die, Cousin Hannah. White Bear walked on.'

'That's a lovely way to put it,' I said. 'Walking on. Where do the Lakota believe people go after they die?'

'To Wakan Tanka, the spirit world in the sky.'

'We'd say heaven.'

'Exactly.' He grinned. 'So would the priests at our school.'

'Can you tell me where my grandfather's buried?' I asked. 'One day, I'd like to visit his grave.'

'That's a more complicated issue,' Nick said. 'These days, we bury our dead in cemeteries and mark the graves with decorated crosses just like everyone else. Back then, though, White Bear would have been dressed in his best clothes and placed on a scaffold, along with his possessions. Food would have been set out for him as if he were still alive. There'd be a wake, too, and it might go on for two or three days. Then his body would have been taken down and buried in the ground under a big pile of rocks. It's hard to say where the grave would be now.

'Wasula kept his soul bundle,' Nick added.

I must have looked puzzled because Nick went on to explain how it was customary for a lock of hair cut from the deceased to be held over burning sweetgrass to purify it. Then it would be wrapped in a piece of sacred buckskin while mourners smoked the Sacred Pipe. 'The buckskin bundle would be kept in a special place for about a year, then carried outside and released,' Nick said. 'Wasula was the keeper of her brother's soul.'

'Golly,' I croaked, overcome by the image. I swallowed, took a deep breath and asked, 'Did Wasula ever marry?'

'Oh, yes,' Nick said. 'A cantankerous old fellow from what I understand, named Jesse Has Horns. He died long before I was born.' He paused. 'Have you ever heard of code talkers?'

'Of course,' I said. 'The Navajo code talkers were famous for stymieing the Japanese.'

'Little known fact. There were more than sixty Lakota code talkers, too,' Nick said. 'Jesse Has Horns was one of them. He spoke three Sioux dialects. Served in the South Pacific. His skills were so critical he had two bodyguards. I gather the Japanese knew about the code talkers and sent snipers out to get them. Jesse came home safely in 1946, but the bullets, mortars and bombs really got to him. He died of alcoholism in the early fifties.'

'What a shame,' I said.

'Alcoholism is a sad fact of life on the reservation,' Nick said.

I simply stared at Nick's image on the screen, not sure what to say.

'Father once told me that White Bear was buried with Wakinyan,' Nick said after a moment.

I searched my memory banks. 'Wakinyan?'

'Wakinyan. Thunder Spirit, his horse.'

A wave of sadness washed over me. Two senseless deaths: first the talented young man, my grandfather, then his magnificent, spirited horse.

'Was that because they believed that Thunder Spirit killed him?'

'It's hard to say, Hannah. I know that the horses of some Lakota, particularly warriors, were sometimes sacrificed at the grave and their tails tacked up on the scaffold.'

I shivered. 'I hate that custom.'

'Needless to say, we don't do that any more.'

'I'm glad to hear that.'

'So, what's happening with the investigation into your brother-in-law's murder?' Nick asked, deftly turning the conversation from two senseless deaths to a third.

I told him about my conversation with Claudia Turner and about the possibility that one of the twins had been home on the day of the murder and had lied about it.

Nick whistled.

'Although it's been days now,' I added, 'and we haven't heard a word from the police about any tape, so maybe . . . well, knock on wood.' I reached out and tapped my solid oak bookshelf three times.

But I guess I didn't knock hard enough.

TWENTY-SEVEN

The telephone rang just after nine a.m., jolting me out of the *New York Times* crossword puzzle. I filled in B-A-L-D for 'barely-there tires' and picked up.

'They've arrested the twins!' Georgina cried.

'Just now?'

'Yes!' she wailed, sounding desperate.

'Miranda warning, handcuffs, the whole bit?' I asked, starting to feel panicky myself.

Georgina took a deep breath. 'Well, no. That detective, what's his name, Evans, and that officer who looks like you. Said they were taking Sean and Dylan downtown for questioning.'

'She doesn't look like me,' I insisted, emphasizing every word.

'Are you listening to me?' Georgina said. 'They. Took. The. Twins.'

In my experience, when the cops *really* come to get you, they arrive at the crack of dawn while you're still in your jammies. No time for phone calls. No time for coffee. Grab you when you're most vulnerable – *Yes, yes, I did it! Now please may I have a cup of coffee?*

'Relax,' I told my sister. 'It's not serious until they get out the handcuffs.'

'I told the twins not to say anything until the attorney got there,' Georgina said.

'Tim?'

'No. I called that guy that Tim recommended. Sydney Foster. I think we need the big guns, don't you?'

'Wouldn't hurt. Is he going to meet the boys at the station?'

'I don't even know where that is!' she whined.

'East Fayette Street,' I said, speaking from personal experience, 'but the attorney will know that.'

'I didn't actually talk to him,' Georgina said, 'but I left a message with his service.' I heard a sharp intake of breath. 'What if he doesn't get there in time?'

'Don't worry, Georgina. Sean and Dylan are not stupid.' After a moment I added, 'Do you want me to come up?'

Georgina heaved a sigh. 'Would you? I don't want to be alone.'

'You're alone?' That surprised me. 'Where's Julie?'

'Working at the day care center. She'll be home around three.'

'Maybe the twins will be back by then, too,' I said, trying to sound reassuring. 'And I'll be there as soon as I can.'

After I hung up, I filled a travel mug with coffee, doctored it with half and half and extra sugar, texted Paul to say where I was going and set out.

I'd driven to Baltimore so often in the previous month that my car could probably navigate there on its own. To keep the drive interesting, I like to vary the route every now and again. That day, I decided to skirt the Inner Harbor and head straight up Charles Street, a slower trip by five minutes or so, but less stress-fraught than the beltway.

I stopped by Eddie's to pick up a continental breakfast tray before heading around the corner to my sister's. Fueled by coffee and Danishes, I helped Georgina address thank you notes while we waited for news, good or bad.

All the mini-Danishes were gone by the time Dylan texted: *Hey! Don't worry. On our way home.*

Georgina collapsed over the countertop, limp with relief.

'Sit down,' I said, when the twins wandered into the kitchen twenty minutes later, looking glum but not suicidal.

'Who pigged out?' asked Dylan, eyeing the half-empty platter.

'Hush up, young man,' I said. 'I'm on a sugar high and could be dangerous.' I shoved the platter in his direction. 'Help yourself. Sit down. Then talk.'

'Did the lawyer show up?' Georgina wanted to know as she watched her sons tuck into the pastries.

'Ms Foster? Yeah, she was super,' Dylan said.

That caught my attention. 'She?'

Dylan shrugged. 'Tall, brunette, around forty wearing wicked don't-mess-with-me glasses.'

I'd forgotten Sydney could be a girl's name, too.

'You were right about the videotape, Aunt Hannah,' Sean mumbled around a mouthful of croissant. 'They questioned Dylan and me separately, but afterwards, Ms Foster got us together and the cops showed us the video.'

'Jesus, Mary and Joseph!' Georgina blurted. 'So? So? Don't keep us in suspense, dammit! Who was it?'

Instead of answering his mother, Sean turned to me. 'It was surreal, Aunt Hannah, like looking in a mirror. My God, it *is* me, I thought. Maybe I drove home in a blackout?'

My heart did a somersault. 'You mean you *lied* to everyone earlier about your whereabouts, Sean?'

'No, no!' He swiped at his bangs, clearing them out of his eyes. 'I was at the beach, like I said. The guy on the tape? He looked exactly like me, but he couldn't have been.'

On the next stool over, Dylan nodded. 'I thought it was Sean, too.' He turned to his brother. 'Sorry I went off on you like that, bro, but when I saw the tape, I thought you'd been shitting me.'

'We asked them to run the tape again, and there was something not quite right about it.' Sean wiped his hands clean on a napkin, balled it up. 'Whoever the guy was, he was wearing a light-blue windbreaker. I don't even *own* a windbreaker, let alone a light-blue one,' he said with a tone of distain, as if owning such a garment would be a fashion *faux pas*.

'But if he looked like you, Sean, why did the police let you go?'

Dylan answered for his brother. 'Because the tape doesn't prove anything, Mom. Let's say, just for the sake of argument, that it was actually Sean on the tape. All it proves is that Sean talked to Dad around one-fifteen and that he lied about it for some reason. There can't be any physical evidence connecting Sean to Dad's murder or Sean would be sitting in the slammer as we speak.'

'Sydney Foster asked if I was being charged with a crime, and they said, "Not at this time". She told me there's a possibility they'll come back to me later, so I shouldn't get too complacent.'

'What does the tape actually show?' I asked. Sean had just bit into another croissant, so I aimed the question at Dylan.

'It was really hard to watch,' Dylan said, his voice choked with emotion. 'I really miss him, you know?' His Adam's apple bobbled as he swallowed hard. After a moment, he said, 'Dad walks down the driveway with this guy who looks like Sean, they talk a bit over by the trampoline, then Dad walks down the lawn toward the shed.'

'The guy follows him,' his brother continued without missing a beat.

'Did either man seem angry?' I asked Sean.

'No, they were just talking. But Dad has this body language, you know, like he wishes the fellow would just go away.'

'Then Dad gets out his cell phone,' Dylan continued. 'Looked like he was taking a call. Anyway, he turns his back on the guy.'

'After Dad finishes the call,' Sean went on, 'he sticks the phone back in his pocket, turns around, looking surprised the guy is still hanging around. Then the guy takes a piece of paper out of the pocket of his windbreaker, unfolds it, and shows it to Dad.'

'They talk for a couple of minutes, then the guy walks away,' Dylan said.

'Which way did he go?' I asked.

'Back toward the house and down the driveway,' Sean said.

'And your dad?'

'Went into the shed and came out with the hedge clippers, then . . .'

'Fade to black,' added his brother.

Georgina, who had been listening silently while her sons told their story, finally spoke up. 'What I don't understand is this. If your father was killed in the shed, how come the actual murderer didn't show up on Claudia Turner's videotape, later on when it actually happened?'

'You're not going to believe this,' Dylan said, 'but a pigeon flew up and perched on the camera, skewing it down. All it recorded after that was Mrs Turner weeding her mint patch.'

'Then they shouldn't be bothering my children,' Georgina huffed. Turning to the twins, she asked, 'Does that mean you're both off the hook?'

Sean shrugged, his face turned serious. 'They told us not to leave town.'

Georgina snorted. 'I thought cops only said that on television.'

'I'm not going anywhere anyway, Mom. I'm working on a team project and they'd kill me if I ran out on them.'

'What kind of project?' I asked, genuinely curious.

Sean made quote marks in the air. 'Land Use, Parking, and Post Internal Combustion Settlement Patterns.'

Dylan grinned. '"If this young man expresses himself in terms too deep for me, why, what a very singularly deep young man this deep young man must be".'

Quoting Gilbert and Sullivan, I thought, smiling to myself, was a refreshing change from slinging Bible verses about like weapons.

I had opened my mouth to ask Sean what in blue blazes his project was about when, correctly reading the puzzlement on my face, he clarified, 'Urban planning. We're looking for cures for Parkageddon.'

'Ah,' I said, trying to sound wise.

'We're not quite finished here,' Sean said, reaching for his cell phone and tapping it to life. 'The cops isolated a frame from the videotape, enhanced it and made a still. They gave the still to our attorney, but she let me take a photo of it after we got into the cab.' He hopped off his bar stool, walked around to our side of the counter and set his cell phone down between his mother and me.

I stared at the image on the screen. My nephew, Sean Cardinale, stared right back.

Next to me Georgina gasped and grabbed my arm. 'No way!'

I leaned closer, squinting at the tiny screen.

Like looking in a mirror, Sean had said earlier, and yet . . . I flicked my fingers to enlarge the image. 'This isn't Sean,' I said, trying to keep my voice calm. 'Take a look.' I circled my hand in the air until I had everyone's undivided attention. 'Sean parts his hair on the left. This guy, whoever he is, parts his hair on the right.'

'Maybe the image's reversed?' Georgina suggested.

'Nope,' I said. 'The numbers painted on the garbage bins are right way round.'

'It's not Sean!' Georgina whooped.

'No, it's not.'

'Then who the hell *is* it?'

'That's a very good question.' I looked up at Sean. 'I think you better call Ms Foster, don't you?'

'They say everyone has a doppelgänger,' Dylan mused. 'Someone who looks exactly like you, down to that annoying mole you've been meaning to have removed.'

'Story of my life,' Sean snorted.

'I didn't mean twins, obviously,' his brother said.

'Time out, boys,' I said. 'One of you call Sydney Foster now. Let her know what we've discovered about the guy in this picture. In the meantime, keep looking. I think Lacey will be easier to find than doppelgängers.'

TWENTY-EIGHT

Several days later, I met Georgina for lunch at Atwater's Belvedere Square Market, a popular eatery featuring home-made soups and artisanal sandwiches. After picking up our order at a counter inside the sprawling market, we managed to snag one of the sidewalk tables, shaded from the noontime sun by a green and white awning.

The police had been strangely quiet, and we hadn't heard anything more from the twins' attorney, but rather than feeling relieved, our nerves were humming with unresolved tension.

'I think we need some time away. Just us sisters. You, me and Ruth,' I said after we sat down, emphasizing my point with a spoon of corn chowder.

Georgina harrumphed. 'Remember how well our last sister trip turned out?'

'All the more reason to try again,' I said.

Georgina nibbled on her avocado toast, apparently mulling it over.

'How long has it been since you visited our place on the Eastern Shore?' I asked.

Four years previously, Paul and I had purchased a fixer-upper on Chiconnesick Creek near Elizabethtown, Maryland. We'd repaired, renovated and laid its ghosts to rest and now spent almost every summer weekend enjoying our cottage retreat.

Georgina sipped her chai latte. 'Honestly, Hannah, I can't remember. A year ago maybe?'

'I rest my case,' I said, sliding the soup bowl aside and reaching for my grilled ham muffaletta. 'Ruth cleared her schedule for this coming weekend. Say you can, too.'

'I thought you and Ruth were going to tackle Dad's storage unit this weekend.'

'We were, but Dennis called and needed his truck so we had to postpone. It's not like there's any rush. Nobody's touched anything in there for years.'

'You'll probably run up against rust, mold and mildew,' she grumbled.

'Climate controlled,' I told her. 'Stop changing the subject. Are you coming or not?'

Her brow furrowed. 'Gosh, Hannah . . . I don't know. What about the kids?'

'What about them? The twins are in school, Julie's filling out job applications . . .'

'Aren't you forgetting about Colin?' she cut in.

'Colin can stay with Emily. I've already checked with her. A little cousin time with Timmy will be fun for both of them.'

She still looked skeptical. 'Ganging up on me again, are you?'

I confessed that we were. 'The older kids are grownups, Georgina. And they won't even have to cook. You have more casseroles than they could eat in a month of Sundays. I know, because I stowed them in your freezer. Thaw and bake. Easy peasey.'

She dredged up a smile from somewhere. 'OK, Hannah, you've talked me into it.'

'Great!' I said. 'So, here's the plan. If we're going to avoid weekend traffic on the Bay Bridge, you'll need to bring Colin down to Emily's early on Friday morning.'

'Wait a minute!' she said. 'He's got school!'

'Missing a day or two of fifth grade will not screw up Colin's chances of getting into Harvard, Georgina.'

She laughed, the first genuine laugh I'd heard from her since before Scott's death. 'OK, you win!' And she tucked into her lunch with enthusiasm. Both the laugh and the appetite were promising signs my sister was coming back from the dark place where she'd been living lately.

Mid-afternoon on Friday, after a provisioning trip to Harris Teeter outside Easton, Ruth, Georgina and I arrived at the cottage we'd named *Our Time*. I'd phoned ahead to give Laurie, our caretaker, a head's up. She'd put out clean towels, made up the beds with fresh linen and opened the windows to the balmy, late summer breeze. When we arrived, Laurie's husband, Rusty, had just finished cleaning the barbeque grill. He greeted us with a breezy, 'Have a great weekend, ladies,' tossed his tools into a compartment on the back of his Harley and took off in a shower of gravel.

After stowing the groceries, I kicked off my shoes and padded barefoot out onto the deck that overlooked the creek. A great blue heron posed at the end of our dock as flocks of geese honked noisily overhead. 'Ah, that's what I'm talking about,' I said.

Georgina came up behind me, carrying a tall glass of iced tea. 'Thanks for talking me into this, Hannah.' She settled into a deck chair, turned her face toward the afternoon sun and closed her eyes.

'What room do you want me to take?' Ruth shouted from an upstairs window.

'Either one,' I yelled.

'I have dibs on the yellow room,' Georgina shouted back without even opening her eyes.

I would be sleeping in the master suite I usually shared with Paul in a wing addition just off the living room.

After cheeseburgers on the grill, we relaxed in chairs on the deck listening to the keening of the frogs. Ruth unearthed a second bottle of Oyster Bay merlot which paired perfectly with the dark chocolate-covered caramels I'd picked up at Trader Joes. I'd been hiding them from myself in the cottage pantry.

'When it comes to religion and politics,' Georgina said, breaking the companionable silence, 'I have nothing in common with Church of the Falls people, but they couldn't have been kinder to me and the kids after Scott died.'

'"Freely you have received, freely give",' Ruth quoted. 'Book of Matthew, I believe.'

Georgina smiled. 'Scott would know. He could quote chapter and verse.' After a moment she added, 'The Johnsons sent a beautiful peace lily in a pot and the nicest handwritten note.'

'The Johnsons?' Ruth asked.

'Our Native American cousins,' Georgina reminded her. 'I'm sorry I didn't get to meet them.'

This was a welcome, one-hundred-and-eighty-degree turnaround from her previous attitude.

'I'm kicking myself, too,' Ruth said, 'but at least I have an excuse. I was out of the country. Have they gone back to South Dakota, then, Hannah?'

'They've been home for a couple of weeks. Everyone had to get back to work.'

'Do you think they'll ever come back?' Georgina asked.

'They hope to,' I said. 'But until then, there's no reason you couldn't visit them.'

'Julie's talking about going,' Georgina said. 'She's rather taken with the twins, I gather. Mai and Nick.'

'They're great kids,' I told her. 'Properly brought up.'

Thinking about the mystery surrounding the death of our common ancestor – Joseph White Bear – I reminded my sisters that I still had the key to our father's storage unit. 'I'm looking for a good time to reschedule the work. Ruth, are you still in?'

Ruth raised a lazy hand.

'Georgina, do you want to help us look through it for clues?' Ruth turned her head. 'Come on, Georgina. Be a sport.'

'I just can't right now,' Georgina said. 'Just about everything sends me off on a crying jag. Looking at old family photos will do me in for sure. Maybe later?'

'Wasula's a hundred and two,' I reminded her, 'so I'm not inclined to dilly-dally.'

'No worries,' Ruth said. 'I'm all in. Name the day, and I'll be there, as long as it's not Thursday. That's my yoga day.'

A buzzer rudely rent the air. I excused myself to transfer a load of sheets from the washing machine to the dryer. When I returned, Ruth was silhouetted by the setting sun, leafing through the *Tidewater Times*, a purse-sized booklet that included feature articles, tide tables and a monthly calendar of local events sandwiched between ads for local businesses.

'Here's something I'd like to see,' Ruth said. 'It's an exhibition at the Blue Crab Art Gallery in Elizabethtown.' She glanced up from the page. 'Have you ever been there, Hannah?'

'Yes, once. It's lovely,' I said. 'They bought an old pharmacy and converted it.'

'What kind of show?' Georgina asked lazily.

'It's called "Arts by the Shore",' Ruth said, referring to the booklet. 'Showcasing over fifty regional artists and craftsmen. Maybe I'll find some merchandise to sell at the shop.' She closed the booklet over her thumb, marking the place. 'How about we have lunch somewhere in town, then check it out?'

'Cool,' Georgina said, looking more relaxed than I'd seen her since the August we'd spent at Rehoboth Beach shortly before her marriage to Scott. 'I'm in.'

My wine glass was halfway to my lips when a silent alarm brought me up short. Scott and Georgina's wedding had been in early September. They had an anniversary coming up soon. I drained my glass and reached for the wine bottle, thinking *Beware: Dangerous Shoals Ahead.*

Around ten o'clock, with dishes done, my sisters having retired for the evening and a last load of sheets and pillowcases tumbling in the dryer, I set about the routine of putting the cottage to bed for the night. As I flipped on the nightlight in the upstairs hallway, I noticed that Georgina's door was open and her bed hadn't been slept in. I poked my head in the doorway. 'Georgina?'

Her room was empty.

She wasn't in the bathroom, either.

No need to panic, I thought as I hustled downstairs to search for my sister.

I found her outside, dressed in her nightshirt, sitting at the end of the dock, dangling her bare feet in the water. Moonlight glistened off the tears that streamed down her cheeks.

'Keep that up,' I said as I settled down next to her, 'and you'll raise the water level in the Bay.'

Georgina swiped tears away with the back of her hand, and then surprised me by laughing.

Grief affects people in unique and mysterious ways, I'd found. I wrapped my arm around my sister and drew her close. 'I know you loved him, Georgina.'

Surprisingly, she began to giggle. 'But that's just it, Hannah! Do you want to know why I'm crying? It's not because I miss Scott, it's because for the first time in my life I feel truly *free!*'

If I had been sitting any closer to the end of the dock, I might have tumbled straight into the water. 'What?'

'Shocks the hell out of me, too, just saying it out loud.'

'But tears?' I said.

'Because I feel guilty about it.' She turned to me, eyes wide. 'Am I a terrible person?'

I assured her that she wasn't.

'You won't tell anybody, will you?'

'Don't be silly. Of course not.' After a moment, I asked, 'Are you going to be OK, Georgina? Financially, I mean.'

'Scott took good care of us, Hannah. He had a huge life insurance policy and some sort of mortgage insurance that paid off the house. Turns out Scott was worth more to us dead than alive.' Georgina's voice quavered. 'I feel horrible about that.'

Georgina scissored her legs, splashing water over her calves, sending mini-waves rippling into the creek. 'Can I share something else?'

'If you think my heart can take it.'

'It's good news,' she said. 'I got an email upstairs just now. In October, I'll be playing the organ again at All Hallows.'

'I thought you couldn't stand the warden there, Lionel Streeting?'

'It's not nice to say, but Lionel had a stroke and had to retire, thank God. The new church warden is a woman, someone I know from before, in fact. She sought me out when their organist moved to Seattle. I'd told her no at first, but after Scott . . .' She let the thought die.

'That's fabulous, Georgina,' I said, meaning it.

'It is, isn't it?' Another tear slid down her cheek. 'I'm *so* happy.'

I bumped her arm with my elbow. 'Little Sister, you are hopeless.'

TWENTY-NINE

The next morning, I awoke early. I poured myself a mug of coffee, stirred in sugar and a splash of half and half and carried it out to the end of the dock to watch the sun rise.

Ruth and Georgina slept in. When the aroma of fresh-brewed coffee didn't lure my sisters downstairs, I tried the nuclear option: frying bacon. Twenty minutes later, still dressed in our nightshirts, we were enjoying breakfast on the deck and planning our day.

At ten thirty, casually dressed in jeans, T-shirts and sensible walking shoes, we piled into the Volvo. With grass *swish-swishing* under the car, I drove cautiously down the rutted track that led from the cottage to the main road. Five miles of corn and soybean fields later, we reached civilization – the colonial town of Elizabethtown.

Carefully avoiding jaywalking Saturday shoppers, I steered the car down High Street, through the town's single traffic light where High intersected with King and parked on the town square between the war memorial and the gaily-painted bandstand. Retracing our route down High Street on foot, we found the Blue Crab Gallery where I was pleased to note that the new owners, out of respect for the building's history, had retained the 'Wm Chase & Son' spelled in black and white tiles on the sidewalk out front.

When Ruth pushed the door open, a bell jangled, announcing our arrival. 'Wow!' she said as we stepped inside.

Wow, indeed. For the 'Arts by the Shore' event every square inch of floor and wall space had been given over to local artisans.

To our right, panels of painted silk fabrics undulated like Salome's veils in the breeze wafting in through the open door, complementing the stained-glass mirrors that Alison Young had on display in an alcove just beyond.

Ruth, immediately taken by Susan Woythaler's whimsical blown glass ornaments, stopped to chat with the artist about them. When the discussion turned to consignments and invoicing, Georgina and I drifted away. I deserted Georgina at Deborah Kelchner's jewelry stall where she decided to purchase a necklace crafted of silver, polished shells and fresh water pearls, but was having a hard time selecting a pair of matching earrings, and refusing to take my advice anyway. Let Deborah deal with Georgina, I thought.

I was inexorably drawn to a section near the back of the gallery by the torso of a mannequin decked out in a bikini made of vegetables. The area beyond the mannequin had been dedicated to low-brow pop art, including colorful Cinco de Mayo-style skulls painted on a recycled skateboard deck. Two large wooden panels, mounted on the wall, depicted surfer dudes captioned with graffiti-style puff lettering: Amped! Froth! Goofy Foot! My taste in decorating was eclectic, but not so eclectic as to include surfer dudes. I wandered on, past the artist who specialized in dog portraits and the mustachioed gentleman who crafted fish out of wine bottles and twisted metal, heading instead for a separate room marked Fine Photography.

Yes! This was more my speed. Roger Miller's vibrant, color photographs of Fourth of July fireworks over the Annapolis skyline, the Chesapeake Bay Bridge at sunset, and the Thomas Point Lighthouse decorated a moveable partition to my right. Black and white photographs by Pete Souza of Naval Academy men and women going about the serious business of being midshipmen hung on a similar partition set at right angles to Miller's work. The wall to the far left, however, had been dedicated, not to photographs, but to a special long-term exhibit of seven beautifully matted and framed etchings, each signed by the artist, James A. Earl.

I had never heard of James Earl, but the man was talented, no doubt about that. I was particularly taken by an exquisitely detailed etching of plovers skittering in the surf entitled 'Can't Catch Me!'. I noted the price – affordable – and decided it would be perfect for the blank wall over my desk at *Our Time*, then moved on to the next etching.

A great blue heron dominated the foreground of 'Ready for My Closeup', its every feather meticulously executed. The magnificent bird had a rapt audience of two: a middle-aged couple shared an Adirondack loveseat in the background. For some reason, the couple looked familiar. I stared at the etching for a long moment, then stepped closer, hoping I wouldn't set off any security alarms. If the couple in the etching hadn't been holding hands, I would have sworn I was gawking at a portrait of Pastor Robert Thomas Selden and Judee McDaniel. No, don't be silly, I told myself. You saw them only that one time, at the reception following Scott's funeral. You're probably mistaken. I needed to consult an expert.

Georgina was no longer at the shell jewelry booth. Deborah Kelchner had last seen my sister heading in the direction of Beaded Magic. I wandered through the maze of exhibits looking for her, but when I got to Beaded Magic, she'd already moved on.

If I were correct, and both married-to-other-people Brother Bob and Judee Two-Es had been caught by an artist canoodling on Maryland's eastern shore, it would be important to know when. It was impossible to tell from the etching itself; the only assumption I could make from the shorts and flip-flops the couple wore was that it was summertime. I'd need to consult the artist.

Earlier, I'd noticed a forty-something guy wearing an oxford button-down shirt belted into a pair of chinos, holding forth near the front of the gallery. Since he stood behind a table smiling, greeting and dispensing champagne in three-ounce paper cups to all comers, I assumed he was one of the owners.

'Those amazing etchings in the back room?' I asked as I accepted a cup of champagne from the man's outstretched fingers. 'What can you tell me about the artist?'

'Jim Earl? He's one of our favorites. Retired a few years ago from the University of Maryland. He was a physics professor.'

'I'm thinking about buying the plovers,' I said truthfully, 'and I'd like to know a little more about him.'

He reached for a loose-leaf notebook on a shelf behind him and laid it on the table in front of the ice bucket. 'This has information about each of our artists.'

I chug-a-lugged the champagne then tossed the empty cup in the wastebasket near his feet. 'Thanks,' I said, reaching for the notebook. 'I'll take a look.'

'It's got Jim's CV and contact information in it,' the owner said, 'but why don't you go talk to him yourself? He's over there, by the display window.'

Sometime in my youth or childhood, I must have done something good.

James Earl sat at the front of the store in a tall-backed wicker chair, sipping from a cup of coffee that I knew from the logo had come from the High Spot Café directly across the street. He seemed to be sketching in a small, leather-bound book.

From the information in the gallery's notebook, I learned that Earl had a degree from MIT and had earned a second degree in studio art, one semester at a time, while teaching Astronomy at the University of Maryland. Blessed by a financially conservative father and a mother who was a canny investor, Earl's family foundation generously supported music and the arts as well as local environmental causes.

If the information in the notebook was correct, the philanthropist was ninety-three years old, but from where I stood, about ten feet away, he didn't look a day over eighty. I returned the notebook to its place on the shelf and walked over to introduce myself.

'Hi, I'm Hannah Ives. May I talk to you about your work?'

Earl looked up from his sketchbook – a leather-bound book about the size of a paperback – and holstered the pen between the leaves. 'Always delighted.'

I got straight to the point. 'I love your etchings, Mr Earl. I'm planning on buying the plovers, but one of the other etchings caught my attention. I think you've drawn a couple of my friends. The couple in the Adirondack loveseat? With the heron?'

'Could be,' he said.

'Do you know who they are?' I asked.

'I thought you said they were your friends.'

I smiled ruefully. 'They *look* like my friends,' I said, but from the twinkle in his dark eyes, I knew he was teasing me.

'I didn't ask them,' he said. 'Frankly, I was more interested in the heron, the way he stood still for so long, like an artist's model, posing for me.'

'Do you work from photographs?' I asked.

He frowned and shook his head, as if suggesting such a thing was sacrilege. 'I draw from life. You probably noticed me sketching just now. There was a pretty redhead looking at jewelry a few minutes ago . . .'

He had to be talking about Georgina. 'She's my sister,' I told him.

He opened the sketchbook to the page he'd been working on. In the short time Georgina'd been standing in front of the jewelry counter, Earl had captured her perfectly, down to the details of the claw that held up her hair, the flowered design on her T-shirt and the fact that her left shoestring was untied.

'You're very good,' I said.

'Thank you.'

'May I have a closer look?' I asked, holding out my hand for the sketchbook.

With a smile, James Earl placed his sketchbook in it.

Earl had sketched Georgina on the right-hand page, and on the left side, facing it, Earl had written, 'Redhead, Blue Crab Gallery, Elizabethtown, Maryland, September 2, 2018.'

I started to turn back a few pages before thinking to ask permission. 'May I?'

'Of course.'

He'd drawn each of his sketches in the same format – a drawing to the right with the subject, place and date documented on the facing leaf to the left. 'Did you do a preliminary sketch for the heron etching?' I inquired.

'I always do preliminary sketches,' he said.

'Would it be in this sketchbook?'

'I'm not sure,' Earl said. 'It was some time ago, but you can check. I run through sketchbooks fairly quickly, but if it's in this one, it will be toward the beginning.'

Sometimes you get lucky. The preliminary sketch for 'Ready for My Closeup' appeared on the third page: Great Blue Heron, Chesapeake Bay Hyatt, Cambridge, MD, July 29, 2018.

'Here it is!' I announced triumphantly. 'I see it was done in Cambridge this summer.'

The Cambridge Hyatt's full name was a mouthful: the Hyatt Regency Chesapeake Bay Golf Resort, Spa and Marina. It was also an upscale conference center. In a picturesque setting overlooking the Choptank River, it attracted groups from all over the country who could afford the costs.

'Refresh my memory,' he said, holding out his hand for the sketchbook.

He studied his work, brow furrowed. 'Ah, yes. I was speaking at a physics symposium in Cambridge that weekend. There was a golf tournament going on, and the place was crawling with visitors.' He paged forward. 'Here's a sketch of some kids playing giant chess near the Grand Fireplace, and another one of seagulls at the bar on the Breakwater Pavilion.'

I checked out those sketches, too, just to be polite. Wearing what I hoped was a disarming smile, I said, 'Do you mind if I take a photograph of the heron sketch? To show my friends?' I added hastily.

'Not at all.' Earl paged back to the heron. Using both hands, he held the sketchbook open in front of my iPhone.

'Thank you,' I said as I aimed, framing both pages on the screen, and touched the button to capture the image. 'My friends will appreciate it.'

After I finished, James Earl closed his sketchbook and slipped it into his breast pocket. He smiled up at me from his chair. 'But I'd rather they bought the etching.'

I tapped my temple. 'I'll see what I can do about that, Mr Earl.'

'It's Bob and Judee, for sure,' Georgina said when I finally tracked her down and dragged her to the back room to view Earl's etchings first-hand. 'See that butterfly on the woman's ankle? Judee's got one just like it.' She took a deep breath, then let it out slowly. 'Well, I'll be *damned*!'

'Not you,' I said reasonably. 'It's Brother Bob who needs to be worrying about damnation. Last time I looked, *Thou Shalt Not Commit Adultery* was still on the list of Ten Commandments.

'One problem. I checked out the date with the artist,' I told her. 'July 29th was a Sunday. Wouldn't Brother Bob have been in church?'

'Not necessarily. One of the assistant pastors takes over when Bob is away. But, there's a way to find out. Church of the Falls posts their sermons online. It'd be easy to see who was preaching that Sunday.'

Prompted by Georgina, I logged onto the Church's website on my iPhone. A search of the sermons revealed that Brother Bob's slot on the 29th had been filled by Brother Vernon speaking on 'Storm-Proofing Your Life'.

'If Brother Bob was doing what we think he was doing that Sunday, he might need a bit of storm-proofing himself,' I said. 'Tamara didn't strike me as the Live-and-Let-Live type.'

'Tell me about it,' Georgina snorted. 'Ever wonder why the church secretary looks like your maiden aunt? Tamara hired her.'

I had to laugh.

'Click on the pull-down menu for News,' Georgina suggested, leaning in close. 'Let's see what Bob *said* he would be doing that weekend. There should be a newsletter for July.'

'What's KidMin?' I asked after the newsletter filled the screen.

'It's short for children's ministry.'

I turned the iPhone screen in her direction. 'According to this, he and Judee were attending a KidMin conference in Cambridge that weekend.'

'Let me see that.' Georgina practically snatched the phone out of my hand. As I watched speechlessly, she initiated a fresh Safari search and tapped a few keys. 'Then he's a big, fat liar. The KidMin Conference was in Dayton, Ohio this year.'

We exchanged glances.

'Do you suppose Scott discovered they'd lied about where they were that weekend?' Georgina said. 'And if he knew about their affair, my God, was Scott killed to keep him quiet about it?'

'That seems extreme,' I said, 'especially in this day and age. Was Scott bothered when a serial adulterer married a nude model and moved into the White House?'

Georgina snorted. 'Not particularly. He even voted for him.'

'Then it's possible he wouldn't have been troubled by learning that his pastor was having an affair with a co-worker,' I said. 'Perhaps something was going on here that had nothing to do with Scott.'

'Better safe than sorry,' Georgina said. 'Open your email, attach that photo and type what I tell you.'

A minute later, my email swooshed. If Dick Evans, the homicide detective in charge of the investigation into my brother-in-law's murder was on top of his inbox, a copy of James Earl's sketchbook and what Georgina and I knew about it would soon be in his hands.

THIRTY

I'd been so busy providing the police with suspects in my brother-in-law's murder that I was barely able to keep up with my email via iPhone let alone any heretofore unknown relatives who might be trying to connect with me through Gen-Tree. And I'd completely forgotten about my custodial arrangement with Julie's family tree, until a message popped up on the email account I'd linked to it.

Dear JLC2000.

Twenty-five years ago, my mother underwent in vitro fertilization at the Great Lakes Center for Fertility and Women's Health in Chicago and became pregnant with sperm from Donor #7135. Through Gen-Tree DNA testing, I have located fifteen half-siblings, also children of Donor #7135. Your DNA results indicate you may be a donor sibling, too. Were you a child of Donor #7135? Hope to hear back from you soon. DavidM23

I sat back, stunned, trying to take that in. When I could breathe again, I clicked back through the Gen-Tree menus to Julie's test results. In the weeks since I'd first uploaded her data, DavidM23 and at least ten other individuals were showing up as 'close family' with 'high probability'.

Scott was definitely Julie's father: you had only to look at her to figure that out. Her glorious hair came from the Drew side of our family, true, but her green eyes and the dimpled chin were pure Cardinale.

I explored some more and discovered that while I shared DNA with Julie, as expected, none of her donor sibling matches shared anything with me.

For Julie and her donor siblings, then, Scott had to be the common denominator.

Where had Scott been twenty-five years ago – I counted backwards – in 1983? Nineteen years old, studying for an undergraduate degree in Economics at the University of Chicago, that's where. We'd all heard, time and time again, 'poor me' stories of how he'd worked his way through college waiting tables. No surprise he failed to mention that he'd supplemented the income from his part-time job in a campus dining hall by selling his sperm.

No wonder Scott had been so squirrelly about Julie being tested. Despite all privacy assurances that presumably had been given by the clinic at the time, Donor #7135 had just been outed to at least one person: me.

I felt like a bomb had gone off in the basement. Fifteen matches and counting. Donor #7135 had apparently been a bestseller. How many other little #7135s were out there? How many children did my late brother-in-law have?

And what's more, what was I going to do with this information?

Do I answer DavidM23?

I decided to leave that up to Julie. 'Do you want to tell your mother or shall I?' I wrote, attached David's email and hit send before I could change my mind.

'Let me get this straight,' Julie said when she phoned, 'because this is totally freaking me out. I have sixteen half-brothers and sisters, all around twenty-five years old.'

'So far,' I added helpfully.

'What if I had married one of them?' she wailed.

'Now you won't,' I said.

'So I emailed the guy and he got right back. They're planning a reunion.'

'Reunion!' Georgina shrieked in the background. 'That's a funny way to put it.'

'I'm putting you on speaker,' Julie said. 'Mom's really pissed.'

'Pissed is putting it mildly, Hannah. If Scott weren't already dead, I'd kill him.'

'I warned you,' Julie said, lowering her voice.

'You tell that David person that I have absolutely no interest in joining his sister-mom club, either, Hannah. I got my sperm donations the regular way, thank you, by cutting out the middle man.'

'Oooh, that's harsh,' her daughter said.

'Georgina, stop sputtering and listen to me. Do you think Scott knew that his donor kids had connected?'

'If he did, do you think he'd tell *me*?'

'I'm worried that one of them may have tracked him down. Think about it. Somebody was seen in the backyard talking to Scott on the day he died. Somebody who looked exactly like Sean.'

'It wasn't DavidM23,' Julie cut in. 'He sent me a photo. He's got masses of dark hair.'

'Are you thinking that one of Scott's donor sons tracked him down and Scott blew him off?'

'Oh, Scott would deny it if confronted, that's for sure,' Georgina snarked. 'Sixteen kids out there, maybe more? Shit!'

'Dad could deny it all he wants, Mom, but DNA doesn't lie.'

'Maybe the kid couldn't deal with rejection,' I said.

To me, Julie said, 'Should we tell the cops?'

'I think you'd better.'

'That'll take their mind off Sean,' Julie said.

'We can hope so,' I said.

'OK, Aunt Hannah,' Julie said, her voice unnaturally loud. 'I'll get that number for you now. Let me put you on hold.'

What on earth? But I was dealing with Julie, so hang on for the ride.

After a brief silence, my niece returned to the call. 'Hi, I'm back. Had to get rid of Mom.'

'What did you do with her? Lock her in the bathroom?'

'Ha ha, I wish. No, I wanted to talk to you about something. In private.'

'Why do I have the feeling I'm about to be sorry you called?'

'I want to go to that reunion,' she said without preamble.

'Then go,' I said. 'What's stopping you?'

I figured Julie was going to ask me for money, but she surprised me by saying, 'I want you to go with me.'

'Julie!'

'I do, I'm completely serious, Aunt Hannah. I'll even pay your way.'

'Don't be ridiculous. You don't have that kind of money.'

'Do, too. I've been saving up from my day care job.'

'Well, I wouldn't accept it.'

'Then you'll go?'

'I didn't say yes, Julie.'

'But, you didn't say no either.'

'What does your mother say about it?'

'She says those children have nothing to do with her, and that I should do whatever I want. And what I want is to go to that reunion. Besides, maybe this guy who looks like Sean will be there.'

'Where is it?' I asked, feeling my resolve weakening.

'A place in Illinois I've never heard of called Des Plaines.'

'Bummer,' I said. 'If you'd said Honolulu . . .'

'Please?' Julie begged. 'If you were in my situation, wouldn't you need moral support, too?'

I had to agree that I would, and I was curious about the Sean lookalike, too.

Which explains why three hours later I found myself on the American Airlines website booking two flights to Chicago. On my VISA.

THIRTY-ONE

O'Hare Airport: the tenth circle of Dante's hell. Four terminals, nine concourses and a complex so large that it spans both Cook and DuPage counties. You need wizardry, not moving walkways, to get from one concourse to another.

I had planned on a rental car for our trip to Des Plaines until DavidM23, the organizer whose last name turned out to be Moody, told us about the Best Western courtesy airport shuttle, so I signed us up for a round trip.

After a forty-minute drive, the shuttle pulled under the portico of a Best Western by the BP Station, just past Mr Pup and directly across the street from Burger King. Modest accommodation to be sure, but clean and comfortable, and the seventy-nine dollar rate suited my pocketbook just fine.

Julie didn't want to be seen until she'd had a chance to freshen up, so we checked in at reception and hustled up to our room on the second floor

'Which bed do you want?' I asked as the door clicked shut behind us. 'I'm not particular.'

Julie dropped her rucksack and fell backward, like a tree, onto the bed nearest the window. She bounced up and down a bit, testing out the mattress. 'This is cool,' she said. After plumping up several of the pillows and propping them behind her back, she opened the Welcome Envelope we'd been given at the front desk.

'What's in the envelope?' I asked as I unzipped my carry-on and removed my toiletry bag.

Julie shuffled several pages. 'There's a schedule of events.' She looked up from the page. 'We're due in the conference room at four for a meet and greet, followed by cocktails at five and dinner at six at a restaurant called the Silver Stallion.'

'It's practically next door,' I said. 'We drove by it on the way in.'

Julie looked up. 'Sounds like a gay bar.'

I laughed. 'It's a family place, I think. Steak, chicken, chops.'

'A vegetarian's delight,' she said.

When I returned from hanging up my toiletries on a towel rack in the bathroom, Julie said, 'Here's a list of my known half-siblings with contact information. The ones with an asterisk are supposed to be here,' she said, starting to count. 'Six boys and five girls, including me. None of these people live anywhere near Baltimore,' she said. 'And look! I have a half-ling in Australia! I've never been to Australia.'

'When do you want to go downstairs?' I asked my niece.

'A little after four, maybe?' She grinned nervously. 'I plan to be fashionably late.'

'If it's all right with you, then, I'll put my feet up for a little while.'

'Go for it,' Julie said. 'I'm going to wash my hair again. There's a hair dryer in there, I hope.'

After repeated shampooing, Julie's hair had nearly returned to its natural apricot color, but another washing couldn't hurt. 'Go for it,' I said.

Two hours later, my niece and I, both freshly showered and smelling like Best Western's Aromae Botanicals bath bar, presented ourselves at the door to the hotel's single conference room. Julie vibrated with excitement.

'Welcome!' David Moody said. While he beamed at Julie, I searched his face for a resemblance to my late brother-in-law, but with the exception of his ice-blue eyes, David had the dark-haired, olive-skinned good looks of his mother, Karen, who stood next to him behind the table.

'Welcome,' Karen Moody said, handing me a 'Hello, my name is' stick-on name badge and a Sharpie. 'You must be one of the sister-moms.'

'I'm with Julie,' I told her, neatly side-stepping the question.

Karen peeled a gold star off a roll of stickers and pressed it onto the upper right-hand corner of my nametag. Since she wore a similar gold star, I figured the star identified me as a sister-mom whether I liked it or not.

'Take off a shoe,' Karen said after I'd finished writing 'Hannah' on my nametag and returned the Sharpie.

'I beg your pardon?'

'It's an ice breaker.' She grinned, revealing a row of impossibly even, improbably white teeth. 'Take off your right shoe and throw it in that pile in the middle of the room. As soon as everyone gets here, we'll have some fun.'

Swell.

Julie and I did as we were told.

About two dozen chairs had been arranged around the sides of the small conference room. Julie and I limped over to claim two chairs next to a small table set with a tub of ice studded with small, eight-ounce bottles of water.

'Diddle-diddle-dumpling,' I muttered.

'What?'

'Never mind, Julie,' I said. *Doesn't anybody read nursery rhymes to their children any more?*

As we waited for the 'fun' to begin, Julie and I sat quietly, observing as her half-siblings and their sister-moms arrived and the pile of shoes in the center of the room gradually grew.

'So far, nobody looks the least bit like me,' Julie said, sounding disappointed.

'That's because you're the image of your mother,' I reminded her. 'But, look. The Cardinale genes are pretty strong. Check out all the dimpled chins.'

Julie touched the dimple in her own chin and smiled. Suddenly, she grabbed my arm. 'Oh my god, that guy over there?' She nodded in the direction of the door. 'He looks just like Colin, but all grown up! Like one of those pictures of missing kids on milk cartons all, um, what do you call it?'

'Age progressed?'

'That's it.'

As the room filled up Julie pointed out the various traces of Scott she detected in his offspring. The blue-gray eyes, the sandy hair, the fair skin, the square-shaped ears and the dimple, always the dimple. 'And that guy over there with the buzz cut? Jeesh! He looks just like Sean and Dylan the summer they went whitewater rafting with Outward Bound!' After a moment, she added, 'I'm getting seriously weirded out, Aunt Hannah.'

In truth, I was, too.

'How can I connect in any *real* way with so many siblings?' she whispered. 'I feel like I'm part of a *herd*, not a family.'

'It gives a whole new meaning to the concept of family, doesn't it, Julie?' I said, reaching out for her hand and squeezing it affectionately.

Nearly every chair had been taken by then: half-lings and sister-moms sitting in a ring, eyes darting about, sizing up one another. Eventually, Karen Moody strolled to the center of the circle and clapped her hands for attention. 'Welcome, diblings and sister-moms!'

Julie turned to me and mouthed, 'Diblings?'

'Ugh,' I muttered.

Karen continued to *clap-clap-clap* which we took as a sign we were to join her, as if applauding ourselves for turning up.

'OK, now,' she said after the applause died away. 'When I say "go", everybody run to the center of the room and grab a shoe. Then, you have to find the owner of that shoe and get acquainted!'

I'd played this game before, back in my corporate days, so I'd already set my sights on the turquoise and gray Keens of a sister-mom who came in with her daughter and retreated shyly, like Julie and I had, to a corner.

Karen shouted 'Go!' and the scramble began. After everyone had been reunited with his or her shoe, I found myself back in the corner near the ice tub with Gloria, owner of the Keens, and her daughter, Nevada. Gloria, far from being shy, turned out to be a cheerleader for the Donor Sibling Registry.

'Next game!' Karen announced.

'I'll sit this one out on the sidelines, if you don't mind,' I said.

'Me, too,' Gloria agreed. 'I have enough of touchy-feely HR exercises back at the office. I once had to convince a co-worker to drink blue buttermilk.'

'Bleah!' I said. It made my toes curl just thinking about it.

I did not regret my decision: the next ice breaker involved a jar of M&Ms and a game of twenty questions.

'My favorite food is nachos!'

'The cartoon character that describes me best is Superman!'

'Describe my personality in one word? Oh, that's so hard
. . . bubbly!'

While that went on around us, Gloria turned to Julie and
asked, 'Have you signed up at the DSR?'

'No, I haven't,' Julie said. 'David found me on Gen-Tree.
com. Tell me about DSR.'

'Sixty-thousand members strong and counting,' Nevada
explained. 'You put in your donor number and get matched up
with half-siblings who share the same donor number. Donors
can register, too,' she added. 'If they want to, of course. Our
donor, Number 7135, hasn't gone online yet.'

Julie's eyes grew wide and she turned to me as the significance of what Nevada had said sank in. No way Scott would
have gone online, Julie knew that. And no wonder he had acted
so negatively when he learned about Julie's DNA test kit.

'The largest half-sibling group match they've found so far is
two hundred,' Gloria informed us, her face serious. 'The guy
keeps track of his kids on an Excel spreadsheet.'

'That's creepy,' Julie said.

'Donor 7135 lived in Chicago, or so I assume because that's
where the clinic was,' I said. 'Julie noticed that a lot of her
half-siblings still live in the Chicago area. Doesn't anybody
worry about incest?'

'Part of my sex education has always been knowing my donor
number,' Nevada said, looking directly at Julie.

'I've only just found out,' Julie said, sounding defensive.

Nevada shifted her steely-blue gaze to me. Clearly I'd come
up short in the sister-mom department.

'Well,' Julie said, moving on. 'That'll certainly take the zing
out of a first date. Hi, I'm Julie and my father was sperm donor
number 7135. How about you?'

I was still mulling over the ego maniac sitting in his office
and keeping track of his offspring on an Excel spreadsheet.
'Isn't there any law to limit how many kids a donor can
father?'

'In my opinion,' Gloria said, 'there should be a cap on sales,
but so far, nada.'

'But the sperm banks keep track of everything, right?'

Gloria wagged her head. 'Here's the scary thing: less than

half the women who come to a sperm bank end up reporting their pregnancy back to the bank.'

'Well, there ought to be a law,' Julie said.

'I agree, but the Food and Drug Administration doesn't. We tried to get a law passed that would limit the number of times an individual donor's sperm could be used. It would also mandate the reporting of donor conceived births and require post-conception medical updates about the offspring, you know, in case there turned out to be medical issues with some of the donors.'

'That sounds like a no-brainer,' Julie said. 'What happened?'

Gloria smiled grimly. 'You're gonna *love* this. The FDA determined that such a law would infringe on the right to privacy and the right to procreate, giving the government control over who has children and with whom.'

I'm afraid I laughed out loud. 'Sorry,' I said, feeling everyone's eyes turn from their M&Ms to me. 'And this is coming from the same government that wants to tell women when and how they can have access to birth control, or to a legal abortion?'

'God Bless America,' Nevada said.

The M&M game eventually drew to a close and we were herded into the lobby for drinks. In the area where the hotel normally served breakfast, the reunion organizers had set up cartons of Box-o-Wine – both red and white – a frosty pitcher of margaritas, and a bowl of fruit punch. They'd whipped up onion-herb dip for the potato chips and cut up veggies, and someone had put small bowls of mixed nuts out on each of the little, square tables. I lost track of Julie as I grazed among the hors d'oeuvres; I hadn't eaten since the pretzels on the plane.

When I caught up with Julie again, she and Nevada were giggling over something another one of their half-sisters, a girl named Beth, had said.

'Brothers!' Julie hooted. 'I should know. I have three of them.' Julie didn't add that they would be half-siblings to the others, too. I'd leave it to her on when, and if, to blow Scott's cover.

'Come with me,' Nevada said to her sisters. 'You need to meet Andy Zimmer. We've known about each other for a couple of years. He's been trying to track our donor down, and he's so close.'

Leaving me to nurse my Pinot Grigio in relative solitude.

Andy turned out to be the Outward Bound version of Sean and Dylan who Julie had singled out earlier at the ice breaker. I watched from a distance as he was backed into a corner near the fireplace by the trio of half-sisters who fluttered around him like groupies.

I studied Andy's profile, so eerily like that of my nephews. If I painted a full head of floppy, Sean-style hair on his short-cropped head, Andy could easily have passed for the lookalike captured on Mrs Turner's video. And if he *were* the donor son who had confronted my brother-in-law in his own backyard on the day he died, Andy would have to know from her nametag that Julie was Scott's standard-issue daughter. How many Cardinales can there be?

'He's close to tracking our donor down,' Nevada had said. If only she knew how close.

I managed to catch Julie's eye by waving my plastic wine glass in a please-fetch-me-another kind of way. When she returned with a refill, I shared my suspicions about Andy.

'No way,' Julie said.

'Way!' I said, 'Turn around and take a good look at him.'

Julie squinted in Andy's direction. 'Maybe from a distance,' she said. 'But if you're right, Aunt Hannah, how can we prove it?'

'Maybe one of us can corner him at dinner,' I said, just as Karen Moody appeared in the lobby ringing a small handbell.

'Better you than me,' Julie said as we joined the parade heading next door to the Silver Stallion, where I was dismayed to see that Karen had arranged assigned seating for our dinner. Tented name cards decorated with the DNA helix placed me at the far end of a long community table and Julie at the other. Andy was seated near the middle, next to Nevada's mother, Gloria, and I ended up with bubbly Beth. If there was a method to Karen's madness, it totally escaped me.

By the time dessert rolled around (homemade rice pudding!) even Beth's wild-and-crazy stories about growing up with a succession of five stepfathers failed to keep my eyelids from drooping, so I excused myself from the table. 'Over to you,' I whispered in Julie's ear as I left. 'You can tell me about it in the morning.'

THIRTY-TWO

S unday morning, an hour before the shuttle that would take us back to the airport, I parked my luggage next to a square, marble-topped table not far from the fake fireplace in the hotel lobby and headed for the breakfast bar. While I waited for Julie to shower, dress, finish packing and join me, I filled a bowl with corn flakes from a dispenser, grabbed a cup of blueberry yogurt from a mini-fridge, snagged a cup of coffee and sat down.

About five minutes later Julie managed to find me. She'd stopped at the make-your-own waffle machine and was carrying a banana and a chunky Belgian waffle swimming in syrup, topped with a generous swirl of whipped cream. 'How do you stay so thin?' I asked, eyeing her breakfast and silently calculating the calories.

Julie scooted her chair forward, leaned over her plate and whispered, 'Hardly any of Dad's children are fat, did you notice?' Wielding a plastic knife and fork, she sawed a corner off the waffle, popped it into her mouth, closed her eyes and chewed appreciatively. 'High metabolism must run in the family,' she said, waving her fork. 'Thank you, Dad.'

I dumped the yogurt onto my cereal, stirred and dug in with a spoon. 'Sorry to run out on you last night, but I just couldn't keep my eyes open. Did you get a chance to talk with Andy?'

'No such luck,' she said. 'He bugged out shortly after you did.'

'Darn,' I said. 'Maybe he'll show up for breakfast.'

'It still feels totally surreal,' Julie said. 'I keep wishing my brothers were here, the ones I grew up with, I mean.'

Because of his age, Georgina had decided not to tell Colin. Dylan had zero interest in meeting his extended family; he'd expressed anger at his father, in fact. Sean had been keen, but even if he hadn't been warned to stick around town by Baltimore's Finest, his class schedule would have kept him away from Des Plaines.

'I hope they come around,' I said, remembering the fury with which Dylan had greeted the news that his father had been a sperm donor, treating it as an act of betrayal.

Julie must have been thinking the same thing because she said, 'You'd think Dad had been unfaithful to Mom the way Dylan carried on. But, Dad hadn't even *met* Mom yet!'

'Give them time to . . .' I began, and then I spotted Andy Zimmer, carrying a duffle bag and looking spiff in slim jeans and a long-sleeved polo shirt that brought out the blue in his eyes.

'Julie!' I whispered. 'There's Andy. Go ask him to join us.'

Rather than leap to her feet as I would have done, Julie unfolded herself casually, stood and wandered in Andy's direction, waylaying him just short of our table.

'Mornin', Andy.' Julie's smile dazzled. 'Would you like to sit with us?'

Andy grinned and dropped his duffle bag next to her chair. 'Thanks. Watch that for me, will you?' With a glance at Julie's plate he said, 'There's a waffle over there just calling my name.'

Julie sat down and scooted her chair forward, nudging Andy's bag with her foot to make room. Her brow furrowed. She reached into her pocket and grabbed her cell phone. After a quick glance around the room, she ducked her head under the table. As I watched, mystified, I heard the distinctive sound of a shutter closing.

When her head surfaced again, I whispered, 'What the heck are you doing?'

Instead of answering, she handed me her cell phone and refocused attention on her waffle.

I studied the screen. Julie had photographed the checked baggage tag wrapped around the strap of Andy's duffle. I raised an eyebrow. Julie made a flicking motion with her thumb and forefinger, indicating I should enlarge the image. I did.

BWI to MDW.

Midway is the airport in downtown Chicago, and BWI . . .

My heart did a quick *rat-a-tat-tat* as my eyes focused on the date. On August 18, the day that Scott Cardinale was murdered, Andy Zimmer had flown from Baltimore back to Chicago on Southwest Airlines Flight 2097.

'He told me he'd never been to Baltimore,' Julie said. 'Liar.'

'I wonder what time that flight was?' I said, calling up the Safari app and doing a quick search. 'Six p.m.,' I told her.

'Time enough . . .' Julie began, then, 'Shhhh. He's coming back.'

'Let me handle this, Julie.'

Her eyes narrowed, but she nodded.

'So, tell me about your family, Andy,' I said as he joined us at the table. 'We didn't get much time to chat last night.'

'I had two moms, never a Dad. My moms were great, don't get me wrong, it's just . . .'

He smiled. 'Mom always said I was conceived on the corner of Drexel and 57th during her lunch hour. No man involved.'

'Did you miss not having a dad?' Julie wanted to know.

Andy shrugged. 'Sometimes, like if there was a father-son event at school. People should be more sensitive, you know? But mostly my father was like a relative who died before I was born.'

Julie's smile turned from disarming to dangerous. 'Donor number 7135 was my father.'

'The father of us all,' Andy said.

'No, I mean my actual father, Andy. My dad. First tooth, first communion, first don't-you-dare-keep-my-daughter-out-late kind of dad.'

Andy sat back abruptly, feigning shock.

'I guess the secret's out now,' Julie said, skewering him with her eyes, 'but you knew that already, didn't you, Andrew?'

'W-what are you talking about?' he stammered.

'The date on your baggage tag, Andrew Zimmer,' she said, her voice dripping acid. 'You were in Baltimore, Maryland. You met my dad.'

Andy's eyes flicked to the duffle at his feet, then back to Julie. He melted into the back of his chair, looking defeated. 'Yeah, it's true. Ever since my mother died, I felt like half of me was a big question mark. I decided to look for my donor. I wanted to see his face. Is it like mine? I wanted to hear my donor laugh, see him smile, you know? I hoped to be able to shake his hand.'

I tried to imagine what it would have been like never to have known my own father – the smart, big-hearted, funny scientist I called Dad. My heart ached for what Andy had missed.

Andy paused for a sip of coffee, his hand shaking. 'I put my DNA up early on. Every time there was a match, I'd think, this might be it, but the matches always turned out to be donor kids, too. So I decided to try another tack.'

'Which was?' I asked after several long seconds of silence.

'There was this lab tech at the clinic. I don't want to get her into trouble, so all I'll say is I got a name. Once I had the name . . .'

I filled in the blank. Unlike Smith, Brown or Jones, Cardinale wasn't exactly your garden variety family name. It must have been easy after that. And it was.

'I did a search on Google,' Andy said, addressing Julie. 'There was a picture of your dad up on that church website. Once I saw the picture, I knew.'

'Yeah, spitting image,' Julie said dryly. 'Well, I hope you got to shake his hand.'

He smiled. 'I did.'

Julie attacked without mercy. 'Because he died. A month ago.'

Andy fell back in his chair as if he'd been shot. 'My God, no!'

Julie let him mull that over. I think we were both surprised when a single tear rolled down Andy's cheek. He swiped it away. 'Sorry,' he sniffed. 'I don't know how I can miss someone I never really knew.

'He's dead?' he repeated, as if he'd misheard. 'I simply can't believe it. All those years of wondering, then searching and I get to spend fifteen minutes with him, now . . .' His eyes misted over. 'Shit. Dead.'

'Murdered, to be exact,' I said.

His head jerked in my direction so quickly I thought he'd get whiplash. 'I think I want to go back to Chicago and start this weekend all over again. Murdered?'

I nodded, deciding to skip the details.

Andy turned to his half-sister, his eyes pleading. 'I didn't kill him, Julie. When I left your house he was definitely alive.'

'We saw that,' Julie said, letting him off the hook inch by painful inch. 'You were caught on a neighbor's security camera.'

'I see. Well, if that's the case, then you know I had nothing to do with it.'

'Somebody did,' I said. 'What can you tell us about your visit, Andy? It might help track Scott's killer down.'

'OK.' He pushed his breakfast, now stone cold, aside. 'I got there around one. Your dad was pulling weeds out of the flower bed in front of your house, Julie. I just walked up to him and introduced myself.'

'That must have been difficult,' I said.

Andy managed a smile. 'I'd practiced it for years, Hannah. Hi. My name is Andrew Zimmer. Twenty-five years ago my mother became pregnant with the sperm you donated to a clinic in Chicago.'

I was trying to picture Scott's face when confronted so baldly, but failed.

'So, what did Dad say?'

'He was really nice about it, Julie. He invited me into the backyard. I told him about my background and he seemed genuinely interested. Then he asked me for time to break the news to his family, in other words, you.'

'And he honored that commitment, Julie,' I said, thinking she'd been a bit brutal with him. 'Andy could have revealed Donor 7135's identity to everyone this weekend, but he didn't.'

'I kept thinking I'd hear from him,' Andy said, sounding lost.

Julie nudged him gently. 'What happened after that?'

'He got a call on his cell, answered it, then told me he had to go.'

'What time was that?' I asked.

'I don't know – one thirty or so.'

'Did he say who was calling him?'

'No, why should he? He just apologized for cutting our talk

short. Said it was business.' Andy reached into his back pocket and pulled out a thin plastic case. 'I gave him my card, and he told me he'd be in touch after he'd had time to think things over.'

He handed Julie one of his cards and waited while she studied it.

'You're an accountant,' she observed.

He flushed. 'Yeah. The apple doesn't fall very far from the tree, does it?'

'My brother, your half-brother, Sean, he's working on a masters in Economics at Hopkins.'

'Brigham Young for me,' Andy said.

Julie wrapped her hand around Andy's wrist. 'You need to talk to the Baltimore police, Andy. They think my brother, Sean, might have killed our dad.'

'You say I'm on tape?'

'Yeah. Looking exactly like my brother.'

'I am your brother.'

The remark made Julie smile.

Something was still puzzling me. 'We mistook you for Sean on the tape because of the floppy hair.'

'I got a haircut,' Andy said simply, rubbing his hand over his fuzz.

Julie cocked her head. 'How do we know you didn't come back later?'

'I took an Uber, Julie, both coming and going.' He reached for his cell phone, tapped the screen and called up the Uber app with the record of his past trips. 'See?'

'OK, then,' Julie said, after studying the screen. 'I believe you.'

'You want to freshen up your breakfast?' I asked, indicating his long-neglected plate.

'Not really hungry just now,' Andy said.

'Let me show you something.' Julie reached into the knapsack hanging off the back of her chair and pulled out a thin paperback photo album. *The Cardinale Family Summer, 2018* was scrawled across the cover in elegant calligraphic script. 'I had it printed at Shutterfly,' Julie explained.

I had to hand it to my niece – she'd come to the reunion

prepared. At least four additional copies of her family album remained in her bag. I wondered who she planned to give them to.

Julie pushed the paperback across the table and watched silently as Andy opened it and began to leaf slowly through. 'It's like looking in a mirror,' he said.

'You can keep it,' Julie said.

Andy wagged his head sadly. 'I have so many questions.'

'And I'll do my best to answer them,' she said.

Suddenly she popped up from her chair. 'I know we did a group shot last night, but Aunt Hannah, will you take our picture?' She looked at Andy. 'Do you mind?'

'Not at all.' Andy stood up, too, wrapped his arm around Julie's shoulders.

'How do you take such wonderful pictures?' I'd once asked my artist friend, Naddie Gray. 'Stand as close to the subject as you think you need to be,' she'd advised, 'and then step closer.'

Brother and sister smiled as I framed the shot, stepped closer, then pressed the button.

'Will you email it to me?' Andy asked.

Julie took the phone from my hand and, referring to the business card he'd given her, did so on the spot.

'I'm grateful to your dad, Julie,' he said, tucking the photo album carefully into his duffle. 'It bears repeating that I wouldn't be here without him.'

'I don't know why my dad decided to donate his sperm to the fertility clinic,' Julie said. 'Maybe he needed the money? But, one thing I know for sure. When guys donate their sperm it's not like slam-bang you're done. They need to understand that they're actually making people.'

'Will you give me permission to tell our diblings?'

'Hell,' Julie said, 'tell the *New York Times*, if you want, but promise me one thing.'

'What's that?'

She screwed up her face. 'Don't *ever* call me a dibling.'

THIRTY-THREE

The Saturday after Julie and I returned from Des Plaines, Illinois, I invited Georgina to join me at *Our Time* on the Eastern Shore. I told her I needed help washing, drying and rehanging the curtains, which was true in a way, but the Housekeeping Police wouldn't have shown up to give me a citation if I'd put off the task until Spring. I felt Georgina needed a break from Baltimore, is all, and she readily agreed.

With Andy Zimmer almost certainly out of the picture, we'd stayed up late that night drinking red wine and mulling over our only other suspects in Scott's murder — Bob and Judee. 'But what was their motive?' I'd asked my sister.

'They were having an affair,' Georgina said flatly, waving her wine glass.

'The only proof of that is the sketch,' I said.

'But we saw them arguing at Scott's funeral, remember?' Georgina said.

'Neither would hold up in a court of law, Georgina. Besides, just because they'd been having an affair and Scott got wind of it, isn't much of a reason to murder him.'

'Well, they were fighting about *something*,' she insisted.

'That could have been about anything,' I told her, pouring myself another glass. 'Maybe Judee needed more money for playground equipment and Brother Bob was being stingy about it.'

So we'd gone to bed a little tipsier and no closer to a solution than the moment we walked through the cottage door.

When I wandered out for coffee late the following morning, I was astonished to find Julie sitting at the kitchen counter.

I pressed a hand to my chest. 'You nearly gave me a heart attack,' I teased. 'What are you doing here?'

'I think I found the smoking gun,' Julie said, her voice quavering with excitement. 'It was hidden in plain sight,' she rattled on, 'tacked up on Daddy's bulletin board the whole time.

It wouldn't have meant a thing to the police, of course, so that's why they didn't take it.'

I held up a hand. 'Whoa! What on earth are you talking about?'

'It's the roster of kids attending day care at the church,' Julie explained. 'The monthly report the Day Care Director submits to the pastor and the pastor sends to the treasurer.' She hoisted her backpack onto the counter, unzipped a pocket and pulled out a wodge of pages. She plopped them on the counter, smoothed out the top sheet, then stabbed at it with her finger. 'This is total bullshit!'

'Bullshit is a two coffee problem,' I said as I headed for the Keurig machine. 'Can I make you a cup?'

'No, thanks,' Julie said. 'I stopped at Starbucks on the way over.'

While I waited for water to gurgle through the coffee machine, I studied the roster over my niece's shoulder. It looked like a perfectly ordinary list of children, arranged alphabetically by last name, followed by a grid of seven dated columns with checks to mark attendance.

When the coffee was done, I dosed it quickly with cream and sugar and then gave my full attention to Julie.

'Explain,' I said.

'How many children do you see there?' she asked.

That was easy. The list was numbered one to twenty-five. Twenty-one lines had names after them. 'Twenty-one,' I said.

'Look at the next sheet down,' Julie instructed.

'Nineteen,' I said.

'And the next?'

'Twenty.'

'I work part-time in the day care center,' Julie reminded me. 'And we always have at least twenty-five kids. Always!' She slapped the top of the pile. 'According to these reports, we didn't have a single week with more than twenty-two children.'

'Maybe I need more coffee, Julie, but I'm not sure where you're going with this.'

'OK. When I first saw the roster, and it didn't add up, I looked at the individual names. Where's Jamie? Where's Declan?'

'Maybe they were away that week?' I suggested.

'No way! Declan's a little monster. He kicked me in the shin.' She tugged on her pant leg, revealing a convincing bruise. 'See that?'

'If I understand you correctly, there were usually twenty-five children in day care, but only twenty on that week's report.'

'Five children unaccounted for,' Julie interrupted. 'You got it. The day care isn't free, Aunt Hannah. They may be a church and all, but they're not that charitable.

'So, I decided to look into it,' Julie continued. 'The teacher has a contact list for all the parents, for emergencies and stuff, so I called Declan's mom.'

'To complain about the kicking?'

'Fat lot of good that would have done,' Julie huffed. 'Anger management issues? Not her little darling.'

'So what *did* you tell her?'

'I said that the church was planning to offer parents the opportunity to pay day care tuition by direct deposit, and if so, would she be interested. Then I asked her how she paid tuition now – cash, check or credit card – and she said, "the usual way".' At this point, Julie paused, drawing the story out, keeping me in suspense.

'Which was?'

'Judee McDaniel told Declan's mom that since she runs the day care center, the church had set up a special account in her name, so the checks should be made payable directly to her.'

'Ah, the light is dawning.'

Julie slapped the countertop. 'It's unbelievable! I called Jamie's mom, too, and Justin's, and Ashley's. Same story.'

'So, the roster that Judee submitted to the church didn't include the names of the children whose tuition she stole.'

'Yup.'

'How much does the day care cost?'

'They charge thirty-two dollars a day, which works out to $972 a month, more or less. The way I figure it, Judee had to be skimming close to five thousand dollars a month off the top.'

'Do you think someone at the church tipped your father off?'

Julie flushed. 'I think I did. I told him about Declan kicking me. Declan's an unusual name. When he didn't see it on the roster, maybe he got suspicious. I mean, why else would Dad have the day care rosters tacked up on his bulletin board?'

'Julie?' Georgina shuffled into the kitchen, rubbing sleep out of her eyes. 'I thought I heard your voice. What the hell are you doing here?' Her eyes grew wide. 'Has something happened . . .?'

'Everyone's fine,' I assured her. 'Sit down. Let me get you some coffee while Julie explains.'

After Julie finished telling her mother about Judee McDaniel's day care scam, Georgina said, 'Scott had introduced best practices at the church. They were about to conduct their first external audit, and everyone had until September 30 to submit their reports.' She pointed at the pages Julie had brought with her, still spread out on the counter in front of us. 'That must be one of them.'

'Do you think Brother Bob knew that Mrs McDaniel was stealing from the day care center?' Julie wondered.

'I think it's a question the police are going to want to ask him, Julie, especially since he seems to have been sleeping with her.'

'You are shitting me! They were having an *affair*?'

'Julie! Language!'

'Sorry, Mom, but eeeuw! Can you imagine having sex with Brother Bob? Gross.' After a moment of apparent reflection on the nastiness of sleeping with the pastor, she said, 'Are you sure?'

I fetched my iPhone from the charging station and showed Julie the photo I'd taken of the sketch of Brother Bob, Judee and the heron.

'That's them all right,' she said, pointing out, as Georgina had, Judee's distinctive tattoo. 'Damn!'

'This is serious,' I said. 'If Scott confronted Judee about the embezzlement, she certainly had a motive to kill him. And if Scott knew about Judee's affair with Brother Bob . . .' I paused. 'Not exactly career-enhancing for an aspiring televangelist, is it? He'd fall from grace faster than a skydiver without a parachute. Maybe Brother Bob wanted to shut him up.'

'Maybe both,' Georgina said.

'What are we waiting for? Somebody needs to make the call.'

Julie shot from her stool, my cell phone in hand. 'I said I never wanted to talk to that detective again, but this time, I'm going to enjoy it.'

THIRTY-FOUR

A t six o'clock the following evening, in the middle of dinner, Georgina called me back. I got up from my chicken piccatta to take her call.

'Scott's biological minions can rest easy,' she began.

'So Uber confirmed Andy's story?'

'They did. Are you sitting down?'

'No,' I said.

'Detective Evans just called. They're charging Judee McDaniel with Scott's murder.'

'Hallelujah,' I said. 'How'd they catch her?'

'Anyone who works with kids in Maryland needs to have a background check,' Georgina explained. 'They tracked down the security firm that did the work and matched her prints to a partial the FBI lifted from the handle of the garden shears.'

'And the money she stole?'

'Oh, it's perfectly safe, wherever she and her duffle bag are.'

'She's not in custody?'

'Flew the proverbial coop. Judee's husband, of course, has no idea, which I totally believe, by the way. She'd been squirreling the money away in an offshore account. Nobody knows what she was planning to do with it.'

Thinking about the incriminating etching, I asked, 'What about Brother Bob?'

'Threw Judee completely under the bus. That man in the picture? Not him, no way. There wasn't enough evidence for the police to charge him with anything, but there was plenty of evidence for Tamara. She kicked him out. Last I heard, Brother Bob is camping out in his office.'

'Amen,' I said.

'Exactly.'

'Are you OK, Georgina?' I asked. 'You sound exhausted.'

'I'm fine, Hannah, really, but I'll really perk up when that bitch is behind bars.'

Twenty minutes later, Julie called. 'They took me, Aunt Hannah, they took me,' Julie bubbled.

'Who took you where?' I teased, although I could guess. Julie'd applied to AmeriCorps, a kind of domestic Peace Corps that sent volunteers out to do good work in impoverished communities.

'I've been accepted into AmeriCorps. I filled out my wish list, now I just have to wait for an assignment.'

'What's your first choice?' I asked.

'Secret,' Julie said coyly. 'I don't want to jinx it. Oh, I forgot to tell you that Lacey turned up,' she rattled on. 'Lacey confirmed Sean's story, not that he needs an alibi now.' She paused to take a breath. 'Lacey doesn't do Facebook, can you imagine? One of her friends told her Sean was looking for her. I'm afraid we're going to be seeing her around.'

'Is that a bad thing?'

'Well, his Virginity Pledge is toast, so what's to lose?'

'Good night, Julie,' I said firmly, but I was smiling.

'Goodnight, Aunt Hannah,' Julie said, but I could tell that she was smiling, too.

THIRTY-FIVE

Dressed in our grubbiest work clothes, Ruth and I drove north on Route 2 in an elderly Ford F-150 pickup truck we'd borrowed from my brother-in-law, Dennis Rutherford. Just north of the South River Bridge, I rattled and jolted into the parking lot of the commercial storage facility where Daddy had been keeping the household contents of his former home. Once inside, I used the key Daddy had given me to open the padlock on his unit.

Ruth raised the roller door. 'Good Lord!' she said.

We faced a daunting wall of furniture, boxes and storage containers, stacked six feet high. 'I don't know where to begin,' she added.

'One step at a time,' I said as I pulled a folded aluminum lawn chair with a broken plastic seat strap off the top of a charcoal grill and set it aside in the hallway.

Ruth grabbed a blue bicycle by the handlebars and eased it out of the locker. Both tires were flat. 'This used to be mine,' she said, 'until I got the ten speed for my birthday. I can't understand why he kept it.' The kickstand was missing, so she leaned the bike against the door of the adjoining locker. 'Why didn't he have a garage sale?'

'Too busy, I suppose. Besides, after Mom died, you remember how he couldn't be talked into parting with anything. "Save it for another day", he'd say.'

Ruth hauled out a second lawn chair and the cushions that matched it and piled them next to the bike, followed by the charcoal grill. 'I guess another day has finally come.'

For the next ten minutes, my sister and I relocated furniture and household items from the storage unit to the hallway, gradually clearing a path through the center of the unit. It was like an episode of *Storage Wars*, except that nobody was bidding on the contents.

'What are we looking for exactly?' Ruth asked.

'I'm not sure,' I said. 'If we're lucky, it will be a box labeled "Charlotte's Things".'

'Hah,' Ruth snorted. 'Do you ever remember seeing anything like that in Mom and Dad's attic?'

I had to admit that I hadn't, primarily because I'd never been in my parents' attic except one time accompanying the pest control man who had been hired to check out a squirrel invasion.

'Maybe there'll be something that will help solve the mystery surrounding White Bear's death,' Ruth said.

'Here, take these,' I said, handing two kites – a dragon and a bird of paradise – over to Ruth.

'Ah, these bring back memories,' she said. 'Remember flying them on the beach that summer before I went to college?' She set the kites carefully aside. 'Maybe your grandkids would like them now.'

'Into the truck, then,' I said.

Stacked to my right, in two columns five high, were cardboard boxes labeled: 'Books'. I eased between the books and a drop leaf table that had once been in our mother's kitchen. It, too, was stacked with boxes marked, appropriately, 'Kitchen'.

What was I looking for? A vintage trunk, maybe? A carved wooden hope chest? An antique safe?

A handle protruded from under the kitchen table. I moved a floor lamp in order to kneel down and check it out. 'Oh my gosh,' I said, 'it's my Chatty Cathy doll!'

Blue-eyed Cathy sat bolt upright in a miniature baby stroller. She was still dressed in the bright yellow gingham dress she'd worn when I last played with her, and a ruffled crinoline with lacy bloomers underneath. Her blond ponytails were tied with matching yellow ribbons. I reached under her dress, grabbed the plastic ring I knew I'd find there and pulled the string. 'Please brush my hair,' Cathy said. I laughed. 'I don't remember her being that whiney.' I pulled the string a second time. 'Give me a kiss,' the doll said. I kissed the top of her head, smoothed her dress and settled her back into her stroller. 'This is a keeper,' I said as I rolled it out into the hallway on its miniature wheels.

On a pair of stacked end tables just beyond the kitchen table I found three boxes marked 'Ruth', 'Hannah' and 'Georgina'. While Ruth wrestled with a Queen Anne chair, I ripped the packing tape off the top of the box marked 'Hannah' and looked inside. In neatly labeled folders Mom had saved my juvenile artwork and every report card and school photograph from kindergarten through twelfth grade. Records of my immunizations, too, and a packet of letters postmarked Oberlin, Ohio, held together by a rubber band that disintegrated when I touched it. In the days before the Internet took over our lives, I wrote home from college once a week.

Tears pricked at my eyes.

Ruth noticed. 'Hannah?'

I looked up helplessly. 'There's a box here for you, too. And one for Georgina.'

Ruth eased the box gently out of my hands. 'Why don't we save these for later?'

'All those memories,' I said, feeling defeated. I eyed the upholstered chair, longing to curl up in it as I had when it sat in the corner of our living room, next to the fireplace.

'You're the one who set us off on this fishing expedition,' Ruth scolded. 'You can't wimp out now.'

'Right.' I took a deep breath, let it out slowly, squared my shoulders and waded back in bravely.

'If I were Grandmother and I wanted to keep personal things private,' Ruth called out, 'I'd keep them in my bedroom.'

'I'm remembering a cedar chest that sat at the foot of Mom's bed,' I said.

I stood on tiptoe, peering over an ancient television – with rabbit ears! – toward the back of the unit. 'I see a four-poster back there, but it will take me a while to get to it.'

With Ruth's help, I moved a mattress and box springs to one side and carted a headboard and footboard out into the hallway so we could gain access to an oak chest of drawers that had once been my grandmother's. The two small drawers at the top held nothing but flowered shelf liner, a paperclip and two blond bobby pins. Except for shelf liner, the three large drawers below them were equally empty. Two bedside tables that were part of the same bedroom suite held no surprises other than a desic-cated trap-door spider.

While I was disposing of the spider, Ruth uncovered two oversize plastic storage containers of sheets and towels. 'Didn't Daddy take anything with him?' she complained, shoving the containers, still stacked one atop the other, aside.

'I think Neelie was fully stocked with linens,' I said. 'I know he took his Navy memorabilia.'

'What about his desk?' she asked.

'That, too,' I said, venturing deeper into the unit.

'It's always the last place you look!' I yelled in triumph.

I'd found Mother's cedar chest, resting on top of an uphol-stered loveseat and covered with a quilted shipping blanket. By the time Ruth joined me, I'd already raised the lid and was pawing through its contents. I found my parents' 1952 wedding album and a square box about the size of a dinner plate containing the wedding bells from the top of their wedding cake. A Lord & Taylor shirt box held a christening gown, ivory with age, wrapped in tissue paper. My sisters and I had worn it, each in turn, for our baptisms. 'I wondered where this gown had got to,' I said, folding the tissue paper back around it again. 'They were moving when I needed it for Emily.'

'Look at this.' Ruth had unearthed a red leather-bound book with 'Autographs' embossed in gold script on the cover. She flipped the book open to the flyleaf. 'It was Mom's in seventh grade.' She chuckled, then paged forward. 'Oh my gosh, listen! Someone named Polly wrote:

> *Lois and John,*
> *Sitting in a tree,*
> *K-I-S-S-I-N-G.*
> *First comes love,*
> *Then comes marriage,*
> *Then comes Lois with a baby carriage.*

'I wonder who John was?' I laughed out loud at the silliness of the verse.

'I don't think we need to know,' Ruth said, setting the autograph book aside in the pile destined for the truck.

The cedar chest was too heavy for Ruth and me to carry out to the truck on our own, so we systematically sorted through its contents. At the bottom of the chest, under a garment bag containing my mother's wedding suit, was an oversized padded mailer marked KEEP. The mailer was sealed.

I glanced up at my sister who was looming like a vulture.

'What are you waiting for?' she said. 'You don't need my permission.'

So I seized the string tab and tore the mailer open.

'If we're lucky,' I had quipped to Ruth earlier that morning, 'it will be a box labeled "Charlotte's Things".'

We'd been incredibly lucky. Nestled inside the mailer I found an old-fashioned scrapbook, its manila pages pre-punched to fit over posts in a black cover which was fastened on with shoestring, tied in a neat bow.

'Charlotte: Her Book' was written on the title page in Gothic letters using India ink. Charlotte had been practicing her calligraphy.

My sister and I stared at each other, then at the scrapbook in reverent silence. I turned to the first page. 'It seems to start in mid-high school,' I said, noting a corsage flattened between the pages next to a booklet titled, 'Spring Formal'. Charlotte had been a popular girl. Every slot on her dance card was filled, but the first and last dances of the evening had been claimed by the same young man, S. Smith.

'That has to be our grandfather,' Ruth said.

I closed the scrapbook carefully and held it close to my chest. 'Let's take this out where the light is better.'

A few minutes later, my sister and I sat side-by-side on folding lawn chairs, watching our grandmother's early life scroll by. Tickets to a concert by Ben Pollack and His Californians. Postcards from Quechee Gorge near her home in Vermont as well as places farther flung like New York City and Niagara Falls.

Charlotte had graduated from high school in June of 1928 and almost immediately bought a train ticket from White River Junction, Vermont to Pierre, South Dakota, with a stopover in Chicago (during the height of Prohibition). Matchbooks and ticket stubs suggested she'd stayed at the Allerton Hotel and attended a showing of 'A Mysterious Lady' with Greta Garbo at the Biograph.

She'd owned a camera, too. At some point Charlotte climbed to the top of a building on Wacker Drive overlooking the Chicago River and the massive construction works that had been required to straighten it. Further on in her journey, blurry photos captured Midwestern towns from her window as the train sped through.

She'd saved a menu from the dining car. Oyster stew cost seventy-five cents, deep dish blueberry pie (baked on car today!) was thirty cents and a special prime rib dinner with all the trimmings would have set Charlotte back just a dollar ten.

Eventually she documented her arrival in Pierre, moving into the boarding house on North Huron, a sprawling Victorian with a front porch large enough to hold all the residents who posed for a group picture there in the summer of 1929. I spotted Charles Keene at once, lounging casually on the steps, straw boater in hand. Dressed in a lacy white frock, Charlotte stood directly behind Charles, leaning against a pillar. The ample, apron-clad woman to the far right had to be their landlady, Mrs Lumley. If I referred back to the 1930 census data, I might be able to sort the others out eventually, too.

Charlotte had chosen to wear a short jacket and wide-legged pleated slacks for a photo while standing on the running board of a Model T, her head cocked to one side, smiling shyly for whomever held her camera. 'She looks so like Amelia Earhart in that shot,' Ruth observed.

I agreed. 'A kindred spirit.'

Some Lakota lived in teepees then, we learned from Charlotte's photos, and as Wasula had told me, rodeos had been big, with a capital B. It's hard to capture a bucking bronco, but Charlotte had tried: she'd dedicated four pages of her scrapbook to action-packed rodeo scenes.

I turned the page and uncovered a treasure – Joseph, Henry and a teenaged Wasula posing against a split-rail fence. At Wasula's feet sat a black and white dog. Everyone was smiling, even the dog, except for Henry who had turned his face away from the camera and seemed to be glowering at something beyond the frame.

'Thank goodness she labeled everyone,' Ruth said. 'What kind of dog is Scout, do you know?'

I squinted. 'Some sort of mixed collie, I guess.'

'So, which brother did Charlotte favor?' Ruth asked. 'Joseph or Henry?'

'Joseph, for sure,' I said. 'Henry looks like a sourpuss, wishing he were anywhere else but.'

After turning to the next page, however, the answer to Ruth's question was obvious: Joseph alone, posing before the same fence, Stetson pushed back on his head.

Joseph grinning broadly, showing off his trophy, a silver belt buckle.

A newspaper article on the Calgary Exhibition and Stampede where Joseph White Bear had won the saddle bronc event. Charlotte had underlined his name three times.

'She was sweet on him,' Ruth said.

Tucked between the next two pages we found a slim packet of notes, written on notebook paper in what I assumed was Lakota, with the exception of a thank you note in English from

Mrs Two Knives who was grateful for Charlotte's help with a school fair. 'I'll have to ask Sam or his aunt to translate these for us,' I said, setting the packet aside for the time being.

The rodeo clipping was followed by several from the *Burlington Free Press* held together by a rusted paper clip. Someone must have mailed them to Charlotte because, 'See what you missed!' was written across the article on top in barely legible pencil.

Wednesday, August 31st, 1932

The curtain will rise on Burlington's great celestial drama – the sun's total eclipse – at exactly 2:16 p.m. today.

The following day's paper reported:

Celestial show races through skies filled with big, slow-moving clouds. Some gazers see corona as a color spectacle, others as a yellow glow. Haze will probably ruin many a plate of scientific photographers. Spectators fared better than astronomers, for the eye was better than the camera in this eclipse, and much that the plates missed excited the admiration of millions.

My eye had been caught by another headline: 'Girl, smoking glass to witness the eclipse, nearly burned to death' when Ruth reached across and ran a finger over the masthead. 'September 1, 1932,' she read aloud. 'Didn't you reckon Mom was conceived around that time?'

My heart did a somersault. 'Ohmahgawd.'

'Dee-dee-do-do, dee-dee-do-do,' chanted Ruth, making 'Twilight Zone' noises. 'I wonder . . .' She turned the pages. Blank, blank, and blank again. The article about the solar eclipse was the last thing Charlotte had pasted into her scrapbook.

'It's as if her life ended with that eclipse,' Ruth said.

I looked my sister squarely in the eyes. 'Act One had come to an end, at least. A little more than a month later, she would start life over as a married woman.'

'A pregnant married woman,' Ruth said.

I closed the scrapbook carefully. When I picked up the padded mailer intending to return the scrapbook to it, a five by seven inch photograph slithered out and fluttered to the concrete floor. I stooped to retrieve it.

A man sits astride a white horse. While the horse seems transfixed by the camera, the man stares into the distance, giving me a clear view of his chiseled, noble profile. He wears dark trousers, a jacket with fringed leather cuffs and a black Stetson hat. The hand resting on his thigh holds a cigarette. He is Joseph White Bear.

I turned the photo over. 'My Knight,' Grandmother had written.

THIRTY-SIX

As my mother was fond of saying, 'You can't get there from here.'

Although I plugged BWI to PIR into every travel website known to the modern Internet, no airline flew direct from Baltimore to Pierre. In the end I accomplished the trip piecemeal, booking a flight to Denver then catching a California Pacific flight to Pierre which, for some reason, didn't fly on Wednesdays and Fridays.

The plane landed at 12:45. I had no checked luggage, so it took only minutes to make my way to the Budget Rental Car counter and pick up my car.

Interstate 90 runs west out of Pierre, straight as a ruler, for mile after hypnotizing mile. I found myself nodding off. I was minutes from pulling off to the side of the road for a catnap, when the interchange with SD73 at Kadoka came into view along with a welcome cluster of gas stations, restaurants and a budget inn.

I purchased a large coffee at the gas station which made the endless miles of widely spaced farms, pastures and ponds south of Kadoka less soporific.

At a stop sign at a cross roads in the vast prairie of nowhere,

I gained an hour when the time zone changed from Central to Mountain time. SD44 eventually merged with the Big Foot Trail on the outskirts of Kyle, a rather soulless sprawl of widely-spaced, one-story buildings.

'Your GPS will do you no good,' Sam had emailed when giving directions. 'When you get to Little Wound School in the center of town, turn left on Allen Road. At St Barnabas Episcopal Church, check your odometer. The dirt road that leads to Wasula's house is exactly one point two miles past the church, on the right.'

Little Wound School, a massive, multi-storied red block of a building, was impossible to miss. St Barnabas Church? Not so much. I'd driven past the barn-like structure twice before I saw it and got myself back on track.

Wasula's modest ranch-style home sat one hundred yards off the road, surrounded by acres of fenced pastureland where a half-dozen cows, two horses and a buffalo grazed in contented harmony.

Mai answered my knock. 'Hannah, so good to see you.'

We exchanged hugs.

'Did you get Julie's message?' she asked in a rush.

'What? No. I haven't had any cell phone service since Pierre.'

'Sucks, doesn't it?' She gave me a what-are-ya-gonna-do kind of shrug. 'Julie's been accepted in an AmeriCorps program.'

I set my overnight bag down on the carpet and shrugged out of my jacket. 'I knew that, actually. She told me she'd applied just before I left to come here.'

Mai grinned slyly. Something was up. 'But you haven't heard the best of it. I don't know how Father did it, but he must have pulled some strings because Julie's been assigned to the Red Cloud Indian School here on the rez.'

Deep down in her DNA, Julie carried the genes of another pioneer woman, venturing out into Indian territory to help better the lives of others. Like her great-grandmother before her, would Julie find her knight? I prayed that unlike Charlotte, Julie's fairy tale would have a happily ever after.

'That's wonderful,' I told Mai, meaning it. 'What will she be doing?'

'Teacher's aide, I think, for the Head Start program.'

'Ah, Julie loves working with toddlers,' I told her. As long as they're not named Declan, I thought to myself.

'She'll homestay with a Lakota family near the school,' Mai babbled on. 'It'll be so cool.'

The reservation, I knew from driving only a part of it, was huge. 'How far away will she be?'

'Only sixty miles.' She dismissed the distance with a wave of her hand. 'I drive more than that to work every day. Speaking of which, I gotta go or I'll be late.' She snatched a fleece hoodie from a peg on the wall. 'Bingo waits for no man . . . or woman.'

Before Mai breezed out the door, slamming it behind her, she pointed me in the direction of the living room where I found Aunt Wasula perched on a loveseat, hands folded in her lap, waiting patiently. She wore her usual uniform – a flowered dress and cardigan – but this time, she'd slipped her feet into a pair of fur-lined slippers.

I wasn't certain of the protocol, but I took her hands in mine and planted a light kiss on her cheek. 'You look well,' I said.

She smiled. 'Every day is a blessing.'

Wasula inquired about my trip, then asked if I wanted anything to drink.

'No, but thank you. I had some coffee earlier.' I grinned. 'Mostly, I could use a bathroom.'

When I returned, carrying my overnight bag, Wasula said, 'You have brought some things to show me.' She moved her feet off the ottoman, indicating that I should sit there.

'I have, and I also need your help.' I dug Charlotte's scrapbook out of my bag, laid it on Wasula's knees and opened it to the first page. I watched silently as she leafed through Charlotte's life, using her hand to smooth each page as she came to it.

At the photograph of Charlotte on the Model T, she paused. 'That's Lottie.'

'Yes.'

'Wasn't she lovely?'

I agreed that she was.

'I found some notes, too,' I said, reaching again into my bag. 'Most of them are written in Lakota.' I handed the first one to her. 'I didn't know my grandmother spoke Lakota.'

Wasula's old eyes sparkled. 'Lottie was very smart. She picked up our language quickly while tending to patients on the reservation, especially the elder ones who did not speak English. By the time she left us, she was almost fluent.'

I called attention to the note, in case she'd forgotten she was holding it. 'Can you tell me what this says?'

Wasula's eyes strayed to the paper. After a moment she said, 'It's from White Bear. He's asking Lottie to bring extra flour when she comes. He tells her he will pay for it.'

'How about this one?' I handed her the next note in the little pile.

'White Bear is arranging to meet Lottie to see a movie when he comes to Pierre with two horses to sell.'

'And this?' I handed her the longest of the notes, written on a single sheet of notebook paper, White Bear's bold capital letters covering both sides.

As Wasula read, her face clouded, her eyelids drooped. At first I thought she'd dozed off. I reached out to nudge her gently awake when her eyes flew open and, startled, I drew my hand back.

'After the rodeos became successful,' she began, 'the Lakota decided to manage the money themselves. One year, after the rodeo was over, the cash receipts went missing.' She turned to me, her face serious. 'You can guess which year that was.'

'1932?'

She patted my hand and nodded. 'One of the young bull riders, Red Shirt, was accused of the crime. Nothing was ever proven, but he left the reservation in disgrace. White Bear is telling Lottie that he knows it was Hawk who stole the money. He's asking her what he should do.'

The room grew quiet as we let the significance of that fact sink in.

'I know what Grandmother would have said,' I told her. 'She would have advised him to talk to his brother, convince him to give the money back.'

'Yes,' Wasula said. 'And I fear that's exactly what White Bear did.'

'Do you believe that Hawk murdered your brother, to keep him quiet about the money?'

'Sixty-three dollars and seventy-six cents, that's all it was,' she said. 'My brothers never got along, but I never thought . . .' Her voice trailed off.

It's all about the money, I thought, thinking about my brother-in-law's murder. It's always about the money.

'A newspaper in Deadwood claimed it was a rodeo accident,' I said, 'that White Bear was injured while riding a bucking bronc.'

'Ah, yes,' she said. 'Father thought it was better that way.'

'What happened to Hawk?' I asked, seething quietly over the cover-up.

'He married, had children, a normal life,' she said. 'Hawk died in 1990. Whatever actually happened that day was a secret he kept all those years and took to the grave with him.'

There was one final note in the pile. 'This is the last one,' I said. 'Can you translate it for me?'

Wasula studied the single page for what seemed like an eternity. 'It's a love letter,' she told me at last. 'White Bear's words to Lottie are private, not meant to be shared.'

'But . . .' I protested.

'I will tell you this, Hannah,' she said, as if to soften the blow. 'White Bear writes this letter to *wínyan-mit-áwa*: my wife, my lover.'

My throat grew tight; I suppressed a sob.

'White Bear won some money at the Celebration rodeo,' Wasula said. 'He could afford to marry. But, after my brother died, I never saw Lottie again. I kept asking myself, why didn't she come to say goodbye?'

A single tear, that of a heartbroken sixteen-year-old girl, rolled down her wrinkled cheek.

'She must have been devastated by his death,' I said. I turned to the back of the scrapbook, to the newspaper article describing the eclipse. I pointed out the date on the masthead. 'She was still in South Dakota then,' I said, 'but this article must have been important to her.'

Wasula closed the scrapbook and laid both hands protectively on the cover. 'In Lakota culture,' she explained, 'a total solar eclipse is the physical manifestation of the sacred union of the Divine Masculine, represented by the sun, and the Divine

Feminine, represented by the moon.' She patted the seat cushion next to her. 'Come, sit by me. I will tell you a story.'

Like an eager toddler at storytime, I moved from the ottoman to the loveseat and sat.

'You may have heard of the peace pipe?'

'Yes,' I told her, 'but everything I know about it comes from movies and television so it's probably not very accurate.'

'Whenever the white men and the Indians got together to talk about treaties, the Indian way was to smoke a pipe first, so the negotiations could be witnessed by the Great Spirit. White men usually associated the pipe with the discussion of peace, so they are the ones, like in the Western movies you saw, who named it the peace pipe. To our people, however, it's always been called the Sacred Pipe because when we smoke it, we are communicating directly with the Creator.

'You are a Christian, Hannah?'

'I am, yes, of the Episcopalian persuasion.'

She nodded, looking wise. 'Think of the Sacred Pipe as a portable altar. Our great Lakota holy man Frank Fools Crow once described praying with the Sacred Pipe as having the same significance to our people as if you, a Christian, prayed while holding Jesus Christ in your arms.

'So, you can understand that the Sacred Pipe was a great gift to the Lakota Nation.'

'You say gift?'

'The Sacred Pipe was brought to us by the White Buffalo Calf Woman. Many have heard the legend of the White Buffalo Calf Woman, but this part of the story is often left out. The Sun and the Moon are husband and wife and they had one daughter: the Morning Star. And it was the Morning Star who came down to earth as the White Buffalo Calf Woman and brought the Sacred Pipe to the Native people.

'So the sun and the moon joining together in a solar eclipse can be a time of Creation,' she said, reaching for my hand. 'Your mother is the Morning Star.'

I rested my head against Aunt Wasula's comforting shoulder and wept.

NEARLY
GONE

NEARLY GONE

GONE

ELLE COSIMANO

Kathy Dawson Books
an imprint of Penguin Group (USA) LLC

KATHY DAWSON BOOKS

Published by the Penguin Group

Penguin Group (USA) LLC

375 Hudson Street, New York, New York 10014

USA/Canada/UK/Ireland/Australia/New Zealand/India/South Africa/China

penguingroup.com

A Penguin Random House Company

Library of Congress Cataloging-in-Publication Data

Cosimano, Elle.

Nearly gone / by Elle Cosimano.

pages   cm

Summary: "A math whiz from a trailer park discovers she's the only student capable of unraveling complex clues left by a serial killer who's systematically getting rid of her classmates"— Provided by publisher.

ISBN 978-0-8037-3926-0 (hardcover)

[1. Mystery and detective stories. 2. Criminal investigation—Fiction. 3. Serial murderers—Fiction. 4. Mathematics—Fiction.] I. Title.

PZ7.C8189Ne 2014   [Fic]—dc23   2013010335

Printed in the United States of America

1 3 5 7 9 10 8 6 4 2

Designed by Nancy R. Leo-Kelly

Text set in Dante

For Connor and Nick
You will *always* be *everything* to me

❖ ❖ ❖

MOST SCIENTIFIC LAWS can be boiled down to a simple mathematical *if-then* equation. If you follow the rules, then you get the desired result. If you deviate, then there is a consequence. The rules of law don't concern themselves with *why*.

My mother really only had three rules: A) no bad grades, B) no trouble, and C) no touching. A + B + C = admission to a good college. In her mind, this was an incontrovertible direct mathematical proof. It wasn't a theory. It was the only possible outcome.

I used to believe that too. But that was before I started to wonder why.

Sometimes, the only way to find a solution is to break the rules.

I

"Who can tell me the purpose of Dr. Schrödinger's experiment?" Mr. Rankin paced between the rows on the other side of the classroom.

I huddled over my open textbook, concealing the *Missed Connections* ad in the personals section, dissecting the words again for some hidden meaning. *Newton was wrong. We clash with yellow. Find me tonight under the bleachers.* It read like a science riddle, and I couldn't seem to stop looking at it. *Stupid.*

"Anyone?" Rankin's chalk-smudged slacks paused beside me. I inched my arm over the ad. I'd never been so careless to read them during class. Especially so close to the end of the semester, with finals only a few weeks away. *Stupid.* No personal ad was worth losing a scholarship over.

He passed on, and I tucked the folds of the *Missed Connections* tighter under my textbook.

At the blackboard, Rankin underlined the words *DEAD OR ALIVE.* He'd scrawled them there yesterday at the end of class, along with a reading assignment, a disturbing preview of today's lecture.

"Dead or alive? This is the question quantum physicists have wrestled with since Erwin Schrödinger first devised his experiment in 1935. Mr. Petrenko, do you care to enlighten us?"

Every head turned to the back of the room, where Oleksander Petrenko reclined, his feet crossed at the ankles, fingers threaded behind his head. The laces on his black high-tops were red, which always seemed out of character to me. Everything else about him—his buzz cut, the sharp angle of his jaw, his brusque Ukrainian accent—was clipped, stark, and ascetic.

He shrugged beneath a dark hoodie. "What is the point?" The consonants rolled off his tongue, stopping abruptly against his square white teeth. He blinked gray eyes, sharply outlined in dark lashes. His lids were hooded, making him look bored when he finally answered. "Schrödinger was a physicist. This is AP Chemistry."

I suppressed a smile. I didn't have one thing in common with Oleksa, but I couldn't agree more. Schrödinger's experiment wasn't about chemistry or even physics. It was a matter of philosophy, and philosophy had no place here. Hard science follows rules. Its assertions are quantifiable and concrete. Clamp down the facts under a bright light and magnify them to the 10x power until the details are so clear, the truth isn't a matter of debate. It just *is*.

Rankin raised one eyebrow and approached Oleksa's desk, drumming his fingers on the surface. Oleksa regarded them coldly, as if he might enjoy breaking them.

"As usual, Mr. Petrenko, you are smarter than you are industrious. This is indeed Advanced Placement Chemistry. I assume this to mean you have the capacity to appreciate the broader implications of Schrödinger's experiment. I am continually amazed that someone with such a large brain can be so small-minded." I cringed, feeling the sting of Rankin's insult. I wasn't small-minded.

Oleksa crossed his arms and slouched lower in his chair.

"Anh Bui, care to take a stab at it?" Rankin turned, and heads shifted to my side of the room. Anh's throat cleared beside me.

"It's a thought experiment," said Anh. "Schrödinger presented a scenario in which a live cat is sealed in a box with a toxic substance to prove that you can't know for certain if the cat is dead or alive until the box is opened."

Rankin waggled a finger in the air and surged to the blackboard. "Proof!" he exclaimed, making Anh and me jump in our seats as he scrawled frantic letters across the board. "Proof by contradiction! An indirect proof by which a proposition is proved *true* by proving it is *impossible* to be *false*." He slapped his chalky hands together. "Schrödinger places a cat in a steel chamber with a device containing a vial of hydrocyanic acid. If a single atom of the substance decays during the test period, a relay mechanism will trip a hammer, which will in turn break the vial and kill the cat. But how do we know for certain?" He paused, looking expectantly from face to face. "Schrödinger presents a paradox. The cat cannot be both alive and dead at the same time, and yet to the universe outside the box, earlier theories of quantum mechanics suggest the cat would be both—dead and alive."

"The cat's dead," muttered TJ behind me. Rankin's eyes swung in his direction, and the class turned collectively to look at him. The brace on his outstretched leg bumped my chair as he shifted in his seat. Five years ago, TJ's mom had locked herself in her Saab inside their garage with the engine running. As far as TJ was concerned, if you poisoned something and put it in a box, it was dead.

"Many would agree with you, Mr. Wiles," Rankin said, brushing over the awkward pause and drawing heads back toward the front of the room. All except TJ, who was staring a hole through his lab table. "Schrödinger himself knew this idea was absurd, and yet he argued that we cannot know the true state of the cat until the box is opened. Until we can prove it."

TJ grumbled something unintelligible. Beside me, Anh's lips turned down. She'd stayed home sick when we'd dissected frogs in biology class, and done extra credit assignments for a week to make up for the grade. Anh was a vegetarian who caught spiders in cups and put them outside rather than kill them. It didn't matter that we were lab partners, or even that we were friends. If Rankin made us do something horrible to a cat for our lab final, I'd be on my own. Which, as much as I hated to admit it, might not be such a bad thing. Our cumulative scores for the year were a little too close for comfort.

I doodled a dying frog on the upper corner of my newspaper, an exaggerated tongue hanging out of his mouth and eyes rolled back in his head, then tipped it toward Anh so she could see it. She clapped a hand over her mouth to stifle a giggle, drawing Rankin's attention toward our end of the room. I slid my textbook to cover the exposed edge of the page.

He frowned at us but didn't bother with reprimands. Instead, he checked his watch and sighed. "Speaking of absurd, there is a pep rally for the soccer team in the gymnasium next period. Lab report scores will be posted on Monday as usual, and we will reconvene to discuss your upcoming practical exam, in which you will design a chemistry experiment that demonstrates your understanding of proof by contradiction. *That*, Mr. Petrenko, is the *point*."

Slamming textbooks and shuffling papers muffled his final instructions. Rankin raised his voice. "Mr. Petrenko, please come prepared to participate next week. And Leigh Boswell, please leave the personal classifieds in your locker, lest they become a distraction in my class." The bell rang and Rankin reached for his mug. "Dismissed."

My lungs collapsed as if the breath had been kicked out of them. I'd made it almost the entire year, and Rankin picked now—the tail end of the fourth quarter—to call me out in front of everyone.

Anh glared at Rankin, hunched over his desk. "Don't worry about it, Leigh. I'm sure no one was paying attention. But you really should consider leaving the love connections in your locker. You're going to get us both in trouble."

I wiped my ink-blackened fingers on the front of my pants. "They're not love connections."

"Whatever." She rolled her eyes playfully, like she knew something I didn't. I adored Anh. Really, I did. But the last few weeks, it had been hard not to resent her crisp white shirts, her hair cropped to perfection over each neat eyebrow, the way she never broke a sweat before a test.

There was only one chemistry scholarship, and I was a fraction of a point behind her, which meant Anh stood between me and a chance for a new life. Alphabetically fated as lab partners for the last three years, we'd been setting the curve since. Which meant that we needed to help each other as much as we needed to crush each other. Most days, the thought of crushing Anh just hurt. And yet, I wanted to out-seat her so bad, I could taste it.

I hated myself for the thoughts I hoped she couldn't read on my face. I felt like Schrödinger's damned cat. It was stupid to think there was more than one possible outcome. To wish we could both come in first. To think of our situation as anything but black and white.

I jammed the *Missed Connections* into my backpack, scooped up my books, and then paused. There was graffiti on my desk that hadn't been there yesterday. I'd been in such a hurry to check the paper, I hadn't noticed it earlier. The letters were blue and bold, and exactly mirrored the words Rankin had written on the blackboard yesterday afternoon. *DEAD OR ALIVE?* I looked up, cradling my books. The room was almost empty.

"I thought I'd go to the library and study for our trig test. Are you going to the pep rally with Jeremy?"

Anh stood waiting beside me. I paused, trailing a finger over the letters. They felt creepy and intentional. The blue ink didn't smudge, but I could still smell a hint of indelible marker fumes. Probably the same blue markers we used during labs. Someone must have been sitting in my seat before class and thought it'd be funny to freak me out. It wouldn't have been the first time a classmate pulled a practical joke at my expense. This one seemed harmless enough.

Anh was still waiting. At this point, I wanted nothing more than to be as far away as possible from Mr. Rankin and the gossip-worthy morsel he'd just served up to my entire chem class. As if they didn't already have enough to chew on. "Pep rally. Sure. See you at lunch."

2

JEREMY WAITED OUTSIDE my class, leaning against the wall and fiddling with his camera case, his baby-blond bangs falling limp over his eyes. He paused his tinkering to push his wire-rim glasses up his nose with a long, slender finger. Someone bumped into him, and when he looked up, his pale gray eyes found mine. He smiled.

I wanted to smile back, but my mood was too dark when I walked out of Rankin's class and I couldn't make myself return the greeting.

"Hello, sunshine." He tossed me a pouch of Twinkies. Jeremy's smiles felt brighter lately. Anh insisted he only smiled now when he was with me. The simple fact that I felt responsible for them made those rare smiles feel like spotlights. And I'd already been under enough spotlights this morning.

He looked past me, over my head, and frowned. "Is Anh coming?"

"She's studying."

I dropped the World News section of my paper into his waiting hands, and kept the rest for myself. World news mattered to Jeremy. His world was bigger than mine. His parents owned time shares in Aruba and the Cayman Islands. I, on

the other hand, never saw much sense in concerning myself
with global headlines when my entire world fit inside a tin
can trailer and the front seat of Jeremy's Civic.

I handed him back a Twinkie and scarfed mine down in
huge bites as I put distance between the lab and me. His camera case bounced against his chest as he tried to keep up.

"Good morning, Jeremy," he mumbled through a mouthful of cake. "Great to see you. How was your morning? Fantastic, *Nearly*, thanks for asking. Hey, that's great. Mine too."

I flinched at the sound of my given name. Back in middle
school, we'd had a writing lesson about eliminating unnec-
essary adverbs, and the class had latched on to my name:
Nearly Boswell. I became an adverb. Expendable.

Jeremy had decided a new name would make me feel
stronger. So he came up with Leigh.

Not that it had mattered. I'd gone from being "Nearly A
Freak" in grade school, to "Nearly Has Boobs" in middle school,
and now "Nearly Invisible" to most of West River High.

Jeremy never called me Nearly unless he wanted to make
a point.

He looked me over thoughtfully. "Don't let Rankin get to
you. He's not going to mess with your grade just because you
were reading the personal ads during lab."

"You heard that?" I glanced around to be sure no one was
listening.

"Should I be jealous?" he chided. "Reading the personals

used to be *our* thing. Since when did you start reading them with Anh?"

"How long were you standing out there? Why weren't you in class?"

He waved a pink slip. "Excused absence. Friday morning therapy with Dr. Matthews."

I didn't break eye contact to double-check his excuse. He'd been seeing Dr. Matthews since he'd tried to OD on a bottle of cough syrup when he was twelve. "So why weren't you in therapy, then?"

Jeremy fanned his fingers and a second pink slip appeared behind the first. "Excused absence. Illness."

I gave him a quick head to toe. He definitely wasn't sick. But he was smiling the same wide-eyed smile he wore the first day he picked me up for school, right after his father forbade him from driving his car anywhere near my neighborhood. The same reckless twinkle in his eyes he'd worn when I dragged him through the back window of my trailer on Friday nights while my mom was at work so our nosy neighbor wouldn't see.

Normally just the thought of cutting class would have had him scrambling for a Xanax. He'd spent his whole life doing exactly what his parents expected of him—well, except for the time he spent with me. His father was wound way too tight for Jeremy to risk anything else. And yet, he was smiling—like he'd tasted his own free will, and he liked it.

"How many sessions have you skipped?"

He ignored my question and started casually toward the gym.

I trotted after him, taking two steps for each of his, growing more anxious when the smile slid from his face. "You're going to be in serious trouble if your mother discovers you bugged out on your shrink appointment."

"First she'd have to care," he grumbled. "She didn't even notice that I paid your rent with my dad's poker money . . ." His Adam's apple bobbed as he swallowed the rest, as if only just realizing he'd said it out loud.

My eyes flew open wide. "You did what?"

"It's no big deal," he said, tucking me under his arm as he walked. "Dad came home from his game last night drunk with a lot of cash. Vince's dad lost big." He arched a brow conspiratorially. "So I snuck a few hundred and gave it to my mom. I told her it was your rent payment. It should keep her off your mom's back for a few days."

"You shouldn't have done that, J. What if you get in trouble?" His parents were our landlords, and ever since my dad left, they hated us. Probably because we always seemed to be late with the rent.

"It's no big deal."

He pasted on a paper-thin smile, but he was holding something back. I didn't see any of the telltale signs that he and his dad might be fighting, but Jeremy'd always been good at concealing the occasional bruise.

My fingers fidgeted in my pockets, wanting to touch him but not wanting to pry. If he wouldn't tell me, then touching him skin to skin was the only way to know for sure what he was feeling. But it felt wrong, like sneaking around in someone's room, or taking something away from them that wasn't mine to take. I'd feel his emotions, taste them like they were some tangible thing I'd consumed.

The first time I touched Jeremy, we were twelve. It was an accident, our fingers grazing as we both reached for the last cookie on the silver tray in Jeremy's kitchen during our dads' poker game. Up until that night, we hadn't really spoken on those Friday nights when my dad dragged me to Belle Green with him so he could play cards with Mr. Fowler. I'd felt out of place in his house. It was filled with delicate and breakable things. Things I shouldn't want to touch, but did, because they were so different from my own. But when I'd touched Jeremy, we felt the same. Alone. He was in his own house, in his own neighborhood, and still didn't fit. I recognized that kind of loneliness, because it was mine too.

We split the last cookie that night, and everything else since. Being together didn't get rid of the loneliness, but somehow, it made it sweeter, because we shared it.

I pulled my hands out of my pockets, and gently took his, letting a painful lump of his emotions swell in my throat. His depression tasted like a dry salt paste. It would have been choking and hard to breathe through if it weren't muted by the anti-depressants Dr. Matthews prescribed. Still, my eyes burned like I'd been crying, and I swallowed the knot until it was a clenched fist inside my chest. "What's going on? You can tell me."

Jeremy shook his head. "It's nothing."

But it wasn't. It was strong, with a bitter after bite that I could feel trying to claw its way up. He was angry, and burying it deep. It seemed to burrow under my own skin.

"It's *something*."

He shrugged it off and didn't look me in the eyes. "I got into it with my mom again this morning. That's all."

I gave his hand a squeeze. Whatever it was, he would tell me when he was ready. "I'll pay you back the rent money, I promise. I don't want to get you in trouble."

He squeezed back, and the brief pulse of affection was laced with doubt. I let go of his hand, and pushed my glasses up my nose, bringing his tight smile back in focus, knowing I'd seen him more clearly a moment ago and wishing I hadn't.

"It's fine. Don't worry about it," he said, as if he could see through me too.

We neared the gym, and the hall erupted with clapping hands and the steady stomp of feet against the bleachers. West River High's varsity soccer team had made the championship playoffs. The athletes gathered by the trophy cabinet to check their reflections in the glass and worship at their own altar before rushing the gym floor. I skirted around the clog of blue uniforms, trying not to touch them.

"Heads up!"

I ducked and held my breath as a soccer ball soared low over Jeremy and smacked into the wall. The rebound caught the side of his head.

"Relax, man. It's just Fowler." Vince DiMorello recovered his lost ball and dribbled it back through the crowd.

"Do you mind?" I hollered.

"Blow me, Boswell," Vince called back, following it up with the finger. I bit back a mouthful of choice insults that would have been completely wasted on Vince's stunted vocabulary and pathetic IQ, and watched as a manicured hand smacked the back of Vince's head. Hard. To anyone else, it might have seemed like a casual flirtation, but I knew this particular cheerleader, and the look on Emily Reinnert's face wasn't romantic.

"Don't be such a dick," she muttered as she stepped out from behind him to head toward the gym.

She didn't look at me when she passed. Not directly. Instead, the corner of her mouth turned up, curling the Wild Cats logo on her cheek. The throng of people narrowed around us and pressed into the wide gym doors. She discreetly slipped a note into my hand and I shuddered at the unexpected contact. A wave of her complex emotions rippled through me. A nauseating prickle I attributed to stage fright. Then the cool wash of gratitude that followed.

I crumpled the note and pulled my hands inside my sleeves while Jeremy watched the hem of her cheerleading skirt disappear into the gym. "Is it just me, or is it shorter than usual?"

"Jeremy!" I tugged on his camera strap. "Why don't you take a picture? It'll last longer."

"I plan to take a few dozen," he said. "You know, for the school paper. Think she'd give me an interview?"

I snorted. "Sure, if you can get past her boyfriend. For your next reckless act of rebellion, you can ask TJ's girlfriend out on a date. Then we can see how long it takes him to beat you to death with his leg brace."

"You wouldn't let that happen."

He said it quickly. Easily. Like he didn't have to think about it. Jeremy was a pacifist—the opposite of his dad—where I tended to react for both of us. When we were fourteen, I'd stood in his kitchen, holding his phone, waiting for social services to answer. Jeremy's hand was on mine, his wrist ringed in bruises, tasting remorseful and uncertain, like maybe he'd deserved it. Drowning out my own feelings and making me uncertain too. I hung up the phone, and Jeremy let go, and I still hated myself for it.

"Are you coming?" he asked, shaking me from the memory. Music and shouts blared behind him, a sea of blue-and-white jerseys and pom-poms.

"No, it's not my thing. Anh's working the store for her brother after school. I wish we could hang out. Just the two of us," I said hopefully. Maybe if it we hung out like we used to, then he'd open up and tell me what was wrong.

"I can't. I'm covering the game at North Hampton." He held up his camera case and waved an apologetic good-bye. People crested around him in blue-and-white waves, and his blond head bobbed over them like the sun. I squeezed my hand where I'd held his a moment ago, and hoped he'd be okay without me for a while. I waved back, walking backward as the gym swallowed him up.

Emily's note crinkled against my palm. I ducked into the nearest girls' bathroom and opened it. Everything about it bubbled, from her loopy letters to the obnoxious circles under multiple exclamation points.

79% on my algebra test. I passed!!!

I sighed, crumpled her note, and tossed it in the trash.

It was *almost* a thank-you. A passing grade meant she could keep her place on the squad, her seat in the social pyramid. Unfortunately, her passing score would do nothing for mine, even though I *had* been the one to tutor her after school.

Every week.

For three months.

Community service. Five days a week. One hour a day. A mandatory requirement of all scholarship candidates. Students with cars and bus money got to volunteer in labs, or hospitals, or at the Smithsonian. Oleksa's dad hooked him up cracking math codes for some government agency. Meanwhile, we who were vehicularly challenged had to tutor students after school.

Of course, it would all have been worth it if they'd paid

me. If I didn't have to slip money from my mother's tip jar for my newspaper and depend on Jeremy's Twinkie donations for my junk food fix

I closed my eyes and thunked my head against the wall, which didn't do anything for the tension headache blooming inside it. Touching Jeremy had stressed me out. The headaches, the nausea . . . they were the reason I'd stopped touching my mother after my father left five years ago. I'd tried, thinking that I could fill the void. That holding tightly to her might ease her pain, and maybe ease my own. But I wasn't enough, and she'd turned so bitter that when we did touch, the pain stayed with me for days and the taste of her made me vomit. I lost weight and missed school, withdrew under blankets and hid inside long sleeves. Worried, my mother took me to neurologists who told her there was nothing physically wrong with me. They suggested I was suffering from stress, that I was emotionally fragile because my father had left us. Relief clung to the stench of my mother's grief— maybe, at least partly, because the doctors had given her one more reason to blame him.

But she was wrong. They were all wrong. What I was feeling wasn't my father's fault. It wasn't coming from *inside* me. It was coming from anyone I got close enough to touch. I wasn't exactly sure how it worked—it's not like they teach this stuff in AP Physics—but I had a theory. Emotion is energy, and if energy is strong enough, it can travel between two points. Maybe I was like a channel, someone other people's energies could pass through. I was somehow experiencing truths about people that others just couldn't. Most of those truths left a sour taste on my tongue that made me wish I'd never gotten close to them at all. So I didn't. I didn't do sports, I avoided parties and crowds, and I didn't date.

And I never told anyone.

I washed two aspirin down with a palm of tap water. Then I leaned on the sink basin and looked hard in the mirror, the bits and pieces I remembered of my father staring back at me through cross sections of my mother's face. Almost, but not entirely either one of them.

I was still just nearly.

3

After school, I spread the newspaper out on my bedroom floor. I wasn't interested in the whole paper, just the section of personal ads called *Missed Connections*. I'd only had time to skim them, sparing glances between labs and lectures, and I clung to the possibility that maybe I'd missed something important.

"What do you think, Doc? Will I find him this week?" I asked the poster on my wall. It had been a birthday gift from Anh, who thought it was hilarious that Albert Einstein was the only guy who'd ever been in my bedroom, until I'd pointed out that this accounted for one more than had ever been in hers.

I'd never told Anh about all the Friday nights Jeremy and I had spent sprawled across my bedroom floor, eating Twinkies and cackling over the personals when we were younger. That was before the two of us had become the three of us.

Looking at the paper now, I saw that the few ads that had resonated with glimmers of hope that morning turned out to be nothing more than empty pick-up lines.

> I saw you on the Blue Line. You got off at Van Dorn.
> You have red hair and a great rack. I think you might have
> noticed me too. If so, same time, same place tomorrow.
> I'll save you a seat.

I snorted into my hand, careful not to attract my mother's attention through the paper-thin walls of our trailer.

> You dropped your stamps at the post office on Wythe.
> I picked them up for you. I was too nervous to think of
> something to say. If you're out there, tell me what I was
> wearing so I know it was you.

I fell backward on the threadbare carpet with an exasperated sigh. Five years gone and still no sign of the man who spent every Saturday with me at Belle Green Park, pulling dandelions out of thin air and making quarters vanish with a wave of his hand.

I reached one hand under my mattress until I grasped a small plastic bag containing a carefully folded personal ad dated five years ago, a worn brown wallet, a gold wedding band, and a train ticket. The wallet and the ring were all that was left of my father's personal effects. My mother'd found them in his car, abandoned in an airport parking garage.

I'd watched Mona cut up the IDs and credit cards and toss everything, even his ring, in the trash. While she wept, locked in her bedroom, I'd fished the remaining scraps of my father out of the wastebasket and tried to tape them back together. There had been far too many pieces. They fit together like a puzzle and when I was done, I had four driver's licenses, each with a different name, all of them similar in looks to my father, but only one of them was him. I'd had all these theories about why he had those phony IDs. I imagined he'd been swallowed up by the Witness Protection Program and that's why he had so many aliases. We lived close to Langley and the Pentagon. I told myself he could have worked covertly for the CIA. My father wouldn't have just left. He must have had a reason. And I believed that one day, he'd come back. That it was all some necessary sleight of hand, and he'd turn up like a card in a trick, right back where he was supposed to be.

I'd returned the broken pieces of the phony IDs to the garbage can and tucked everything else in a plastic bag.

The personal ad was something I'd found when I was in middle school. Jeremy and I read the ads every Friday night while our dads played poker together. I'd always assumed we were drawn to the ads because of our common loneliness. That maybe we were *both* searching for something. But then

one day, about a year after my father left, I found this particular ad that changed everything.

Careful of the brittle paper, I eased it open. I didn't actually need to read it. I'd memorized every word.

N—I'm here and I'm okay. I'll always be *near* you.

I love you,

D.

I had no proof it was my dad. Jeremy insisted N could be
anybody. But I knew this ad was mine. I knew it was from my
father, without proof or probability, all the way through to
my soul. My father had known about our Friday ritual, and
he must have thought it was the perfect way to contact me
discreetly. He'd even included the word *near*, a safe way to
refer to my name without actually using it.

After that, I didn't want to share the ads anymore. I didn't
find them funny, didn't laugh at the desperation. *I* was searching for something. I was desperate. Jeremy didn't really
believe my dad had sent me a message, and the only thing I
cared about was finding another one. Jeremy stopped bringing the *Missed Connections*, and I started buying my own. It
wasn't our ritual anymore. It was mine.

I spent every Friday looking for another ad. Once, I'd
thought for sure I'd found him.

**It's been nearly a year since my last ad. I'm in town and want
to see you. Meet me at our old hangout next Saturday.**

I'd gone to Belle Green Park just after sunup. Spent all

day watching the parking lot and the trailheads, the neighborhood parents watching me suspiciously as they pushed
their kids on the swings. *These are the kids you should be making friends with,* my dad had said when I'd asked him why we
came to this park every Saturday instead of the one at the end
of our street. Their parents looked at me now the same way
they had looked at me then. Like I didn't belong there. They
were right. At dusk, I walked home alone. And a week later, I
found the response to the ad, confirming it wasn't him.

When I was younger, searching the *Missed Connections* had
always been about finding my father. But now? Sometimes
I'd see an ad that so perfectly expressed my own loneliness
that I'd clip it out and save it. Study it, searching for whatever it was that made one ad yield a reaction, and another go
unanswered. I wasn't exactly sure who, or what, I was looking for anymore, but sometimes it felt like I was looking for a
missing piece of myself.

I read the clipping again and carefully folded it back into
the bag, slipping it deep under my mattress. Then I flipped
to the ad that had haunted me all day, the one that got me
busted in chem lab.

> **Newton was wrong. We clash with yellow.**
> **Find me tonight under the bleachers.**

Nothing like the saccharine pleas I'd come to associate with
Friday mornings, this ad left an acrid taste in my mouth. Something about it was just . . . wrong. Not dirty-pervert-at-the-bus-

station wrong. Not even unrequited-lovesick-nerd wrong. This was something different. Something I'd never seen in the *Missed Connections* before.

"Nearly!" My mother banged on my door and I jumped. I cursed under my breath and leaped to my feet.

"Nearly, open the door!"

I scrubbed my hands against my shorts, leaving trails of dark smudges.

Breathing deep, I flipped the lock and cracked the door, blocking the narrow opening. Mona stood in the hall holding an empty coffee mug and a full pack of menthols. A full pack meant she hadn't checked the cookie jar yet. My shoulders relaxed, but only by a fraction. My petty larceny of her tip jar was just a necessary reallocation of household funds—I needed my newspaper fix more than she needed to smoke. But even though *my* addiction wouldn't kill me, I still had no intention of getting caught.

She raised a thinly tweezed eyebrow. If I didn't look at her face, I could pretend her frayed robe concealed flannel pajamas with teddy bears and hearts. If I ignored the rhinestones glued to her eyes, she could be anyone's mother. But she wasn't anyone else's mother. She was mine.

Mona lit up and exhaled a long ribbon of smoke. "I'm going to work."

I paused, torn between slamming the door in her face and locking us both safe inside.

"Jeremy says we're late with the rent again."

She was slow to answer, and for a moment I worried there really might not be enough money this time. Jeremy had bought us a day with his dad's poker money, but I knew I had to pay him back. Where would we go if his parents evicted us? I looked at her, the *what-ifs* written all over my face. Her brows drew together, scrunching up the rhinestones and deepening the lines around her eyes.

"Jim hired a new girl and my shifts got cut back," she said. "I'll have the money tonight. You can take a check to school on Monday." Mona looked past me to the personal ads spread across my floor. Her laugh was derisive like she was coughing up bad memories. The same cutting laughter that made me want to keep the loneliest parts of myself hidden. I pulled the door tighter around me, blocking her view of my room.

"They're not worth it," she said. "I don't know what it is you think you'll find in those papers, but there's not a man in this world you can count on to fix your life."

I wanted to tell her the same thing. That the money they threw at her wasn't worth it. That taking her clothes off for strangers hadn't fixed anything. But we both knew this argument wasn't about just any man. It was about the one who'd left us overextended on credit, without money for bills. About how he was the reason their only car was repossessed and Mona would never be able to leave her job at Gentleman

Jim's, the only job she could walk to that paid enough to hold on to the lease on our trailer.

We had the same argument every Friday—about how men can't be trusted and if you depend on them, you'll be left alone with more problems than you started with. It was the same argument that drove me to buy a train ticket to California two years ago, because I'd started to believe her. "Even if he did come back, it would only make things worse," she said.

"Look around, Mona. Could it really get any worse?"

She sucked in a thoughtful drag. "Be careful who you put your faith in," she said in the sultry deep rasp that sounded ancient and sad, but had everyone else fooled. "You're lucky. Born with a head full of brains. Don't make the same mistake I did." She pointed her cigarette at me. "Your education is the only thing you can count on to get you out of this trailer. If I'd spent more time on mine instead of chasing after a boy, neither of us would be here."

Lucky . . . she thought I was lucky. Of course she couldn't accept the possibility of my father's genetic contribution to my intelligence. He was dead to her. And some days, her grief and anger hurt me more than his absence.

Ash balanced precariously from the tip of her cigarette. She looked tired, and so much older than her thirty-five years. "A diploma. A college degree. That's the only thing that's going to get you out of here." She shook her head and exhaled a long smoky sigh, the ash falling to my floor.

I sighed and pointed at the sign I'd tacked to my door. "Do you mind? This is a non-smoking room."

Mona raised a brow, and amusement tugged at the corner of her mouth. Her smile was painted on and clung outside the natural line of her lip, making it look fuller than it was. But I knew better. Beneath the gloss, she had forgotten how to smile when my father left.

"Don't you ever wonder where he is?" I asked, tossing my own hope at her as though it were a life raft. "If maybe he's thinking of us?"

She leaned against the door. "He's never coming home, Nearly. That much I know." She stubbed out her cigarette in her empty mug, the life raft abandoned and drifting in the murky waters between us. "Get your studying done."

4

I PUSHED OPEN THE DOOR of my trailer, pausing to look up and down the street before dragging the full trash bag onto the front porch and down the rickety wooden steps. Sunny View Mobile Home Village was shaped like a fish. Or at least the decaying remains of one. Run-down trailers lay in parallel rows alongside short alleys protruding like ribs off Sunny View Drive. The crooked backbone of my neighborhood began as a dead-end street, a rutted narrow blacktop that hadn't been tar-coated since the 1960s. Almost as old was the playground, a skeletal collection of rusted metal wrapped in remnants of yellow police tape where the fish's tail would have been. On the other end, Sunny View Drive spit into an intersection of a six-lane highway, and beyond that, the parking lot of a run-down strip mall: Anh's parents' store, a coin Laundromat, Ink & Angst Tattoos, Gentleman Jim's, and a video store that would have been obsolete had it not been for the red curtain room at the back. A half-dozen small businesses feeding the addictions of the chewed-up residents of Sunny View.

Our trailer sat on a corner lot, right in the middle of Sunny View Drive. The trailers across the alley were staggered, set back from the street, and from my front porch, I could see all the way to the traffic light at Route 1. Mona had almost reached the end of the street, the sashes of her long coat dangling beside her heels. I slung the trash bag a little too hard and the dented metal cans rattled together before toppling over. The echo bounced off wall after wall of rusting aluminum. My neighbor's window blinds were drawn shut, her cautious hands prying them back to check the noise.

Mona turned her head, wary eyes checking over her shoulder, heels purposeful over the ruts and loose gravel. I watched until she reached the brighter streetlights at the intersection.

She'd worked nights at Gentleman Jim's as long as I could remember. When I was younger, I'd slept on Jim's couch in the back while she waited tables. Now Jim's phone number was on a yellow sticky note, taped to the phone in the kitchen. I'd called her once when we'd run out of peanut butter for sandwiches. Jim said he'd leave a note in her dressing room, that she was on stage—not waiting tables—and he'd have her call me back between sets. He never gave her the message. And I never called again.

A car turned onto Sunny View Drive, the blue-white halogen beams blinding me. I shielded my eyes until the lights swung back onto the road, and when I looked up, Mona was gone. The car continued its approach, a lean black older-model Mercedes with diplomatic tags that was obviously lost. It drifted down the street, and I waited for it to make a clumsy three-point turn in the alley beside our trailer. It didn't. I stared at the driver's window, surprised to see Oleksa Petrenko slouched coolly behind the wheel. Our eyes met for a brief second as the Mercedes ghosted by, barely crunching the gravel as it eased into a parking space a few doors down beside Lonny Johnson's Lexus.

Lonny was a second-year senior, not that he cared. He was a businessman, not a student, home again after consecutive stints in juvie. He'd been gone longer than usual this time and when we passed each other at the mailbox earlier that week, he was taller. Thinner. Eyes deep set and dark. He had new tattoos that climbed up his neck and met the shadow of a beard that hadn't been there before. A silver bullring hung beneath his nostrils. It matched the barbell under his lip.

A screen door slammed and a security bulb snapped on, illuminating him in a wide halo.

Lonny raked his bleached hair back with tattooed fingers and scanned the street to both sides. His eyes skipped over me like I wasn't there. But when he leaned over Oleksa's window, he angled his back to me, blocking my view of the exchange between them. I could see the glint of metal tucked inside his waistband, a reminder to mind my own business.

I turned around and stooped to pick up the overturned cans, crinkling my nose at the scattered debris. A few feet from the cans, tucked just under the lowest porch step, was a small cardboard box. I picked it up, expecting it to be empty, but something shifted inside. It had been loosely taped shut, and a soft scratching sound rasped against the inner walls of the box when I shook it. I held it under the dim porch light, a strange feeling twisting in my gut.

FOR NEARLY, it said in bold blue letters that felt oddly familiar.

I glanced over my shoulder. No one was there except Lonny and Oleksa, still deep in hushed conversation. Pulling at a loose corner of tape, I slowly opened the top.

I dropped the box and clapped a hand over my mouth. The small mound of rotting flesh was stiff with rigor mortis. Her white throat was crusted with blood.

A dead cat.

The words DEAD OR ALIVE were written in blood inside

the lid. The letters had dried and crackled like finger paint, but the blocky handwriting was the same as the blue letters on my lab table.

I'd seen the feral calico coming and going from a hole under Mrs. Moates's trailer. I looked down the street at her window but her lights were already off and I didn't see any sense in waking her. The poor thing had probably been a stray anyway.

I held my breath and used the box to scoop up the tiny body, dropping her inside the closest trash can and lowering the lid. I breathed through my sleeve and backed away, eyes blurring and throat working from the smell, and stumbled over the other can. The lid crashed to the pavement and wobbled, reverberating through the alley. Oleksa and Lonny stared with narrow eyes. My neighbor peeled back her curtain again when her security light flashed on, her dog barking and scratching through the window. I untangled myself and raced up my front steps, throwing the dead bolt behind me.

Reaching for the metal bat my mother kept propped behind our front door, I slid to the floor, crouching in the dark until the Mercedes's lights passed over the frayed sofa and peeling walls, tossing the room in one quick pass, then dropping it into darkness. I listened for feet on gravel or a rustle against the window. It was silent except for the cars on Route 1.

Leaving the lights off, I crawled into bed with my clothes on and pulled the blankets to my chin. I lay there, unable to get the smell out of my head. Unable to shake the image of the letters written in blood.

I reached down between the mattress and the box spring for my father's wedding band, one ear alert for Mona coming home. But I knew I wouldn't tell her about the cat. I couldn't let some jerk from school freak her out enough to miss her weekend shifts just to stay home with me. We couldn't afford it. Besides, it didn't matter what Schrödinger thought. I'd opened the box and the cat was dead, and there was nothing Mona or I could do for it now.

5

I STOOD ON MY TOES in the crowd clustered by the chem lab. Lab grades were posted next to the door every Monday morning, so we'd all know exactly where we stood. Like I needed any reminders.

There I was.

Boswell, Nearly.

Second place below Bui, Anh Thi. On paper, it was only a few millimeters of space—one half of a percent between friends—but in my mind those millimeters were miles. I had about five weeks left to narrow that gap, or I'd have to shake Anh's hand and congratulate her on walking away with my ticket out of Sunny View.

Hugging textbooks to my chest, I pushed through the pack of hopefuls, trying not to touch any of them skin to skin. I'd almost made it out of the herd when I tripped over someone's shoe and went sprawling across the hall, colliding into something hard. My books scattered over the floor and a tall guy with messy dark hair and multiple piercings in his eyebrow glared down at me, obviously offended. His cold blue eyes were ringed with shadows, like he hadn't slept well in a long, long time and he was looking for someone to blame.

I backed out of his way as he bent to pick something off the floor. He came up holding a black motorcycle helmet, turning it over in his fingers and checking it for scratches before tucking it into the crook of his tattooed arm. Beside him, Lonny Johnson chewed the barbell in his lip, snapping it between his teeth, and I swallowed whatever I'd been planning to say.

I muttered an apology, but the guy just shoved me aside, growling, "Watch it." Then he kicked my books out of reach with a heavy black boot and walked away.

I watched them go, glaring at Lonny's friend as I plucked my books from the floor. The guy had to be new. I'd never seen him in school before. I would have remembered him. As he walked, students spread away from him on either side, like water from an oil slick.

"People say he killed someone." Anh snuck up beside me, watching him with narrow eyes as she bent to help me collect my books.

"People say a lot of stupid things." I should know. Most of them were about me. Lonny's new friend may have been an asshole, but I refused to feed the West River rumor mill solely on principle.

I hadn't realized I was still staring at him until I noticed Anh staring too. Her hair tipped to the side as she studied his retreating form. "Not exactly prom date material, but I guess he's cute, if you're into that whole bad-boy thing. His butt's not bad either," she said, watching it disappear around a corner.

I shot her a surprised look. "I'm not looking for a prom date."

"Well, you're obviously looking for someone."

"I have someone," I said with a grin. "I have Albert Einstein."

"I hear he's a terrible kisser."

"I wouldn't know."

"What about Jeremy? Has he asked you yet?" I looked at her like she must be joking, but she wasn't.

"I told you, I'm not going. School functions give me hives. Big masses of stupid people in a low-volume space increase the density of the whole idea."

"Don't be ridiculous. You can't calculate the probability of having a good time at a dance."

"Sure I can. Me going to the dance is a singular event. Me enjoying myself at the dance is one of only two possible outcomes of said event. If the event and the outcome are mutually exclusive, it is safe to conclude that there is no possible way in hell I would have fun at the dance."

Anh laughed. "You're such a nerd."

"That's why you love me. Since when are you so bent on going to prom anyway?"

"Since my brother decided I don't need to have a life. He won't let me do anything except work at the store and study. He's got me scheduled to work every Friday and Saturday night between now and the end of the school year. The only reason he's letting me go to the play on Friday is because I told him it was a mandatory requirement for lit class. I figure if I can find a date for prom and buy a dress before he says no, then he'll have to let me go to that too." She slumped against a wall and rolled her eyes to the ceiling. "I can't wait until the semester's over and he stops riding me about this stupid scholarship."

The warning bell rang and our smiles faded as our eyes cut to the chem lab door. Monday mornings after rankings were posted were the hardest, when crossing the lab threshold felt like stepping through the ropes to a death match.

Students lingered in the hall, waiting for the bell. I braced myself as I walked past Vince where he huddled quietly with a handful of his teammates. He didn't look up, which made me eerily cautious. He'd never passed up an opportunity to humiliate me before. It was like he hadn't even noticed the spectacle I'd just made of myself, even though his blond head stood several inches taller than the rest of his friends' and I was sure he'd had an unobstructed view. Strange. The hallway hummed with a somber intensity, everyone talking in hushed tones, including Vince, who didn't come with a volume control.

Inside the lab, the air lightened considerably. Oleksa perched on top of a table, one long leg dangled coolly off the side, his red shoelaces grazing the floor. A cluster of boys hovered around him, which was odd. Oleksa was a loner—the kind with a razor-wire wall that said *No Trespassing* in big red letters. Don't get me wrong, the guy wasn't bad-looking. If he ever smiled, he might even be handsome, with his full lips and sharp cheekbones—but those features didn't necessarily equate to attractive. More like he was good-looking in a dangerous, off-putting sort of way.

Oleksa shrugged off his hoodie. "How much?"

His lab partner, a mouthy kid named Eric Miller, whipped out a small stack of dollar bills and slapped them on the desk like some heavyweight high roller.

"Fifteen bucks," he said, rolling his narrow shoulders and looking Oleksa in the eye. I wondered if Eric would've been so ballsy if Oleksa had been standing up. Eric looked like maybe he was having the same thought. He took a small step back and looked away.

"We're in too." Four others dropped their own money on top of Eric's.

Part of me wanted to get closer to see what they were doing, but I stayed back.

Oleksa's clear gray eyes revealed nothing as he glanced at their faces, then at the cash.

"Deal," he said. He didn't move. Simply inclined his head and gestured with a quick curl of his long fingers. "Give to me."

Eric withdrew a Rubik's cube from the pockets of his baggy shorts. He grinned, twisting the sides of the puzzle until it was a jumble of random colors. Another boy drew up a sleeve and poised his watch in the air, fingers twitching over the stop mechanism.

Oleksa's eyes met theirs. He didn't blink.

"Ten seconds," the timer said, shuffling from foot to foot. "Starting . . . now!"

Oleksa caught the cube and his fingers flashed over the surface in quick successive turns, each pass aligning the colors with increasing accuracy. My heart sped up as I counted down in my head.

"There's no way . . ." Eric clenched his hands, glancing at his money. "The world record is just under seven."

I rocked forward, inching up on my toes for a better look. The timer looked from Oleksa to his watch. "Five . . . four . . . three . . ."

Oleksa gave the cube a final turn and slammed it down on the desk between them.

"I win," he said.

The class bell shattered the silence. Mouths hung open,

but no one spoke. The watch's alarm rang, rubbing in Oleksa's victory. Students filtered into the room and took their seats, but my feet were glued in place. Oleksa could give Anh and me both a run for our money for the scholarship. And probably win.

I'd chalked Oleksa's poor grades up to laziness, a lack of competitive edge, but the steel in his eyes told me I was wrong. He clearly had the edge. So why wasn't he leveraging it?

Oleksa turned his cold stare on me, that same gouging look I'd seen in Sunny View on Friday night. Then his hand shot out, smooth and quick, palming the money just as Rankin came through the door.

I hustled to my desk, feeling Oleksa's eyes on my back. The blue ink letters were lighter today, as if the custodian had tried unsuccessfully to scrub them out. I covered them with textbooks, but the words *dead or alive* felt like more than random graffiti and only intensified the feeling of being watched.

"Attention, people," Rankin called the class to order. He stepped through the aisles, pausing to count off sheets of paper. He dropped a stack in front of me and I took one before pushing them to Anh. "You have forty-five minutes to complete this assignment."

The room was quiet as we all read the instructions for today's lab. "We will be identifying mystery solutions. If you completed your homework assignment, then you have already researched the sixteen solutions you will correctly identify today."

Eric groaned. "Hydrochloric again? When do we get to work with something cool, like hydrofluoric?"

Half the room turned to stare at him. Oleksa uttered something in Ukrainian and looked annoyed to share a lab table with him. Rankin raised an eyebrow at Eric. "You are quite obviously behind on your reading or you'd know that hydrofluoric acid is lethally toxic and highly corrosive." His gaze drifted down to the orange juice stain on the front of Eric's white shirt. "And given that you are infinitely clumsy, you would do well to stick with the assignment at hand."

Rankin leaned over his desk and stared around the room, waiting for our laughter to hush. "I'll take a moment to recognize our top three scholarship candidates: Anh Bui, Nearly Boswell, and Thomas Wiles, in that order." He nodded to the seat behind me. "Does anyone know if Mr. Wiles plans to join us today?"

We all turned to TJ's empty chair. As if summoned, his blue-and-white letterman jacket appeared in the door.

"I'm sorry I'm late." He eased into his chair, leaving his stiff left leg protruding into the aisle.

"Do you have a tardy slip?"

TJ frowned. Sweat pinned his dark curls to his forehead and trickled into the neck of his jersey. He didn't have a car and varsity football players wouldn't be caught dead on the bus, no matter how long or hot the walk from Sunny View, or how hard it was on a bum leg.

"No, sir," he said quietly.

Rankin nodded gently. No sarcasm. No witty admonishments. He simply said, "Don't let it happen again." Then he looked at the wall clock. "Forty-two minutes."

A flurry of activity and whispers broke out around me. I looked down at the assignment and started to write my name.

"Miss Boswell," Rankin spoke over the heads of students as they gathered Bunsen burners and titration equipment from the cabinets at the front of the room. "A quick word if I may?"

The tip of my pencil snapped, scattering lead over the page. Beside me, Anh bit her lip and glanced at the clock. I pushed back my chair and walked with my head down. Students in white lab coats hunched in circles, talking in low tones behind cupped rubber gloves as if the odd heaviness in the hall had followed TJ into the room.

Rankin spoke quietly. "You won't be tutoring Emily this afternoon. Miss Reinnert was involved in an unfortunate set of circumstances on Friday. The principal informs me she won't be returning to school for a while."

"Is she okay?"

Rankin's eyes flicked to TJ and he lowered his voice, apparently as aware as everyone else that TJ and Emily Reinnert were dating. The small show of sensitivity was out of character and I suspected Emily's situation was worse than he let on.

"Marcia Steckler is on the waiting list for a math tutor. I'll arrange for you to meet with her on Mondays so you don't fall behind in your community service. I'll send a note to her second period class and ask her to confirm. If you don't hear from me otherwise, please plan to meet Marcia here at two forty-five."

I opened my mouth to ask what had happened to Emily, but he gestured to my desk with his coffee mug. "That is all."

My eyes drifted to TJ as I returned to my table. He looked lost in his own thoughts, absently massaging his leg brace while his partner worked double time to set up their lab. Across the aisle, our classmates whispered to each other as they worked, casting him sidelong sympathetic looks. Emily's name carried across the room in hushed, worried tones.

"Hey," I whispered to Anh. She was labeling glass vials with indelible marker and my eyes watered from the fumes. "Heard anything about what happened to Emily Reinnert on Friday?"

Anh's concentration was focused on the lab. She didn't look up as she set the vials carefully into a rack. "People were talking about it on the bus this morning," she said absently, her voice more than a whisper. "They said she disappeared after the soccer game at North Hampton. She went into the school to use the bathroom and never came back."

TJ's chair screeched, attracting everyone's attention. His

sweaty brow was furrowed, and I couldn't tell if he was angry or if he was going to be sick. He snatched the hall pass off a hook by the door as he limped from the room.

Anh and I looked guiltily at each other. I donned my goggles and rubber apron, determined to forget about it and get back to work, but the whispers around the room were persistent, and I was having a hard time concentrating.

"Did they find her?" I finally asked.

Anh shrugged. "Yeah. Sounds like it was a team prank that went a little too far. The custodian found her naked and unconscious in the gym under the bleachers. People say it was *roofies*." Anh shook her head and capped her marker. "Sick. They painted her."

I scrunched up my face. "What do you mean, they painted her? Like Picasso-painted her?"

Anh rolled her eyes. "Nothing quite so sophisticated. This is the soccer team we're talking about. Think paint by numbers." She poured a solution into the vials, recording their reactions. "They literally painted her. They drew the number ten in permanent marker on her arm and then painted the rest of her body in those creepy oil paints people put all over their faces during the games."

I fought the urge to look over my shoulder at TJ's empty chair, only now beginning to understand the strange shift in the school's collective mood. "Ten? Why ten?"

"No one knows. Probably someone's jersey number." She

waved it off. "A bunch of the players were in the store this morning and my brother heard them talking. The Hornets' captain is number ten, but he's pointing the finger at Vince DiMorello."

"Wait. *Our* Vince DiMorello? Vince-Who's-Overly-Fond-of-His-Middle-Finger DiMorello?" Vince was number ten for our team, but I couldn't imagine him pulling a stunt like this. TJ and Vince were best friends. "Why would they think Vince had anything to do with it?"

Anh pushed a fresh pencil toward me, as if to remind me to get my head back in our own game. "Apparently, Vince and Emily have been fighting a lot lately." I remembered the look on his face before the pep rally, when she'd smacked the back of his head in front of all his teammates. "But it doesn't matter anyway. The rest of the team is standing by him. They told the police Vince was with them after the game. And everyone on North Hampton's team was accounted for."

Of course they'd say whatever they needed to in order to protect their star player. But this sounded like more than a prank. Getting drugged, stripped, and marked, and left under the bleachers was a lot worse than stink bombs in your locker or marker on your lab table. Even worse than a dead cat on your porch.

I shook off the news and concentrated on helping Anh, but my mind had a slippery unfocused feeling. The nagging kind that slinks around behind your thoughts like a word on the tip of your tongue. My brain stuck stubbornly on the image of Emily. Her blue cheerleader uniform. Her limp body under the bleachers.

Under the bleachers.

Newton was wrong. We clash with yellow. Find me tonight under the bleachers.

I eased into my chair as the colors of Newton's wheel spun in my mind. Isaac Newton's color theory was based on a wheel. Colors that appear opposite each other on the wheel are complementary. But if we were talking about school colors, like in the case of Friday's game, the opposing colors wouldn't complement. They would . . . clash. Our school color was blue. The color directly opposite blue on the wheel was . . .

We clash with yellow.

"Their school colors . . ." I muttered, a prickling curiosity creeping through me. I reached for a beaker and kept my voice as matter-of-fact as I could. "Do you know what colors they painted her?"

Anh slipped off her gloves, the lab completed before I'd even had a chance to start. "One side of her was painted blue and other side was—"

Yellow, I thought. Only I must have said it out loud. Anh looked at me, analytical eyes asking all kinds of questions.

I turned away. Began clumsily collecting up the tools, knowing I was stuck with the dishes since she'd done all the work. I shrugged as if I wasn't at all surprised before I answered the question on her face. "Just a hunch."

• • •

That afternoon, I was still thinking about Emily when I felt the light tug on my sleeve.

"Hey, are you okay?"

I withdrew my arm. I didn't like being touched, but Marcia Steckler was an "artist," and they tended to be touchy-feely like that.

"Yeah, I'm fine." I pushed my glasses up my nose for the six hundred and ninety-seventh time. They slid back down again. I thought about taking them off, but I was unfocused enough as it was. "I'm sorry, what were you saying?"

"It's okay." Marcia stretched gracefully. "I'm distracted too. Opening night is this weekend. Algebra is the last thing on my mind."

She looked like a dancer. Her loose cotton tank drifted over pale willowy limbs. How was she so comfortable exposing so much skin?

"Algebra needs to be on your mind for another fifty-three minutes." I glanced pointedly at the clock.

She leaned close as if she was ready to confess a secret and I pressed back into my chair.

"I've got a sixty-nine percent in algebra. If I don't get it up to a passing grade, the principal can pull me from the show. And if Principal Romero doesn't, my mother will."

"So we'd better get to work." I flipped through the textbook, eager to put a pencil in her hands to keep them away from me. She seemed nice enough, but you can't always judge a person by the parts they choose to show you. Touching someone, getting close, always reveals the darker parts they don't want you to see. And I really didn't want to know any of Marcia Steckler's deep, dark secrets. "You know, the play's the thing and all . . ." I mumbled.

"Hey, you know Shakespeare?" She beamed, spine pulled straight as though someone had tugged a string at the back of her head. "No way!"

I answered with a sour smile. Why did everyone assume that because I was good with equations, I was only one-dimensional?

"Methinks thou doth protest too much, Ophelia." I rolled a pencil across the desk. "No more stalling. Time to do some algebra."

6

FOR THE MOST PART, Mona wasn't hard to live with. She slept all day and worked all night. And we generally agreed on all the rules.

The first rule (no bad grades) was easy. I'd always done well in school.

The second rule (no trouble) was a broad umbrella encompassing a dozen overprotective restrictions. Like, don't hang out with the neighborhood kids, don't wear skanky clothes, and stay out of the principal's office. These were easy too. I wore whatever T-shirts and jeans Mona brought home from yard sales and consignment shops. The sizes always ran too big, and covered too much, which was fine by me. And I had no interest in hanging with the neighbor-hoodlums anyway.

Mona and I shared the third rule, which was good for both of us. I didn't need a boyfriend; touching was complicated. But for my mother, it was also dangerous. Butch, the bouncer at Gentleman Jim's, made sure all the patrons respected the only rule at the club. He liked to brag about the time he'd broken a man's arm for trying to touch my mother while she was working. He'd given me self-defense lessons in the alley behind the club when I was old enough to make a fist, and he drove her home each night after closing. I'd hear his van crunch over the gravel, the click of the locks, and know she was home safe when her bedroom door shut.

Butch never came inside. There hadn't been a man in our trailer since the year after my father left, when Mona had brought one home from the club. They'd both smelled like booze and sweat, but her cheeks were flushed for the first time in months, and she was smiling. She'd gone to her room to change clothes. The man sat down on our couch and reached for me. My stomach twisted with the wrongness of his taste, and the cloying, putrid-sweet smell of him. I twisted out of his grip and screamed "Don't touch me!" My mother had come flying out of her bedroom, and kicked him out. She pulled me tight to her chest, saying "it's okay" over and over. I felt the hole open up inside her, wider and deeper than before, like I was eating it away myself. It was the last time I touched her.

Her door was still closed now, and I could hear her soft, breathy sounds through the thin walls. She'd only been in bed for a few hours and slept like the dead. I reached into the ceramic Santa Claus cookie jar. It was full of cash—our grocery money and rent for the month. Thursday nights were busy at Jim's. She rarely noticed the few missing bills I took on Fridays. The way I figured it, the money belonged to men who bought bits and pieces of my mother away from me every day. I was only taking back what was rightfully mine.

The problem with the rules was, while they were designed to get me into a good college, they didn't tell me how to *pay* for a good college. But Mona didn't seem all that concerned. For the last three years, she'd scattered college brochures all around our trailer. Georgetown, Tech, GMU, and Hopkins— top-rated schools, all within a tight radius of home. My own wish-list put more distance between me and Sunny View, but the problem of cost and deferred student loans only grew with every mile I imagined myself out of state. I told myself I didn't care what school I got *into*, as long as I got *out* of Sunny View.

On Sunday I wanted to give a little something back to her. It was Mother's Day. She didn't celebrate her birthday—she was the oldest dancer at Jim's and we never knew how many birthdays there'd be until she was out of a job—but Mother's Day made her smile. She'd wake up early and let me bring her coffee in bed. Then she'd ask me about school and we'd talk about my grades. Her eyes would shine a little.

I pulled the trailer door shut quietly, locking the dead bolt behind me, and headed toward a collection of tables on the next street. Friday was yard sale day in Sunny View, and the trailer park was buzzing as people wandered, poking through boxes, and kids headed to school.

A girl with magenta streaks in her hair leaned against a lamppost, smoking a cigarette while she waited for the bus. It was the same street corner she slouched at in the evenings while she waited for men she probably didn't know to pick her up. We gave each other tight awkward smiles, like we sort of knew each other, both of us probably grateful we didn't.

TJ looked at the ground when I walked by. He sat on the edge of the rusted weight bench that was chained to the axel under his uncle's trailer, his knee brace dangled over his lap. A stack of free weights was padlocked to the bench, and he kicked it with the toe of his sneaker. As usual, neither of us acknowledged the other. Maybe it was too much like looking in a mirror, seeing another version of ourselves stuck where we didn't want to be. As soon as Vince's Camaro blew around the corner, windows down and music blaring, TJ threw on his backpack, scooped up his brace, and bolted off the bench. Vince reached across the passenger seat and threw open the door, and TJ jumped inside like he couldn't get out of the park fast enough. I couldn't blame him.

I waved away the gravel dust kicked up by Vince's car and made my way to the towers of knickknacks and boxes of mismatched trinkets. Nothing on Mrs. Moates's sticky lopsided table was my idea of a treasure, but I paused at a collection of mugs, lingering over one with a kitten dangling by his claws from a tree. A thought bubble from his head said *Hang in There*, and my heart squeezed a little.

"How much for the mug?" I asked. A mangy cat curled around Mrs. Moates's ankles.

"The one with the busted handle?" she lisped.

"No, the other one."

"Fitty cents." I gave her seventy-five. Not that a quarter could replace the cat who'd lived under her home. But the thing had been stuffed in a box with my name on it, and I felt responsible. The gesture, small as it was, made me feel better.

With the mug safely inside my backpack, I went to the Bui Mart. The bells jingled when I opened the door, and a 1980s hair band wailed from the overhead speakers. Bao looked up from the counter and smiled.

Everyone called Ahn's older brother "Bo"—though I'm

pretty sure that's not the way *Bao* was supposed to be pronounced—the same way we all called Anh "Ann."

"Morning, Leigh." He already had my newspaper and
chocolate milk laid out for me. I fished a chocolate donut
from the day old bin. "Heard my little sister is kicking your
ass in chem lab." Bao snickered. "Maybe all the crap you eat
rots your brain."

"That crap is the breakfast of champions." I took a bite
of the donut and headed for the cheap greeting card display,
licked the frosting from my fingers, and picked a ninety-nine-
cent Happy-Mother's-Day-and-thanks-for-putting-up-with-me
card. I stacked it on the counter with the rest of my loot.

Bao keyed them in and counted out my change, without
looking at the register or the coins. He had to be bored out
of his mind, running the family store. Bao was wicked smart.
Maybe smarter than Anh. It was one of the reasons I liked
him so much. I could forgive him his music and the obnoxious skinny jeans he'd paired with his Bui Mart polo T, and
the fact that he was an incessant flirt.

"You should come over for dinner with the family sometime. I'll show you what you're missing." Bao looked me up
and down like he was mentally removing my clothes. When
he got to my baggy pant legs, he frowned. "You're too skinny.
You're spending too much time with that country club kid. I
know his parents don't feed you."

"Jeremy's parents won't even let me into their house. For

that matter, neither would yours," I snorted, stuffing my purchases into my backpack. "What's your mom so afraid of, anyway? That I'll take my clothes off and dance on her table?"

Bao blushed.

"Don't worry about it," I said before he forced himself to suffer through some bogus apology. We both remembered the look on his mother's face when Anh brought me home after school in seventh grade. Anh had asked her mother what was so bad about being a waitress. Bao had kept his eyes on the floor. He'd understood more than I had back then. At least now we could joke about it. "Besides, I'm storing up all this fat and calories for my end of the semester sprint. Your sister will never see me coming."

"Don't make me poison your Yoo-hoo." He leveled a finger at me. "She's got her heart set on that scholarship. The whole family does. I might have to go all big-bad-ass brother on you." His playful voice didn't match the rest of him anymore. College had never been an option for Bao. He would work here for the rest of his parents' lives because that's what was expected of him.

He slapped the cash drawer shut. A wallet-size photo of Anh was taped to the register. He was as proud as any parent. Anh didn't need that scholarship as much as she thought she did. She already had so much. I wondered what it would be like to have someone like Bao looking out for me. Someone

proud and protective and strong. Someone who would sacrifice his own future for mine. I tucked my newspaper under
my arm. It felt unusually light.

"Here." He slid seventy-five cents across the counter.
"Donut's on me. My money is still on Anh."

I opened the paper and thumbed through the sections.
The classifieds were missing. I folded it up and set it on the
counter. "Can you swap this for another paper? It's missing
a section."

"All the important stuff is in there. Besides, what do you
need the personals for? Everything you need is right here."
Bao leaned against the corn dog machine and waggled his
eyebrows at me.

I felt my face grow hot. "I don't need the personals," I lied.
"There's a lot of other stuff in the classifieds too, you know."

I jumped as a package of Twinkies dropped to the counter
in front of me.

"Should I be offended that my cheap cake offerings have
been trumped by a fudge cruller from the day old bin?" Jeremy
leaned over my shoulder and piled breath mints, a soda, and
a candy bar beside the Twinkies, giving Bao something to do
other than harass me about the paper.

"What are you doing here?" I asked, surprised.

"Taking you to school."

"But it's Friday. Aren't you supposed to be at—"

Jeremy coughed loudly into his hand, cutting off what I

was about to say. "I need someone to share my Twinkies with me. If Anh makes me eat one more carrot stick, my hair will turn orange." He gave me a pointed look that said *Please don't go there.* He didn't want Bao to know he was seeing a shrink. Since when did he care? Then again, I didn't want anyone to know I was reading the personals, so I guess we were even.

"Maybe I like redheads. Ever think of that?" Anh emerged from an aisle balancing a cup of fat-free cottage cheese, a banana, and a bottled water. She leveraged her items onto the counter and Bao wrote them all down on an index card rather than ring them up. All the while his eyes were fixed on Jeremy.

"Sharing produce, Anh? Sounds serious." Bao glared at Jeremy, sizing him up.

Jeremy looked at me with an awkward smile. "Just a few carrot sticks between friends."

"Ew." I held out the last bite of my donut to Jeremy. He probably needed it more than I did. He stuffed it into his mouth, looking relieved to have an excuse not to say anything.

"Jeremy's been giving me a ride to school on Fridays. And in return, I'm trying to save him from a slow death by high triglycerides."

Jeremy stopped chewing and looked at me sideways. His Adam's apple bobbed as he swallowed. He hadn't told me he'd been driving Anh to school on Fridays. And missing appointments with his shrink to do it. Anh kept talking, clueless to our silent exchange.

"Do Mom and Dad know about this?" Bao asked, looking all serious and parental.

"He's only driving me to school," she said. "And to the school play—"

"Wow! Would you look at the time! We should probably go . . . to school . . . before we're late." Jeremy made a show of looking at his watch, clearly uncomfortable.

An awkward silence passed and we all turned at the sound of the bells when Lonny Johnson pushed open the door. His new friend followed, the one who'd shoved me at school. They drifted in like two dark clouds, and changed the climate of the store.

Jeremy paled and dropped a five on the counter. "Keep the change," he muttered. "I'll wait in the car." He walked quickly toward the door, his eyes lowered. Lonny watched him blow past with a peculiar interest. When the bells hushed, Lonny moved wordlessly to the cooler in the back.

His friend turned his back to the counter and began to browse, walking lazily through the aisles, and pausing in front of the greeting card display. Lingering at the Mother's Day cards, he grazed one with the tip of his finger, hesitating before he moved on. Then he reached for an item on the snack shelf instead.

"You planning to pay for that?" Bao said loudly. The guy's fingers hovered over a strand of beef jerky. Bao's hand reached under the counter. "You girls should get to school," he said without taking his eyes off the guy's back.

Anh took a tentative step and gave her brother an anxious look. He jerked his chin to the door, and she followed Jeremy out.

Lonny's friend snatched up the jerky and strolled slowly to the counter beside me. If he recognized me, he didn't seem to care. I held my breath when he reached under his jacket. All that came out was a worn leather wallet.

He looked to me where I stood blocking the register, then to Bao, then back to me. One side of his lip curled up and he arched a pierced brow. "Are you in line, or what?" His voice was deep, like he'd just woken up. It sounded more like a growl.

I cleared my throat to get Bao's attention, but he wouldn't look away from the guy's face. "My paper?" I nudged.

Bao reached under the counter and pulled out a fresh copy without looking at me. It was heavier than the one I passed back to him, and I decided to trust the personals were all in there, rather than open it in front of Lonny's friend, who looked like he was running out of patience.

I folded it under my arm, grabbed my milk, and made a beeline for the passenger side of Jeremy's car. But Anh was already in my seat. I wrestled with my backpack and got in behind her, struggling to get comfortable. Anh's seat was set far back, the way I usually liked it, and now it left very little room for me.

Jeremy pulled out of the space before I had time to fasten

my seat belt and made a rolling stop out of the parking lot, ignoring oncoming traffic. A horn blared.

"Do you think we should make sure Bao's okay?" Anh asked, clutching her armrest and craning to look back at the store window.

"I'm sure Bao can handle those guys. Besides, you don't want to be late. Bao and I have money riding on the two of you." Jeremy's eyes found mine in the mirror. He was looking at me when he said it, but sitting in the backseat, I wasn't so sure who he'd put his money on.

7

Archimedes knew the play wasn't really the thing.
Do the math and find me after the show.

I drew a wide blue circle around the ad with my lab marker, careful not to touch the print. I had no doubt the ad was written by the same person who wrote the Newton one. The tone and cadence felt so similar. Both read like a puzzle waiting to be solved. But what did it mean?

Someone grumbled behind me. I flipped the ad facedown on the desk and looked over my shoulder to see TJ fighting with his leg brace, looking exhausted. He was early today and I'd thought I was alone. Class didn't start for another ten minutes.

He stretched forward, struggling to capture the bottom strap. It was unfastened and dangled just out of reach. The weariness on his face, that flat and colorless veneer—the one my mother painted over with makeup—reflected every loss he'd sustained. His father was gone, in prison since TJ was in middle school. His mother had killed herself shortly after. And now he was stuck living in Sunny View with his drunk uncle, maybe indefinitely, since he'd lost any shot at a football scholarship when he'd hurt his knee last season. We weren't all that different really, and turning my back on him felt wrong.

"Do you need a hand with that?" The words were out before I realized I'd offered to touch him. I tucked my hands under my legs.

He noticed. "No, thanks anyway." He gave a forceful heave, his face reddening as he grabbed the Velcro strap and secured it in place.

"I've been meaning to ask about Emily," I said, guilty that I hadn't at least tried to look helpful. "I hope she's okay."

"She's okay," he said, frowning as though it hurt to think about her. "She's just freaked out. I'm going to see her after school. I'll tell her you were asking about her."

I stared at my fingers, rubbing at the dark smudges, curious about the glue that held Emily and TJ together. Emily was really all he had. She'd stayed—through his move from Belle Green to a trailer in Sunny View, through the breakdowns that followed, through the countless rejections when the last of the college scouts and recruiters stopped coming for him. For some reason I desperately wanted to understand, Emily had stayed, knowing a future with TJ might not be all she'd dreamed it would be.

A handful of students filtered in and I curled my fingers over the edge of the newspaper, studying their faces for the hundredth time this week. I was still trying to figure out who had left the dead cat on my doorstep and the graffiti on my desk. It had to be someone in one of Rankin's chem classes— or someone who'd seen the Schrödinger assignment on the blackboard and knew where I sat—but that could be anyone. I looked over just as Oleksa Petrenko was sliding into his seat. He'd been absent the last three days and a not-so-small part of me had hoped he wouldn't come back. Our stares held as he eased back in his chair, amusement clear in his eyes.

"Stop staring. He's going to think you like him, and that's just plain scary." Anh dropped her backpack and settled in beside me. "And you'd better put those away before Rankin sees them."

I looked down at the exposed corner of the *Missed Connections* and blushed. I squirreled them away, crossing my arms and staring straight at the blackboard before she could say another word.

She raised an eyebrow. "If you need a date—"

I opened a textbook, pretending to read it. "Don't you have extra credit to do?"

"Fine. But if you *did* need a date," she whispered. "Like maybe to the school play tonight? I could set you up with my brother."

I opened my mouth, ready to tell her that was the dumbest idea she'd ever come up with and no freaking way I was going on a date with Bao. But the words stuck in my throat. I had that slippery feeling in my head again.

"What did you say?" I whispered, careful not to attract Rankin's attention.

"I said my brother can take you to the play tonight if you need a date. We could double."

The school play. *Hamlet.* It was tonight. I flashed back to my conversation with Marcia. *You know, the play's the thing and all.*

The play's the thing.

Archimedes knew the play wasn't really the thing.
Do the math and find me after the show.

What did it mean?

Rankin pounded away on the blackboard. I threw my backpack over my shoulder and whispered to Anh, "I'm not feeling well. Tell Rankin I went to the nurse."

I was gone before he turned around.

8

I PICKED UP THE CITY BUS at the corner of Route 1, got off as close as I could to the police department, and walked the remaining three blocks. I presented my school ID and signed the police log book, then fidgeted in my seat while I waited to be called, avoiding eye contact with the weary faces in the corridor. Each one eventually disappeared through the thick metal door. A phone rang over and over behind the Plexiglas window and I chewed my nail, waiting for someone—anyone—to pick it up. I'd never been in a police station, and being here made me twitchy, like I'd broken one of Mona's rules.

"For chrissake, who the hell drank the last of the decaf and didn't put on a fresh pot?" The office chatter died, and the booming voice became louder. "Where the hell are all my detectives? I don't have time to be taking statements from snot-nosed kids. That's what I hire all of you for!" The metal door buzzed and slammed open, and a scowling bear of a man filled the frame.

"Nearly Boswell? Come with me."

I followed him into a sterile gray room with mirrored walls, a sturdy table, and two metal chairs—like the setting of every cop drama I'd ever seen on TV. I clutched my backpack, feeling smaller than usual under my oversized clothes. I wanted to tuck my knees up into my shirt like I did when I was in middle school. Mona used to get so pissed, saying I'd stretch my clothes all to hell. I'd hollered back that at least I was wearing clothes. No back talk wasn't one of Mona's rules, but being anywhere near a police station was.

Coming here was stupid. What was I going to say? *Hello, Officer. I think there may be a crazy stalker at my school.* My suspicions were literally paper-thin, based on two lines of text from a newspaper clipping. There was no quantifiable evidence to suggest my theory had anything to do with Emily at all, and it was probably just a dumb prank anyway.

The officer set a small bottle of water in front of me and sat down. He crossed one leg and locked his hands behind his head, the butt of a very large holstered gun casually revealing itself through the gap in his jacket. He introduced himself as Lieutenant Nicholson.

"So, Miss Boswell." He snapped my ID down on the table. "I understand you are a junior at West River High School and you think you have information about an incident that occurred last weekend? Are you friends with Emily Reinnert?"

"No." Jeremy was a friend. Anh was a friend. Emily was more of an acquaintance who I was forced to talk about algebra with.

Lieutenant Nicholson sighed and his eyebrows drew together. "Did you witness something you think is relevant to the incident?"

"No . . . I mean, yes . . . I mean possibly." I shook my head. "What I mean is, I think I may have witnessed something, sort of."

"Let me get this straight." He glanced very deliberately at his watch and crossed his arms over his chest. "You *think* you *may* have witnessed something, *sort of*? What *exactly* do you *think* you *may* have witnessed?"

When I didn't answer right away, his stare burrowed into me, like he was digging around in my head. The harsh fluorescent lighting accentuated the tight wrinkles around his mouth. It wouldn't matter what I said next. He wasn't going to believe me.

"I'm sorry to waste your time. This was a bad idea. I shouldn't have come." I stood up and started to sling my pack over my shoulder.

"Sit down, Miss Boswell."

I looked between the lieutenant and the door. I was sure there was some law that said they couldn't detain me if I hadn't done anything wrong. Wasting the lieutenant's time wasn't a criminal offense.

"You know, I hate writing truancy reports. It gets messy. Too many people involved. Parents, teachers, principals . . . Whatever you have to say must be pretty important. Otherwise, you wouldn't have skipped school to come and say it. So why don't you just say what you came to say and let me be the judge of what's a waste of my time." He looked pointedly at my chair, making it clear he wasn't giving me a choice. If I walked out of here now, my mother would get a phone call, and a truancy report would definitely blow my chance at the scholarship.

I dropped into my chair and laid the two *Missed Connections* ads side by side on the table.

"What is this?" The lieutenant turned them one by one, to face him. His expression didn't change, but I sensed the slight shift in his posture as he drew the first ad toward him. The one about the colors.

"I know about what happened to Emily under the bleachers at North Hampton. I know about the blue and yellow paint."

He pushed the ad back in line with the other one and looked at me, confusion written all over his face.

"I don't think she'll be the only one. I think these ads were written by the same person. This was in today's paper." I tapped the table above the second ad. "That part about the play not being the thing is a reference to *Hamlet*. It's a play on words." I slid the *Hamlet* flyer across the table. "Tonight is opening night. I know this sounds like a stretch, but I think something bad is going to happen tonight during the play."

The lieutenant stared at me blankly. He didn't look at the flyer. The only sound was the second hand on the wall clock over the door. I fidgeted in my seat and fought the urge to look at it, staring him straight in the eye until the first beads of sweat trickled down my back.

Lieutenant Nicholson drew the flyer toward him, his face as expressionless as the room. "Why did you come?"

I wondered the same thing. Why had I come? I wasn't close to Emily. And I didn't owe her any favors. I should have minded my own business. Too late now.

"Telling someone seemed like the right thing to do, that's all." I wiped my palms over my jeans.

The lieutenant watched me. "What makes you assume these ads are related?"

I shrugged, not having any plausible answer for that.

"Do you know the person who wrote these ads, Miss Boswell?"

"How would I know that?" I wiped my lip, uncomfortably aware that I was the only one sweating. The small interrogation room felt stuffy and hot.

"I don't know. That's a really good question. Maybe you should tell me." He thought I was lying. "Who are you rolling over? An ex-boyfriend? What happened? He piss you off and now you're going to air his dirty laundry?"

Of course that's what he thought. What kind of person would report a crime before it happened? Unless they were somehow involved. Normal people don't make a habit of studying the personal ads.

I crossed my arms and leaned back in my chair. His smile

was supercilious, and it put me on the defensive. "I don't have a boyfriend. And I have no idea who wrote the ads."

"Then how can you assume they're connected to Emily?"

"It's not rocket science. Emily was found under the bleachers at North Hampton on the same day this ad came out." I shoved the ad back toward him. "Our school colors are blue. North Hampton's are yellow. You know . . . Newton? Isaac Newton?" The lieutenant either didn't remember or hadn't passed this particular class in high school. His face was impenetrable. "And then today's ad about *Hamlet* . . . it seemed too coincidental." I pinched the bridge of my nose. This conversation was giving me a headache, and I hadn't even touched him.

Lieutenant Nicholson stared a hole through me, as if the answer to some question was hidden inside my skull. "Do you make a habit of reading the newspaper cover to cover . . ." He paused to read my ID card. "Nearly, is it?" The corner of his lip turned up, like he was amused. Like I was a joke.

I crossed my legs, knees tight together, feeling exposed. "No."

"Just the personals, then?" He cocked a silvering eyebrow.

"No." I jammed my fists into the pockets of my hoodie.

"I thought all you kids were into the online dating thing. I thought only old farts like me still read the newspaper." He lowered his voice and leaned toward me. "Why were you reading the *Missed Connections,* Nearly?"

Heat crawled up my neck and my head began to pound.

The metal chair legs scraped as I stood up. I'd come voluntarily. I could leave on my own terms as well. If he slapped me with a truancy report, I'd find a way to deal with it. I threw my pack over my shoulder. "I found the ads by accident. I was only trying to help."

I stepped toward the door, but the lieutenant's meaty hand beat mine to the knob. He handed me a card, his face softening. He pinched the card. "Look," he said, waiting for me to meet his eyes before letting me take it. "If you think of anything else you *think* may be important, call me at this number. I want to help you."

For a second, I thought maybe he did. That maybe I'd done the right thing by coming. I reached for the card, letting our fingertips brush, then yanked it from his hands.

He didn't believe me. Not at all. And his distrust clung to me like smoke.

I pocketed the card without looking at it, and trained my eyes on the door. He stepped aside, but his suspicion held fast, all the way to the exit.

• • •

My relief fizzled as soon as I realized I'd left my school ID behind. I backtracked through the maze of desks and offices, retracing my steps.

The narrow hall was lined with identical doors under cold fluorescents. Police escorted disheveled prostitutes and gang-bangers up and down the hall. I kept my head down and walked like I had a clue where I was going. I couldn't remember which door I'd come from, so I peeked in each one. Some were shut.

Laughter echoed, becoming louder as I approached an open door.

"I don't see much money on the table." A man's voice—not Nicholson's.

"I got my money on my man, the Game Boy."

"How much?"

I paused in front of a room identical to the one I'd been in. Peeking my head around the opening, I couldn't tell who was speaking. A group of four uniformed officers stood on either side of the metal table with their backs to me. My ID wasn't on it. Instead, the bright sides of an un-solved Rubik's cube sat in the center, surrounded by small bills. Oleksa Petrenko slouched in a metal chair. His steel-gray eyes flickered between the gaps in the blue uniforms, finding mine.

"I say no more without my attorney," he said in his brusque Ukrainian accent. The laughter in the room fell silent and four sets of eyes turned to me. I jumped when the door slammed shut.

Walking faster, I checked the next two rooms. At least I didn't have to worry about Oleksa spreading rumors. He didn't talk to anyone, as far as I knew. And obviously, whatever crime he'd committed, including hustling police officers out of their donut money, was far worse than any reason I had for coming in on my own.

I stopped just outside the next door. Lieutenant Nicholson grumbled in a low voice.

"Emily Reinnert's father sits on the city council. He's been all over me for answers and we've got nothing. I want a plain-clothes at the play at West River High tonight." I heard the *tap-tap-tap* of plastic against the metal tabletop. My ID card. "And I want to keep an eye on this Boswell girl. She knows more than she's letting on. Who do we have inside West River?"

A woman answered. "This is everyone we've got working inside the local high schools." A heavy thud, like a stack of files hitting the surface of the table. A quiet rustling.

"No, I don't want a cop," Nicholson growled. "I need some-one who can get in close to the girl without giving Internal Affairs one more reason to crawl up my ass."

"We've got a C.I.—Whelan—at West River," she said. "Sprung him from juvenile about three weeks ago."

A brief silence and a shuffling of papers.

"Wasn't the Whelan kid involved in the shooting at North Hampton?" Nicholson asked.

"We cut him a deal. He stays in school and keeps his nose clean, and in exchange we registered him as a confidential informant. His file says he's got an apartment in Hunting-ton. The kid's parole officer says he's back in school as of this week. She's got him checking in daily by phone. Meets with him on Saturdays."

Nicholson grunted. "And what do we get out of the

arrangement, aside from charitable warm fuzzy feelings and another paycheck against my budget?"

"He agreed to help us bust Lonny Johnson."

I held my breath. More papers shuffled in the silence.

"Toss him a bone. Tell him to get in tight with this Boswell girl and we'll expunge the last assault and battery charge from his record. And make sure he stays in line."

"We met with him this morning and debriefed him on the Reinnert case. He's cocky, but he doesn't seem like such a bad kid. Asked him to keep his eyes open in case he hears anything. Lonny's mostly distributing speed and coke, but he'll try to get us something on the local rootie dealers. The lab found ketamine residue in Emily Reinnert's water bottle."

Tap-tap-tap . . .

"I want more than that. I want Whelan to get me everything he can on Nearly Boswell."

I abandoned my ID and crept back from the door.

9

HE WASN'T HARD TO SPOT. The man in the navy suit came out of the auditorium at least a dozen times during the performance, his jacket buttons straining over something bulky near his waist. He walked to the water fountain without looking at it, eyes roving the hall in both directions as he drank. A thin comb-over flopped in an arc from his head, flirting with the fountain spray when he leaned over. When he stood up, he checked his watch and yawned.

Nicholson had sent one pathetic verge-of-retirement cop, but I guess that's all my skinny prank theory was worth. I'd been observing his unimpressive stakeout for almost an hour from the courtyard. It was the perfect vantage point, dark enough to conceal me, with panoramic views of the halls in each direction. Nicholson was suspicious of me, and I wouldn't add fuel to his fire by flaunting the fact that I was here.

The cop disappeared into the red hues of the theater and I crept back into the hall just as the auditorium doors pulled slowly closed. I withdrew the ad from my pocket. The clue suggested two possible scenarios.

The first—the reference to the play and the invitation to meet up after the show—was an obvious one. Almost too obvious. But the second?

Archimedes knew the play wasn't the thing.

Was the play a decoy? Was the real prank happening somewhere else? Somewhere Archimedes—one of history's greatest mathematicians—would likely be? *Do the math . . .* I couldn't be in two places at once.

The cop already had the auditorium covered, so I followed my gut to the math department at the far end of the school on tiptoe, pausing every few feet to listen.

I ducked under the stairwell where I could see most of the

wing, and since I wasn't sure what I was looking for, I waited. The ad just said "find me after the show." I checked the clock above the fountain. Ten. The show was ending. *After the show* was now. I squatted low, my breathing shallow. The wing was quiet and still.

The second hand crept slowly over the face of the clock, and each passing second I felt more and more like an idiot for being there. My knees began to ache where they pressed against the cold tile, and a cramp pinched my calf. I shifted positions, stretched my legs, checked the clock again. The whole thing was probably a complete waste of time. I wasn't even sure I was in the right place, or what I would do if I spotted someone, or exactly what I thought they might be doing, but I stayed put, remembering what had happened to Emily. If there was a chance something like that could happen again, I couldn't abandon my suspicion and walk away. I urged the red hand of the clock forward with my mind, wanting to get this night behind me.

By eleven o'clock, I was sure the audience was long gone. The actors were probably washing off their stage makeup and heading to the after-party. The cop was probably shaking his head, chalking the wasted night up to a paranoid girl.

I stepped out from under the stairwell, stretched, and scanned the dark passage. All closed doors.

With the exception of one. Room #112. My AP Physics class.

It was barely cracked, but I kicked myself for not having noticed it sooner. I eased it open, listening. The room was silent. Pitch-black. The hair on my neck prickled.

I reached inside and flipped a switch. The fluorescents flickered to life, turning lumpy shadows into recognizable shapes. Chairs stacked neatly upside down on tables, the blackboard wiped clean, trash can empty.

Everything neat. Nothing out of place. Except one chair.

Mine. It rested on the floor, flipped over as if someone got up in a hurry. I walked over and saw my desk.

Jagged deep letters were carved into the wood.

YOU LOST THE GOLD CROWN.
BETTER LUCK NEXT TIME.

Goose bumps rippled over me. The last message on my desk led to a dead cat on my doorstep. And that message was only in ink. This one had been carved in angry-looking purposeful lines, deep enough to splinter the wood. And this time I had no doubt it'd been left for me.

You lost the gold crown.

I paced, filtering through memories of lectures and texts, sorting what I knew about math and Archimedes.

Archimedes' Principle was based on the story of a gold crown. He'd written his *Treatise on Floating Bodies* after discovering he could determine the weight of a gold crown by measuring the volume of water it displaced.

So what? What did that have to do with anything? Or with

the play? What could the gold crown possibly have to do with . . . *Hamlet?*

My brain worked fast, outpacing my pulse as it divided out all the factors until just one common denominator was left. A chill raced down my spine. There was a floating body in *Hamlet* . . . Ophelia.

I took off at a run, my footsteps echoing back at me down halls that seemed to go on for miles. I flew around the corner of the gymnasium and slipped into the girls' locker room. The door closed behind me and I waited, winded, while my eyes adjusted to the dim yellow lights. I headed for the moist hot scent of chlorine until the concrete gave way to rubber floor runners.

When I came to the door, I took a breath before inching it open.

The light around the Olympic-size pool was a steamy green. Watery lines danced on the ceiling, refracted light from below the pool's surface. I stood, listening. The huge space was silent, as if the water muted all the sound except the ragged breaths I couldn't quiet. I stepped slowly toward the pool, scanning the bleachers for shadows or movement.

"Marcia?" I called quietly.

My own voice came back in soft echoes.

"Marcia, are you here?"

I perched on the curved lip below the diving boards, beside the depth markings . . . twelve feet. I looked down the length of the pool, following the lap lines that wavered like long black threads, marking the distance to the opposite end of the pool. Except for one, which seemed to stop, disappearing prematurely into a blur of shadow by the far wall.

My skin prickled as I rounded the corner of the pool. The shadow in the water grew as I neared, a dark mass floating above it. As my feet picked up speed, the shadow cleared, the dark mass becoming black tendrils of hair, drifting like cobwebs over a pale face and tangling between purple lips.

"Marcia!" I ran to the edge.

Her eyes were closed, as if she was sleeping. She lay on the shallow bottom, mouth open and legs spread, her big cotton dress billowing up around her. Her gray fingers reached for the surface but didn't quite touch.

I dropped to my knees and plunged both arms into the water. Her hand was cold and slippery and didn't grab back. The dress, flowing and weightless below the surface, clung to a drain at the bottom of the pool. I pulled hard, but the dress was like an anchor, weighing her body down.

"Come on, Marcia! Please!" I dropped my grip to her wrist, leveraging all my weight. Her elbow scraped the lip of the pool. Then her head broke the surface, heavy hair tipping her head back on her neck. First her nose, then eyes, then lips. Then her face emerged, blue and green under the light. I pulled again, catching her underarm on the concrete. Her head rolled toward me, water spilling from her mouth and draining down her chin.

I whispered frantically, begging her to wake up, begging her dress to stop fighting me, but the harder I pulled, the more I was losing her. I looked at her wrist, feeling her frail joints strain. Her wet sleeve fell back, revealing a mark.

A number.

Through the water, the number eighteen appeared, clear and dark against her forearm like a blue tattoo. I stopped breathing, unable to move as her wrist slipped through my fingers. I watched her mouth and nose slide under. Watched the number drift slowly to the bottom, her sleeve stuck stubbornly in the crook of her elbow, dark hair floating above her.

I covered my mouth with my sleeve, icy streams of pool water trailing down my chest.

The locked exterior doors rattled on their hinges.

"Marcia? Are you in there?" came muffled voices from the other side.

I scrambled to my feet and looked down at Marcia one last time as the next set of doors shook, louder this time. I had minutes, maybe seconds, before they found another way in. And there was nothing I could do for her. She was gone.

• • •

I took a back stairwell to the second floor and hid in a remote girls' bathroom, retching into the sink. When I was done, I washed my face and wrung out my sleeves, too afraid the automatic dryers would attract attention. I needed to get out of the building without being seen.

Someone had wanted me to be here tonight. Someone wanted me to find Marcia's body. Maybe even get caught with it.

And he'd marked her. But why? What did it mean? The number looked like it had been written in blue ink, but it wasn't smudged or faded by the water. Permanent marker.

They drew the number ten in permanent marker on her arm . . .

Like the number ten on Emily's arm.

Like the blue markings on my chem lab table . . .

DEAD OR ALIVE . . .

I slumped to the floor.

The person who wrote those ads knew me. He knew I read the *Missed Connections* on Friday mornings. He knew exactly where I would go, leaving the door to my physics class open. He carved the message in my desk, and left the chair down to make sure I saw it. He knew how to communicate with me.

Somehow, this was all about me.

I needed to get out of here. I snuck out of the bathroom and down the stairs, emerging in a corridor near the auditorium. Blue lights flashed through the windows from the parking lot outside and walkie-talkies squawked muffled commands. I backed around the corner and peered around the wall, listening to the chaos on the other side.

Theater students lingered in tight groups as EMTs and police cleared a path. Jeremy stood a head taller than the crowd, watching through his camera and snapping pictures until a uniformed officer put a hand over the lens. Part of me wanted to grab Jeremy's attention, wanted to pull him behind the wall with me and tell him everything. But a short girl with dark hair stood close to him. He tucked her under his arm, holding her close while she dabbed her cheeks with a tissue. Anh.

My reflection stared back from the darkened courtyard windows where I'd stood only an hour ago. I was too close, too visible here. I backed slowly away from the blue flashing lights. When I rounded the corner, I ran, cutting through dim halls I could navigate blind, stopping at each exit, checking the doors. All locked.

When the front hall came into view, it was silent. Empty. I smacked into the release bar and it yielded easily, sending the metal door flying into the wall outside. I jumped out of my skin at the crash. It was dark. Steam rose off the cooling blacktop. I pulled my hood low over my face, but the police by the auditorium were busy interviewing the students who remained and didn't look over.

The parking lot was empty except for a handful of cars, including Jeremy's Civic. I needed to get home. I was sure the police were anxious to speak with me, or at the very least would keep a close eye on me after tonight. I'd reported a crime before it had happened. Nicholson would be an idiot not to suspect me.

I felt eyes on me. A figure stood just beyond a weak halo of light. I sped up as we made eye contact. Lonny's friend, the guy I'd crashed into, reclined against a motorcycle, silently taking in the scene.

I kept my head low as I veered from the sidewalk and slid into the shadows, avoiding the security lights, cutting through the ball fields, not caring that this route through the backyards of rough neighborhoods might be more danger-ous than where I'd just come from. Wanting only to make myself invisible. But I couldn't.

He'd been watching.

And he'd seen me.

IO

THE SPEED LIMIT IN SUNNY VIEW was a heart-stopping twenty miles an hour, and most people treated the three stop signs as suggestions. From my front steps, I watched the Civic come to a complete stop at each one. I checked my wrist in an aggravated pantomime for Jeremy's benefit. I didn't actually own a watch, but I knew we were going to be late and I wanted to get to school early. I needed to know what everyone saw or heard on Friday night and by now, the rumor mill would be churning out the details. Jeremy grinned weakly at me through the windshield as he pulled to a careful stop at my feet.

I threw open the passenger door. The air felt heavy and thick and seemed to press in from all sides. I rolled up my window and Jeremy flicked on the AC without a word, angling his own vent at me.

"I guess you heard about Marcia Steckler?" He looked hard at the road, his hands perfectly positioned at ten and two.

I swallowed before answering. "No, what about her?"

"She never showed up at the after-party on Friday. There was an . . . accident."

I stared out the window, the world moving too fast, lines blurring. I shut my eyes. "What happened?"

"The police found her . . . in the pool."

I fought to keep my voice from breaking. Only one person had seen me in school that night, and that was already one too many. If the police asked questions, Jeremy shouldn't have to lie for me. "Was she hurt?"

"She's dead, Leigh," he said gently, as if placing something delicate in my lap. "I wouldn't have believed it myself except Anh and I watched them carry her out."

Ahn and I. I bit my lip, letting a penned-up tear spill over. It was partly for Marcia and partly for me. I was in trouble. And Jeremy had been with Anh Friday night. When I'd needed him. When he should have been with me.

"Did you have a date or something?" They hadn't even asked me if I wanted to go with them. I never had the chance to tell them no. He hadn't just offered her a ride. He'd taken her to the play. Put his arm around her. And he hadn't told me because he didn't want me to know. Because they didn't want me there.

"A date? With Anh? No." He scrunched up his nose. His glasses slid down and he pushed the wire rims back in place with his index finger, a nervous habit. "Why?" he asked. "Would it matter to you?"

I didn't answer, afraid I'd say something I'd regret. Something that might slice too deep to fix.

"Of course not," he muttered to himself.

The silence was hard to breathe through.

"I was covering *Hamlet*," he finally said, sounding tired. "For the school paper. Anh was just . . . there . . . with me."

Anh was there with me.

And I wasn't, was implied. I wanted to tell him that I *was* there. That I saw *everything*. That I touched Marcia's blue fingers. That I held her cold hand and screamed at her to wake up while he was comforting Anh. But I couldn't tell him anything.

He pulled into his assigned space, set the handbrake, and plucked the key from the ignition. We listened to the engine cool, an awkward and terrible tension between us until I couldn't take it anymore and reached for his hand.

His skin burned, hot and anxious. His anxiety tasted like stomach acid and smelled like sweat. I hadn't felt Jeremy like this in years. The mood stabilizers his shrink prescribed mellowed the sharp tang I'd come to associate with stress. Usually I could feel the way they cushioned his moods, leaving only mildly astringent aftertastes. Today Jeremy's anxiety was bitter enough to make me gag. It was pure and unfiltered. "You stopped taking your medication." It should have been a question, but I knew it with complete certainty.

"I'm fine," he said, without looking at me.

"You're not fine. I can tell. You're skipping your appointments and you're off your meds. Why?"

He didn't answer. Just brushed back the thin blond hairs pasted to his temple.

"Does this have something do with Anh?"

He looked at me sharply. "Can we just drop it?"

I gave a single curt nod. If he didn't want to share what was going on inside his head, I wouldn't push him. But I couldn't shake the feeling that all these awkward unanswered questions between us that seemed inconsequential alone, might build into something insurmountable.

Reluctantly, I let go of his hand. We both stared straight ahead. The gymnasium stared back, its doors sealed shut with strips of yellow tape.

"Why's the gym taped off?"

Jeremy shrugged. "The police don't think Marcia killed herself. She was drugged before she drowned. I was listening to their radios in the parking lot on Friday night. They're calling it a probable homicide."

Probable. There was nothing probable about it. She'd been murdered and left there for me. "Does anyone know who did it?" I asked, piling one more omission on my growing mountain of lies.

"I don't know."

"Did anyone see anything?"

"I said I don't know," he snapped.

"What kind of crappy reporter are you?" I snapped back, the sharpness of his mood still lingering in me. I only meant to be sarcastic, but it came out sounding frustrated and critical. Maybe because that's how I felt too.

He got out of the car.

"Hey," I called after him, but he walked away. I hadn't meant to hurt his feelings, but he was so tense—so on-edge without his meds. I should have been more careful. I was stupid. I should never have touched him. "Would you stop and look at me?" I just needed to see his face. He stopped, his sigh obvious in the fall of his shoulders before he turned. We stared at each other over the roof. I tucked my hands in my pockets and lowered my voice. "Whatever it is, you can tell me." Inside I cringed, feeling like a hypocrite. Here I was, expecting him to share what was happening inside his head, and I hadn't been willing to do the same. He was silent, and I didn't push. I hadn't earned that right.

Instead, I told him what was in my heart. "You know I love you, J. Don't you?"

He thought for a minute, then said, "I'll see you at lunch?" and walked away without waiting for an answer.

II

THE BELL RANG, marking the end of seventh period, and Rankin's last chem class of the day. I stood in front of the bulletin board, waiting for the room to clear, staring at my most recent test score. The one that solidified the gap between Anh's and my final grades and perfectly positioned her for a stronger lead. Cumulative scores wouldn't be posted until Friday, but it didn't take a genius to figure out what a ninety-four percent would do to my grade.

When the last of the students filed out, I slumped into my chair. Why was I even there? Marcia was gone, and no amount of wishful thinking would bring her back. You don't get credit for just showing up.

Without a word, Rankin placed my graded test on the table in front of me.

I stared at the exam. Through it. To the blue graffiti on the surface of my desk. The words *DEAD OR ALIVE* showed through the paper, less like a fading memory than a lingering promise, making it impossible to think about anything else.

Rankin tapped my test with his lab marker. "I expected a closer race. You're letting Anh get ahead of you. And TJ's not far behind."

I stopped looking through the paper to look at it, all the blue notations where half points had been deducted for stupid mistakes. The blue ink. Rankin's standard-issue indelible blue marker. We all had them. Every chemistry student. The same kind that was scribbled all over my test. All over my desk. On Marcia's arm. Emily's had been ten. Marcia's was eighteen. But why? What was the connection? The message carved in my lab table in physics suggested there'd be others.

Better luck next time.

"I know what you're thinking," Rankin said, "but you've still got four weeks, and the scholarship is based on cumulative scores."

I nodded. The largest scholarship in the history of West River—$25,000 dollars for one qualified junior, based on academic achievement and community service. Straight A's in chemistry and five hours per week volunteering . . . and *voilà*! A big fat college tuition. One every year for one lucky student until the bucket ran out.

This was my year. My only year. My ticket out.

And I was blowing it.

"Well," Rankin said decidedly, "we can't have you falling behind in your community service. It's deeply troubling, and I know it's hard, but try not to let this loss distract you for long. You've worked hard, and I'd hate to see you lose your momentum so close to the end of the year." He patted my shoulder gently. The touch was unexpected and I bit my lip trying not to jerk it from his hand, grateful for the barrier of fabric between us. I didn't want to feel his disappointment in me. Or his pity. "I'm late for a faculty meeting." He checked his watch, and lumbered to his desk. "I took the liberty of making other arrangements for you today . . ." He paused, raising an eyebrow. ". . . if you feel you're up to it."

I nodded again.

"Good. Your new mentee will be here shortly. He needs basic chemistry." He bent to scoop up a stack of books and muttered, "Very basic . . ."

As Rankin shuffled out the door, another figure shuffled in. They exchanged polite hellos in an awkward dance, Rankin clasping his disheveled stack to his chest and a short, square-figured boy squeezing in around him. I tutored Teddy Marshall on Thursdays and I was surprised to see him so early in the week. His special ed class was in a small wing on the other side of the school, and we rarely saw each other outside of our weekly lessons. He beamed, his small eyes shining behind thick corrective lenses, his tongue peeking through the gaps in his teeth.

"Hey, Leigh!"

I forced a small grin, but wasn't able to make it stretch further than that. "Back at you, Teddy," I said, trying to be cheerful for his sake.

He extended a stubby fist in my direction, leading me through a complex handshake involving a lot of knuckle thumps and hand slaps that had him laughing as I struggled to keep up. Teddy was a toucher, but I'd never tried to dissuade him. His joy was pure and sweet, like honeysuckle blooming, the sun-warmed taste of it on my tongue.

"What are you doing here?" I asked, feeling a cloud lift. "I thought you were my Thursday date?"

"Yeah, I'm your man on Thursdays all right. But my mom says I have to go to the cardiologist this Thursday, so I won't see you."

"Oh." I scratched my head, remembering Rankin's comment about "very basic chemistry." "So you're here today instead?"

"Nope." He tucked his thumbs under the straps of his backpack and rocked on his heels. "I've got soccer practice today. We'll need to find another day for our date."

"Soccer?" I paused, sensing an opportunity to ask the question I hadn't been able to ask Jeremy that morning in his car. Teddy was the water boy. He probably knew everyone on our team. Anh said the police thought Emily's number might have been connected to the soccer team. That maybe it tied to a jersey number. "Do you know who number eighteen is?"

Teddy scratched his head and blinked. "There is no eighteen on the team."

"How about North Hampton's?"

He thought for a minute. "They don't have an eighteen either."

So much for the police's theory on jersey numbers. *Better*

luck next time. I hated to think there would be a next time, or that I'd have to wait until Friday to find another clue.

"Everything okay, Leigh?" Teddy frowned.

"Everything's fine." I pulled out a calendar, shaking off an image of Marcia on the bottom of the pool. "We can't meet this Friday. It's the junior class trip to the amusement park, and you and I have a date to ride the carousel instead. How about the Friday after that?"

Teddy stripped off his backpack, reached inside, and handed me a permission slip bordered with stars and space shuttle clip art. The bottom portion for his parents' signature of consent had already been cut away, leaving only the flyer for a field trip to the National Air and Space Museum. "Mrs. Smallwood is taking us to the Smithsonian next Friday. I asked if I could bring a date, but she said it's just for the special ed kids." He blinked both eyes in lieu of a wink. "*I* think you're special, but she says you can't go."

I ruffled Teddy's hair, soaking him up. "Don't worry about it. I'll talk to Mr. Rankin and see what we can figure out. I'll see you at the carousel."

Teddy flashed an enthusiastic thumbs-up and raced off, leaving behind his field trip flyer.

"Teddy, you forgot your—" I started to call after him, before I spotted the writing on the back of the yellow page. The details of our "date" to ride the carousel. Beside it, two stick figures held hands. They both wore glasses, and one had frizzy hair. I bit my lip and smiled, despite my foul mood. When I looked up from his drawing, he was gone.

I sunk back into my chair and rested my head against the tabletop. A mild headache was starting just behind my eyes. I couldn't afford to miss any hours, and my mentees were dropping like flies. I smelled indelible ink where my forehead rubbed against my blue test score, and it felt like salt in a wound.

I wasn't sure how long I'd been lying there when something eclipsed the fluorescent light, casting a long shadow over the length of the table. The sharp, oily smell of leather bit my throat and I raised my head.

Lonny's friend stood over my desk, staring at my test. His hair fell over his forehead, framing his face in knife-like points long enough to brush his collar. Two silver loops pierced his right brow over the same steady blue eyes that had watched me leave school Friday night.

I sat straighter in my chair. No one else had seen me. He couldn't prove I was there. I had nothing to be afraid of. I flipped my test over, sliding it a few inches down the desk. He didn't register the hint.

"Can I help you?"

He looked me over, starting with my hair. It was twisted into a tight knot at the back of my head. His eyes continued down with little interest and paused at my T-shirt. It was two sizes too large and the sleeves hung to my elbows, but right now it didn't feel big enough. I crossed my arms around myself.

"You're Nearly?" His voice was dark and rough around the edges. A perfect fit.

"What do you want?" Somehow I doubted he'd come to apologize.

He glanced at the clock. "It's three o'clock. I'm here."

"So?"

The corner of his mouth pulled into a grin. "So, you're supposed to tutor me. Rankin told me to be here at three."

No. Freaking. Way.

His eyes bored into mine, a whole conversation passing before either of us could blink.

"Rankin was mistaken." I snatched up my book, determined to find some other way—*any* other way—to fulfill my community service requirement.

"No problem." He shrugged, watching me wrangle textbooks and calculators into submission. "How about tomorrow?"

"Booked," I said without looking up.

"Wednesday?"

"Geometry with Kylie Rutherford."

"Thursday?" he asked with a sarcastic undertone that put me even further on edge.

I zipped my pack closed.

"Let me guess. You're washing your hair on Thursday?"

He reached for a stray lock. My whole body tensed and something on my face must have changed his mind. He paused, his hand inches away, and a slow grin crept over his face. He leaned over the desk, his voice low. "Or is it swim practice?"

I couldn't speak. Up close, his eyes were suffocating and deep. I flashed back to Marcia's dead blue face. He was too close, he'd seen too much, and my thoughts scrambled and blurred.

"No!" It came out loud enough to wipe the smile off his face. I cleared my throat, hiding my bare hands under the table. His eyes trailed after them. "I tutor Teddy Marshall on Thursdays."

He shook his head and half smiled, as though he found me entertaining. "I get it. You're busy." He slid something across the table. "Maybe a few hours after school sometime?"

I waited for his hand to retreat before reaching for the scrap of paper. A phone number. His phone number. I shoved it back across the table, and his hand closed over mine, trapping it between us. I sucked in a surprised breath as his emotions crept into me. He was suspicious of me. And conflicted. Guilt and self-doubts simmered just below the surface, under that cocky self-assurance he wore like a leather skin.

I jerked my hand from his, dropping the number. He hadn't wanted to give it to me anyway. I'd tasted his regret when he did. "What's your name?"

"Reece." He gave me a skeptical once-over, then extended his hand. "Reece Whelan."

I didn't take it. I watched him, brain skimming around the edges of a memory.

He dismissed the rebuff. "So, are we cool or what?"

Whelan . . . We've got a kid inside . . . get me everything he can on Nearly Boswell.

I stood up, gears clicking in place as I grabbed my pack and made a beeline for the door. No, we were absolutely not cool.

12

The next morning, when I opened my locker, a wad of paper and a pink slip ruffled between the vents. The pink slip was from Rankin, telling me I needed to reschedule two hours of tutoring this week, for Teddy Marshall . . . and Reece Whelan.

The wad of paper had been folded and crushed to fit through the vent. I peeled it open. Chapter one of a basic chemistry textbook had been ripped from its binding, and blocky blue ballpoint letters were inked over the top of the page.

I NEED YOU . . . PLEASE.—RW

I balled it between my hands and pitched it onto the floor of my locker. Reece Whelan could forget it. I knew he was working for Nicholson. No way was I letting him follow me around and spill the details of my miserable life to the police just so he could hold on to his *Get Out of Jail Free* card.

The first period bell rang. I set my mental timer for five minutes, barely enough to cross the length of the school and up two flights of stairs before the tardy bell. If I cut through the courtyard, I'd make it with seconds to spare. I turned, smacking into a wall of black T-shirt.

I leaned back against my locker, my pulse sky-rocketing. "Do you always sneak up on people like that?" I angled to shove past him, that too-close feeling snaking through me.

"Hey, wait up." He grabbed my wrist and I snatched it away with a curse. The rush of his emotion was cold and sudden, like someone had dumped ice cubes down my back.

"What the hell is wrong?" He lowered his voice. "I'm sorry. I don't know what I said to make you so mad yesterday. If you don't want to hang out after school, it's cool. I get it."

I drew in a deep breath, passing it off as impatience. It wasn't a psychic smell. It was him. A spicy masculine-smelling soap mingled with the tang of his leather jacket into something warm and appealing. I massaged my wrist. "It's not *cool*. Just leave me alone." I pushed past him, careful not to touch him, and kept walking.

He followed me and I had to work twice as hard to stay ahead of his long strides. He was almost as tall as Jeremy.

"Hey," he said, his tone carefully measured. I could actually hear the effort in his restraint. "Can you slow down a little?"

"No."

"Why?" He hovered, one step for every three of mine. I slipped between snuggling couples, jostled through groups of broad-backed jocks. He was impossible to shake. The throng of oncoming traffic parted for him with a reverse magnetism.

"I'm late for class," I snapped.

"So?"

"So, maybe it's okay for you to ditch. You can just take it again. Some of us have scholarships to worry about."

Reece jockeyed himself in beside me. "I don't want to take it again. That's why I asked you to tutor me."

I stole a quick glance at his face. He was clean-shaven and his hair was combed neat.

"I'm not going to tutor you," I said. "I told you yesterday."

He muttered something under his breath and raked a frustrated hand through his bangs.

"Look, can we start over? I'm not sure what I did to piss you off. All I did was introduce myself and ask for help."

"Yeah," I said, recalling my visit to the police station. "I can totally relate."

"What's that supposed to mean?"

"Never mind."

"Fine, I'm starting over."

"Good luck with that," I mumbled.

The burr was back in his smile, his voice bristly. "It's nice to meet you, Nearly."

"Don't call me that."

"Don't call you what?"

I stomped past the library doors, marking the halfway point to class. I wished I could move faster, but my legs burned and my lungs were tight. I was all elbows and knees, hands in my pockets as I pushed through the crowd.

"Leigh. You can call me Leigh."

"Leigh?" He wasn't even breathing hard. "Why? Don't you like your name?"

I rolled my eyes. "Just trying to blend." A point a narc should sympathize with. "And for the record, no, I don't like my name."

"So, Leigh," he said. "Can I ask you something?"

In two minutes this conversation would be over and I'd walk into a class he wasn't qualified to set foot in. "What?" I kept my pace brisk, taking the stairs two at a time.

"Why do you hate me so much?"

"I don't hate you."

"Well, you obviously dislike me."

"That's not true," I said. "I'd have to know you to dislike you, and I don't know you at all."

"That's exactly my point!" He blocked me with a long, deliberate stride just before I reached the door to the science wing. "I'm trying to get to know you. Why are you making this hard?"

I tried to step around him, but he wouldn't let me pass. "I

didn't think *easy* was part of the job description." I cringed, berating myself for saying it out loud. I told myself I should just walk away, ignore him and he'd lose interest. But he kept pushing. And even though it was stupid, something inside me couldn't resist pushing back.

He shook his head. "You're not making any sense. I don't follow."

"Yes, you *do* follow me. You've *been* following me. And I'd like you to stop!"

I looked at the clock behind his head. I had thirty seconds to end this conversation and get my butt to class. I felt the curious onlookers hovering nearby. "This is a complete waste of my time," I muttered.

He ground his teeth and glared at me, looking insulted. "What are you saying? You think I can't learn this stuff?"

"Move!"

"Not until you tell me why helping me is a waste of your time." His peppermint breath touched my face. Who was he trying to impress?

"Seriously?" I threw my hands up. "One day you're kicking my books across the hall. The next, you're giving me your phone number. Who the hell do you think you are?"

His dark eyes flashed back and forth between mine.

"What do you want me to say?" He raised his arms over his head in surrender. "You're right. It's no secret where I've been. I did some pretty stupid shit and spent a whole semester in juvie. I'm probably not worth your time." He rested his hands loosely on his hips, glanced furtively around, and lowered his voice. "But aren't you being a little hypocritical?"

I stiffened, darting nervous glances as people walked by. "What's that supposed to mean?"

He answered in a low rumble, the words barely a whisper. "I know where you live. What your mother does for a living. That's no secret either. So why is it okay for you to try to make something of your life, but not me?"

I'd expected him to bring up what he'd seen on Friday night—my daring escape from the crime scene at school. Not my mother. I wasn't sure which was worse.

"Rankin says you have to tutor me to qualify for some scholarship."

"I don't have to do anything," I snapped. But he was right. If I refused to take Reece on, I'd fall short on my qualifying hours. The door to my future would zip shut like an empty suitcase and I'd be stuck in Sunny View for eternity. I let out a long breath, taking in the winding tattoo on his arm and the piercings in his eyebrow, already regretting what I was about to agree to.

"What?" His half grin curled like a beckoning finger. "Do I look dangerous?"

"You could say that." I looked away from his lips. "I just want to pass chemistry. Please."

Passing chemistry wasn't all he wanted, but Rankin had

me between a rock and a hard place. Whelan's eyes widened, sensing an opening. They were lighter, warmer with his smile, and dangerous enough to make me forget about everything—even Marcia. "So what do you say? Meet me after school?"

I bit my lip. Nicholson set this up so Reece Whelan could spy on me. Get close. Get information. But I wasn't guilty of anything, so what did it matter? Maybe the solution to my problem was the narc standing right in front of me. If he saw that I was just a boring, normal person with a boring, normal life, that information would make it back to Nicholson. Getting to know Reece might get the police off my back.

"Just chemistry," he promised, palms raised in mock subjugation.

Right. Just chemistry. It all boiled down to one undeniable truth. Reece Whelan held my scholarship in his slippery lying fingers.

"Fine," I said before I could change my mind. "Four o'clock."

He flashed a self-satisfied one-hundred-watt smile and turned to go.

"I hope you're worth it," I called after him without thinking.

Reece's boots paused on the tile. He turned to look at me, and his smile was gone.

• • •

I took my bag lunch to the library and headed to a small table in the back. Jeremy was at our usual spot, hunched over his iPad. Several large maps were open and spread all across the table. I set my backpack on the floor beside him with a heavy thunk.

"Where were you after first period?"

"Why? Did you miss me?"

"Of course."

"And all this time I thought you only loved me for my Twinkies." A slow smiled curled his lip, and I was relieved that whatever tension there had been between us the previous morning seemed to be forgiven. He looked from his iPad to one of the maps, carefully marking a point with a yellow highlighter. "Tell me again why we're doing this?"

"Because I won't survive the summer if we don't."

"Syracuse is only six hours away. I have a car."

"And I don't. So we need to figure out how we can spend weekends together while you're away on this internship."

He dropped his chin in his hand. "I have a better idea. How about if I just don't go."

"Are you kidding? This photojournalism program is the perfect opportunity for you!"

"It's at Syracuse. I don't want to end up at Syracuse for college. My *mother* wants me to." Because it was far away. Because it's easier to push someone away than to look at them too closely and see the pain you've inflicted reflected back in their eyes.

"Does it matter that it's what your mother wants? Syracuse is a great school." And a chance for him to finally get away from his father. "You'd be a fool to pass up a chance to live on campus for a summer. You'll be a shoe-in when you apply in the fall."

"I'm not going to New York." He tossed the highlighter on the map. It was a local map. Maryland, DC, and Virginia. He'd highlighted all the schools I planned to apply to.

I shouldn't have been happy about that, but I selfishly smiled. I didn't know what I'd do if Jeremy left for four years—he was my best friend. I picked up the highlighter and a bus map and asked, "Where do we start?"

"University of Maryland," he said, studying me sideways. My smile widened. College Park was just over thirty minutes away.

"Your mom is going to throw a fit."

"My mom doesn't have to know."

I picked up the route map where Jeremy left off, plotting bus stops and transfer points between bites of my sandwich.

"Nearly," Jeremy said after a few quiet minutes.

"What?" I asked. "Do I have jelly on my chin?"

He was quiet for a minute and then reached inside his backpack. When his hand emerged, he was holding a photograph. "Remember when I took my dad's poker money and paid your rent? When I went back to return the cash, I found something. I wasn't sure if I should show you. I didn't want to make you sad."

He set the photo down in front of me. A group of men stood arm in arm in front of a banner. It read *Belle Green Poker Club*.

I recognized my father immediately. It was like catching my reflection in a mirror. His eyes, his nose and cheeks and smile, were mine. Warmer than his sterile face on his driver's license photo, it was like he was looking at me. I touched the glossy surface, memories of him coming back in a rush.

His arm was thrown over the shoulder of one of his teammates. As if reading my mind, Jeremy reached over my shoulder to point them out. "That's Vince's dad. And the one to Mr. DiMorello's left is my dad. The short one is Eric Miller's dad. And the one on the end is Emily Reinnert's dad, I think. I'm not sure who this one is," he said, pointing to the man my father had his arm around. The man's face was partially torn away.

"It was stuck to the back of another photo. I had to pull them apart, and tore a piece. I'm sorry." He shrugged.

"Are you kidding? This is amazing, Jeremy." I threw both arms around his shoulders before I realized what I'd done.

Jeremy's shock hit my skin first. Then his pain. It was physical. He sucked in a breath and winced. His arms remained rigid at his sides.

I shut my eyes, wanting to cry for him.

"He caught you returning the poker money, didn't he?" I whispered without letting go.

Jeremy slowly lifted his arms and wrapped them around

me, his emotions distilling into something tender and confused. "It's okay. The look on your face when you saw that
picture made it all worth it."

A throat cleared behind me. Jeremy and I pulled apart and
Anh set her bag down on the table, covering our maps. "Am
I interrupting something?" she asked. Jeremy glanced guiltily at the folder Anh carried under her arm. She set it on the
table. It was a summer internship application. To Syracuse.

We all took turns staring at one another through an
uncomfortably long silence.

"You're not interrupting anything," I told her. "I was just
leaving."

13

LATER THAT AFTERNOON, Posie Washington looked at her
watch and shrugged. A damp breeze turned the leaves upside
down, revealing their bright undersides and blowing debris
over the sidewalk. I tried not to stare at the remnants of yellow tape that tumbled along with them. Four days had passed
since Marcia's murder. That's what the police were calling it.
The police tape had been cut from the gym doors, and it was
no longer cordoned off as a crime scene, but the details of
the ongoing investigation were quiet.

We both stared at the storm clouds, neither of us mentioning the subject that hung over West River like a pall. "Twenty after four," she said apologetically, rubbing her coffee-milk arms.

"No worries, my next student is late anyway."

An older model minivan turned into the school parking lot and pulled to the curb. Posie's little brothers and sisters were wreaking havoc in the backseats and her Mom's tired face smiled through the window.

Posie was the oldest of five children, and would be the first to go to college. And at the rate she was going, she'd be the youngest student at West River ever to graduate. She'd skipped ahead two years, and was a gawky and slight fourteen-year-old junior. She didn't really need the tutoring, but Posie had spent every Tuesday afternoon with me since the beginning of the year. It couldn't have been easy for her to make friends, and as she sailed through her lessons each week, I suspected she needed the companionship more than the mentoring.

Posie's little brother made blowfish lips against the glass and I smiled, resisting the urge to make a funny face back. Must be nice, coming home to a house full of giggles.

Posie climbed into the passenger seat, reaching over to wrap her arms around her mother's neck. She waved with a sad smile, and watched me disappear in her rear-view mirror, as if maybe it was really me who needed the companionship after all.

The minivan rolled out of the lot, and thunder rumbled in the distance.

Obviously Reece wasn't going to show up, and despite needing the tutoring hours, I was relieved. I secured my backpack tighter over my shoulders, zipped my hoodie against the humid gusts, and began the long (and soon to be wet) walk home.

A motorcycle growled to life in the parking lot. It rounded the corner, grumbling louder, and my stomach knotted as it neared the curb. Reece hadn't been a no-show. He'd just been late.

He wasn't wearing a helmet and his eyes were obscured behind aviator sunglasses even though the sun wasn't out. I waited for him to shut off the engine.

He didn't.

Instead he revved the throttle, just enough to make a point, and idled at the curb.

I turned on my heel and headed for the doors. If he wanted to study, he could park his death machine and come inside. I pulled the handle but it didn't budge, already locked from the inside.

I turned back with a look that could kill and a fat raindrop plunked down on my cheek.

Reece shook with laughter I couldn't hear, and he dangled a helmet from his fingers, crooking one in a "come here" gesture that made my knees slightly numb.

Thunder crackled a few miles away, the sky a deepening purple.

"I'm not getting on that thing with you."

He glanced up at the sky, shrugged a shoulder, and kicked the bike into gear.

"Suit yourself," he said, fingers loosening on the clutch. A fork flashed low across the sky and the wind kicked dirt devils across the pavement. In a few minutes, I'd be a wet human lightning rod tromping down Route 1.

"Oh for god's sake." I snatched the helmet, wrestled it onto my head, and fumbled with the chin clasp, muttering profanities as fat drops splattered the pavement.

Reece reached out, grabbed me by the front of my shirt, and dragged me closer. The heat of the pipes bloomed against my ankles, creeping up to settle in my cheeks. He fastened the clip with practiced hands, and his finger accidentally brushed my chin.

"Have you ever been on a bike before?" He spoke loudly over the engine.

I shook my head.

"It's easy. Just relax. Hold on to my waist. Lean when I lean." Reece waited for me to ease onto the seat behind him. My fingers fumbled for a handhold, but there were no handles. He reached back and grabbed my arm through my sleeve, drawing my hand toward his waist where the hem of his T-shirt met his jeans. My wrist grazed the warm skin of his stomach, and I think I forgot how to breathe. His emotions were suffocating and heavy, regrets mingled with guilt so deep, I was sure I'd never get the taste off my tongue. "Try not to fall off."

He revved the engine and I held tight with both hands as the bike lurched forward.

I squealed, grasping for finger holds and finding them in the belt loops of his jeans. As we neared the first turn out of the parking lot, I dropped my face between his shoulders and squeezed my eyes shut. Icy drops pelted the back of my neck. We zoomed down streets, the bike leaning into the curves, wind whipping over me. The faster we went, the more Reece's bitterness faded. I pressed into his back until all I could smell was the leather tang of his jacket, and all I could taste was the sweet thrill of flying away.

• • •

When we finally stopped, I smelled French fries. My legs wobbled and my ears thrummed, but I was alive in the parking lot of a diner.

Reece stepped over the bike, unhooked my helmet, lifted it off my head, then laughed.

"What's so funny?" I smoothed back the static fly-aways.

"Nothing. You did great. It's just a little helmet-hair." His own hair fell around his face in effortless, orderly chaos.

"I thought we were going to study."

"We are."

Reece freed his backpack from the bungee cord behind the seat and I followed him into the restaurant. A waitress led us to a quiet, high-backed booth in the back.

I waited until he was engrossed in his menu before I set mine aside.

"What's the matter? You're not hungry?"

"No." My stomach growled and I wrapped my arms around it to stifle the sound.

"Order whatever you want." He pushed the menu back at me with a smirk. "Consider it payback for scaring the crap out of you."

"I wasn't scared," I lied.

The waitress returned with two sweating water glasses, and took our orders. As she cleared the menus, Reece took out his chemistry book and set it on the table between us.

I raised a brow. "You remembered your book?"

"Maybe I'm not as stupid as I look." The crease between his eyes was real and made me feel small. I pulled the book closer.

"Sorry, I'm just surprised."

"Why?"

"No reason." I bit my lip. This conversation was treading on dangerous water. Lieutenant Nicholson was already suspicious of me. If Reece figured out that I knew he was a narc—using me to get close enough to feed information to Nicholson—it wouldn't look good. But my curiosity was getting the better of me. "I don't know many juniors that haven't taken basic chemistry."

He turned his glass in lazy circles, slowly enough that I could study the tattoo on his arm. The leaves of some bristly plant climbed up his skin. "I already told you, I spent some time in the system. Missed a few classes."

The waitress arrived, balancing two large plates and a basket of fries. Reece slammed the book shut as she set the food on the table between us, his interest in studying overshadowed by a mountain of patties with melted cheese. I supposed in this way he was like every other normal high school guy. My stomach growled again and I scarfed down a handful of fries, scalding my tongue and making my eyes water. I'd had trouble eating since Friday night, and that hollow feeling had finally caught up with me.

Reece watched with a curious smile and I almost shrank under the table.

"Guess I was hungrier than I thought." I hoped I didn't have ketchup on my chin and I was desperate for a subject change, anything to take the focus off me. "So, what were you in the system for?"

His eyes drifted down to his own plate. "Nothing I'm proud of."

"Assault and battery" rippled in my memory. I wondered how many times he'd been locked up, and for how long? Looking at his face, it was hard to guess his age. The shadow of his beard was dark and full, broken by a faint white line where an old scar cut across his chin. He was at least as old I was. Maybe older. But basic chemistry was freshman year curriculum. Sophomore year for the really slow kids. He must have missed at least a year of school. He was hard, but there was nothing slow about him.

"Why didn't you go back to your old school?" I asked.

He chewed more slowly, thoughtfully. I got the distinct impression he was stalling, weighing his words. "Got kicked out of North Hampton. They wouldn't let me back in, so I got sent to West River."

"Sent by who? Your parents?"

Reece's brow furrowed. "Parole officer."

Nicholson had said Reece was involved in a shooting, but a shooting was bad. Very bad. And yet they let him free. Something didn't add up. "If they let you out of juvie, it couldn't have been that bad, could it?" I kept prodding. I don't know why I needed to hear him say it. That Anh was wrong and he hadn't done anything too terrible. After all, the charges were only assault. Assault wasn't the same as manslaughter. "I mean . . . it's not like you killed someone, right?"

Reece didn't answer.

The hamburger gelled in my throat. No, he was probably just trying to screw with me. The cops never would have sent a known killer to follow me around . . . unless maybe they knew as little about Reece Whelan as I did.

I shoved my plate aside, my appetite gone, and reached for his textbook. "Aren't we supposed to be studying or something?" I flipped the pages clumsily. The spine gaped where chapter one had been ripped out. I buried my head in my hands. "We're not going to get very far—"

"Relax." Reece pulled the missing pages from the pocket of his jacket and smoothed them across the table. The edges of the periodic table were curled and webbed with crinkle marks.

I stared at it. "Where'd you get that?"

"I found it on the floor in front of your locker."

"But I could have sworn I'd tossed it *inside* my locker."

"Must have slipped out," he said, answering the question on my face. He raised an eyebrow. "You're supposed to teach me how to balance equations," he offered, as if I were waiting for some direction. When I didn't answer, he pointed to the handwritten note on the first page.

I NEED YOU . . . PLEASE.—RW

"Please." He dipped low, that uneven smile back on his lips.

"Fine." I scowled at the mess on the table, remembering the pink slip that landed me in this situation to begin with. "You've got one hour, so pay attention. I'm only doing this once." I reached into my backpack for a spiral notebook, a calculator, and a pencil. The waitress came by and cleared away the plates, refilling our water glasses while I scrawled out a simple equation.

$$Al + O_2 \rightarrow Al_2 O_3$$

I turned the paper toward Reece. "This is a chemical equation. Aluminum and oxygen are the reactants. The product is aluminum oxide. Your job is to balance it."

Reece nodded and watched, like maybe he was actually interested.

"We need the same amount of aluminum and oxygen on both sides. So how would you do that?"

"Easy." He grabbed my pencil and drew a two in front of the symbol for aluminum. Then slapped the pencil down, triumphant.

"Okay, hotshot. So you've got two aluminums on the reactant side. Now how do you balance your oxygen?"

He frowned over the notebook. Then he scratched 1.5 in front of the oxygen, but held on to the pencil this time, a little less sure of himself.

I'd seen that coming. It was a common mistake. It was human nature to look for the quick fix, not necessarily the right one, and Reece was no exception. "That would work if you could have half of an atom, but you can't. Atoms are indivisible. You can't cut an atom to make it fit into an equation."

He stared at me for a long moment. "Why not? Isn't that what you're doing?"

I looked at the equation, confused. "What are you talking about?"

"Changing your name just to fit in?" Reece studied me

through the rain-slicked ends of his hair. "I mean, aren't you glad you're not a Jennifer or a Susan? Why do you hate your name so much?"

What the hell? He had no idea how it felt to grow up with a name like Nearly. "Isn't it obvious?"

"No." He kept digging, ignoring my don't-go-there glare. "What's the story? A name like that has to have a story."

I dropped the pencil and slouched back in the bench. "I was born premature, and I almost didn't make it. My mother didn't have a name picked out, but when the doctor told her they 'nearly' lost me . . ." I rolled my eyes over the air quotes. Why the hell was I telling him anyway? Just chemistry. That was the deal. I didn't have to tell him anything about me. "Stop changing the subject," I said, poking the equation with a finger. "Besides, we're not just talking about changing the *name* of an element. Even if it were possible, your solution would change the fundamental *nature* of the element. It would be like turning it into something else."

Reece looked from the paper to me, trying to look serious, but the gleam in his eye gave him away. "So you're saying an errant—and maybe slightly unbalanced—element can't fundamentally change?"

"That's what I'm saying."

He leaned over the table. "Even if it really, really wanted to?"

I drummed my fingers, patience wearing thin. "Can we please just focus on the equation?"

"Okay, fine." He slouched back against the booth. "So the elements are different. Big deal. Why don't we just put the elements together as they are, and mess with outcome later?"

I wasn't biting. This was all a big game to him. "You can't do that. The aluminum oxide molecule is what it is. You can't change the elements within a compound to force the fit."

He tossed the pencil down. "Are you always so rigid?"

"This is chemistry. The rules don't bend for good behavior."

"Well, it's a shitty rule." He glared at me across the table. "I'm just trying to get to know you."

"Getting to know me wasn't in our agreement." That was his agreement with Nicholson, and I'd be damned if I wanted any part of that.

"What if I want to change our agreement? What if I wanted to take you out sometime?"

"You're not my type."

"And that Jeremy guy I've seen you hanging out with? Is he your type?"

I stood up and reached for my backpack. Watching me was one thing. Involving Jeremy in this was where I drew the line. "We're done."

"Wait, I'm sorry." He reached across the table and grabbed my hand.

My mouth grew dry with thirst and a void opened like a cold pit inside me. Loneliness. He was contrite. Even curious. But mostly, he was alone.

I pulled my hand out from his and eased back into my seat.

After a moment of silent contemplation, he leaned in, elbows resting on the table. "Look. I know we're different. I know you probably don't want to have anything to do with a guy like me. Assuming I can't just erase the parts that don't balance . . . assuming I can't change anything . . . fundamentally—" His eyes locked on mine and held. "How am I supposed to make this work?"

I reached for the pencil. He held the other end a second too long, forcing me to meet his eyes before letting it go. How were we supposed to make this work?

Easy. He pretends to like me. I pretend to let him. He realizes I'm boring—and rigid. The police figure out who killed Marcia and my life goes back to normal. That's it.

I erased the 1.5 in front of the oxygen and the 2 in front of the aluminum, brushing away the eraser dust with my sleeve. "We can't get rid of the unwanted parts of the element—no matter how much we might want to . . " I let my eyes flick back to his. "But we can build up both sides until they balance each other. Try multiplying the entire equation by two."

I was surprised when he took the pencil and followed my directions. He scratched out a few numbers, laying down the pencil and turning the notebook in a slow circle toward me. "So . . . if a wayward element is willing to give twice as much of himself, he might have a shot?"

The booth suddenly felt a little too close. "A shot at what?"

"You know, this whole balance thing."

He looked serious. As serious as the person I'd felt hiding underneath when he touched me. I wondered how difficult it must be, to walk a tight rope between two lives and two identities. Unless those two people weren't actually different from each other at all. "I think it would depend on how bad the element really is."

Some nameless emotion crossed his face, making me regret letting go of his hand. He picked up a dull knife and balanced it between his fingers, letting it hover over the fragile silence between us. "I got busted in a drug raid."

"Dealing or buying?"

"Dealing."

"Did anyone get hurt?"

He winced as if the question caused him pain, but didn't answer.

"If you really want to change, why are you hanging out with Lonny Johnson?"

"It's complicated," he said almost to himself. "But it doesn't really matter, does it? You know, once a bad element, always a bad element." The words were empty. Hollow. As though he'd heard them so many times they'd lost their meaning.

I watched him fall into a dark corner of himself and I resisted the urge to touch him, not wanting to feel the depth of emotion I saw on his face. Expunging his past was as much his ticket out of a life he didn't want as my scholarship.

"That's bullshit." I turned the page, starting the lesson again. "Just because it's complicated, doesn't mean there isn't a solution."

14

MARCIA WASN'T COMING BACK. That much was certain.

But Thursday, we knew that Emily wasn't either.

Jeremy and I stepped through the front doors as VOTE FOR ME FOR PROM QUEEN posters of Emily were stuffed into oversized trash bags, discarded like yesterday's news. Posters of new faces immediately went up in their place. Their smiles seemed to say: "Nothing to see here, folks. Everything's back to normal." But I knew better.

Everything wasn't back to normal. The note carved into my table in physics class promised this was far from over. *Better luck next time.* Emily's disappearance under the bleachers was directly connected to Marcia's murder, even if the police *had* been careful not to reveal any information about the marking on Marcia's arm that matched the one on Emily.

"What do you think happened?" A gravelly voice spoke close behind me and I lurched. Reece leaned over my shoulder, close enough that his hair tickled my cheek.

"Don't *do* that!"

He just laughed.

"I'm heading to class." Jeremy swallowed hard, Adam's apple catching on his good-bye. "See you later, Leigh." He disappeared behind a row of lockers before I could say a word.

Reece sidled up beside me. "I don't think he likes me very much."

"You might consider softening your image a bit . . . if you care, that is." I picked up my pace and he walked beside me in silence.

"So . . ." he finally asked, "what do you think?"

I risked a sideways glance, seeing only his left side in profile. It was like looking at an entirely different person. From this side, I couldn't see the two barbells in his brow, the scar that leaned to the right of his chin, or even his tattoo. He looked smooth and deceptively charming. Even his smile seemed to hug the left side of his face. It was like all he had to do to soften his image was turn around. "I don't know . . . Maybe the facial piercings are a bit much."

He touched the studs in his brow. "That's not what I meant. What do you think about Emily and Marcia? A lot of rumors flying around. What do you think happened?"

I'd been listening for days for the quiet conversations between classes, and the whispering clusters in the halls. The school had been so preoccupied with Marcia's death, everyone had more or less forgotten about Emily until this morning when her Prom Court posters came down. Nothing in any of the wild rumors linked the two. Which meant the police had told Reece that the cases were connected. And now he was fishing. Waiting for me to slip up and say something that he could take back to Nicholson.

"I think their families have probably been through enough. And talking about it isn't going to change what happened to either of them."

I cut Reece a quick glance out of the corner of my eye, hoping I'd sounded vague and uninterested enough to be convincing. I wasn't paying attention and smacked headlong into Vince DiMorello. He stood over me with a broad, dimpled, shit-eating grin, like an opportunity had just fallen into his lap.

"Hey, Boswell." His smoothed his jersey, his green eyes twinkling. I lowered mine to the floor. Vince was hard to look at, perfect in ways that made the world seem that much more unfair. "The team's going out on Friday night. Thought we'd go see your mom."

Freshman year, Vince's older brother used a fake ID to get into Gentleman Jim's. He managed to take a few incriminating photos on his cell phone before Butch kicked him out. None of them showed my mother's face, but it wasn't her face they were interested in.

"Let it go, Vince." The jokes about my mother got old years ago, and I just didn't have the patience for it today.

"I've got a stack of Washingtons," he boomed, loud

enough to turn heads. A loose circle formed around us and necks craned for a closer look. Vince was the center of his own universe and as usual, all the popular stars revolved around him. He pulled a roll of cash from his pocket and peeled off a crisp twenty-dollar bill, waving it in the air high enough for everyone to see it. "Where do you think your mom will let me put *this*?"

A few people laughed, the circle tightening. Hot tears burned behind my eyes and I refused to blink.

"What about you, Boswell? What would you do for a dollar?" Vince grabbed his crotch and rocked his pelvis, showing off his best "O" face for the crowd.

If I walked away now, the crowd would part for me, even if they did laugh behind my back. But I refused to turn my back on Vince and let him have that satisfaction. Instead, I stepped toward him. "Let me by," I said as firmly as I could. If he laid one finger on me, I'd have him expelled. He didn't move and I took another step forward, into him. His hand twitched.

"Don't touch me," I warned.

His breath was hot on my face as he peeled another bill from the stack. "I hear your mom charges extra for that too."

I stiffened, ready to tell him to go to hell, but someone yanked me back. The laughter died and a hush fell as Reece stepped between us.

"Leave her alone," Reece said quietly.

TJ's hand rested on Vince's shoulder and he spoke into Vince's ear. "Come on, man. You don't want to do this."

Vince jerked his arm, dislodging TJ's grip and making him stumble. TJ righted himself and took a step back, and I knew he wouldn't try to hold Vince back again.

A whisper rolled through the crowd, the air thick and electric between them as Vince's eyes flicked from Reece to me, and then back again.

"No shit, Whelan. Is Nearly A Virgin your new girlfriend? I didn't realize charity work was a requirement of your parole." Low whistles rose over muffled laughter. Someone shoved me into Reece's back.

Reece balled his fists.

"You don't have to do this," I whispered to his shoulder, too short to speak into his ear. I tugged his sleeve. He didn't move.

"You owe Leigh an apology," he said in a tightly controlled voice.

"That's pretty fucking chivalrous, Whelan. You're a real gentleman. Does that mean you haven't done her yet?"

Reece's fist shot out and Vince's head snapped back. I was pitched forward as teachers shoved their way through the mass and grabbed Reece's and Vince's tangled bodies from behind. Faculty shouted orders, but the crowd had erupted into chaos.

"DiMorello! Whelan!" Principal Romero and two security

guards clawed their way into the nucleus. Romero's face was red, a map of forking purple veins. "In my office! Now!"

Faculty ordered everyone to return to class. Vince sneered at me with bloody teeth and dropped the twenties at my feet as security herded him through the crowd. I didn't pick them up. A shoulder bumped against me, and I looked up into Reece's expressionless face as security marched him past.

He didn't even look at me, his words cold enough to burn. "I hope you're worth it."

15

I TOOK MY SANDWICH and retreated under a willow on the quieter side of school. The branches dipped low enough to brush the dirt and concealed me in a veil of green shadows. But I knew Jeremy would find me. The same way he'd found me that Friday morning at the train station two years ago, when I ran away, determined to find my father after a particularly bad argument with Mona.

I hadn't called Jeremy. Never told him where I was going or why. I had just taken my ticket from the counter and turned to see Jeremy's face, standing in line behind me, a duffel over his shoulder and his wallet in his hand.

"What are you doing here?" I'd asked him.

He'd replied, "I'm going with you." And in that moment, everything changed. Finding my father—figuring out who David Boswell really was—didn't seem to matter as much as the fact that Jeremy was there. He'd stay with me, no matter what it cost him, even if his father beat him for it. And I couldn't leave him any more than I could take him with me.

As if stepping out of my memory, Jeremy parted the willow branches and eased down into the grass. I smiled, tears brimming over again, and I wiped them with my sleeve.

"Are you crying?" He wore a surprised expression. Like he'd never seen me cry before.

I blew my nose on a torn corner of my lunch sack. "It's been known to happen."

Jeremy sat close, our arms and legs not quite touching. "I heard about Vince."

"I guess everyone heard, huh?" I rested my chin on my knees. A warm breeze blew over the campus, rustling new leaves and scattering cut grass over the sidewalks.

"They say"—Jeremy leaned in close—"they, of course being the collective unconscious of the West River populous—that you beat the crap out of him. That you gave him a bloody lip and wiped the floor with his ass."

I gave him a playful shove. "Vince did get a bloody lip, but it wasn't from me. He mouthed off to Reece Whelan. Reece got one good shot in." I wouldn't begrudge myself a little smug satisfaction, even if Reece's parting words had cut deeper than anything Vince said about my mother.

"I know. It's all over school, how Prince Pierced-A-Lot came to your rescue." Jeremy put his hand to his head and went limp against my shoulder, a mock swoon. "How'd it feel to be the damsel in distress?"

"Shut up." I knocked his knee with my own. "What else did you hear?"

"Just that Vince got off with a warning. He didn't throw a punch and administration doesn't want to screw up his spotless athletic record . . ."

I threw my bag lunch into the dirt. In the school's eyes, as long as Vince DiMorello scored goals, he could do no wrong. No one cared that he was showing naked pictures of my mother or picking fights in the hall. They refused to see him as a criminal, but I knew better. Vince DiMorello was as evil as his twisted bloody smile.

"Whelan got a week of suspension and a one-strike-you're-out warning."

I closed my eyes and leaned my head against the bark, letting that bombshell sink in. A week of suspension. I should have been happy, thrilled even, to have Reece off my back for an entire week. But I couldn't shake off a sense of guilt.

We sprung him . . . for good behavior . . . cut him a deal . . . stays in school and keeps his nose clean . . .

I felt sick. If Reece had been expelled, he'd end up back in jail. And—underlying motives or not—he'd fought Vince because of me.

I hope you're worth it.

Jeremy's elbow knocked mine, drawing my attention as he drew up his sleeve. He flexed a wiry bicep.

"You know, if *I* had been there, *I* would have taken care of Vince for you."

I arched a weary eye. If Jeremy had been there, we'd have suffered the verbal smack-down together. Vince was an equal-opportunity destroyer.

"Seriously," he insisted, holstering his pathetic guns. "I'd have challenged him to a spelling bee. Total jock obliteration. I'd have been ruthless in defense of your honor." He pressed a fist over his heart and tipped his head to mine.

A laugh bubbled over the lump in my throat. I leaned on him, resting my head between his chin and shoulder. He felt warm and familiar, and surprisingly serene. He tasted like chamomile and honey. I soaked up his feelings for me, letting them radiate through me like the sun.

"You seem . . . better than you did last week." It was easier to say, when neither of was looking right at the other. I felt him shrug. Felt the deep breath he took before speaking.

"Yeah, about that," he exhaled. "I just wasn't myself."

"Don't apologize. I never should have called you a shitty reporter—"

"Oh, so now I'm a 'shitty' reporter?" My head bobbed on his shoulder.

"You know that's not what I meant." I tipped my chin up to make sure he was laughing. He was. He gave me a peck on the forehead, then looked away, before either of us could second-guess his reasons.

At least Jeremy was honest with himself. He never tried to be anyone he wasn't, accepting each of us for who we were, flaws and all. He was a real friend, not a paid one. I knew he wouldn't mind when I asked him to skip lunch to drive me home so I could pretend to be sick for the rest of the day.

I knew he'd share half of his sandwich with me on the way.

And we both knew I wouldn't have anything to give in return.

16

THAT NIGHT, I PULLED BACK THE SHEET, a makeshift curtain tacked to the paneling over my window, while I balanced the phone under my chin. I was only half listening to Anh while she bitched about her brother. ". . . so he refused to sign the permission slip. He says it's a waste of time to spend an entire school day at an amusement park. Instead, he's making me go on a bunch of college tours out of town all weekend. I'm so pissed!"

Mona disappeared beyond the circle of the neighbor's security lights. They flickered on and off in succession, the dark snapping at her heels as she stepped in and out of each one, and approached the traffic light at the end of the street.

From the point where she disappeared, a single headlight turned, blinding me as it drew closer.

"I think he just has something against Jeremy . . ."

Reece. He cruised under the same security light Mona had just tripped. My stomach twisted in a tight knot. Was he here to blame me, to tell me it was my fault he got suspended? Or was he here to pick up our conversation where we left off, before his fight with Vince, when he'd asked me what I'd really thought had happened to Emily and Marcia?

"Leigh, are you even listening?"

I dropped the sheet and leaned against the wall. "Sorry, Anh. I'll call you back. I have to go." I disconnected, heart speeding up as I listened for Reece's bike to slow. But he didn't stop at my trailer. His bike rumbled past and I counted beats until he killed the engine at the dead end of the street.

What the hell was Reece Whelan doing? No one parked at the playground at the end of Sunny View Drive after dark, unless they had business there. And there were only two kinds of business in Sunny View. My mind spun with a sick curiosity. I'd watched men pick up rent-a-girls on the corner by the playground all my life. I was numb to it. But something inside me clenched when I pictured Reece with them.

Or when I considered that the alternative might actually be worse.

What if he wasn't here for the girls? He said he'd been sent to juvie because he'd been busted in a drug raid. How far could he fall if he thought he'd lost everything?

Make sure he stays in line.

Shit.

I pushed off the wall and threw open my bedroom door. The stale reek of Mona's cigarettes assaulted me in the hall. I grabbed the metal bat and slid back the dead bolt, taking a last deep breath.

I kept to the shadows, careful to avoid the light sensors and trailers with barking dogs, and looped around the block, emerging behind the broken-down playground. Rancid trash gagged me as I crouched low behind a Dumpster and peered around it.

Reece stood near the metal frame of an old swing set. Three car doors slammed in quick succession. The interior lights of Lonny's Lexus never came on, but the bleached spikes in his hair and white-blond goatee glowed under the dim light of a full moon when he stepped out. He was flanked by two figures, their faces concealed under hoodies.

Hair rose on my forearms. If this was just business as usual, why didn't they meet at Lonny's trailer, like he had with Oleksa? Why meet here, in the dark, with two of his thugs?

"You're late," Lonny growled.

"I'm here." Reece shrugged, unconcerned. "Are we going to do this or not?"

Lonny nodded and the hooded figures stepped forward. Reece raised his arms, locking his fingers behind his head. He seemed relaxed, comfortable even, like he'd done it a million times before. Until one of them—the tall one wearing bulky high-tops with red laces—pushed back his hood and Reece stiffened.

Oleksa.

He smiled a rare, cold smile at Reece. Whispered something in his ear. Reece answered with a barely perceptible shake of his head. Oleksa frisked him down both legs, hands running over and inside his leather jacket, quick and sure as they'd been with the Rubik's cube. Satisfied, he lifted Reece's T-shirt, offering Lonny a view of his bare chest.

Shadows outlined the muscles of Reece's abdomen. A nipple ring glinted from his right pectoral and a pendant hung to his sternum, hovering over a dark line that started at his navel and dipped into the top of his jeans.

Lonny nodded. Oleksa dropped the shirt and stepped back. Reece lowered his hands slowly, eyes never leaving Oleksa's face.

"Excuse the formalities." Lonny smoothed his goatee thoughtfully.

Reece pulled his shirt in place and rested his hands at his sides. "We're cool."

"I believe we've already agreed on the terms?"

Reece nodded, glancing cautiously at Oleksa before reaching into his pocket and withdrawing a small envelope. Oleksa grabbed it and thumbed through the contents. He signaled to Lonny with a jerk of his chin, then stuffed a bag into Reece's pocket.

"It's been a pleasure doing business." Lonny turned, goons at his heels. "Let's do it again soon."

"Actually . . ." Reece's voice was unwavering. "I was hoping you could help me out with one more thing."

Lonny stopped, but didn't turn. His tattooed fingers laced around the handle of his car. "And what might that be?"

"I'm looking for a little *Special K.*"

Tension crackled in Lonny's pause. When he spoke, his voice was low, deadly. "You're a good-looking guy, Whelan. All the girls are talking about you. Probably drop their panties just looking at you. I have a very hard time believing you need any . . . social lubricant."

Reece shifted, darting glances at Oleksa. Lonny's suspicion was almost tangible. Something between them had turned. Lonny tipped his head, studying him. "It's an odd request from someone like you." He shot Oleksa a look. "And it makes me a little uncomfortable."

The goons lunged. I clung to the Dumpster as the stocky one bent Reece's arms behind his back. Oleksa grabbed the bag from Reece's pocket and tossed it to Lonny.

"Just because you're not wearing a wire doesn't mean I trust you." Lonny stepped up in Reece's face. "See, the cops have been sniffing around ever since Sleeping Beauty fell in the pool. They're asking a lot of questions. But you wouldn't know anything about that, would you?"

A chill crept through me. Crouched low, I stepped back and looked for a way out through the shadows where I could escape unseen. A twig snapped under my foot and I froze, but no one heard.

Lonny paced, tossing and catching his keys. "I've got friends in the system, Whelan. I heard about you. I know who you are. What you did." The keys jangled. Up and down. "What I can't figure out is how you walked." Lonny stopped and ran a palm over his gelled spikes, back and forth. "Only two ways to walk from the shit on your record, kid. You either blow the right parole officer . . . or you narc."

Reece's cover was about to be blown.

Lonny turned to Reece. "So which is it?"

Reece's expression was hard, but the cool steadiness was gone from his voice. "Just time out for good behavior, man."

Lonny pointed two fingers at Reece's chest. "Answer the question."

"I'm not a narc." Reece struggled to free his arms, his chest rising and falling faster.

"I'm glad to hear that." Lonny launched a fist into Reece's

gut. I gripped the bat, squeezing my eyes shut as Reece dropped to his knees.

"It doesn't change anything. I don't trust you, and it wouldn't matter even if you were a narc. Cops got nothing on me. I've learned a few things. My hands are clean . . ." Lonny wiped his knuckles and scrutinized his nails. ". . . Always clean. See, I have a business to run. I don't like when things get messy." A smile crept over his face. I wasn't sure which was more frightening, watching Lonny inflict violence, or the promise of something worse in that smile. "I'll need time to check your . . . credentials . . . before we try this again."

Reece rolled onto his side, grunting and struggling for breath. Lonny motioned to Oleksa and I panicked when they hefted Reece to his knees. I wanted to run. Lock myself in my metal box and pretend this wasn't happening. But I couldn't make myself leave.

Oleksa's fist smashed into Reece's face. His head rocked back, blood flowing in a thick, dark stream. Lonny watched, tossing and catching his keys. I fisted the bat, hiding in the shadows like a coward, waiting for the police to come and save Reece—or arrest him. But they weren't coming. He wasn't wearing a wire. They had no way of knowing he was in trouble.

Oleksa hit him again.

I hope you're worth it.

I grabbed the bat, creeping through the shadows in a wide

arc and coming behind them near Lonny's car. I pressed one hand on the hood and hauled myself up, planting my feet wide, steeling myself for the stupid, crazy thing I was about to do.

I raised the bat over my head.

"Let him go!" I shouted. "Or I'll destroy your fucking car!" Loose hair whipped around my face. I looked into their eyes, one by one, then held Lonny's stare. I wouldn't let go.

Reece's chin rested on his chest, bleeding into his shirt. Oleksa looked back and forth between me and Lonny, hands twitching at his side. Lonny shook his head with a bemused disbelief.

"My, my." His voice was silky sweet and it terrified me as much as his smile. "Isn't this something?"

He stepped toward me and every cell in my body screamed at me to run. Reece raised his head slowly, his eyes half closed and unfocused. His gaze sharpened on the hood of Lonny's car. On me. His face paled, as if he were looking at a ghost. He opened his mouth to speak and struggled to one knee, but Oleksa kicked him in the gut, doubling him over.

"I said let him go!" I raised the bat higher, aimed at the windshield.

Lonny chuckled, but nobody moved. He was stalling. Calling my bluff. I tested the weight of the bat, letting it roll in my palms. Lonny raised an eyebrow.

"I heard about your run-in with DiMorello today. Heard

Whelan came to your rescue. Is he your man now? Or are you just here to return the favor?"

I calculated my words carefully. Lonny was already suspicious of Reece. The wrong answer could get him killed.

"What I do with Reece is none of your business."

"Maybe it should be, Boswell. Your boyfriend is looking for some pretty nasty little pills. Nasty little pills that make sweet girls like you do really nasty things." Lonny shrugged. "But what do I care? Maybe you already do."

His eyes skimmed over me, lingering on my breasts and hips in a way that made me feel sick inside. He ran his tongue over his teeth and toyed with the barbell above his chin, pushing and pulling it through the hole in his lip while he considered me.

"You keep your boyfriend on the right side of my street. I'm not sure I like him." Lonny gestured to his goons. The stocky one tossed Reece's limp body to the ground.

"You, however . . ." Lonny shook his finger at me. ". . . I am definitely beginning to like. Now get your skinny ass off my car. Next time you pull a stunt like this, I'll break your pretty legs."

I had no doubt he'd make good on the threat. Bat in hand, I jumped down the side of the car farther from him and backed away.

"You have your girlfriend to thank for this," Lonny said, tossing a clear bag of pills between Reece's knees. Reece swayed, slick with blood and sweat, red drops spattering against the plastic.

Lonny's gaze was heavy on me as he angled into his car. "I won't forget this, Boswell."

The Lexus ghosted out of Sunny View. I tossed the bat and dropped to the ground beside Reece, afraid to touch him. He cradled his ribs, each breath harsh and shallow.

"What the hell were you thinking?" He spit blood in the dirt, then snatched up the bag and jammed it in his pocket. "He could have killed you!"

"What the hell was *I* thinking? What the hell were *you* thinking? Look at you!"

An angry gash split his lip and dripped off the end of his chin, and blood trickled from his left eyebrow. He was caked in dirt and blood, but he'd been lucky. Oleksa had been right-handed, sparing Reece's piercings. "We need to get you to a hospital. Can you stand?"

"No! I can't go to a hospital. They'll call the cops." His face contorted in pain as he tried to straighten himself. "I'm fine. Just help me up."

Reece wrapped his left arm around his ribs. I grabbed his right, and together we eased him to his feet. Groaning, he maneuvered himself out of his jacket and peeled his T-shirt over his head. Angry black bruises were blooming over his ribs.

I watched, helpless, as he balled up the shirt, then pressed it to his head to staunch the bleeding. With labored breaths, he worked his arms back into his jacket and eased himself onto the bike.

"Come on." The order rasped in his throat as he released the kickstand.

He could go to hell. I kicked through the tall grass, snatching my bat off the ground. "I'm going home."

"Leigh, wait!" The kickstand snapped back into place and I heard his boots behind me.

I kept walking.

"Leigh! I'm sorry." His apology echoed off the trailers. "You can't go home. You shouldn't be there alone tonight. It's not safe."

I swung around. His blood was streaked across my hoodie and my hands. "I can take care of myself!"

He looked at me—really looked at me—for the first time. And I wanted him to. I wanted him to understand what I had been ready to sacrifice, though I wasn't sure why.

He blinked away blood and wiped his eyes with his balled-up shirt. "You didn't have to get involved. Haven't you ever heard of a cell phone?"

"I don't have one!"

"Well, you should. What if something happened to you? You'd be a lot safer carrying a cell phone . . ." He gestured to the bat I still gripped.

My vision blurred with angry tears. "Next time I won't

bother!" The adrenaline slipped away, leaving me raw and cold all over.

He let out a long, tired breath. "I'm sorry I yelled at you. I should have said thank you. Now will you please put down the bat and come with me?" He held a hand out, waiting.

I let the bat fall to the ground and looked down at my fingers. At the blood under my nails. My hands were shaking, and I stared at them, half expecting them to crumble. Reece grabbed the front of my hoodie and pulled me to him.

"I need . . ." He looked in my eyes with a raw and tangled expression. Then he pulled away and it was gone. He cleared his throat. "I need you to hold this while I drive." He pressed the crumpled bloody T-shirt into my palm.

I looked toward home, down the rows of metal boxes with dead bolts and security lights that never felt like enough. I didn't want to be alone.

I straddled the bike, legs unsteady. He reached behind and took my sleeve, lifting my hand to his wound. I wrapped the other around his chest, tucking my hands inside my sleeves to keep from touching the bare, hot skin under his jacket.

"Where are we going?" I asked.

"To see a friend. And then I'll take you home."

17

REECE KNOCKED ON THE DOOR of a rattrap row house. I drew
my hoodie tighter around me. The sounds of this neighborhood weren't too different from my own; thumping sub-
woofers of an old beater with its windows down, neighbors
yelling and glass breaking next door, dogs barking. Familiar
sounds aren't always comforting.

Reece banged again, harder this time. Someone rustled
behind the peephole.

"Gena, it's Reece. I brought a friend." The slide chain and
dead bolts were already in motion.

Gena stood in the doorway and gave Reece a head-to-toe
scan, her face blank. Then she stepped aside to let us in. The
narrow room was sparsely furnished with a worn-out sofa
and two overturned milk crates for end tables. A small TV
in the corner cast moving shadows against the scuffed walls,
and pizza boxes littered the kitchen.

Gena leaned back against the locked door, watching me.
I guessed she was at least eighteen, maybe older, with cinna-
mon skin and chocolate-almond eyes. Crimped sections of
her hair fell below her shoulders, chunked with multi-toned
highlights. She was flashy. Too much makeup. Too much

perfume. Too few clothes. Before a word passed between us, I knew I wouldn't like her. She inclined her head in my direction.

"Nobody," Reece muttered, dismissing me with a wave of his hand. "Just someone from school."

My cheeks burned. Screw him. I extended a bloody hand to Gena. "I'm the nobody that just saved his ass. Nice to meet you."

Gena looked at my hand and raised an eyebrow at Reece.

"Gena Delgado. Leigh Boswell," he announced through gritted teeth. "Leigh is a friend from West River."

I waited, awkward, while a meaningful glance passed between them. A silent conversation I wasn't privy to.

She turned and swayed into the kitchen with a fluid motion that drew my attention and Reece's, and I hated her even more for her rear view. Her trendy clothes were the barely there kind, breasts pressed into sexy curves that peeked suggestively out of her halter top, jeans hugging low around her hips, revealing curvy pelvic bones and a gold hoop in her midriff.

"You look like hell," she said. "Who put you in a meat grinder?"

"One of Lonny Johnson's lackeys." Reece followed her, dabbing blood from his cheek.

"You're lucky he kicked your ass pretty good then." Steam billowed around her as hot water spurted from the tap. "It'll save Nicholson the trouble. He's gonna freak out when he sees you."

I tensed. How did Gena know Nicholson? Unless she was a

narc, like Reece. I kept my face impassive. As far as they were concerned, the name held no significance for me.

"Who's Nicholson?"

"He's a cop," she said smugly, bending to rummage through a cabinet. "Reece isn't supposed to be fighting."

"Nicholson isn't going to know."

"Oh yeah? Says who?"

"Says the guy who just made dog food out of my face. Maybe you know him?" Reece spoke up over the rustle of pots and pans. "Some asshole named Petrenko."

The clanking pans fell silent.

For a moment, nobody spoke.

Gena shut the cabinet and stood with her back to us. "What happened?"

"Lonny got spooked."

She set the bowl in the sink and turned. "How?"

"No idea. Everything was going down fine. Then I asked him for some K and he just . . . I don't know . . . freaked out. Accused me of being a narc." Another meaningful pause. A brief lock of their eyes. Reece nodded. "I think we're cool, though."

"What changed his mind?"

"Not sure, exactly." His meaningful glance was directed at me this time.

Gena carried a bowl of hot water, some clean towels, and a first aid kit to the living room. She pulled a milk crate to the couch and pushed Reece into the sofa, then scooted between his legs. I looked the other way while she helped him out of his jacket and sponged down the worst of his wounds. He winced and cursed, and she swatted him playfully on the shoulder. My stomach clenched each time she touched him or leaned in to examine the cuts on his face.

Reece told her I was *nothing* and it stung more than it should. I told myself I didn't want to know if she was actually *someone* to him.

He looked at me out of his good eye and touched my leg. I jumped.

"You okay?" he whispered. I nodded, inching away from him. I was edgy and drained. I didn't want to feel anymore. He withdrew his hand, wiping both on his jeans, hiding the blood and dirt that wouldn't wipe away inside clenched fists.

Gena evaluated her handiwork. "Keep the butterfly clean and dry. I don't think you'll need stitches. You've got a few bruised ribs, so don't do anything crazy for the next few days." She tossed him a clean shirt. "You left this in my car last weekend. I washed it for you." She grinned, another silent message passing between them. I needed some air.

"I'll wait for you outside." I was already halfway to the door. I didn't want to be there when he kissed her good night.

His hand beat mine to the doorknob. "That's not necessary," he said sharply. "Good night, Gena," he grumbled. "And thanks a lot."

"Ten cuidado, mi hermano."

I didn't speak Spanish, but she winked and smiled wryly. He gave her an admonishing look as he bent down to peck her cheek, then he pulled the door shut behind us.

• • •

"Drop me off here." The bike rumbled through Sunny View, stopping a block from my trailer. Mona's shift was eight to four. She wouldn't be home for at least an hour, but I didn't need the neighbors ratting me out. Reece killed the engine and waited for me to get free of the helmet. My hair was wild with snarls and I smoothed it down with filthy hands, cringing as I imagined what I must look like to him. He was staring at me.

"What were you doing in that park tonight?"

I thrust the helmet at him. "Aside from rescuing you?"

He caught it against his sore ribs and clenched his teeth. Then fisted it like he wanted to throw it. "That's not what I meant."

"I could ask you the same question."

He lowered his voice. "You know exactly what I was doing."

"Yeah. I saw the whole thing. And it scared the hell out of me!"

"I just need to know . . . were you there to meet Lonny?" He looked hard into my eyes, waiting for my answer as though a life hung in the balance. Why did I feel like that life was mine?

"I was looking for you." I blushed, grateful for the darkness. "I saw your bike. Thought you might be here . . . you know . . . picking someone up . . ."

"Picking someone up?" It sounded ridiculous hearing him say it out loud. Seeing the stupefied expression on his face. "And you thought it would be okay to follow me?"

I winced. "I don't know what I thought. I guess I thought you might need . . . help . . . or something."

"That was stupid," he muttered.

"You're right. It was stupid. It was stupid to care if you're getting yourself killed. Stupid to think you might need my help."

He hung his head, stared at the helmet clenched to his chest, as if he wanted to say something, but didn't. I had that crumbling feeling again and for a minute I wished it was me he was holding.

"Whatever." I ran home, sprinted up the stoop.

The baseball bat was propped against my front door.

18

We all fall down. The tower will point the way.
It's 68 ft. higher than three times a side of its square base.
If the sum of these two is 1,380, at day's end you'll know
where to find me.

I was on the chartered bus on the way to our class trip to Kings Dominion. I leaned against the bathroom sink for balance while the narrow walls rocked and rolled. The enclosed space smelled like a sewer, and the fumes weren't helping my motion sickness. I copied the numbers and tested a few equations on my palm.

$$\text{Height} = (3x + 68)$$
$$(3x + 68) + x = (4x + 68)$$
$$(4x + 68) = 1380$$
$$x = 328$$
$$\text{Height of tower} = 1052 \text{ ft.}$$

Something didn't add up. These numbers were as meaningless as the one on Marcia's arm. I was tired—exhausted after the late night with Reece and three hours of fitful sleep—but there was no possible way I'd screwed up the calculation this badly. I checked the equations. Cross-checked them against the numbers in the ad.

The math was infallible, but the solution was impossible. A tower more than one thousand feet high didn't exist in the state of Virginia, or anywhere in Washington, DC, for that matter. The closest tower over a thousand feet was in fucking France.

I crumpled the page. Let it go, I'd told myself. The answer to this whole thing was so simple. Just leave the newspaper in the bathroom and walk away.

I smoothed it flat. Ran the numbers again.

Someone banged and jiggled the door handle. I tore out the crinkled ad and shoved it in my back pocket, folding away the rest of the *Missed Connections* for later.

Back in the seat next to Jeremy, I sniffed my sleeve, hoping I didn't smell like a hot bus bathroom.

"You feeling okay?" he asked.

"Just a little queasy." It wasn't a lie.

"What's all over your hand?" Jeremy scrunched up his face and reached for me. I pulled away.

"It's just a test problem I'm working on."

"I wasn't talking about the numbers."

He was talking about the other ink—the newsprint smudges all over my fingers.

"Were you reading the personals in there?" His voice rose in disbelief.

"No," I said defensively.

"Seriously? You were looking for him in a bus bathroom?" He looked disgusted. "That's completely unhealthy."

"If it'll make you feel better, I'll wash my hands when we get there," I said, trying for levity.

Jeremy shook his head. "It's been five years, Leigh. Are you ever going to just let it go?"

"I can't. What if he comes back?"

"He's not coming back, and you're wasting your life waiting for him. The guy's not worth it." He sounded like Mona. If I closed my eyes and touched him, he'd probably taste just like her. I scooted closer to the window and crossed my arms over my hands.

"Just because your dad's an asshole, doesn't mean everyone else's is too."

"No, *yours* is a deadbeat. He *left* you."

"I'm sure he had his reasons."

"Yeah, like two hundred forty-seven thousand of them," he muttered.

My head snapped up. "What did you say?"

Jeremy turned away. "Forget I said anything."

The number was too specific, his tone had been too certain. I reached for his arm, certain there was more he wasn't saying. When I touched him, his alarm was a hot spark against the tip of my tongue and he tried to pull away. His emotions were all over the place, fleeting scents I couldn't quite catch. He was hiding something.

"What aren't you telling me, Jeremy?"

The sadness in his eyes wasn't his. It was for me. I felt him make a decision. Tasted it, a crisp bite of resignation.

"You know how you asked me to set up those search engine alerts? I created an alert for each of the names on those driver's licenses you told me about. Every few weeks, an alert will pop up, but they've always been pretty random. Until the last three months, when I started to see some patterns." Jeremy pulled his arm from mine to reach in his backpack. He set his iPad in his lap and swiped the screen a few times, pulling up a page of search alert results. He scrolled through them, pointing out names that matched the ones on my father's fake IDs. "But that's not all. Check out the posts the names were found in."

I read the headlines. Each of the men had been announced a winner in a high-stakes professional poker tournament. One in Vegas. One in New Jersey. And one in Los Angeles. Winnings totaling two hundred forty-seven thousand dollars. "This can't be right," I said, even though something in my gut told me it was. "My father's a professional gambler?"

"I'm sorry, I never meant to tell you," Jeremy said quietly, reaching for my hand.

I tucked it under my arm before he could take it, needing time alone in my own heart to process what I'd learned. I pressed my forehead to the glass as the peaks of the roller coasters came into view and the bus became charged with a thrill-ride buzz.

"Are you mad at me?" he asked.

I wanted to be. He'd kept things from me. Important things. But I'd be a hypocrite to be angry with him. Of course Jeremy resented my father. Jeremy'd stolen from his dad to cover our rent. He bought me breakfast and drove me to school. And in five years, I'd never missed a class trip— because Jeremy always paid for my ticket, never asking anything in return.

He was still looking at the empty place where my hands had been. The expression on his face made my chest ache a little. I pulled on my hood and folded back the armrest so I could curl up against his shoulder. He rested his cheek on my head.

"Thanks for today," I said quietly.

His sad smile said my gratitude was almost but not quite enough.

19

TEDDY'S LAUGHTER WAS CONTAGIOUS. He'd nagged me about this "date" on the carousel all semester, and it had loomed like an obligation for the past three months. Just one more expectation to fulfill.

But it ended up being strangely freeing. Everything—the creepy ads, the scholarship, Jeremy's moods, what I'd learned about my dad, Reece's fight . . . even Marcia—all just slipped away as I gripped Teddy's hand, content to be with someone who didn't expect anything more from me than this moment.

I almost didn't notice Jeremy's reflection in the mirrored hub. Almost didn't see Reece leaning against the metal rails. The weight of their combined stares seemed to drag the ride to a stop.

Teddy swung my hand back and forth as he escorted me down the platform. Jeremy stepped forward to meet us.

"I can take it from here, champ." He looked at our joined hands and gave Teddy a wan smile.

Part of me wanted to drag Teddy back on the carousel for another round, but the look on Jeremy's face told me he wasn't in the mood to wait.

"Thanks for the date, Teddy." My face hurt from laughing and I squeezed his hand one last time. He darted in and kissed my cheek, blushing hot against it.

"I had a very nice time with you, Leigh." Teddy spoke with formal precision, as though he'd practiced each word. He let go of my hand, taking his joyfulness with him as he skipped off. His voice rose high over the crowd where his friends waited. "I had a date! With a girl! I had a date!"

I smoothed down my sticky grin, but it popped back in place. I watched him disappear into the crowds, part of me already missing him.

Jeremy glowered and I put my hands in my pockets, returning my attention to his impatient face.

"What's eating you?"

"I don't get it," he said sourly. "You'll hold hands with someone like Teddy . . . let him kiss you. . . ."

"What's that supposed to mean?"

The carousel's organ started again. Jeremy scowled, refusing to say more. Which was probably smart. I didn't like his implication that there was anything wrong with Teddy. Or the assumption he had any right to decide who I should be kissing.

"Am I interrupting something?" Reece peeled off his sunglasses and assumed a relaxed pose by my side. Jeremy's face was a flipbook of emotion. He took in Reece's battered eye and swollen lip, his expression morphing from anger to confusion, then fear.

"No," I said, my eyes still drilling a hole through Jeremy. "You're not interrupting anything."

"Then he won't mind if I borrow you for a while." Reece turned up his palm in invitation.

I looked down at Reece's hand and a thrill raced through me, but I couldn't do it. I left it hanging in the air.

"What are you doing here?" Jeremy asked him, emboldened by my hesitation. "I thought you were suspended."

Reece shrugged. "It's a public park. I bought a ticket."

"Yeah, so did I! For Nearly!"

I stepped back, jaw hanging open as if Jeremy had slapped me. He'd crossed a line. I was no rent-a-girl.

Without a word, I slipped my sleeve over my fingers and reached for Reece's hand.

• • •

Reece guided me through the sweet fried funnel cake smells, past roller coasters and bumper cars, until we were climbing to a shady wooden platform. I stopped midway, holding up the line for the log flumes.

"What are we doing here?"

"What's it look like we're doing?" He squinted at me through his puffy purple eye, and the butterfly bandage crimped the skin.

"I'm sorry." I gestured to his broken face. "Does it hurt?"

"I'm fine. Believe me, I've been through worse." He tried to smile, but the split in his lip was tight and swollen, threatening to crack. "But if you want to make me feel better . . ." He arched an eyebrow toward the ride. People barked behind us to keep the line moving.

"Okay! Just quit bleeding already!"

Reece laughed, and I followed him up the ramp to the boarding platform. He took the backseat of a narrow boat, and I dropped a cautious foot into the front, but the attendant stopped me. "Oh, no, sweetheart. Two to a seat." She ushered the next couple into the front and nudged me. There was only one seat left, and it was in Reece's lap.

"What are you waiting for?" he teased.

My stomach did that flip thing. The attendant nudged me again and I fumbled my way into the boat. Reece grabbed the back of my sweatshirt and pulled me down between his legs.

My face was on fire as the boat rocked away from the platform and sluiced down the flume. I leaned forward, gripping the metal rails. After a few easy turns, the boat lurched onto the first incline and the gears ground us upward with a slow steady *click, click, click*. Gravity pulled me back against his chest. It was hard and soft at the same time, and even as I clenched my stomach muscles, I felt myself sink into him as the boat climbed higher. My head rested in the hollow of his shoulder, his neck too close to my temple. I concentrated on the water, reminded myself of the steep drop at the end of the ride, but all I could feel was the rise and fall of his breathing, how steady it was compared to mine.

"Are you scared?" He breathed in my ear, but I felt it everywhere.

I was petrified. "Maybe."

The flume creaked, suspended for a heartbeat before it fell, and my stomach dropped. I screamed and pressed into him.

We sloshed, giggling and dripping wet through a few mellow turns and eased back to the platform. My knees wobbled when I stood up.

Reece shook out his hair as we descended the wooden ramp, spraying me with droplets that rolled down my glasses. When I looked up, Reece was looking at me again, the way he had in the booth at the diner.

His smile fell away and he stepped in close, closer. Too close until I couldn't breathe. He lifted a hand to my face.

"Don't," I whispered.

"I didn't mean to . . ." He pressed his lips shut, then tried again. "I wasn't going to . . . your face is . . . wet. . . ." He spoke softly and looked at me through one deeply sad eye.

I didn't move. Didn't turn away. Didn't stop him when his hand came up slowly this time. Would it be so bad to let him touch me, right now, when I knew he was thinking about

me? To know what he really wanted? To know if any of this
was real?

His hand cupped my face, thumb sliding between my glasses
and my cheek, smoothing droplets of water over my skin.
Heat radiated under his fingers, like sunlight. Brushed over
my sunburned skin like a warm wind. I closed my eyes and
inhaled summer, heard laughter over the screams and shouts
from the rides.

Reece's thumb pulled away first. I grabbed on to his wrist,
wanting to hold on to the unexpected and beautiful piece of
him I'd just tasted. But it was gone. An icy sensation trailed
down my spine, hair prickling over the back of my neck. I
opened my eyes, confused, and found Reece staring angrily
over my shoulder.

His rage slid into my veins. I let go of him and turned to
see Oleksa and Lonny sitting on a park bench, watching us.
Lonny reclined with one arm swung casually over the seat-
back. Oleksa perched next to him, elbows propped on his
knees. He massaged his bruised knuckles, his eyes locked on
Reece's. A silent conversation passed between the three of
them. Were they really so different? Reece and Lonny and
Oleksa?

"Wait for me," Reece growled. "I have to take care of
something." He stalked to the bench, hands ready at his sides.

There I stood, waiting. While the people and the colors
and the sky swirled around me until I all I could picture was

a tiny black-and-white portrait of Sunny View. Reece was in the middle of it, making me forget what he was, sucking me in, telling me to wait.

I'd let him touch me. Had broken all my own rules.

A bag exchanged hands. Then a wad of dirty green bills.

I ran. I flew into the crowd, parting it with my shoulders until it swallowed me.

"Nearly!" Reece called after me.

But I was gone.

• • •

The sun was low in the sky when I trudged to the park entrance, where we were counted off, waiting to be herded to the buses. Jeremy leaned against the iron filigree, staring into the fountains, cones of uneaten cotton candy in each hand. He didn't look up. Sometimes, it was better to say nothing at all. He handed me the pink one. I reached for the blue instead.

We stood that way for a while, picking apart the fibers, letting them dissolve on our tongues. It felt late, like we'd been waiting too long and we were all growing restless. I shielded my eyes against the setting sun. It stung my forehead as I scanned the promenade, searching for a clock. My eyes climbed the green metal structure beyond the fountains, a replica of the Eiffel Tower. Its lengthening shadow was the only clue to the late hour.

"What time is it?" I asked Jeremy. Shopkeepers had begun

pulling down the chain-link gates. The park was near closing.

"We were supposed to board thirty minutes ago."

Teachers wearing blue-and-white West River T-shirts carried clipboards and weaved through the crowd. "We're missing Posie," they called. "Has anyone seen Posie Washington?"

I hadn't seen Posie all day. That wasn't unusual in a park this size, but it was unusual for Posie to be late. I kicked at the pavement, the blisters on my heels screaming. A toddler in a stroller laughed as the teacher repeated Posie's name. "Has anyone seen Posie Washington?" they called again, louder. The little girl shrieked Posie's name gleefully and sang behind me.

Pocket full of posie,

Ashes, ashes,

We all fall down.

My mind had that slippery feeling. Then it grasped at something solid, finding traction in the rhyme.

We all fall down. The tower will point the way . . . at day's end you'll know where to find me.

The *Missed Connections* clue was part of a nursery rhyme. *We all fall down. Pocket full of posie.*

Posie was missing.

I checked the equation I'd written on my hand. Height of tower = 1,052 feet high. *It's 68 ft. higher than three times a side of its square base. If the sum of these two is 1,380, at day's end you'll know where to find me.* I squinted at the green replica of the Eiffel Tower, backlit by the setting sun. The real Eiffel Tower was over a thousand feet high. This had to be it.

I shielded my eyes and followed it from base to tip. The observation deck was empty, closed for the night. *The tower will point the way.* No. The tower wasn't pointing the way. Its shadow was pointing, and growing longer by the minute.

I broke out in a sprint.

"Leigh!" Jeremy yelled. I could hear his hard footfalls right behind me. "What are you doing?"

I wasn't sure precisely where to find her, but I followed the angle of the tower's shadow deep into the amusement park, hoping it was far enough. I wove and dodged through the thinning crowd, sweating and swearing. The paths cleared and I pushed myself faster—until I slammed into a wall of people. My knees locked and I fought the forward momentum, freezing in place in front of the bathroom near the thrill ride called The Crypt. Jeremy stopped short behind me.

A crowd formed a tight knot at the entrance to the women's room, stretching up on their tiptoes and craning their necks to see inside. A voice called out from the bathroom, "Call 9-1-1!" Concerned faces looked at one another, and reached for their phones. Someone ran to find an attendant.

"What's wrong? What's happening?" I breathlessly asked the woman in front of me.

Without turning her attention from the bathroom door, she said, "Someone found a body in the ladies' room." A sheet of paper taped to the frame of the open door curled in the slight breeze, angling toward me. *OUT OF ORDER*, it said, in bold blue letters.

I'd found Posie Washington.

20

"I HAVE TO HELP HER! Let me go!" I threw myself against Jeremy, bucking and kicking.

He held me tighter. "Help who, Leigh? You don't even know what's going on! If someone's really dead in there, then this place is going to be crawling with police and paramedics in a matter of minutes, and we shouldn't be here! We've got to get back to the buses!"

I felt like I was drowning, struggling to get my head above the crowd, listening for the sounds of paramedics that hadn't come yet. The words *dead girl* bobbed over and over to the surface.

No, not dead. Posie couldn't be dead. I twisted my wrists, forcing a gap in Jeremy's fingers and wriggling free, then brought my elbow back hard in his rib. I heard him grunt, and I darted into the crowd, plowing through it, fiercely determined to get to Posie. To touch her. I blocked out everything else, the smells, the angry people I bumped aside, the morbid curiosity of everyone I touched, and forced my way into the bathroom. Fumes and sweat and fear assaulted me. I shoved my way farther in. I could hear Jeremy calling my name.

In front of one of the stalls, the crowd of bystanders waved hands in front of their faces, brushing away the noxious scent of something burning. Through the gap, I saw Posie's sandals peaking out of the open stall door. A man knelt at her side, crammed between her body and the wall. He coughed, his eyes watering uncontrollably. I pushed closer. The man held Posie's wrist, unable to find a pulse. A horrified expression came over his face as he drew her arm cautiously away from his body. Ash-gray blisters crept over her skin, a shape materializing on the inside of her forearm.

The crowd gasped, struggling to see as the number three burned into existence, leaving an oozing white path where it consumed her. The man covered his mouth with his sleeve and dropped her hand.

I fell to my knees and reached for her ankle just as two hands grabbed me under my arms and dragged me back.

It had only been a moment. The faintest flicker. But I'd felt her.

I let Jeremy carry me away, the crowd swallowing me as I screamed, "Someone help her! She's alive!"

• • •

An hour later we were on the bus, heading home. The emergency exit lights cast a haunting glow over the somber faces around us. It was quiet except for the drone of the engine. No one spoke. One teacher remained at the park with the handful of students who'd claimed they'd been the last to see Posie hours before. Jeremy had dragged me away before the police arrived, insisting that we needed to get back to the bus. He'd been livid, and walked clutching his bruised rib. When he took my hand, I'd tasted the copper and salt of his anger. He'd pulled me hard through the crowd, repeating himself over and over. If we could make it back to the bus, everything would be okay. Paramedics and police rushed past us, and Jeremy kept his head down, murmuring in my ear to keep walking. Everything would be okay, the soothing words at odds with what he was clearly feeling. "There's nothing we can do for her," he'd said, holding me close to his side until we were herded into the bus.

I curled in on myself with my arms around my knees, forehead down, and I shut my eyes against the image of Posie blistering and the number three burning. Three, eighteen, ten. What did they mean? Where was the pattern? I forced my brain to zero in on the details, to clamp down on the hard facts of what I'd witnessed. But they were clouded in the chaos of the moment, and the confusion of the crowd.

Think.

I took a deep breath, focused. Started with the obvious.

The number in Posie's arm was made by a chemical burn. But it was the dramatic appearance—the well-timed bleaching of the number in her coffee-brown skin, white blisters in necrotized flesh—that gave the only clue to which chemical might have been used.

Bits and pieces of data circled my brain, like puzzle pieces sliding over a tabletop, seeking a logical intersection. Slowly, they began snapping together. The acid was probably lipophilic. Hydrofluoric acid was highly corrosive and yet slow to show burn symptoms on the skin. It could be purchased in most hardware stores, and would be easy to smuggle into the park in a sealed plastic water bottle. A set of rubber gloves and a small mask to protect the lungs would be just as easy to conceal. That's all that would have been needed to administer the poison, and a very small amount, just a few milliliters, would have been enough to kill her.

But somehow, Posie Washington had survived.

"How did you know?" Jeremy startled me. The question was barely more than a whisper in the dark. I pulled my head from my hands and looked up at him, unsure what he was really asking. Was he asking me how I knew where to find her, or how I knew she was alive? It didn't matter. I couldn't tell him anyway.

I let my silence speak for me. For Emily and Marcia and Posie. For the mysterious numbers etched in their skin. There was nothing to say. My puzzle was riddled with holes, pieces

thrown everywhere and none of them fit. I had no answers
for any of this.

Instead, I said, "I'm sorry. I didn't mean to hurt you. I just
needed to see her. Are your ribs okay?"

Jeremy massaged them tenderly. "Remind me never to
sneak up behind you."

"Why were you so mad back there?"

He gaped at me, shaking his head as if he couldn't believe
I'd asked the question. "You were trying to run headlong into
what may or may not have been the scene of an attempted
murder, Nearly."

"But it was Posie!"

"No, it was a mistake!" Jeremy spoke firmly in a tight, low
voice. He wasn't joking, and the stern expression he wore
stole any argument I'd been ready to make. "Getting called in
to the police station for questioning isn't the way today was
supposed to end. If I hadn't pulled you out of there when I
did, that's exactly where you'd be."

It was my turn to look away. He was right. I had made a
mistake, but not the one he thought. I should have figured
out the clue sooner, rather than letting Reece distract me. I
should have been there under the tower's shadow, waiting,
and maybe I could have done something to stop what happened to Posie.

If I'd spent more time studying instead of chasing after a boy,
we wouldn't be here.

I'd left Jeremy for Reece, and let him touch me, wondered if there was a chance he could be something more . . .

"You're right," I conceded to myself. "It was all a mistake."

21

POSIE'S FACE WAS THE FIRST THING I thought of when I woke early Saturday morning. I scrambled for the phone and called Jeremy, desperate for news. Had she made it through the night? Did they have any clue who might have done this to her? Jeremy said he'd searched online, but Posie was a minor, so her case would be kept confidential. For now, all I could do was hope. And wait.

Mona was still sleeping, so I took a few dollars from the cookie jar, hefted the basket of dirty clothes under one arm and my backpack over the other, and headed to the coin laundry across the street.

The Laundromat was always empty on Saturday mornings, and the tumble and slosh of the machines drowned out the street noise on Route 1. I tried studying. Tried letting the machines drown out every other intrusive thought in my head, but I was restless, and couldn't focus. When I was little, my dad and I always did laundry on Saturday mornings. He'd keep me entertained with card tricks while we waited for the wash cycle to finish, then we'd walk next door to Bui's for donuts while it dried. But that memory of him that used to be so clear in my mind had become hazy, wrapped up in smoke, smudging what was real and what was imagined.

My father couldn't be these people Jeremy had found. A gambler. A phony. A man who'd run out on his family for no good reason. He couldn't be those people, because he was like me. We had the same sweet tooth. The same nose and eyes. He was smart. He had to be. I pulled the photo of him from my backpack and studied him, arm in arm with his buddies at the Belle Green Poker Club. Touching them, and smiling.

Touching them, like it was easy. Like it didn't faze him at all.

Maybe I'd been wrong. I shut the photo inside my textbook. Maybe we weren't the same person at all.

• • •

Mona was stirring behind the closed door of her bedroom when I pushed open the trailer door later. I set the laundry basket on the table and pulled a fry pan from the rack inside the oven. The pat of butter slid slowly across the pan while it warmed, and I mixed up some milk and eggs with sugar and set two slices of bread in the bowl to soak. While the bread swelled and softened, I found the kitten mug I'd given her on Mother's Day, and heated water for coffee. Mona liked it strong, with one packet of artificial sweetener, and I left it for her, steaming at her place at the table.

Her door opened and she ambled to the kitchen, rubbing her eyes. They were bright green and ringed in old mascara. The whites were bloodshot, making her olive skin look sallow. She pulled her robe shut and smoothed her long, unruly hair—the only thing we had in common—back from her face.

Inhaling deeply, she reached for her coffee and sipped. "Do I smell French toast?" She raised a suspicious brow, but behind the mug she hid the hint of a smile. "What's the occasion?"

I scooped the toast onto a plate and set it in front of her place at the table. "No occasion."

Mona eased into her seat, looking at me skeptically while I washed the pan. "Something you want to talk about?"

"No," I said, rolling my eyes. She took another slow sip of her coffee, still watching me. "Okay, maybe there's this one thing."

Mona nodded knowingly, lip curled as she cut into her toast sideways with her fork. She took a bite and watched me dig around in my backpack. "Ace another trig test?"

I pulled out the photo of the Belle Green Poker Club and set it on the table. Mona stopped chewing. "Where did you get this?" she asked, and set down her fork.

"Jeremy's house," I said. There was no need to go into the details of how he found it. I didn't think she was even listening. She didn't acknowledge me, lost somewhere in her own head. After a minute, she snapped the photo down against the tabletop and slid it back to me. She stuffed another fork-ful in her mouth, chewing and blinking away the wetness in her eyes.

"Who took this picture?" I asked, trying not to let her hear the urgency in my voice. She knew this picture. She'd seen it before. I was certain of it. She glanced at it bitterly.

"Jenna Fowler," she answered quietly.

I took a moment to process what she'd just said. Jeremy's mother had taken this photo. And the only way my mother would know that is because she was there. I looked again at the smiling faces in the photo, the men arm in arm wearing matching team shirts. These were my parents' friends. Which meant she should remember the man whose face was missing. If he was close to my father then, maybe this man would know where to find him now. Maybe they were still connected.

"Who is that man Dad's holding? The one whose face is torn away?"

My mother scraped her plate absently. I reached for her hand to make her look at me. She dropped the fork with a clatter and stood up, pulling her hand away. But not before I felt it. The grief, and loss, and shame. She clutched her robe and looked down at the table. "Get that picture out of my house," she said, low and angry. "I don't ever want to see it again."

22

After the final bell rang on Monday, the chem lab was empty, and uncomfortably quiet. Rankin leaned back in his chair and sipped his coffee with a frown. Then he got up and shut the classroom door.

"Your mentees seem to be disappearing," he said, returning to his desk and perching on the edge of it. His salt-and-pepper eyebrows arched over his mug, waiting for an answer. I didn't have one. And he wasn't asking me anything I hadn't already asked myself. I'd spent the entire weekend trying to make sense of something that made no sense at all. Why me? Why my students? And who might be next?

"With Emily, Marcia, and now Posie no longer in need of your services—and with Mr. Whelan on suspension until Thursday—I daresay this will put you several hours behind in your community service. With less than three weeks until finals, I might add."

A bubble of panic rose through me. It was only a matter of time before the police began connecting the same dots Rankin already had. All three victims had been connected to me. I closed my eyes and dropped into the chair behind me.

"I can see this bothers you as much as it concerns me." He

tapped his fingers on the side of his mug. "Therefore, I've come up with a solution."

A desperate and almost hysterical giggle slipped out. "A solution?" He made it sound so simple, as if it was only a scholarship at risk.

"You can make up the hours sorting, cleaning, and taking inventory of the lab equipment. You may start immediately." He looked at me expectantly. I sat motionless, anxiety chipping away at my blank expression. "Unless you have more important things to do?"

I shook my head.

Rankin handed me a stack of inventory forms.

"You may start with those boxes." He gestured to a mountain of cardboard with his mug. "I'm going to the teacher's lounge for more coffee. I'll be back in a few minutes should you have any questions." He paused in the open door, then turned hesitantly and said, "Principal Romero called a rather interesting meeting. With the Fairfax County police. They appear unable to connect Emily, Marcia, and Posie in any way that might shed light on what happened, though they seem quite certain they are indeed connected. They're interviewing faculty this afternoon, to uncover any missing link between them. I suppose, since you are no longer their tutor, I have no reason to mention it. I'm quite confident that information would only serve to disrupt your studies and waste their valuable time." He raised an eyebrow. "I do hope you agree?"

I nodded, looking at the stack of boxes, feeling both surprised and grateful.

When I raised my eyes to thank him, Oleksa stood in his place.

"What are you doing here?" I looked past his shoulder down the empty hall. My heart skipped a beat. How long had he been standing there, and how much had he overheard?

He slid into his usual seat. "Detention," he said flatly. If he had overheard my conversation with Rankin, he didn't seem concerned. "We seem to find trouble together."

"I'm not here for detention." The implication burrowed under my skin. I hadn't done anything wrong, but this whole lab-cleaning business felt like a punishment. And he was right. It wasn't the first time Oleksa and I had been together like this. The police department, the park, and now here.

He smirked and opened a deck of cards, then shuffled them, whisper quiet. He laid a card face-up on the table. "You run with Reece, and soon it will be more than just detention."

"And Lonny Johnson's a saint? Maybe you shouldn't be so quick to judge." I glared at him as he spread the rest of his hand facedown, so fast I could barely see his fingers.

"There are things you don't know about him." He snapped a card against the table. "And there are things he doesn't know about you." His clear gray eyes found mine as he threw down an ace, and I knew he'd heard everything.

I swallowed, my throat suddenly dry.

So what if he knew that Rankin was covering for me? So what if he knew I was the missing link the police were looking for? Who was he going to tell? Definitely not the cops, since he obviously didn't want their attention any more than I did . . . Or would he? What would someone like Lieutenant Nicholson trade for information like this, like they'd done for Reece? The air in the room was too thin and my hands felt shaky. I clenched them into fists.

"You're no angel either." I refused to be afraid of Oleksa Petrenko. I had information too. I could completely discredit him as a witness. I could place Oleksa at the scene of a drug deal, and had seen him assault Reece with my own eyes. Hell, I probably even had his fingerprints. Oleksa must have been the one to put the baseball bat on my porch.

I smiled to myself, feeling more secure in the knowledge that I had something to wield over him if I needed it. "Thanks for returning my bat," I said, turning my back and grabbing the first box. *FRAGILE*, it said in bold red letters.

"I returned nothing," came his reply.

I set the box down silently. I had no reason to believe him. But I did.

"Whatever." I bit my lip and snatched a box cutter off the shelf. The warm, woody smell of newsprint seeped out as I sliced the packaging tape. Objects wrapped in old newspapers filled it to the rim. The cards rustled and snapped quietly behind me. I felt Oleksa's stare. Knew he was watching. A dozen dusty boxes lined the walls, waiting.

Mr. Rankin returned to his desk. Oleksa didn't say anything more.

I thrust a hand in the box and pulled out the first ball of paper. My hands were shaking as I unrolled it, and I dropped it and cursed. The glass vial shattered, startling Oleksa and Rankin and spreading tiny shards across the floor. I looked at the mess and blew out a long slow breath. The glassware had been wrapped in a page of personal ads, and it felt like a bad omen.

I swept up the glass, then resumed my work in silence. Oleksa left after an hour. I only knew because the room felt bigger, and I no longer had the feeling of being watched. After two hours, I'd washed, dried, inventoried, and shelved only three boxes.

I scooped the last of the wadded-up sheets of newspaper and stuffed them in the empty boxes. When I was done, my fingers were covered in newsprint smudges, making it hard to think about anything but the *Missed Connections* and the events that had unfolded since I'd found the first ad. Three ads. Three victims. Three students, all connected to me. Rumors were spreading, facts unraveling from fiction, weaving together to create truths that could almost hold weight. Emily's friends had talked about the number on her arm, even after police had tried to silence them. Marcia's friends had done the same. And Posie's number had appeared in a horrific public display, in an amusement park of thousands, making it impossible for police to conceal the specifics of the crime. Ten. Eighteen. Three. The numbers, random and meaningless on their own, were beginning to add up. Sooner or later, a pattern would emerge. And it was only a matter of time before police figured out that I was the only common denominator between the victims.

I closed and locked the cabinet, and leaned against it, lost in thought.

The tower will point the way . . . You'll know where to find me . . .

Do the math and find me after the show . . .

Find me tonight under the bleachers . . .

Find me . . .

I'd found Posie where the tower pointed, I'd found Marcia after the show. But *the bleachers* . . . I'd never been to the bleachers. I'd never gone to the gym at North Hampton.

How had I been so blind? I'd missed the first invitation completely.

23

I TOOK THE CITY BUS to the end of its route, then walked the rest of the way to North Hampton. The doors to the school's gymnasium were closed, but not locked. I peeked inside. The lights were on. It still smelled like warm bodies, but the gym was empty, and I slipped under the bleachers, unnoticed.

The air under the stands was at least two degrees cooler. I blinked, waiting for my eyes to adjust. Metal columns slowly came into focus, but it was too dark to make out anything beyond them but shadows. I withdrew a penlight from my pocket and hoped the lights on the other side of the wooden platforms over my head would be enough to keep anyone from noticing the flashlight's thin beam through the slats.

I flipped it on. If there was a message here, hidden in the dark, I'd find it. I started at the high side nearest the wall, illuminating cinder blocks covered in graffiti. Finding nothing unusual, I turned the light toward the splintering underbelly of the bleachers themselves.

Bingo.

A shiver passed through me at the sight of the familiar blue ink.

"Aren't you a little far from home?"

I jumped and switched off the light, dropping it as I spun toward the echoing voice. He stood in silhouette at the bleachers' opening, arms resting on the risers over his head. I could feel his stare, steady on me, even in the dark. Reece ducked under the tiers and I let out a breath.

"You scared me to death." I hid my hands in my pocket. "What are you doing here?"

"I was going to ask you the same thing. *I* used to go to school here," he said.

I jumped at a *snap-click*, like a pocketknife or a switch blade flipping. But it was only a flashlight. My light, that he'd retrieved from the floor.

The beam flashed to my face, obscuring him and blinding me. "What's your excuse?" he asked.

I averted my eyes and took a step back. "Get that thing out of my eyes." I shielded my face with both hands and he lowered the light. I blinked, adjusting to the creepy dim shadows it cast over the walls. I was face-to-face with the bleachers, the exact spot where I'd found the message a moment ago. I risked a glance.

A glimpse of blue graffiti. Like the letters on my chem lab table. Like the letters on the dead cat's box.

Printed. Bold.

Two lines buried in years of old scribble. The cops probably hadn't even noticed it was there.

"Looking for something?" he asked.

He couldn't have noticed. It had only been a glance.

Reese stepped toward me, blocking my exit. He braced a hand on the wooden tier over my head and dipped his face low enough for me to feel the heat radiating off his skin. To smell hot leather and sweat. I swallowed, not sure if it was the closeness of his body or the cryptic blue message that sped up my breath. "I should be going."

He didn't move. I could have stepped around him, but I didn't.

"Why do you do that?" His voice drew goose bumps over my skin.

"Do what?"

"Run away. Every time I get close, you run."

Close. All I could see was his face. Purple shadows, green bruises, and his blue eyes.

"Does it bother you?" he whispered. "Being close to me?"

"No." I barely shook my head, unable to look away from his lips. "Yes." They were too close, disorienting. "Maybe."

He stepped in closer even though there shouldn't have been any space left between us. "Where did you go on Friday? You took off after the flume ride and I spent hours looking for you. Where were you?"

I looked from his mouth to his eyes. Found all the same questions that had been in Jeremy's and Rankin's. Everyone tiptoeing around me while they pointed questions like fingers. Where was I? What was I doing? Why? Why? Why?

"None of your business," I said, feeling cornered. I took a step back and bumped my head on the bleacher. But he wasn't looking at me anymore. He stared past me, his eyes flicking side to side. His body, smooth and relaxed a moment ago, stiffened. He took a step back and straightened slowly, focused on something behind me.

I lurched at the slam of a gymnasium door. A sound, like the squeaky wheels of a mop bucket, made its way across the floor.

Reece was the first to speak. He was distant and cold. "It's getting late. We should get out of here."

I should have been grateful for his shift in focus, but I wasn't. I was humiliated for no reason that made any sense at all. I stepped around him, avoiding his arms as I brushed by.

"I was just leaving anyway." My voice wavered, relief and disappointment warring inside. I focused hard on the white light at the end of the bleachers. But when I got there, he wasn't behind me. I looked back. Reece stood in profile, flashlight shining against the underside of the bleacher where I'd just stood. He turned toward me, his face unreadable in the dark.

I knew he'd seen the same thing I had. Two lines of blue graffiti that read like all the others.

IT'S PERSONAL. I'LL PUT IT ALL ON THE TABLE FOR YOU. ARE YOU CLEVER ENOUGH TO FIND ME IN TIME?

24

I SAT AT THE KITCHEN TABLE, scribbling numbers on a sticky note. Ten. Eighteen. Three. I'd gone over them countless times. Rearranging them. Looking for patterns. Nothing made sense.

It's personal. I'll put it all on the table for you. Could the numbers have something to do with the messages on my lab tables? There had only been two. A reference to Schrödinger's cat written in ink on my chemistry table. And a reference to Archimedes' Principle carved into my table in physics. But there hadn't been any equations. No way to plug in the numbers to come up with a solution. I tapped my pen, making a mental note to check all my lab tables again today.

A familiar rumbling grew louder and died outside my trailer. A motorcycle. I ripped the sticky note off the pad and stuffed it in my pocket while I sprinted to the door, flinging it open and blocking the stoop before he could knock and wake my mother.

"What are you doing here?" I made a roadblock with my hands. Reece rested a hip against the splintered rail and squinted up at me.

His eyes drifted down to my pajama pants. "Suspension's over. I'm taking you to school."

I gritted my teeth. Like if I bit down hard enough, it could block the flow of blood to my cheeks. And maybe keep him off my porch. "I have a ride."

He came up the steps anyway, backing me into the door. "I've seen your ride and he's not doing much for you. He was kind of a dick on Friday—"

"So were you!" I braced my hands on the frame. No way was I letting him inside.

"Yeah, we didn't really get to finish our conversation about that. About where you went when you disappeared on Friday?"

This "where were you the night of Friday May 23" crap was getting old. And I had no intention of telling him I'd gone to the same bathroom where Posie had been found. I didn't owe him anything. "I rode the bus home from the class trip with Jeremy."

He looked at me like I was an idiot. "Yeah, Lonny made a point of mentioning it—"

"Lonny? When?"

He gripped the top of the door frame and leaned in close. "When he promised to put a cap in my ass if he found out we were lying." He didn't blink.

I glanced toward Lonny's trailer, where his Lexus idled. I could just make out the shape of his head, hunkered down in the front seat, watching us in his mirrors.

"You let him think you're my girlfriend, and that's the only reason he didn't impale me with my own ribs that night in the park. He's got his eyes on both of us, waiting for us to trip in our own bullshit. Running away from me at the amusement park and going home with Jeremy just made him suspicious. I had to make up some lie about you being pissed off at me."

"Where's the lie in that?" Our eyes met and held. "I saved you once. No one said I had to do it again."

"Who said anything about saving *me*?"

The bike's engine cooled with a series of soft clicks. Traffic

hummed on Route 1, and the smell of rancid trash was growing stronger as the morning sun glinted hot off the cans. I
looked down the street. Lonny's face was clear in his side
mirror. He looked straight at me, touched his index finger
to his lips, and blew a kiss like it was smoke from the barrel
of a gun.

"Wait here," I said. "I'll get my things." I opened the door
and headed to the kitchen, cursing under my breath as I slapped
together a quick PB&J and shook open a paper bag. Reece
reached over my shoulder and grabbed it off the counter.

"I thought I told you to wait outside!" I hissed.

He inhaled half of my sandwich and wiped his mouth
with the back of his hand. Then he pushed past me into the
hall, paused at the No Smoking sign, and let himself into my
bedroom.

"You can't be here! My mother will have a stroke!" It came
out as a frantic breathy whisper.

"If you're quiet, she'll never have to know." He rummaged
in my closet, shuffling through my scant collection of second-
hand clothes.

A pair of frayed low-rise jeans landed on my feet. A
designer label Mona'd found at a yard sale in Belle Green,
practically a give-away because of the bleach stains. She'd
retired them to the closet a year ago, saying they showed too
much skin. I couldn't agree more.

"What are you doing?"

"Getting you ready for school." Reece examined a stretchy collared shirt, two sizes too small. It had been part of a sweater-vest set I'd worn to middle school graduation. He tossed it to me. "Put this on."

I plucked the hem of my heavy metal T-shirt. "What I have on is fine! It's too hot for a sweater vest."

"You're not wearing a sweater vest."

I held the blouse against my torso. "It's too small!"

He raised an eyebrow and grinned. "I know."

"Why are you making me wear it?"

"Because Lonny doesn't believe you're my type."

I waved the shirt in his face. "And this is your type?"

He looked at the shirt, then at my chest, and smiled.

I made a noise somewhere between a growl and a sigh. A minute passed on my desk clock. He didn't move. He didn't care if we were late.

"Fine!" I started to push him into the hall and paused. If Mona woke up and found him in the living room, I'd be dead. If he was here with me, at least I could shove him out the window. I checked the lock. "Turn around." I twisted him to face the wall.

I slipped off my pajama pants, pulling my shirt down to cover myself while I eased on the ones Reece picked out. I looked twice to make sure he wasn't peeking, then wiggled out of my shirt lightning quick and stuffed my arms into the blouse. The stretchy material was too tight across the chest, pulling the fabric taut between each button. I picked at the fabric, wishing there was more of it, and tapped Reece's shoulder with an exasperated sigh.

"Satisfied? Can we go now?" I looked ridiculous.

He reached toward my chest and I flinched.

Give me a break was written all over his face. "I'm not trying to feel you up."

I narrowed my eyes at him, covering the buttons with both hands.

"Trust me." He reached again before I could object, unfastening the top two buttons and drawing the collar wide across my chest. Blood rushed to my cheeks and I held perfectly still, too freaked out to move. He gave the fabric around my waist a few quick tugs, then reached lower. I swatted his hands but he'd already unfastened the bottom two buttons, the stretchy material pulling apart to reveal a triangle of pasty-white belly.

"What are you doing?" I covered my stomach with my hands, then shot them up, missing his as he mussed my hair with his fingers. I muttered something about all the corners of hell where he could shove himself while he unclasped the thick chain behind his neck and fastened it around mine. It was still warm from his body, as warm as his fingers when they brushed my skin.

Feelings bloomed under his touch, stealing my breath. I closed my eyes against a tender ache, an emptiness beneath the shallow rise and fall of my chest. The pendant ignited a heartache inside him, the same way my father's wedding ring did. He let it go slowly as if it were difficult to part with, making me curious about who he might be missing.

I captured the pendant between my fingers. A class ring. Class of 2013. North Hampton's mascot, the hornet, was carved on one side. I turned it over and saw an odd, thorny-looking flower that matched Reece's tattoo.

"What is it?"

"It's a thistle," he answered, still frowning over my ensemble.

"A thistle?"

"Yeah, you know . . . little . . . prickly . . . pain in the ass. It suits you."

I dropped it and scowled as his gaze climbed back up my body. "I know what a thistle is. What's the story behind it? Why the tattoo?"

"You ask too many questions."

"Maybe I don't ask enough."

His eyes found mine and his sly smile fell away. He looked broken, and I couldn't tell if it was the fading bruises on his face, or the sadness beneath them that kept me from asking any more.

Slowly, he reached both hands toward my face. I caught him by the cuffs. I knew exactly what he wanted.

"No," I said, determined to draw this line in the sand. "The glasses stay."

"Fine," he smirked half-heartedly. "Sexy librarian works for me. My job is done."

He turned me toward the mirror. It was as bad as I'd feared. The shirt clung to me, the pendant hanging like a glaring focal point over my chest. I fidgeted with the collar, trying to tuck the thistle inside, but Reece stopped me.

"Leave it," he said.

"I can't go to school like this," I protested. "People will notice. They'll stare."

"That's the idea. Lonny will see me ride the new and improved Leigh Boswell to school, and by the end of the day everyone will believe we're a couple. Besides, you can't keep hiding from guys like Vince under big glasses and hoodies."

"I'm not hiding from anyone."

"Neither am I." He surprised me, catching my chin on his finger. His resolve bled into me, cool and solid in my veins. "Leave the pendant where it is."

He was invading me like a drug. I could feel him inside me, uninvited and pushing himself closer to my heart. But it was all a lie. I stepped out of reach. "Why?"

He stared at the pendant, worry pulling at the bandage over his eye. "The thistle is mine. There are people who will recognize it and know that you're . . ." A flash of hesitation crossed his face. "They should see you wearing it. That's all."

"Are we talking about Lonny or Vince?" Looking at his face, I already knew. I had more than just Vince and Lonny to worry about. He wanted Nicholson to see me wearing it, but why? Was he trying to show Nicholson that he'd worn me down? That he'd done his job and made good on his end of the bargain?

"Why are you doing this?"

He let out a long slow breath before answering quietly. "Because it's my turn to save you." He grabbed his jacket from my bed and reached for the door.

He was so close. So close to saying something with a glimmer of truth in it, without me having to take it from him. Without me having to feel it. "Save me from who, Reece?"

He paused before twisting the doorknob. "From yourself."

I watched him go, too dumbstruck to speak. The bike roared to life. I threw my backpack over my shoulder and went after him.

25

THE ENTIRE SCHOOL might as well have been watching when we pulled into the lot. It would have been enough just to show up on the back of his bike, but between Reece's battered face and the disquieting buzz around school since the class trip on Friday, it felt like every eye at West River was on us. As well as a few others I hadn't planned on.

Reece wheeled slowly past an unmarked cruiser. The

plainclothes officer was parked directly in front of the cross-walk, taking inventory of the morning deluge behind a pair of dark sunglasses. As we passed, he drew the handset of his radio to his mouth, following our every step from the parking lot to the front door.

I hadn't realized I'd been holding my breath until the door shut behind us. I exhaled long and slow, but that microscope feeling only got worse once we were inside. People looking down their noses, trying to dissect what we were doing together. We were the object of whispers and stares from the moment we crossed the threshold, ten minutes earlier than usual.

Ten minutes earlier . . .

I jerked to a stop, Reece pulling up short behind me.

"Oh, no. Jeremy! I was supposed to ride to school with Jeremy." I calculated the distance home. If I hurried, I could make it in time.

Reece grabbed my hand, dragging me down the hall in the opposite direction. "Tell him it was my fault. He'll get over it." He repositioned my hand in his leather riding glove and slowed to walk beside me. I took a few hesitant steps.

We were holding hands.

In public.

In school.

Intentionally.

"Do you mind telling me what we're doing?" I ignored

the curious eyes and pointed fingers, the whispering behind cupped hands.

"I'm walking you to class."

"I mean what are we doing . . . as in you and I . . . together? As in *this*." I lifted our joined hands.

"I thought we already talked about this." He cocked an eyebrow but kept walking. "What? You don't like holding my hand?"

"No . . . I mean, I do . . . I mean . . . No!" Even if I did like holding his hand, that didn't change the fact that he was using me.

I shook him off and stopped in the middle of the hall, forcing him to turn around. "Don't play games. You know exactly what I mean." My voice bounced, too loud against the blue-and-white walls.

He played it cool, casually stripping off his gloves and stuffing them in his pockets. Holding his bare hand palm up, he waited for me to take it. "I'm not playing any games. I'm just walking you to class."

"Why would you do that?" Fine. If he insisted on denying it, I'd pry the truth out of him. "Who am I? I can't be your girlfriend. You already have one!"

He glanced around and lowered his voice. "What are you talking about? I don't have a girlfriend."

"Really? I'm not sure Gena would agree with you."

"Gena's not my girlfriend!" Curious heads turned our way.

"Do you always leave your clothes in not-your-girlfriend's car?"

Reece dragged me into an empty bank of lockers. His guilt and shame surged through me the moment we touched. "Can we please talk about this somewhere else?" He clenched his jaw and spoke through his teeth. "You're attracting attention."

"I thought that's what you wanted. Why else would you tell me what to wear and how to act?" Two girls in hemp skirts shouted something about girl-power. Bodies lined up at each end of the row, blocking our way out, but I didn't care. I just wanted him to tell me the truth. "When are you going to come clean?"

"Come clean about what?"

I stared hard into his eyes, as if I could hurl the words at him without speaking them. *I know who you are.*

He pulled back an inch, his eyes flashing between mine. His face blanched and pupils dilated, and I could see the exact moment when the realization slammed into him. *She knows who I am.*

A wave of panic crashed over his face.

"You're making a mistake. Don't do this," he whispered. Sweat beaded on his hairline.

I was sick of the lies. I was tired of not knowing what he really wanted from me, or what information he was feeding back to Nicholson. "The only mistake I made was agreeing to tutor you in the first place. But you don't have to fake it anymore."

He gripped my shoulders, fingers digging in. "I promise. We'll talk later. About everything." The truth was close. I could feel something in him about to break, and I couldn't take the pressure anymore. I had enough of my own secrets without bearing the burden of his too.

I needed to hear him say it. "I know you're not who you say you are."

A crowd collected around us.

He shook his head. "Don't."

"I know you're a . . ."

Reece's mouth pressed hard against mine. A rush of emotions rolled through me, a barrage of tastes and smells so tangled, I couldn't make sense of them. My protests muffled against his tightly closed lips.

He pulled away just enough to whisper, "Please, don't do this." His damp forehead rested against mine, eyes searching for understanding. He was terrified. His fear was so thick and suffocating, it drowned out everything else.

He was afraid of me, because I had the power to expose him, and his future depended on me. It hadn't even been a real kiss. He'd just been trying to shut me up. I was just a job, a ticket to redemption he probably didn't even deserve.

What about what I deserved? I brought my foot up hard against his shin. "Just say it! I already know . . ."

Reece stumbled and grunted, pushing me into a wall of lockers and pinning me with his body. His hands tangled in my hair, pulling me into him before I could say another word. He tried to kiss me again and I bit down hard. Felt him flinch. Felt a shocking hot flare of emotion as his mouth crushed mine. His lips parted and I felt his tongue. I froze, startled by the unexpected taste of something decadent and sweet. His fingers loosened in my hair and his mouth softened. He cupped the back of my head, and I clutched his jacket and kissed him back. I wasn't sure if I needed to kiss him or kill him, or if the need I was feeling was his or my own.

Cheers and whistles erupted through the crowd. Reece pulled away, startled and red in the face. I licked my lips, copper and vinegar. His anger and humiliation tasted like a kick in the gut. My chest heaved in the tight space between us, that swollen horrible need threatening to burst.

I slapped him hard across the face. People applauded and shouted, and I looked over Reece's shoulder, spotting Jeremy's pale face. Anh stood beside him, staring at Reece and me with wide eyes. She reached for Jeremy's hand, but he turned and ran, shoving his way through the crowd.

Every inch of me wanted to run after him.

Or maybe just run. The bodies parted and two security officers came toward me. I froze, but their eyes were locked on something behind me.

I turned. Reece was pale except for the handprint on his

cheek and the cut that had opened where I'd bitten him. He swiped the back of his hand across his mouth, wiping the smear of blood on his jeans before the officers could see it.

He shut his eyes. He couldn't even look at me.

"I'm sorry," he said, barely a whisper, as they took him away.

26

I SPENT FIRST PERIOD UNDER the willow tree outside school, not ready to face Anh and the barrage of questions she was sure to fire at me the minute I walked into lab. Jeremy didn't come, and while I'd hoped he would, I guess I really couldn't blame him.

When the second period bell rang, I pulled myself together and crept back in the side entrance I'd used to sneak out, avoiding the cop in the parking lot. I snapped open my locker. Two sheets of paper cascaded out, and a sleeve of Twinkies rested on the top shelf. I couldn't bring myself to open them, so I reached for the notes instead. The first was in Reece's scratchy block print.

WE'LL TALK LATER. I PROMISE.
MEET ME TOMORROW AFTER SCHOOL.

I didn't have time to contemplate the meaning or what he planned to talk to me about, because the second note was more pressing—a pink slip directing me to the principal's office. There was an X in the box marked *Urgent* and several exclamation points next to the word *Immediately*.

I'd known this was coming. Reece had practically body checked me in front of the entire school. And I'd drawn blood. Rumors were bound to get back to administration. I just didn't expect it to be "immediately."

I inspected myself in my small locker mirror. Girls walked slowly past my locker, staring as I scraped away a patch of dried blood from my cheek. My lips were still swollen from the kiss, and I bit them, feeling a momentary stab of guilt over Gena. He'd said she wasn't his girlfriend, but having seen the way she cared about him, I wasn't so sure she would agree.

None of that mattered, though. It hadn't been real. He'd said it before, out loud, in front of Gena. I was nobody. A liability he was forced to silence with an artificial kiss. Lonny had almost killed him over his suspicion that Reece was a narc, and I'd threatened his cover. I'd left him no choice.

The second bell rang.

All I wanted was a ride home.

• • •

Principal Romero did indeed see me "immediately." I sat in the chair across from his desk and looked down at the floor, humiliated.

"You missed first period this morning, Miss Boswell. Care to tell me why?" His tone suggested he already knew the answer, but he'd put me through the act of contrition anyway.

I had the overwhelming temptation to tell him everything. The ads, the numbers, the fights, how I'd seen Posie burning and Marcia on the bottom of the pool. I chewed my lip.

I took a deep breath, decided. I'd be safer under Frank Romero's wing than in Lieutenant Nicholson's custody.

"It's all right, Nearly," Principal Romero said, interrupting my thoughts. "I am aware of what happened with Mr. Whelan, and I assure you I am taking corrective action. He won't bother you again. He's been removed from West River High School."

"Removed?" My head snapped up, my confessions forgotten. "What do you mean?"

"He's been expelled. Security escorted him off campus a few moments ago. Now it's only a matter of some paperwork." He beamed down at me from his stupid faux-leather throne. Even if Reece had tried to fight it, it wouldn't have mattered. Romero wasn't ever going to give him a chance.

"It wasn't his fault."

The smile slid from his face. "Excuse me?"

"I was the one responsible." Romero tossed his pen on the expulsion papers he'd been ready to sign.

I couldn't let Reece go back to jail for something that was my fault. He'd only reacted because I'd provoked him. My behavior hadn't left him any choice.

I cleared my throat, preparing to tell a story that I hadn't quite come up with yet. Some excuse Principal Romero and the rest of the school would be willing to believe. I owed Reece this much.

"I wanted him to notice me," I said, looking at the principal through lowered lashes, trying to gauge his reaction. "So I tried changing my hair and wearing different clothes. It didn't work, so I did something stupid. I practically attacked him in front of a million people." I cringed. It wasn't entirely a lie. I'd threatened him, which could be construed as an attack . . . of sorts. Then there was the kicking, biting, and slapping . . . And plenty of witnesses to corroborate this slightly revised version of the truth.

"I understand there was blood involved? Did he hurt you?" Romero didn't look concerned so much as hopeful. His chair creaked as he leaned into my story, waiting for it to crumble.

"No, sir. The blood was Reece's. I guess I was a little rough." I blinked hard, provoking a tear. It wasn't hard, the truth cut deep. "But it doesn't matter. He made his feelings perfectly clear."

Romero handed me a tissue, studying my hair and my shirt, as if noticing for the first time that something was, in fact, different.

"That's probably for the best," he said. "Mr. Rankin tells me you're awfully close to earning the merit scholarship in chemistry. I would hate to see you throw that away over a boy."

I blew all my disdain into his tissue. He sounded like Mona.

"Besides, he's a bad influence. You would do better not to associate with someone like Whelan. Trouble seems to follow him. Ever since he enrolled, there have been problems."

I looked at him. "What kind of problems?"

"It's none of your concern." He pursed his lips. "The important thing for you to remember is that he's not the kind of boy you should be friendly with."

Something inside me snapped. I was sick of people telling me who I should or shouldn't be "friendly" with. My voice climbed an octave and I stood up before I could rein in my reaction. "Regardless of whether or not he's a nice guy, it was still my fault. It wouldn't be fair to expel him for something I did." I swallowed hard, hoping I wasn't about to dig myself into a hole I couldn't climb out of. "You should expel me instead."

A silence passed.

Romero's face was red and he loosened his tie with a finger. He only had two choices: Expel us both, or go easy on Reece in light of my admission. A vein bulged at his temple.

"I'll take that information into consideration," he said carefully. "Although I can't guarantee it will change the outcome of my decision."

We both knew it would.

I slung my backpack over my shoulder. The motion lifted the hem of my shirt, revealing a few inches of bare midriff, and I felt Romero's gaze linger there.

I reached for Reece's pendant as an excuse to cover my

skin. Mona always said hanging out with boys like Reece would ruin my chances, make me into someone I didn't want to be. And here I was, exposing myself and dressing in lies. I didn't want her to be right.

"Mr. Romero?" I turned, one hand on the door. "Why was Reece in jail?" Something inside me needed to know, to reassure myself it had been a petty crime. A misunderstanding.

Romero fingered the expulsion papers, as if reconsidering. "He was responsible for the death of a student."

"Who?" I heard myself ask.

"A senior. Shot and killed at North Hampton last year."

• • •

I don't know what I had expected to hear, but I walked back to my locker in a daze. The hall was empty, silent except for the murmur of teachers lecturing behind closed doors. I'd missed chemistry and almost all of physics, and for once I didn't care. I walked slowly, taking the longest route through the front hallway and staring out the windows at Reece's empty parking space as I passed. I'd been so close to telling Romero everything, but I'd chosen to protect Reece instead. I'd just saved him again, but why? Every time I thought I knew him—thought maybe I could trust him—I learned something about Reece Whelan that made me realize I didn't know him at all.

I laid my head against my locker. It felt too heavy to hold up anymore. *We'll talk tomorrow*, he'd promised. But what was there to talk about? I had one too many evasive killers in my life already and I wasn't any closer to knowing who I could trust.

I spun the combination. The door rattled open, and I was greeted by Teddy's drawing of the two of us holding hands on the carousel. Unable to throw away the yellow scrap of paper, I'd taped the memento inside my locker. It lifted my mood, but only for a moment. There was a note from Anh, folded to fit through the vent.

Leigh—WTF? You have some serious explaining to do! Call me later. I want details!

Anh

It was stapled to our chemistry homework assignment for the night.

Another folded paper drifted out. I plucked it off the floor and unfolded it. As soon as the first blue letter appeared, my skin prickled, and I peeled the rest open more carefully.

FLOWERS DELIVERED
WHC
RM # 214

It had been written in the same blue marker, the ones we used in chem lab. The same handwriting as the message in the box with the dead cat and under the bleachers at North Hampton.

I shoved the letter in my locker and slammed it shut. I'd wanted to visit Posie, but I'd heard she'd been flown to the burn unit at Washington Hospital Center and had spent the last four days in ICU. No visitors allowed.

Flowers delivered to Room #214. He was tipping me off. Posie must have been moved. And if she was out of intensive care and had her own room, I could talk to her. I could ask her what she remembered, if she had seen who had done this to her. I knew she would tell me if she could. I had to try.

I shook my head, split down the middle. Who was I kidding? That's exactly what the killer wanted me to do. Exactly where he wanted me to be. This note felt like a set-up. I'd be playing into his hands again, and I hated myself for it. But I had no choice. It was time to pay Posie a visit.

• • •

I hopped the Red Line downtown, then took the H4/Tenley Town bus to the hospital. Once inside, I crossed the main lobby and headed straight for the elevator.

"Excuse me," said the woman at the desk behind me. I turned to see her holding out a clipboard and a visitor's pass. "I'll need you to sign in, please."

The elevator doors closed. I approached the desk and took the clipboard, hesitating before writing my name. If the note was a set-up—if someone really did want me here—then maybe I shouldn't use my own name. At the very least, it wouldn't hurt me to use someone else's. I wrote "Mary Jones" in the space marked *Visitor*. The pen hovered over the space for the patient's name, warnings whispering in my head. If the police were keeping tabs on Posie's visitors, something told me I shouldn't use her name either.

"What's the last name of the patient you're looking for, dear?" She was a kind looking older woman with smiling wrinkles. I felt guilty lying to her.

"Smith," I answered.

The attendant henpecked the name into her computer and stared down her nose at the screen. "Would that be Ronald, Evelyn, or William?"

My shoulders sagged with relief. Smith had been a safe bet. "Ronald," I said.

She handed me the pass and said, "He's in 263. You can go ahead up."

I clipped my pass to the hem of my shirt and darted into the first open elevator. Posie's room was easy to find. I peeked in the small window inset in the door, relieved to find Posie alone. A jacket hung over the back of an empty chair beside her bed. I didn't have much time. I rapped softly on her door and pushed it open a crack.

She replied in a jagged whisper, as though she were talking through broken glass. "Come in."

I stepped quietly inside. Posie sat propped on a mountain of starched white pillows, her eyes taped shut with cotton pads. A clear tube hung below her nostrils and an IV dripped from a stand near her headboard. A clip hugged her finger, and a monitor beeped steady with the rhythm of her heart. Her other arm, the burned one, was concealed under a sleeve of bandages.

"Posie?"

She tipped her head, turning in my direction. "Leigh?" She smiled weakly. "You made it. I knew you were coming."

I stopped halfway to her bed. A cold sensation slithered over me. "Yeah, it's me," I said quietly, my throat dry. "How did you know I was coming?"

She pushed a button, elevating the bed. "One of the nurses said you called."

I didn't answer. I hadn't called or spoken to any nurses, but I didn't want to scare her.

Her smile faltered. "You didn't call?"

My mind raced. I looked at the clock. "I don't have much time, Posie."

She drew her call button tighter against her hip and pulled herself straight against the pillows. I heard the strain in her breaths.

"I know," she rasped. "The police have been asking all kinds of questions about you. I told them there was no way you could be involved in something like this. But they keep asking, like I might change my mind. I told them I won't." She took a few thin breaths and sunk back into the pillows. "I'm glad you're here, but it's probably better if you go. My mom will be back any minute and I'd hate for you to get in trouble."

I looked between Posie and the door. Someone called the nurses' station pretending to be me. I knew I should leave, but I had so many questions. "Is there anything you remember . . . anything at all that might help me figure out who did this to you? Did you see anyone? Talk to anyone?"

She shook her head. "I don't remember a thing. The police said I was drugged. They said someone put something in my soda. I remember eating lunch, and then feeling dizzy and sick to my stomach. I left my friends to find the bathroom, and then everything just went blank. I woke up here. They said I have to stay until my burns are better." Her brief recollection seemed to drain all of her energy, and I helped settle her back on her pillows. She couldn't help me. It had been a mistake to come.

"It's okay," I said, as much to comfort myself as to ease the worry on Posie's face. "You don't have to say any more." I straightened her blankets. A medical chart hung at the foot of her bed. "Posie? Would it be okay if I looked at your chart?"

She nodded and I hurriedly flipped through the pages of a toxicology report. Posie's bloodwork had tested positive for ketamine, the same drug the police said they'd found in Emily Reinnert's water bottle.

The rest of the report held no surprises. Just as I'd expected, hydrofluoric acid burns. The fumes were strong enough to damage her respiratory system, but as long as there was no direct contact with her eyes, the cotton and tape should be temporary and her lungs would get stronger and heal over time. I couldn't say the same about her arm. That scar would stay with her for the rest of her life. I thumbed through the rest quickly—her vitals, which seemed fairly stable, and a treatment plan showing an estimated discharge date a few days from now. She'd be fine.

A series of loud beeps erupted from her IV monitor and we both startled. Her bag hung empty, the last drops sinking close to her hand. "You should probably go," she said. "The nurses will be in soon to change my IV."

A stack of fresh gowns and surgical caps were folded neatly on a chair. I grabbed a set quietly and pulled them over my clothes.

Posie wheezed and started coughing. I didn't think, just reached for her hand, needing to know she would be okay. "I'll be fine. Just go. I won't tell anyone you were here." Her strength ebbed through my fingers in steady, reassuring waves. Posie would be fine, and now I was one step closer to understanding the person who'd done this to her. Emily, Posie, and Marcia had all been drugged.

I gave her hand one last squeeze and cracked the door before slipping into the hall. I walked quickly toward the end of the hall, away from the nurses' station, looking for emergency exit signs that might lead me another way out. A police officer emerged from the stairwell and walked toward me. Every nerve ending screamed at me to run. He was on his phone and didn't seem aware of me, so I kept my head down and shuffled past. I took the stairs fast and threw open the door, emerging in a hallway near the hospital chapel. I darted into the nearest bathroom, stripped off the gown and tucked it into the trash bin, plucking the visitor's pass from my shirt. I was about to toss it in the can and find a less conspicuous exit than the one in the main lobby, but then I paused. Would it be suspicious if Mary Jones never signed out?

I carried the pass to the visitor's desk, darting looks through the lobby to make sure I hadn't been noticed. The wrinkled attendant smiled and held out a basket of used passes. I dropped it in and thanked her, reaching for a pen.

I found my name, Mary Jones, and signed out. Several unfamiliar names followed, but I gripped the clipboard tighter when I recognized my name. Not Mary Jones. My real name. Nearly Boswell had signed in, visited with Posie Washington in Rm #214, and signed out. Three minutes ago.

I wanted to tear off the sign-in sheet and stuff it into my pocket, but the attendant was watching, politely waiting to see me off. I held the clipboard too long. "Good day," she said, lifting it from my hands. I looked up at the high ceiling as though I could see through the floors. Nearly Boswell wasn't in class or with friends. She was officially logged in the hospital record as a visitor.

I never should have come.

27

I COULD ALMOST SMELL the tight stack of newsprint on Rankin's desk, more aware of those pages than the blank one in front of me. I tapped my pencil and tried to focus on the pop quiz. My knee bobbed up and down, shaking the table. Anh kicked me without looking up. It was Friday morning and the Bui Mart had been sold out of *City Posts*—as was every store in a three-block radius. Bao said the front page had been some kind of smear campaign against a local politician, and his supporters had combed through every store in town that morning, buying up every copy on the shelves. I stared at the *City Post* on Rankin's desk, took a deep breath, checked the clock, and forced my attention to my quiz.

Two more problems and I was out of there. Maybe Jeremy had a copy . . . if he was speaking to me at all. I'd taken the bus home from the hospital yesterday, and walked to school that morning, like I did every Friday. I hadn't seen Jeremy since I'd stood him up yesterday, and I had no idea what to expect.

A cold rush of air moved past my desk. Oleksa sauntered down the aisle and set his quiz facedown. I looked at the clock again. Anh finished, sliding her chair back without a sound. TJ was behind her.

I jabbed the buttons of my calculator, scratched out numbers, and finished just as the bell rang. My quiz was the last
one on the stack, but I was certain I'd nailed it, even through
all the distractions.

I approached Rankin's desk, where the newspaper was
now spread open. Somewhere in it was a message for me. I
knew it. The note in my locker and then the sign-in sheet in
the hospital were building up to something.

Better luck next time.

No. No more next times. I needed that paper.

"Question, Miss Boswell?" Rankin stared at me over the
drooping pages of his newspaper.

"No. No question."

"Very well then." He snapped the paper up, teasing me
with the front and back pages. Definitely today's paper.

"Where did you get it?" I heard myself ask.

He looked at me with a curious expression. "You mean
this? Yes," he said, brows shooting up as he rustled the pages.
"I had quite a time finding one this morning. This copy was
waiting on my desk quite unexpectedly when I arrived."

My spine tingled, as if someone drew a finger over it. The
only *City Post* in school was left on Rankin's desk before first
period, where I'd be sure to see it. Someone wanted me to find
it, like they'd wanted me to find all the others. I had to get my
hands on that paper.

"May I borrow it?" The ice I was treading was thin. He'd

expressly forbidden me from bringing the paper to class, but class was over and I couldn't walk away without asking. If he didn't agree, then I'd find another way. I wasn't leaving school without that paper.

He flipped the corners down. "No, you may not. I'm sure your physics teacher would not appreciate you reading it in his class any more than I want you reading it during mine."

"But—"

"However," he interrupted, raising a finger, "there is plenty of inventory yet to be counted. I'll see you at two forty-five. If the paper is still here when you return, you may take it if you wish."

• • •

At 2:43 p.m. I sprinted through the chem lab door. Rankin was gone, but his newspaper was there.

I flipped through the sections with shaking hands, snatching the *Missed Connections* out of the stack. The pages clung together, reluctant to separate. I dropped into my seat, skimming the fine print for an equation or theorem. But the numbers were all bust sizes and addresses of bars.

Whoever had written the ads wasn't making this easy. If there was an ad in today's personals, I'd have to read them all to find it.

I laid the paper across my desk and studied them, one by one, reading the cryptic ones slowly, listening for a familiar cadence or the suggestion of a clue.

And there it was.

I don't know how I knew, or why I was so sure, except that it was the only ad that didn't seem to fit with the others. The tone of the ad seemed to resonate with malice, where all the others resonated with hope. Grabbing a lab marker, I circled it.

> **I'm serious. I'm done chasing my tail, trying to be the big dog.**
> **I'm the brightest. Lie back and watch me shine.**

What did it mean? I'd expected a number, a formula . . . something concrete. This was as maddening and nonsensical as the message under the bleachers.

I'm the brightest. Fine. Whatever. I shoved my chair back and stuffed my hands in my pockets. If he wanted to prove he was smarter than me, why not give me a problem I could solve?

Or had he?

I scooted back to the desk. I read it again, dissecting each word for some corresponding value. Scrutinizing each letter for patterns or hint of a code. No key emerged.

I took a step back and rubbed my eyes. They burned with fatigue and frustration. I was too emotional. Too eager to find it. The ad felt like a damn Seurat painting. Like I needed distance to see it clearly.

Unless the clue wasn't something I could see at all.

Skeptical, I closed my eyes and took a breath, exhaling my anxiety and muting the distractions in my head. Then I spoke the words aloud. I listened to them, imagining them from thirty thousand feet.

"I'm serious. I'm the brightest," I repeated softly. "I'm serious."

I'm serious.

I'm Sirius.

My chair flew out behind me. I snatched up my things, and headed to earth science. The map of the solar system spanned the interior wall of the classroom. I searched the constellations, my head swimming, full of tiny dots and lines that formed shapes and patterns of animals and warriors, until I found it. Sirius, the brightest star in the sky, in the constellation Canis Major—the big dog.

I'm serious . . . the big dog. I'm the brightest.

I cried out, a victorious shout that echoed and died in the empty room.

Now that I knew what I was looking for, where the hell was I supposed to find it?

Lie back and watch me shine.

I mapped streets and bridges in my head. There were hundreds, if not thousands of places to stargaze in and around the city. Riverfront parks, historic battlefields, ball fields, beaches . . .

But the last three ads reflected a pattern. They had one common denominator. Each of the victims had been people I knew. More specifically, people I'd tutored. I'd worked with dozens of students through the year, and I counted them off in my head, grasping for any connection. Where they lived, their interests, their hobbies, their classes. Nothing fit. I had no clue where I was supposed to find Sirius and I only had a few hours until dark.

I slogged to my locker, folding the newspaper into a tight square around the circled ad. I spun my combination and opened the door, dropping the newspaper on the shelf inside. Teddy's drawing drew my attention like a bright yellow flare. My stomach dropped as I plucked it from my locker door. I turned it over. The flyer for the Smithsonian field trip was rimmed in clip-art planets and stars. It was dated today. My hands shook as I set it down on top of the ad.

Lie back and watch me shine.

Teddy Marshall was at the Air and Space Museum.

28

I SHOVELED ALL MY LOOSE CHANGE from my pockets into the machine and it spit a ticket into my waiting hand. I jammed it into the turnstile and bolted down the escalator, where the next train was already waiting. Departure lights flashed at the edge of the concrete, and I slipped between the closing doors, breathing hard.

The Yellow Line out of Huntington Station was mostly

empty, heading into the city against rush hour. Full cars packed with standing passengers in suits rushed by in the opposite direction. I grabbed the handrail as the train picked up speed, leaning against the route map by the door. I ticked off the landmarks in my head, counting down the stops, and grateful every time we surfaced that daylight remained.

I changed trains at L'Enfant Plaza, pushing past suits and ties, bumping into briefcases at every turn. When my Blue Line train finally stopped at Smithsonian Station, I ran up the escalator, squeezing past slow movers. Early-evening sun filtered through the escalator shaft. I stepped out into a wall of humid city heat and jockeyed past a cart of hanging souvenir T-shirts that blew in my way, stopping briefly to orient myself against the National Mall.

The Washington Monument pierced the sky to my left. The Capitol Building stretched the horizon on my right, a mile of museums and galleries flanking the lawns between. I flew past them, crossing 7th Street and following the manicured perimeter. The dipping sun cast a long, narrow shadow before me like the second hand of a clock. Taxis blared horns when I jumped between two parked school buses, emerging before the sprawling white walls spanning an entire block of Jefferson Avenue. The National Air and Space Museum.

I stood on the steps, doubled over with runner cramps,

sweat trailing down my shirt. When I straightened, I was
staring up two stories of glass and stone. The sleek face of
the building seemed to reflect the enormity of my mission.
I turned back to the long line of yellow buses at the curb
and found the small bus marked *Fairfax County Public Schools*
sandwiched between countless others.

Teddy was still here.

I took the steps two at a time. I knew this museum, like I
knew all the others from years of countless school field trips.
The familiar sterile smell hit me as I pulled open the heavy
glass doors. I walked right through the security checkpoint,
carrying only my hoodie through the scanners and grateful
I'd had the presence of mind to leave my backpack in my
locker. A bag search would only slow me down.

I darted through the lobby to the welcome desk.

"Excuse me," I said, breathless and damp. "I'm looking for
a tour group from West River High School. Do you know
where I can find them?"

The woman behind the counter looked at me, her face
pinched and her posture rigid in her starchy Smithsonian
blazer. Conscious of her stare, I withdrew my newsprint-
covered hands from the desk.

"I'm sorry, dear." She eyed me, taking in every detail of
my appearance with a tight smile. "I have no idea where they
might be. Would you like me to have someone paged?"

"No," I said quickly when she reached for her phone. "That's okay. I'll find them." I couldn't have him paged. Couldn't attract that much attention to myself.

I turned, pausing at two stories of thousands of people. The killer wanted me to find Teddy. He would make it easy. There had to be a message, a clue I wasn't seeing.

I turned back to the clerk.

"Has anyone left a message? Maybe an envelope?" Doubt clung heavy to each word.

The woman opened a drawer. "Let me check. What's the last name?"

I hesitated, remembering the visitor's log at the hospital, my gut telling me it was pointless to lie.

"Boswell," I finally said, turned away to scan the crowd.

"Here you are, Miss Boswell." The woman slid a white envelope across the counter, my name printed in crisp blue letters across the front. "This must be for you."

My arm was heavy as I reached across the desk. I drew a narrow ticket from the envelope.

"Oh, no." She frowned over my shoulder. "You're too late. That ticket was for the four thirty show." She looked at her watch. "It's already over. The planetarium is closed."

I sprinted for the stairs, barreling through the descending wave of tourists. Shoving them aside, my sleeves clutched tight around my hands, I bumped past them like a pinball. When I reached the top, I looked out over the gallery wall and caught the high, agitated voice of Mrs. Smallwood,

Teddy's teacher. Mall security officers gathered around her in the lobby below, her arms gesturing wildly with her clipboard. My heart sped up. Teddy must already be missing.

Across the gallery, the double doors of the planetarium were closed, the ticket windows shut for the night.

Too late.

I slipped between the velvet ropes, checking over my shoulder as I tugged the handle. Locked. I leaned back against the door. There had to be a way in. Every theater has more than one exit. I looked right, then left. Another set of doors. I ducked under the rope, staying tight to the wall. I tugged the handle and it eased open with a quiet sigh.

Inside, it was night. The hall was narrow and close around me, dark except for tiny blue-white runners illuminating the way. A light glowed at the end, the hall opening into a high domed theater where hundreds of empty seats radiated from a projector in the floor.

There was no movement. No sound but the rush of blood in my ears.

"Teddy?" My voice cracked. "Teddy, are you in here?"

I took a tentative step, then another. The theater was cavernous and dim.

Beyond the doors, a muffled overhead speaker repeated, "Teddy Marshall, please meet your party at the welcome desk in the first-floor lobby."

The projector cast a swirling pink-and-purple glow against

the ceiling, but the rows and rows of folding seats were cast in deep shadow. I gripped the rails, following the diffused blue glow of the runway lighting through the room. Taking slow steps, I searched each aisle, and had almost given up when I caught a faint green glow near the floor. I walked toward it, tripping over something hard.

Teddy Marshall's shoes. Teddy lay face-up between the rows, his feet breaching the aisle. My heart leaped into my throat. I pulled myself to my knees. Whispered his name and reached for his hand. It was nothing but cold when I touched it.

The green light emanated from his right arm. A cluster of glow-in-the-dark stars—the kind they sold in the gift shop downstairs—stuck to his forearm. They twisted into a shape. A number. Five.

I pushed myself farther into the aisle toward his face, wedging myself between his shoulders and the seats. His glasses hung askew inside a clear plastic bag that clung to the opening of his nostrils and stuck in his mouth. The plastic sucked tight over his face—and didn't move. I couldn't breathe. The bag was knotted at Teddy's throat, tied with his own shoelace. I reached out to tear it, to rip it away from his face. Breathe, Teddy, breathe!

A dark hand shot in front of me before I could reach the bag. A glove clamped over my mouth and I screamed into it. Bucking and kicking, I grappled with the arms around my chest. They dragged me down the aisle, away from Teddy, pushed me against the tunnel wall, and cupped my mouth tight. My breath raced in and out my nose, whistling over the leather glove.

"What the hell are you doing here?" The voice was deep and angry, but familiar. Reece released his grip. "You shouldn't be here." He peered anxiously down the mouth of the tunnel before bringing the full force of his gaze back to mine.

"Teddy Marshall is in there. He's dead!"

"I know. And you can't be here when they find him!" He grabbed me under the arm and pulled me toward the exit. I planted my feet.

"What do you mean, you know he's in there?"

He jerked a furious finger toward the door. "In a few minutes this place is going to be crawling with cops. We've got to get out of here. Now."

"We can't just leave him here! We have to do something!"

"There's nothing we can do for him. He's gone, Leigh. But if we don't get out of here now, you're on your own." His face was cold and impatient. He waited two beats, then headed for the door, dragging me with him. He flung it open and I squinted against the flood of light as the doors whispered shut behind us.

I tugged against the pull of his hand, and started to turn back for the theater, but he was right. There wasn't time. Blue uniforms shuffled past. Security guards and chaperones swept through the exhibits, calling Teddy's name. I followed

Reece into an elevator. He pounded the lobby button with his fist.

"We go fast. You do what I say and no one will see you." Reece crossed the elevator toward me, his body arched possessively over mine with his back to the doors to shield me from view. He was hot and damp under the heavy leather, his sweat fetid with fear. The doors slid open to the first floor and he held the doors with one hand, and glanced over his shoulder.

"Come on." He hustled me under one arm, tucking me in close to his body. I tried to look behind me, at the planetarium gallery over our heads, heart tearing with every step, but Reece snapped me around, directing me with a hand at the small of my back and clipped commands no one else could hear.

Turn left, go right, head for the exit.

We threw the doors open and stepped out onto Independence Avenue, breaking apart the second we hit the stairs. Reece grabbed my hand and dragged me behind him with quick strides, dipping between two parked tour buses. His bike was there, illegally parked between them.

"Put this on." He practically threw the helmet at me as he straddled the bike and started the engine. "Hurry!"

I didn't move. "But Teddy . . ."

"We've got to get out of here," he pleaded from the bike. His eyes widened as he looked over my shoulder. I turned back toward the museum, torn. A traffic cop was staring, heading toward us.

"Now, Leigh!" Reece revved the engine.

I snapped the chin strap and jumped on behind him. The bike roared and I threw my arms around his waist as we leaped into traffic, weaving between buses and cabs until the museum fell away. An ambulance flew past, heading toward the museum, but Teddy was already gone.

29

REECE TOOK ME TO A PARKING SPACE near a grassy peninsula just north of the runway at Reagan National Airport. He set the kickstand, and headed toward the river's edge without a word. I plodded after him, tears streaming down my face.

Reece took off his jacket and spread it on the ground. He lowered himself to one side and gently patted the spot next to him. I didn't move, so he tugged my sleeve, and I dropped down beside him. Runway lights blinked red across the inlet. He stared at them, forearms resting on his knees while I wiped my nose on my sleeve.

"How did you know?" I clenched my jaw, afraid I'd start crying again. There wasn't enough room inside me for my anger and grief.

Reece reached into his jacket, unfolding Teddy's yellow

permission slip, and the ragged edges of the *Missed Connec-tions* ad tucked inside. I snatched them away from him.

"These were in my locker!"

He didn't look at me. "Just add breaking and entering to the long list of things I'm not proud of. I found the field trip flyer and the ad, and figured that's where you'd gone. I thought I could beat you there on my bike, but I was too late. I saw you run up the stairs. Hell, I could see you on the gallery, but I was stuck in the damn security line and I couldn't get to you in time." He dropped his head between his knees. "I owe you an apology. Not just for breaking into your locker. I never should have—"

"It's okay." I already knew he regretted kissing me. I didn't need to hear him say it. His guilt was one more emotion I didn't have room for. "You don't need to explain. I know why you've been following me." I watched the shoreline. Tried not to look at the lights that twinkled behind it. Tried not to think of stars.

"How'd you figure it out?" Reece asked softly. His skin glowed faintly pink, the violet and gold sunset casting color across his cheeks. The answer seemed so obvious to me.

"Because insanely hot transfer students don't ask girls like me to tutor them in chemistry . . . much less ride me to school, buy me dinner, fight my battles, pick my clothes, or hold my hand in public." I shook my head, giving in to a sad smile.

The one he returned was lopsided, and maybe a little self-conscious. "I think a few people might disagree with you. We've convinced the whole school we're dating. Maybe it's believable to everyone but you."

"Don't. Not now."

He nudged me gently with his elbow. "Tell me how you *really* figured it out."

The leather under my legs was heavy and warm and I wanted to crawl inside it and tell him everything. Instead, I hugged my knees to my chest and told him only what he wanted to know. "It was an accident. I went to the police station to tell them what I knew, and I overheard a conversation I shouldn't have."

"What did you know?" he asked quietly.

"The same stuff I already told Nicholson."

"How'd you know all the stuff you told Nicholson?"

I bristled, and just like that, the urge to confide in him was gone. Like someone turned on a light, and I could see him for who he was. A narc getting paid to snitch on me.

"Does it matter?" I snapped. "Two people are dead! And someone's making it look like I killed them. It's only a matter of time before—"

"Three," he whispered.

Everything stilled.

"Three people are dead." He looked in my eyes, worry lines digging deep. "Posie. She's gone, Leigh."

"No!" I shouted. "That's impossible! I saw her yesterday. She was fine. Her chart said she was—" My mouth hung open, breath held. The words were out, and I couldn't take them back. But it didn't matter. My name was on the visitor's log at the hospital anyway. The police would know I'd been there. "How?"

"Poisoned. Through her IV bag."

"When?" I already knew the answer. Posie had been murdered right after Mary Jones left her room. Right after I fled down the stairwell, and a nurse had come to change her bag.

"It was a slow-working toxin." Reece reached into his pocket and withdrew a folded paper. He held it between his thumb and forefinger, hesitating before he gave it to me. "She was pronounced dead this morning."

I peeled open a long list of handwritten names. On it were Mary Jones and Nearly Boswell. It was the visitor's log from the hospital. My stomach rolled. I stared at the flashing runway lights, half listening for sirens in the distance. "How much time do I have?"

Reece's cell phone rang in his pocket.

"I never gave that to you. It doesn't exist." He walked away, putting a few feet between us before taking the call.

"What?" he snapped into his phone.

Pause.

"None of your business . . . No, she wasn't there either . . . I know because she was with me all day, same as yesterday. So we ditched class? Big freaking deal . . . They told me to get close. I'm just holding up my end of the bargain . . . I already told you, I'm not in the city . . ." A jet blared overhead, swooping in low with its landing gear down. Reece plugged the microphone with his thumb and swore, waiting until the plane touched down to release it. ". . . No, I'm not at the airport . . . No, I'm not leaving the state . . . I'm hanging up unless you have something to say . . ." Reece listened, his eyes flicking to mine. His voice lowered. ". . . The planetarium? Seriously? Was the kid okay?" He massaged one temple while he listened, presumably to the details of the crime scene we'd just fled. "Yeah, about that, Lonny called. It goes down next Friday . . ." Reece turned his back, pitching his voice low. ". . . A warehouse downtown . . . I need you to hold up your end of the deal. . . . Friday night. You promised . . ."

Pause.

Reece's head snapped up, eyes fanning over the parking lot as an older model Mercedes with diplomatic tags—Oleksa's Mercedes—eased out of the lot. We were being watched, and not just by the cops. How could Oleksa have known where we were?

"I can't talk now. I'll call you later." Reece pocketed his phone and exhaled a string of curses. He dropped down beside me and stared out at the water. "We can't stay. They know where we are."

I folded the paper, a critical piece of evidence I wasn't supposed to have. "How did you get this?"

He hesitated before answering. "Today wasn't the first time I broke into your locker," he confessed, glancing at me sideways as if gauging my reaction. I remembered our conversation back at the diner the first time I'd tutored him. How he'd pulled the crumpled first chapter of his textbook from his pocket and made up some story about finding it on the floor.

"Why?"

He jerked his hand through his hair. It stuck up around his head in a prickly halo. "The cops told me to keep an eye on you. Get information. They didn't tell me how. After Romero kicked me out of his office, I came back to find you. I wanted to thank you for sticking up for me, and apologize for . . . you know . . . what happened." He squeezed his eyes shut as if blocking out the memory. "But you weren't there, so I broke into your locker. I was only going to leave you a note about meeting up to talk, but I found the message. The one with Posie's room number on it. By the time I got to the hospital to find you, I was too late."

"So you stole the visitor's log?" I waved the folded paper in his face. "Lying to the cops, tampering with evidence? This is obstruction of justice, Reece! You'll go back to jail—"

"I wouldn't have to break any laws if you'd just stop running from me and be where you're supposed to be for once!"

"What the hell is that supposed to mean?"

His face wrinkled with disgust. "You're really not getting this, are you? You were supposed to be with *me* after school today. I was supposed to be your alibi!"

"My alibi?" I asked, only now remembering the note he'd left in my locker yesterday. *Meet me tomorrow after school.*

Reece's head dropped into his hands, muffling his frustration. "Did anyone see you between the time school let out and the time Teddy went missing?"

"What are you saying?"

Reece raised his head. "I'm saying you're the number one suspect in the case of three"—he lifted three fingers—"count them—THREE homicides! All the evidence points back to you, Leigh! And today, when you should have been teaching me chemistry in a packed restaurant full of witnesses who could place you there at the time of Teddy's death, you traipse right into the damn crime scene! It's like you're walking into an ambush and I keep trying to keep you clear of the fire, but you just won't listen! You were supposed to be with me!"

I hugged my knees. "I didn't do any of this. None of this is my fault," I whispered.

"Look," he said through a long exhale. "The police think you're involved. They just can't prove anything. They're looking for any connections. Motives. Accomplices. Even if you didn't do it, they think you know who did. They're watching you, waiting. They figure you'll either do something stupid and incriminate yourself or lead them to the person behind this."

He took a deep breath and rubbed his eyes. "Leigh, I know you didn't kill anyone, and I know a set-up when I see it. You need to start thinking like the cops. It all boils down to motive. Think of everyone you know. Look for connections to the ads or the victims. Who has a reason to kill people you care about? To put you behind bars? Who would want to ruin your life, Leigh?"

I put my head in my hands. "I've never hurt anyone. I've never done anything wrong. My life isn't all that great to begin with. It's not like someone would have to work all that hard to ruin it."

"They're working hard because it's personal, or they wouldn't be risking so much. There's got to be someone who wants to hurt you. Keep thinking. I'm just buying time—picking breadcrumbs off the trail until we can figure this out."

He was covering for me. Which meant he believed me. And if he believed me, he could make the police believe me too. "Why not just give Nicholson the note the killer left in my locker? Tell him I'm being framed. I can't do it, but he'll believe you if you tell him you found it in my locker."

Reece shook his head. "I can't. It's inadmissible. I stole it from a locker that the police didn't have a warrant to search. Besides, the case isn't Nicholson's anymore. Homicide took it over weeks ago. The only reason I'm still involved is because I'm the only one who can help the cops connect the sale of the Special K to the killer."

"Emily, Marcia, and Posie were drugged."

"Roofies," he explained. "I'm guessing they'll find traces in Teddy's blood too. The killer is using ketamine to subdue the victims. Lonny's the only known ketamine dealer at West River, and he's willing to sell it to me. He heard I was back on suspension and decided my credentials were solid enough. If I can prove he's the one supplying it, the cops can squeeze him for a list of his buyers. Whoever's responsible for Posie and the others will be on that list."

I sat up, hope lifting me by the shoulders. A list of Lonny's buyers would exonerate me. I'd never bought drugs, and I couldn't possibly have a connection to any of Lonny's clients. We needed that list.

"So you're meeting him next Friday?"

He thought before answering. "At a rave. In Old Town."

Perfect. He wanted me to stay close to him, and I wanted that list. "Okay, what do we do?"

"No." He shook his head in big exaggerated sweeps. "There is no *we*."

"Yes, there is. You just said so. I'm going with you."

"No!"

"Give me one good reason why. You just told me I'm supposed to stay with you. For my own protection." I was determined to hold my ground. It was my life on the line too.

"Gena's taking you shopping Friday night. Lots of store cameras and receipts. Lots of witnesses. A bulletproof alibi in case anything happens. You'll be fine."

My legs shot out in front of me. "No way! I'm not bonding with your girlfriend at the food court while you screw up your shot with Lonny because I'm not there!"

"She's not my girlfriend, for chrissake!" He massaged his eyelids. "Look, I can't involve you in this, Leigh. If the details of the investigation leak, I could get in a lot of trouble."

"Fine. If you won't take me with you, I'm not cooperating anymore."

"Ha!" He chuckled bitterly. "When have you ever been cooperative?"

I leveled a finger at him. "You need me."

"I need you?"

"You need me."

His eyes dropped to my lips until that too close feeling sucked all the oxygen out from between us. A wicked thought seemed to root behind them. "Chemistry notwithstanding, in what ways do you think I need you?"

I ignored the hot rush of blood to my cheeks. "You said it yourself. Everyone thinks we're a couple, and Lonny's going to expect you to bring your 'girlfriend' to the party, which is convenient since Nicholson expects you to tail me anyway. That was one of his people on the phone, wasn't it?"

A muscle ticked in Reece's jaw. He didn't answer.

"Face it," I said. "You're in too deep with me. And if you don't take me with you, then I'll . . ."

Reece raised an eyebrow, his crooked smile challenging me to finish that sentence. I couldn't turn him in for tampering with evidence because that evidence was enough to get me arrested. And I couldn't blow his cover without getting him killed. I settled for the next best thing. ". . . I'll ditch Gena and go on my own." I raised my chin, looking him straight in the eye.

His face fell. "You're a pain in the ass, you know."

"That's my offer. Take it or leave it."

He gazed thoughtfully over the water, shaking his head. "I'll take it, but there's one catch . . . and one condition."

"What's the catch?"

"If you're in this as my cover, then you agree to play the part my way. We do it together. No more running off on your own."

I cringed, wondering what he might make me wear to school on Monday. "Fine," I muttered. "What's the condition?"

"You do anything to blow my cover, my paycheck, or my freedom, and the deal's off." His tone was stern, non-negotiable.

"Fine. I accept."

He clenched his teeth and glared at the river. "Then it's a date."

A plane took off, roaring over our heads. So close I could almost make out the individual faces of the passengers in the cabin windows, their foreheads plastered to the glass. Were things really any clearer from thirty thousand feet?

Hot air rustled the grass and rippled the water's surface, whipping my hair back from my face.

"You never answered my question," he said softly when the air finally stilled.

"What question?"

"How did you figure out that the ads were connected to all this?"

I settled for more half-truths, even if they hurt coming out. "The first—Emily's—was just random. Dumb luck, I guess. The second—about the play—seemed too obvious to ignore."

"What were you doing reading the ads in the first place?"

I searched him for signs of condescension, expecting the thick and dripping sarcasm Nicholson reacted with when he asked me the same question.

"I mean . . . are you looking for someone?" His expression was curious.

I turned away, feeling foolish for the childish hope that made me steal money for newspapers on Fridays. The one that brought this whole mess crashing down on my head.

Reece's bangs fell forward, concealing his face. I wondered what he was thinking. If he was disgusted with me. If he thought I was the kind of girl that trolled for dates in the personals. I didn't have the energy to explain.

He stood and reached down for my hand. I was afraid to take it. Afraid to know how he felt. But more afraid to seem ungrateful, after all he had done for me. I hesitantly placed my hand in his, letting him pull me to my feet. He tasted like worry and sadness—slightly salty and mildly acidic, the bitterness of that persistent nagging regret I'd come to think was always part of him. But no judgment. We stood there, hands touching for an awkward long moment.

"It's late," he said, letting go first. "I'll take you home."

30

JEREMY'S PARENTS WEREN'T HOME on Saturday morning. His white Civic was the only car in the driveway, so I found the hidden house key under the rock in the flowerbed and let myself in. I could have knocked, but I wasn't entirely sure he would answer, and after two days of not speaking, I missed him.

I found Jeremy in his bedroom, bent over a thick binder at his desk. I waited as he applied adhesive to a newspaper clipping and smoothed it against the page.

"Wow, that's quite a project." I craned my head over his shoulder. "What is it?"

He didn't look up. He knew it was me, and I didn't need to see his face to know how he felt about that. The minute he heard my voice, he sagged. He always slouched in school, as if his shoulders bore the weight of the social tiers above him, but something inside me broke to see him bend at the sound of my voice.

He didn't turn around. "It's my portfolio."

"Can I see it?"

He pushed it toward me. I picked up the book and turned the pages, pausing to admire the articles, ordered chronologically, beginning with the first day of school. Each school event had been photographed and memorialized. The name Jeremy Fowler appeared beneath each one.

"It's fantastic. How many are there?"

"One for every school event this year."

"What's it for?"

"My application to the journalism program at Syracuse."

He looked up at me, deep creases in his brow. For a moment, neither of us spoke. I set the portfolio on his desk.

"Syracuse? What happened to University of Maryland?"

"Changed my mind." He stroked the binder and closed the cover.

"Your mom must be happy."

He fingered the edge of a blue-and-orange admissions folder, and didn't look up.

"Why are you leaving?"

He choked out a harsh laugh. "Are you going to give me a reason to stay?"

There was a dare in his eyes. They asked questions he was too afraid to voice out loud because he already knew the answer. He wanted more than what we had. More than I could give him. I didn't know what to say. I set my backpack on his floor and dropped onto the bed. My own selfish desires collided with what was best for him. If he went to Maryland, Jeremy and I would stay close, but not the way he wanted.

I reached into my backpack and held out an unopened pouch of Twinkies. He stared at them, puzzled. "What's this for?" he asked.

"For standing you up on Friday." The plastic sleeve crinkled, a small sound that felt louder in the silence while I waited for him to accept both the gift and the apology.

He turned back to his work. "I know you've got a boyfriend. I get that you don't need me to drive you anymore."

"He's not . . . Reece isn't . . ." I stammered, shook my head, too afraid of losing him to pile on one more lie. But I'd made a deal with Reece. "It's not like that, Jeremy."

"Did he break up with you or something?" There was a glimmer of hope beneath the sarcasm, and I hated myself for disappointing him again.

"No, I just told him I needed some space."

Jeremy's lips moved, started to form words and then paused as if he'd changed his mind.

"Forget it. It's none of my business." He turned back to his desk, opened his iPad, and began scrolling through photos. I was about to answer him, to tell him he was being ridiculous, when one photo made me pause.

"Wait, flip back," I said, reaching over him to brush a finger across the screen. I scrolled backward through a few shots of a soccer game and the pep rally at school and stopped at a photo of two people, locked in an embrace. "Is that Emily Reinnert?" Her long blond ponytail gave her away, but who was she kissing? I couldn't make out his face, but he was too tall to be TJ. And he wasn't wearing a leg brace. I parted the curtain over Jeremy's bedroom window and held the iPad up against the house across the street—Vince's house. It was a match to the front porch in the photo. "When was this taken?"

Jeremy shrugged. "About three months ago, I think."

"Does TJ know?"

"Of course he does. Why do you think I took it?" He snatched the tablet from my hands. "What better way is there to express my appreciation for all those years of humiliation and public beat-downs? I gave a copy of the picture to TJ. He was pissed! Completely lost it. You should have seen him."

"What happened?"

"I kept waiting for him to pick a fight with Vince and break up with Emily. But nothing happened. Instead, Vince and Emily started fighting, and TJ and Emily made up and got over it. Nobody's mentioned it since."

"Weird."

"Maybe not, if you think about it. Vince and TJ have been best friends as long as we have. It's not like they're going to let one stupid kiss come between them. Maybe it didn't mean anything. Maybe it was just a one-time thing. A mistake." He looked at me for a long time, trying to convey more than he was saying. I wondered if this was his way of telling me we were cool. That he was over it, and I was forgiven. Or if he was asking me to say it was all a mistake. That I shouldn't have kissed Reece and it wouldn't happen again. His stare was heavy with expectation. I changed the subject and looked away.

"So TJ thwarted your wicked retribution plan by not going ballistic on Vince, and not dumping his girlfriend. Why didn't you just print the photo in the school paper, or blast it out to everyone by e-mail? Why let him off easy?"

"We came to a gentlemen's agreement." Jeremy rolled his eyes and grinned sheepishly. It was the first smile I'd seen him wear in days. "I agree not to broadcast the photo of his girlfriend kissing the hot rich guy whose legs are still working, and he agrees not to break both of mine."

I laughed. "Gentlemen, huh?" Feeling like the pall had lifted, I reached over his shoulder and playfully started flipping through his photos. "What other crazy incriminating shots are you hiding in this thing?"

A gap-tooth smile caught my attention. I reached slowly, turning the screen toward me.

A group of students posed in front of a building with tall glass sections. Teddy's face smiled back at me and my gut clenched.

"You were at the museum yesterday?" I clicked through a short slide show, scanning the handful of pictures, looking past the smiling faces, searching the figures in the background for my own. Finding no sign of either myself or Reece, I let out a shaky breath and scooted it back to him.

Jeremy's face was paler than usual and he looked tired. "I had permission to leave school to cover it for the paper. I guess you heard about Teddy," he said, closing the picture and looking awkward and uncomfortable. "I'm sorry for that stuff I said about him at the amusement park. I didn't mean it like it sounded."

I nodded. I doubted anyone knew about Posie yet, but it was only a matter of time. Monday morning, the entire school would be buzzing over it. As if reading my thoughts, Jeremy said, "You should get to school early on Monday. The police are auditing attendance records and I heard teachers are giving detention if you're late without a pass. There's supposed to be some big announcement and a lecture on personal safety in every first period class. And I'm pretty sure all after-school activities are canceled until further notice. Counselors from all six high schools have been called in and they're supposed to be making the rounds. You know . . . grief counseling for anyone who needs it." He massaged his eyes under his glasses, then pulled them off and dropped them on the desk. "I'm not a big fan of shrinks, but I thought you should know about it. Just in case . . . you know . . . you needed to talk to someone."

"How'd you know about all this?"

Jeremy opened the Twinkies and lay down beside me on the bed. "Contrary to popular belief, I'm actually not a shitty reporter." He smirked it off. He knew he was a great reporter. I was just lucky he hadn't seen me at the museum.

"So what was it like?" he asked around a mouthful of sponge cake.

I bit into my own. "What was what like?"

"You know . . ." he mumbled, "your first kiss?"

I stopped chewing. Jeremy stopped too. We lay staring at the ceiling instead of at each other. I searched for tiny imperfections in the surface—imperfections I knew weren't there—while I thought about what to say.

"It's okay. You don't have to answer that." I felt him reach for his glasses, to push them up the bridge of his nose, even though he wasn't wearing them. It was something he always did when he was uncomfortable—like some people chew their nails or pace or twirl their hair. I hated that I was the one making him feel that way.

"That wasn't my first kiss." My first kiss had been with Jeremy, when he'd gotten drunk at a party and made an unexpected pass at me six months ago.

Jeremy frowned as if the memory stung. "That one doesn't count."

"Just because you were too shitfaced to remember it, doesn't mean it doesn't count."

"For the record, I remember very clearly. My face hurt for two days."

"That's called a hangover."

"No, it's called an upper cut. It doesn't count because you didn't kiss me back."

Of everything that went wrong that night, this is what bothered Jeremy most. Not the fight with his father that'd made him want to get drunk in the first place. Not that he'd been too inebriated to listen when he tried to kiss me and I said no. Not that I'd hit him, or the fight we'd had before I took his car keys and walked myself home. No, what bothered him most was that I hadn't returned that kiss. Not at all. It may have started out like my kiss with Reece, but it ended very differently. It never had any traction. Never turned me inside out like Reece's kiss had. I hadn't lost myself in Jeremy's kiss for a single minute. Because I'd never wanted it to begin with. But I'd never told him that. Instead, I'd hidden behind Mona's rules. To tell him that now, when we were so close to finding our way back to normal, felt unnecessarily cruel.

"Well, it counted to me. And I'm sure if you hadn't been such a sloppy drunk, you would've proved yourself a much better kisser than Reece Whelan anyway." I teased a sad smile from him. Jeremy's kiss may have been a disaster, but it had been real for him. He'd wanted it. He'd wanted me. And I wasn't sure I could say the same for Reece.

I fell back onto the mattress and stretched. Let my muscles melt into the thick down comforter. They ached, swollen and knotted with the tension of the past few weeks. With the door shut and the blinds closed, the house quiet and Jeremy lying beside me, I relaxed.

Jeremy cleared his throat softly. "So I heard Reece got expelled . . ."

"Suspended," I corrected before he could finish.

"Right . . . suspended. I was thinking maybe you'd need a date for prom? We could go together . . . if you want to?"

For a moment, neither of us spoke, and the look on his face was two parts regret and one part hope. I opened my mouth to speak, but couldn't find the right words. I hadn't intended to lead him on when I told him he was probably a better kisser, but it was too late to take it back.

"I kind of assumed you'd be taking Anh to prom."

Jeremy frowned. "I haven't asked anybody yet. I was hoping maybe you'd want to go. I mean, I know you hate crowds. And I know there's going to be like a thousand people there, but I just figured maybe . . ."

The thought of a crowd that size made me cringe, but throw alcohol, drugs, and touching into the mix and it made the prom seem like a tame alternative when I considered Friday night's rave. The difference was the matter of choice. I didn't have a choice about the rave—I had to be there, like a mandatory graduation requirement. Prom felt more like an elective.

"You should probably go ahead and ask Anh," I suggested as gently as I could. "I hate those things. Wouldn't be caught dead at a school dance." I looked over at Jeremy. He stared at the ceiling, his chest motionless. I twined my fingers in his and felt the thin ray of hope slip out of him, making room for heavier emotions that tugged down the corners of his smile and pulled the color from his face. He was still angry with me, and it was a sour and metallic knot in my throat, but I made myself swallow it like medicine. I deserved it.

"It's okay," he said numbly. "I figured as much."

We lay quietly, hand in hand until his disappointment started tasting more like bitter determination.

"There's a rave on Friday night." His fingers twitched with an eager thrill that covered me in goose bumps.

I sat up, letting go of his hand. "You're not going, are you?"

"I thought it would make a really cool piece for my portfolio. It's kind of edgy. I thought a little grit might make me look more . . ." He paused, choosing his words carefully. "Might get more attention in a college application than something as lame as another canned food drive."

"Are you sure that's a good idea?" Translation: *This is the worst idea. Ever.* Jeremy had no idea what he was getting into. "I mean, you do know what goes on at a rave . . . don't you?"

He looked insulted. "Jeez, Leigh. I may be a loser, but I'm not an idiot!"

"I wasn't suggesting that you're an idiot . . ."

"And I happen to *enjoy* doing Sudoku and watching the History Channel on Friday nights. There's nothing wrong with that."

I laughed, kicking him gently with the tip of my shoe. "I didn't say there was. I just don't want you to get in trouble."

"I won't." He kicked me back. "I already talked to our sponsor. She said I can run the article as long as there aren't any photos of 'questionable content.' Besides, I'm not going to print any recognizable photos of anyone's face, and I'll change the names to protect the innocent."

My laughter evaporated as I considered the best way to tell him . . . tell him what? That I'd be posing as a narc's girlfriend to facilitate a drug deal? That it might be my name he had to change?

"Fine, but if you snap any pictures of me, I might have to kill you."

"You're going?" He sat up, looking confused. "But I thought you just said you wouldn't be caught dead . . ." He smiled, thin and brittle. "Oh . . . I get it. You wouldn't be caught dead at a dance *with me*."

My heart hurt. I wanted to explain. To fix what I couldn't stop breaking over and over.

"Jeremy," I began, unsure how to say what needed to be

said. "You know I love you. You're my best friend . . ." I took a breath, and forced myself to speak the truth I'd never had the guts to tell him. Not part of it. Not half of it. All of it. "But that's all you are to me."

He lay back down, eyes glued to the ceiling.

My voice trembled, but I needed him to hear this even though I wished he didn't have to. "I need that to be enough for you too. I can't make myself love you more than I do. And it's not fair to either of us to try."

He flinched, a movement so small I might have missed it if I hadn't been looking so closely at his eyes, waiting for them to blink.

"Can you understand? Will you please just look at me?"

His silence was disorienting. I'd navigated my life by him. Had always counted on him swinging back to me, his true north. But he'd turned away, and wouldn't look back.

Even as he said "I think you should leave."

31

I SPENT SUNDAY MORNING with the shades drawn tight, sagging into our creaky dirt-brown sofa. I was still in my pj's, buried under a faded afghan that smelled like mildew and cigarette smoke. The TV was bright in the dimly lit room. I poked the remote through a gap in the blanket where it was pulled up

to my ears, flipping between channels with the sound muted
so it wouldn't wake my mother. News stations had footage
from the Air and Space Museum on a loop, each showing
different angles of the front of the building, rows of yellow
buses, and flashing police lights. The police hadn't released
many details to the press, only that an unidentified minor was
found dead during a school field trip, and police were investi-
gating the possibility of foul play.

Possibility. No mention of how he'd been asphyxiated with
his own shoelace, or the mysterious number left in stickers
on his arm. Five.

Emily . . . ten.

Marcia . . . eighteen.

Posie . . . three.

Teddy . . . five.

I'll put it all on the table for you.

I looked past the reporters' faces searching for someone
familiar in the background, someone who might have a
reason to frame me for murder. Someone who might stay
through the chaos to see me carted off to jail. But the media
was careful not to show any students on camera, and the
police barricades kept the press from getting too close.

Who wrote the ads? What did he want from me and what
was he trying to tell me?

I flipped the TV off and sat in the dark for a while, listening to Mona snore in the next room. Then I threw off the

quilt, padded to my room, and flopped on my bed. Einstein stared back at me from the poster on my wall, as if to say: "Why the hell haven't you figured this out yet? It's four lousy numbers. Not the Theory of Relativity, for crying out loud."

But those four numbers were impossible to solve. I had no idea what factor connected them. It's like I was missing the value of x, because I couldn't figure out what x was supposed to represent.

The phone rang on my nightstand and I reached to grab it before the second ring.

"What are you doing?" Anh asked before I could say hello. She knew I'd be the one to answer this early on a Sunday.

"Talking to Albert."

"I bought you that poster to demonstrate the correlation between frizzy hair and scientific brilliance. Not so you'd become all codependent upon Our Holy Father of Modern Physics."

"It's Sunday. Let me worship in peace."

"Fine, what are you doing after nerd-church?"

"Sleeping."

"Want to study for finals?"

"Can't. I'm out of bus money and I don't have a ride."

Anh sighed. "Jeremy's just upset. He won't keep you in pedestrian purgatory forever. You can walk."

It felt wrong that Anh should be the one telling me how Jeremy was feeling. "I don't feel like it."

"Come on. I'll bring lunch. I made hummus and gluten-free dippers."

"No can do. My brain's a carb- and fat-oiled machine. It runs on these crazy little alkaloids called theobromine and phenethylamine. They're found in nature in something called Snickers bars. Maybe you've heard of them?"

"Very funny. Will you come if I promise to bring chocolate?"

I didn't feel like leaving my room. All I wanted was to climb under my covers and try not to think about Teddy's face in that bag, and the last words I'd spoken to Posie. But my stomach growled at me. I thumbed through the syllabus on my desk and grumbled, "Throw in a Coke?"

"Adding caffeine to your growing list of vices?" Anh chided.

"Fine. I'll stop at Bao's and pick up chocolate and soda. And if your arteries haven't spontaneously combusted by then, you can meet me at the library in an hour, where I expect to hear all the gory details of your scandalous affair with Mr. Scary Hot New Guy."

"Fine." I rolled my eyes, as if she could hear it through the phone. I was getting ready to hang up when something occurred to me. "Hey, Anh. What do the numbers ten, eighteen, three, and five have in common?"

Anh was quiet for a moment. I couldn't hear anything but the rattle and drone of the small rusting air conditioner duct-taped to the frame of my window. "No idea. I need more information."

"Yeah," I said. "Me too." Even if I wasn't any closer to solving the numbers, at least I didn't feel as stupid as I had a moment ago. Anh couldn't see a connection either. I could only hope the next ad would reveal the missing link. And that I wouldn't be too late to solve it.

I said good-bye to Anh, got dressed, and packed up my books. When I grabbed my hoodie off the back of my desk chair, something crinkled in the pocket. The torn page from the hospital log book still smelled like the inside of Reece's jacket. I should have destroyed it or flushed it down the toilet, but I looked around my room for a place to hide it instead. I reached under my mattress and withdrew the plastic bag. It was the one place Mona was sure to avoid.

I put the hospital log sheet inside it, adding it to the old photo of my dads' poker club. A mystery for another day. I shoved them all under the mattress. This week was all about being normal. Laying low. I threw my backpack over my shoulder and recited the rules that would get me through the next six days: No bad grades, no trouble, and no touching.

• • •

I'D WANTED TO GET TO RANKIN'S CLASS EARLY on Monday, but that didn't happen. I was still in purgatory. Jeremy hadn't picked me up and I didn't want to call Reece for a ride. Despite my best efforts, our kiss had landed him in suspension for another week and I didn't need to give Romero one more reason to expel him. Reece had given me an alibi and confiscated the evidence from the hospital. I was safe at least for now. I just needed to keep a level head. To be on time when attendance was taken, and to be as shocked as everyone else when the rest of the school figured out that the unnamed minor found murdered in the planetarium was Teddy Marshall, and that Posie was dead too.

A reporter stood on the front steps of the school, holding a microphone and talking into a TV camera. School security guards and police flanked the front doors, and I slipped in with the last of the students to arrive.

Inside the lobby, a line of parents waited to speak with administration, talking animatedly to each other about emergency PTA meetings and the need for increased security at school events. The secretaries politely nudged them out of the office, telling them they'd have to schedule an appointment to speak with Principal Romero.

I dodged around the tail of the line and headed to my first class, trying not to notice the red PERSONAL SAFETY flyers on every bulletin board I passed.

I flew into the chem lab as the second bell blared. No time to check Friday's test scores, or the rankings for the week. Curious heads turned and followed me to my seat. Anh sat hunched over, her face uncharacteristically pale. She didn't look at me when I sat down. My test lay facedown on the desk. I took a deep breath, turned it over, and felt Anh's eyes dart to the score circled on top.

103%. A yellow sticky note beside it read: "Please meet Kylie Rutherford at 2:45pm today. You will be tutoring her in geometry through Thursday."

I stifled a strange involuntary noise.

"Congratulations, Miss Boswell." Rankin's back was to the class as he copied the day's homework on the blackboard. "You and Mr. Petrenko both achieved perfect scores on this exam. You both also solved the extra credit question." He slapped his hands together, a cloud of chalk dust fanning out as he turned to address the class. "It was quite a puzzle. I must say, I was rather impressed."

I rotated my head slowly toward Oleksa's table. He reclined in his seat, assuming his usual I-couldn't-give-a-shit slouch. His test scores wouldn't be enough to sway the rankings. His lab partner was hopeless, he'd never completed a homework assignment, and his attendance was sketchy at best.

I wanted to savor the moment. I'd aced the test and I had four tutoring sessions booked to keep me on track this week. I should have felt buoyed by Rankin's confidence in me, but I couldn't shake the image of Kylie Rutherford, strung up and tied like a lamb for slaughter.

Anh turned her test facedown and tried to hold a smile, but it wavered, and she gave up. I opened my mouth to apologize, a stab of guilt prodding me to say something. But I stopped. Anything I said would sound clumsy and insincere.

The silence was deafening as Rankin marked his attendance log. Finally he said, "I'm afraid I must share some rather grave news with you today." I imagined every eye in the room darting in my direction, but when I looked up all eyes were on Rankin. "Some of you may already know that two students passed away this weekend under tragic and uncertain circumstances. Posie Washington and Teddy Marshall are no longer with us. There will be a memorial service for them here at the school on Friday."

A roar of whispers erupted, rumors confirmed behind cupped hands. Oleksa's head rotated slowly in my direction. Our eyes locked, and I turned away.

Rankin went on to disclose the events of the weekend in vague detail. I slunk down, kept my eyes low. It wasn't hard to look broken by the news. I picked at the corner of the sticky note, wondering if Kylie Rutherford had any idea what she'd signed up for.

• • •

"I'M SORRY! I JUST CAN'T DO IT." Kylie dragged her fingers through the magenta hair at her temples and squeezed her head. As if that might somehow expel the information from her brain and spray it across the page.

"You can do it. We have all week to practice. The test isn't until Friday." I pushed the book at her. She looked up through a jagged veil of bangs. Her raccoon eyes were shiny and wet.

"I'm not smart like you." The pathetic whine seemed out

of character with her tough-girl face. She wrestled a finger under the dog collar at her throat, like she was loosening a tie. Or a noose. I closed my eyes and shook off the thought, but not before seeing the mud-colored hickey behind the leather band.

"You are smart," I lied, unable to stop staring at the bruise on her neck. Kylie lived a few doors down from my trailer. She was seventeen and already a rent-a-girl. She'd be lucky to finish school at all, much less pass this test. "You can pass this," I said anyway. "You just have to memorize a few simple equations." *And stop letting losers suck away your future.*

Kylie smeared the black stream under her eyes with her sleeve. "You're really nice. I don't believe anything people are saying about you," she said between sniffles. "I mean, not the bad stuff. You don't seem like the type."

I stiffened. "What bad stuff?"

"You know, all that stuff about how you think you're so much better than the rest of us just because you're smart. I think it's cool that you're smart. Gives the rest of us a reason to hope, right? Everyone's talking about you maybe getting some big scholarship—that you might make it out of the park. I hope you do." She smiled. It was a sad smile, like the corners of her mouth had to fight to pick themselves up.

I wasn't sure what to say. I was used to people talking about me, but not like this. Usually, the comments felt like hands grabbing at my ankles, dragging me back down into the slag. I'd never thought anyone in the park would care enough to offer a push from below. Like it might lighten their burdens if just one of us could make it out.

"Thanks." I took one last look at her neck, feeling protective for reasons I didn't want to think about. Her face flushed, splotchy and streaked. She fidgeted with her dog collar, pulling it up to conceal the mark, ashamed—the same way my mother tugged up the collar of her robe. Kylie would be someone else's Mona someday. "I hope you do too."

She looked down at the desk. "Can I give you one piece of advice?" Her brow lined with thoughtful creases. "Lonny says you're seeing that new kid, Reece?"

I nodded, feeling a little more cautious now that I knew who'd been sucking the life out of her.

"Be careful," she said. "Boys like him . . ." Kylie cocooned her hands in the cuffs of her sleeves. I wondered what secrets she was hiding under them. "Just be careful."

I wanted to tell her the same, but I couldn't. Not without saying too much. So I changed the subject instead.

"What are you doing on Friday night, to celebrate after the test?" I asked casually, as if I wasn't so anxious to know the answer. As if her life didn't depend on it.

32

BOTH POSIE'S AND TEDDY'S FUNERALS took place on Wednesday, one after the other, and the school announced a liberal absence policy for those who wished to attend. I didn't wish to. I wanted them both to be alive and well. But I'd go.

That morning, I fished in Mona's closet for a simple black blouse and paired it with a pair of black jeans. My only shoes were my sneakers, but no one would see them if they were tucked under the pews.

I dropped some change in my pocket and walked to the bus stop at the end of Sunny View Drive. The clear plastic shelter felt like a magnifying glass in the sun, and I stood beside it, with my toes on the curb. A car slid to a slow stop at my feet. I looked up and saw Anh's face in the passenger-side window of Jeremy's Civic. The glass rolled down. She was perfectly polished in a sleeveless black sheath and a strand of delicate pink pearls. Her nails were painted pale pink to match and in her small hands, she held an elegant black clutch that shone like her patent leather heels. She said nothing about my jeans and sneakers. Just looked at me with a sad smile.

On her other side, Jeremy wore a dress shirt and tie, and looked hard at the steering wheel.

"You shouldn't go alone," Anh said quietly. "Get in. We'll take you."

The city bus rolled to a noisy stop behind the Civic, a trail of suffocating exhaust blowing over me. The air brake released and the bus doors swung open, but the choice Anh was offering didn't feel like a choice at all. I knew they were going to the funerals, same as I was, but they looked like a matched pair, and I felt like I was crashing their date. But if I took the bus, I'd seem ungrateful.

I pulled open the Civic door and scrunched myself into the backseat. "Thanks."

We rode to Posie's family's church in silence. Neither of them asked the questions I knew must be on their minds. Why my mentees? Why me? Because how can you ask a question like that without it sounding like some kind of accusation? So instead, they said nothing.

I sat beside Anh in the back of the church with my hands tucked under me, and my legs folded tight at the ankle. Jeremy sat on her other side, her leg crossed at the knee, angled toward his. She cried silently into a clean lace hanky. My own tears slid steadily down over my chin.

When it was over, Posie's family took up quiet places beside her open casket. The receiving line moved slowly, relatives and students pausing to hug or shake hands with her parents. I wiped my palms over my jeans as we neared the front of the line, made an excuse about needing to use the bathroom, and waited outside until it was over.

Silent and numb, we loaded into Jeremy's car and followed a caravan of students to Teddy's graveside service on the other side of town. We stood on the outside edge of a large circle of mourners. The soccer team was there to acknowledge the loss of their water boy. Vince stood tall in a dark designer suit, hands folded and head bowed. I watched, bitter, as he approached Teddy's mother and reached for her hand. He held it while he spoke to her, paying day late respects to her lost son, a kid he never had a kind word for until he was lying in a hole.

As if reading my thoughts, Jeremy shook his head and whispered, "Amazing, isn't it? How they all see him now?" He watched the endless receiving line with a look of fascination. His hand wandered to his chest where his camera would normally be.

Anh took a deep, shaky breath and rested her head on Jeremy's shoulder. The thought of getting in the backseat of Jeremy's car again was unbearable. When I walked away from the service, across the cemetery, I was pretty sure neither of them noticed.

• • •

IT WAS DUSK WHEN I GOT OFF the city bus and stared down the potholed mouth of Sunny View. Every inch of me felt heavy, and I walked slowly toward home. Music blared from Lonny Johnson's trailer, and strange cars lined both sides of the street. Kylie hung over the railing of his front porch.

"Boswell!" she called, heavy-lidded and unsteady on her feet. "Come party with us!" After two funerals, I didn't have the energy to shout back. I half smiled and kept walking. "Come on," she sang loudly after me. "Your boyfriend's here!"

I slowed and looked at the line of parked cars, finding Reece's motorcycle wedged in it. I hesitated, unsure, and glanced back at my own trailer. The shades were drawn tight. Mona might not notice. Even so, I'd rather gouge my eyes out than step foot inside Lonny Johnson's front door. But how would it look to him if I turned away now?

Lonny's door flung open and Reece stepped out, a cigarette dangling between his lips. He held a beer can in his hand, laughing and talking with one of Kylie's friends, a bleach-blonde with dark roots and heavy eye makeup, and boobs too big for her frame. Kylie elbowed him hard in the ribs and jerked her chin at me. Reece's eyes found mine and his face sobered. He handed the blonde his beer without looking at her. Then he flicked his cigarette and directed his exhale to the ground in a move that looked entirely too practiced.

"Leigh, wait up," he called, but I was already walking. He vaulted the porch rail and caught me halfway down the street. "Leigh, wait."

I made it two steps before Reece grabbed my wrist and dragged me behind my neighbor's trailer, out of sight of Kylie and her friend. I swayed a little at the touch of his fingers on my skin, my lips tingling and my head suddenly light. He stopped short, pulling me in close, steadying us both. He was drunk. I ripped my hand from his, bracing myself against the trailer while I waited for the fog in my head to clear. His face was flushed and he looked at me with glassy eyes. "I can explain."

"You don't need to explain. I know who you are."

"Do you? Because that would make one of us." He scrubbed a hand over his face, as if trying to sober himself.

I stepped back. He was entirely too close. No good could come of this conversation. "I'm tired, Reece. I just came from two funerals. All I want is to go home."

"Is it so unbelievable that I want the same?" He threw an arm toward Lonny's trailer. "I have to be here. I don't have a choice."

"There's always a choice. You can choose to leave."

"I can't."

"Why not?"

"Because I'm not like you! I'm like them. A year ago, I was just like Lonny. I was at the bottom of the food chain and I was hungry. I wanted the big car and the hot girls and the fat wallet and I didn't care who got hurt. There are only two ways out of places like this—the quick way or the right way. I chose the wrong one. And now I'm stuck here. And the only way to fix what I've done is to keep guys like Lonny from stealing that choice from people like you." He rubbed his eyes and cussed. They were bloodshot and weary. "Don't you see? I have to go to his screwed-up parties. I have to drink his booze and hang out with his friends and put up with girls that don't have half the guts or brains that you do. I have to be someone I don't like—someone you don't trust—to make him trust me—"

I put a hand up to stop him, still buzzing from his touch. I didn't want to know what he was doing behind Lonny's closed doors. It was painful to think about, and I didn't want to overanalyze why. "I know, I know . . . so we can get Lonny's list of ketamine buyers. I get it."

"You don't get anything! I can't keep making this about you! I came to West River for one reason. To destroy Lonny. To set him up for a big fucking fall and put him behind bars for good. I can't lose sight of what side I'm on, just because you show up on the hood of Lonny's car and turn everything upside down."

Reece was suddenly quiet. He swallowed hard, looking like he'd said too much. If he was so angry, why was he standing so close? If I turned everything upside down, why wasn't he walking away?

"I don't understand," I said, wanting to touch him without feeling drunk. Wanting to feel the things I saw in his eyes that his lips weren't saying. "I thought we were on the same side. I thought . . . I thought we wanted the same thing."

We did, didn't we? Want the same thing?

His eyes crinkled, confused. "Maybe I don't know what I want anymore."

He leaned in slowly, lips parting and hesitating close. His breath was warm against my face. Beer and other things that blurred the lines between us when he touched me. The way Jeremy had blurred the lines the first time he got drunk and tried to kiss me.

"I should go," I said, pulling out of reach. He looked down at his feet as I turned to leave.

"Why'd you do it, anyway?" He wore a self-deprecating look, hands stuffed in his pockets while he kicked at the gravel.

"Do what?"

"Why waste your time saving someone who can't be fixed?"

I folded my arms over my chest, tucking my hands under them as I backed away, wishing I could kiss him without caring how he felt. "Maybe you're not the only one who's broken."

• • •

When I got to school on Thursday morning, my locker was buzzing. I jerked my hand from the lock and looked around. A cluster of girls from my trig class stood at the end of my locker bay. They lowered their voices when they saw me watching, slammed their lockers shut, and hurried away. People were beginning to connect the dots. Rumors were spreading about the bizarre connection between the dead students, bringing curious eyes around to me. It felt like those dreams when you're sure that you've come to school naked. Only this wasn't a dream. And no one was laughing.

I rose up on my toes and peered into the vent. A red light blinked inside. I sucked in a breath and spun my combination. Slowly, I opened the door. A cell phone rested on a folded sheet of paper.

4 *New Text Messages* flashed across the screen.

I reached for the folded paper and peeled it open. The handwriting was immediately familiar.

> IT'S MORE PRACTICAL THAN A BASEBALL BAT.
> MINUTES ARE PRE-PAID.
> TRY NOT TO WASTE THEM.
>
> — RW

A cell phone? Why would I need a cell phone? I looked for a hidden message, turned it over, but nothing had been written on the back.

The phone vibrated again. *5 New Text Messages* flashed across the screen. The first message popped up.

R U THERE?

I scrolled down to the next one.

WHERE R U?

The screen flashed *Incoming Call from REECE.* I pressed the green TALK button. "Hello?"

"I guess you got the phone?" There was a drowsy quality to his voice. It was gravelly and deep, like he'd just woken up.

"You mean the one inside my locker? Note the emphasis on *lock*," I snapped.

"Don't shout," he groaned. "My head's splitting. Where have you been?"

"You're the one still in bed." I shook my head to clear that image.

"Cut me some slack. It was kind of a late night."

I wondered who he'd been up late with. I bit my lip. "Yeah well, I was out late too."

"No you weren't. You were in bed by nine, and I didn't want to leave the phone with your mom—"

"Wait . . ." I couldn't get enough air. I hunkered behind my open locker door and whispered, "You talked to my mom?"

"Relax, Leigh. I didn't talk to your mom."

My body tingled with receding panic, like I had narrowly missed a disaster. Until a curious thought occurred to me. "If you didn't talk to my mom, how did you know I was in bed by nine?" The thought both fascinated and horrified me. "Were you watching my trailer last night?"

No answer.

"We need to talk about Friday," he said, changing the subject.

"Did Nicholson tell you to watch me?"

"I told you, Nicholson's team is off the case—"

"Then whose team are you on now?" It was the wrong thing to say, and I regretted it the minute it came out of my mouth. But I needed to know where his loyalties were, and if I could trust him. All those things he'd said yesterday, about how he didn't know whose side he was on . . . Was he watching my trailer because he wanted to or because some homicide detective was paying him to?

"I'm on the team that's trying to keep you out of jail. What are you wearing tomorrow night?"

"Excuse me?"

"To the rave? On Friday? We had a deal, remember?"

I felt lost in the conversation, still preoccupied with the fact that he'd been watching my house.

I glanced down at my faded T-shirt. It was two sizes too large and fit me like a muumuu.

"No clue." I squeezed my eyes shut. I knew what was coming.

"Don't worry. I'll take care of everything. I'll pick you up at your place tomorrow at eight. Bring your phone."

The bell for first period rang. I plugged a finger in my ear and pressed the cell tight to my head.

"You've only got five minutes and a long walk to class. Better get moving. I'll call you later." He disconnected.

He was right. I was going to be late. But I still had so many questions. I scrolled through the contacts. Gena and Reece were both on speed dial. I gnawed the inside of my lip. Why would he program Gena's number into a pre-paid phone he'd bought for me? My finger hovered over the delete prompt, but at the last minute, I changed my mind. Reece said he was on the team that was trying to keep me out of prison. If there was any chance Gena was on that team too, then I needed all the help I could get.

33

JEREMY'S CAR WASN'T IN THE PARKING LOT at the Bui Mart and I hoped that meant he'd gone to see Dr. Matthews. Bao didn't look up when I walked into the store. Metallica blared through the overhead speakers, loud enough to drown out the bells on the door, but my chocolate milk and paper were already waiting on the counter. Bao's spiky hair bobbed up and down to the beat of the music while he mopped up a spill beside the coffee machines on the other side of the store.

I stretched up on my toes and leaned over the counter. Felt around underneath for the volume control on the stereo. My hand passed over something cold and metallic, mounted to the underside and pointed at me. I carefully removed my hand.

The music died suddenly. The only sound was the whir of the slushie machines.

Fingers gripped my shoulder and I jumped. "Looking for something?"

Bao stood behind me, a remote control in his other hand. The mop handle lay across the floor, its wet strands making a gray puddle in the aisle.

"I was looking for the volume," I said, wriggling out from under him. "They've done studies, you know. Eighties hair bands are hazardous to your health. They should put a warning label on that stuff."

"They do. It says *Listening at High Volume Makes You Dangerously Cool and Lethally Attractive to Members of the Opposite Sex.*"

I reached into the day old bin and plucked out a jelly donut to settle my nerves. "Maybe you should consider toning it down a little. Two hundred decibels is loud enough to kill you."

Bao lifted the opening in the counter and stepped in behind it. "Know what else can kill you? Snooping around under the counter of a convenience store that's been robbed three times already this year." His expression was grave. He rested his hands on the counter above where he kept his handgun, and I didn't feel so hungry anymore.

I tucked the donut into a bag and set my change on the counter. Then I thumbed through the paper and checked to make sure it was all there.

"Are you going to this rave I keep hearing about?" Bao folded his arms and leaned against the counter while he watched me pack up my loot. I responded with an indeterminate shake of my head.

"Anh wanted to go with your friend Richie McRich. I told

Dad I need her to mind the store for me tonight. She's pissed, but she'll get over it." He shrugged. "I don't know what she sees in that guy. She should take a lesson from you and just not date. She doesn't need the distractions. You, on the other hand." He shook a finger at me. "You've got your eye on the prize. You know how to play the game and I respect that. That's why you're such competition for her. If she's not careful, you might pull that scholarship out from under her."

"I'm counting on it," I said quietly, not sure how I felt. I left, clutching my newspaper to my chest.

• • •

The halls were empty when I got there. Regular classes had been canceled for a memorial assembly honoring Posie and Teddy. I was in class when Rankin took attendance, but no one had noticed when I veered off to the social studies wing instead of following the others to the memorial service. I carried the *Missed Connections* to the civics classroom, my soft soles too loud on the tile, but no one was there to hear me.

A laminated street map of Alexandria was mounted on a bulletin board in the hall, just outside the classroom. I traced a finger over the intersecting lines, checking them against the clue in my other hand.

> **Isosceles had the right angle.**
> **The Torpedo is a straight shot to the Yards.**
> **Follow my tracks.**

The Torpedo Factory was a collection of boutiques, galleries, and restaurants on the waterfront in Old Town, spread over the top right corner of the map.

Clearly, the ad was a problem of triangulation, accounting for two points of an isosceles triangle—the Torpedo Factory and Potomac Yards, the old rail yard that lay almost due north of it. But the clue didn't reveal the location of the right angle. If the ninety-degree angle was located at Potomac Yards, that would put the unknown angle somewhere in Fairlington. But if the vertex of the right angle was at the Torpedo Factory, the clue would take me several miles south, on the other side of town. The killer was giving me one more chance to screw up, just like I'd done the night of the play. But if I screwed up this time, I wouldn't be on the wrong side of school. I'd be on the wrong side of town.

I pushed up my glasses, certain I'd missed some subtle clue hidden in the text. I held the torn ad against the map and read it again, pushing my finger into Potomac Yards, then dragging it south along the railroad hash marks that paralleled the Torpedo Factory . . .

Follow my tracks.

"Bingo, you bastard."

I changed direction at the factory, tracing the railroad west and pressing a finger into the center of an industrial park in Cameron Run. A grid of at least a dozen warehouses. I tapped the spot thoughtfully. With a yardstick and a few quick calculations, I could probably narrow the location of the vertex to a particular street.

A reflection appeared, a ghostlike shadow against the glossy laminated surface of the map. I stiffened as a dark sleeve reached over my right shoulder. Fresh pink scars crisscrossed the calloused knuckles of the large hand that disappeared under a black hoodie. An expensive cologne tickled the back of my throat, a cloying combination of musk and menthe.

Oleksa braced against the board and arched over me, close but not touching.

"You think too much about these things." His clipped accent rappelled down my spine. "And not enough about others."

I moved left, but his other arm rose to block me, boxing me in between him and the map. I held my breath, mind rolling through the self-defense moves Mona and Butch had insisted on teaching me. Heel to shin, elbow to ribs, head to chin . . .

"Why aren't you at the memorial service?"

My jaw clenched. I didn't owe him any explanation.

"Three students are dead. You should be more careful," he said. I raised my head slowly to see his face reflected in the map. "Whelan's more dangerous than you think."

I shot a deliberate glance at the scars on his hand. "Reece isn't the one with anger management issues."

His chest brushed my back. Too close. "There are a lot of

things about Whelan you don't know." He whispered into my hair, making me shiver. "Everyone has secrets."

"Was Reece too close to your secrets? Is that why you beat him?" I met his reflection eye to eye.

"I beat Whelan because Lonny doesn't trust him. Lonny trusts you. So why weren't you at his party on Wednesday?"

I wanted to tell him to screw off, but it felt like a test. Like Reece might pay the price for the wrong answer. "I had two funerals to go to, and I was tired."

"Reece said as much when we asked him. But make no mistake, Lonny's expecting you to be with Whelan tonight. No excuses. No tricks. If you care about him, you'll come." His cheek brushed my ear as he whispered, "But be careful." He pushed off the bulletin board and backed away, leaving a chill on my skin and the nagging aftertaste of sour mints. He believed me, but there was an acidic undertone to his unease. I watched his reflection disappearing in the map. A pink flyer hung by a thumbtack where his hand had been. The bottom edges lifted in the breeze of his departure.

I pulled the thumbtack. The flyer was drawn in code. A rave flyer. I ran my hand over the map, finding the pin-sized hole where Oleksa had placed it. A strip of warehouses in Cameron Run. It couldn't be a coincidence. The *Missed Connections* clue was leading me to the rave. That's where the killer would strike next. Where he wanted me to be. Where Kylie would be.

I spun around, but Oleksa was gone. I slumped against the wall, feeling completely screwed.

• • •

I called Reece as I walked home and told him Kylie might be in danger. We talked about going to the police, but Kylie would probably stick close to Lonny and we couldn't risk drawing a swarm of undercover cops to the drug deal. If the Homicide team knew Kylie was a target, they'd hover way too close and step on Narcotics' toes. And Narcotics wanted that list as badly as I did. If Lonny got spooked or if the deal went bad, we might not get the list of ketamine buyers at all, and that was the whole point of being there. Besides, if I went to the police now, to report another crime that hadn't even happened yet, they'd have no choice but to hold me for questioning.

No, we would do this ourselves. This time would be different. This time, we'd be ready. We'd be close to Lonny, and Lonny would be close to Kylie. Between the three of us, she'd never be out of sight.

"I'll keep an eye on Kylie," I said.

"No," Reece argued. "The only person I'm worried about keeping safe tonight is you. Lonny can take care of his own. We make the sale. We get the list. We use the list to prove you're not involved. That's it. I can't be responsible for Kylie, and neither can you. Remember, you agreed to do this my way."

"Right." I let it go, sensing his doubt. I couldn't let him

change his mind. Not when we were so close. This whole
nightmare could be over in a matter of hours. "I'll be careful." And hopefully I'd find the killer before the killer found
Kylie.

• • •

At home, Mona was awake, hair dryer blaring on the other
side of the bathroom door.

I slipped into my room, fell onto the lumpy mattress,
and threw an arm over my face. Jeremy and I hadn't spoken
all week, despite the fact that we'd essentially gone to the
funerals together. Even Anh was growing distant. Studying together was becoming awkward, each of us looking
over the other's shoulders, wondering what the other was
doing to gain an edge. The silences in our conversations
seemed to say more than we did. I'd clammed up when
she'd asked me to dish on my relationship with Reece, and
neither one of us wanted to broach the topic of the murders.
I couldn't blame her for wanting to spend more and more
time with Jeremy. I'd kept my promise to Reece by protecting his secret, at the cost of my relationship with my
best friends.

It hurt to think about it. A peculiar feeling fluttered low in
my stomach when I remembered Reece's lips. I rolled onto
my side and curled my body around the frayed comforter. I
squeezed my eyes shut and dreamed.

• • •

I woke to the sound of a man's voice. Strange, because Mona never brought men home. I blinked, trying to place it in the dark, and bolted upright in bed.

Reece.

I fumbled with the lock and threw open the door.

Reece stood in my living room, his height more pronounced under the low ceiling, his features more severe in the dim light. Mona paced a slow circle around him to shut the door, and then came around his other side, giving him a stern once-over.

She didn't look at me. Her rhinestone eyes rested squarely on Reece.

"This *boy* . . ." She drew the word *boy* into a question. "Says he's a friend of yours?"

Reece lowered his eyes. Mona's stare took in all of him.

I swallowed hard.

"I can explain." My mind reeled for a plausible story. One that might explain why he was standing in my living room.

"Don't bother. You're not leaving." She crossed to the kitchen and slapped her cigarettes against her palm, shaking one loose from the pack.

"Why not?" I'd intended to sound indignant and rebellious, but it came out more like a whine.

"Don't think for a minute I don't know what's going on at school. When the principal cancels after-school activities and sends a letter to all the parents recommending curfews, then

I have a damn good reason to keep you home on a Friday night."

"I'm not going out alone—"

"You're not going anywhere with him! He reeks of trouble. He came on a motorcycle, which I forbid you to ride!" She drew the collar of her robe higher. "And I know for a fact he has a fake ID."

Reece wiped his upper lip. My eyes flicked back and forth between the proud angle of my mother's chin and his downcast face.

Mona tapped her ash and gave him a long, hard look. "Ask him, Nearly. Ask him about his record. Boys like him always have one." She held her robe shut with one hand and sucked in a drag. "Your father certainly did."

My eyes cut to Mona's. They glistened as if that one sentence had turned a lock and loosed a secret. "What are you talking about?"

Reece shuffled, twitchy and uncomfortable. "I should go," he said quietly.

For the first time I noticed the silk collar under his leather, his buffed boots, his clean shave, and the gel in his mussed hair. He could have texted me. I could have sneaked out and met him down the street, but he came in to meet my mother. And she was the pot calling the kettle too black.

I repeated myself louder. "What do you mean?"

She smoked and didn't answer, that whispery secret scratching behind her eyes.

Reece opened the door. "It was a bad idea anyway," he muttered. "I'll see you Monday." He slipped out, head down. I turned back to my mother, torn between uncovering my past or fixing my future.

"We're leaving," I said.

The ashtray clattered to the floor behind me, scattering filth into the air. I threw open the door, calling Reece's name over the roar of the bike. My mother's robe filled the security door as I swung a leg over behind him. I glared at her through the bars and leaned in close, wrapping my arms around his chest. If he was leaving, he was taking me with him.

34

I CLOSED MY EYES and rested my helmet between his shoulders, anchoring myself in leather and the smell of his cologne. The rest of the world blurred around me.

He downshifted to a curb and I lifted my head, blinded by the light on Gena's front porch. I unwound myself from Reece's waist and unfastened the helmet, waiting for him to lead the way.

"I'm sorry," he said. "I didn't mean to get you in trouble." He scratched the back of his head and looked at me sideways, abashed for some reason I couldn't figure out. He hadn't done anything wrong.

"She shouldn't have said those things."

"She's your mom. She cares about you."

I perched on the edge of the curb and shoved the helmet into his hands. "She's an overprotective hypocrite—"

"At least you have one." He looked at me with a sadness that felt transparent and locked me out at the same time.

"Where's your mom?" His secrets felt so close, just under the skin. I wanted to reach out and touch them, even the ugly ones.

He stared at the pavement, slow to answer. "I took something from her. She won't see me anymore."

I thought about Mona, my fingers in her tip jar. How balance could be found in something as simple as a chipped mug on Mother's Day. Even after our fight tonight, I'd go home and wait up for her. "Can you give back what you took? Try to make it right?"

His eyes lifted to mine. "I'm trying," he whispered.

We both jumped as a door creaked open and Gena poked her head out. I took a guilty step back from Reece. She rolled her eyes and slammed it again.

"Are you coming in?" I crossed my arms over my chest. Everything about me felt inadequate, standing in front of Gena's house.

"I've got something I need to do before the rave. Gena'll take good care of you while I'm gone." He took both porch steps in one long stride and rapped on the door.

"Gone?" Suddenly the thought of being alone with Gena dropped my stomach into my shoes. "You're leaving me here? But—"

"Relax." He knocked again, looking me up and down with a wry smile. "You need to lose that shirt. I'll be back to pick you up in two hours."

"Two hours? I don't need two hours to change my shirt!"

The door opened. Gena scrutinized me, blinking slowly, nails tapping her hip. "Oh, sweetheart. We're going to do a hell of a lot more than change your shirt." She grabbed me by the collar and dragged me over the threshold.

Reece chuckled softly as the door slammed shut.

• • •

Gena ushered me down the hall.

"Bathroom. Second door on the right. Hot water's on the left. Towels are under the sink."

Cold fingers brushed my ankle and slid up my calf, Gena's smoky skepticism raising goose bumps on my skin. I rounded on her. "Hey, what are you doing?"

"I might as well be filing my nails, girlie. You need to shave those legs. There's a disposable razor in the medicine cabinet." She mumbled something in Spanish and I was grateful I didn't understand a word of it. "Pits too!" she called out as I slammed the bathroom door in her face.

When I finally caught a glimpse of myself in the mirror, I cringed. My face was tear-streaked and puffy, and my hair was sticking up in every direction. I sighed and looked around. Every inch of counter around the sink basin was packed full of scented soaps, perfumes, lotions, and cosmetics.

Her medicine cabinet was full to near bursting with beauty products. I grabbed a fresh disposable and was about to close the cabinet when I spotted something on the highest shelf.

Aftershave, an extra toothbrush, men's deodorant . . .

I shut the cabinet.

Then I opened it again.

I reached for the aftershave and sniffed the inside of the cap. It was cool and heavy with menthe. It tickled the back of my sinuses and stirred a memory. But not of Reece. Feeling like a total creep—and relieved for reasons I didn't want to think about—I shut the cabinet and turned on the hot water.

When I was done, I wrapped one of Gena's plush pink towels around my chest, careful to cover the pendant that clung to my damp skin. I tiptoed into the hall, following my nose to the kitchen, where I found Gena spooning rice over a steaming thick stew. My stomach growled through the towel.

"Sit." She ordered me to a chair and shoved the bowl into my hands. "Eat."

I scooped in the first mouthful cautiously. It was full of meat and vegetables and gravy and I'd never smelled anything so good. I hoisted my towel up with one hand, shoveling the spoon to my mouth with the other, barely letting it cool before I worked in the next mouthful. With a snort, Gena snapped a chip clip over the knot in my towel.

"You don't got much to work with up top, huh?" She smirked as she adjusted the clip. When she pulled her hand away, Reece's pendant came with it, and her smile fell. We looked at each other. Neither of us spoke. Then she looked away. "Eat."

I ate in silence, scraping every last drop of gravy from the bowl, and accepted another helping. Gena watched, scrutinizing my figure, face, and hair as I devoured it.

"You've got no boobs and no butt because you don't eat enough. You should eat. You skinny white chicks got it all wrong, starving yourselves. Men like a little something to hold on to, you know what I'm saying?" She patted the fleshy part of her backside with a manicured hand.

I licked my spoon. "Not all of us skinny white chicks starve ourselves on purpose. You know what I'm saying?" I felt bad for mocking her at her own table, but her lashes curled up, amused, even if her smile wasn't quite there yet.

"*Tranquilo*, I didn't mean anything by it." She grabbed my dirty dish and set it in the sink. "I can see why Reece likes you."

Blood raced to my ears and I tucked the pendant back into the folds of the towel. I didn't want to have this conversation with her. The pendant didn't mean anything. It was a costume. An act. "It's not like that. He doesn't . . . like me that way."

Her eyes flicked to the silver chain. "Doesn't he though?"

I set the spoon quietly on her table, too guilty to look her in the eyes. How much had he told her? She couldn't possibly know that I'd almost blown his cover at school, or she never would have been this kind.

Without warning, Gena yanked the front of my towel up . . . with me in it. "Come with me."

Too full to protest, I let her pull me down the hall and plunk me in a chair in front of the bathroom vanity. After blasting my hair dry, she worked a straightening iron through the long sections. In the silence between us I heard the clack and release of the iron working over and over in her hands.

"How long have you known Reece?" I asked.

Gena looked at me in the mirror, a hint of distrust in the lift of her brow. "About a year."

If they'd known each other a year, then she'd know why he was in juvie to begin with. "People say he's dangerous." I studied her face for a reaction.

"People say a lot of stupid things."

I bit back a smile. I didn't want to like her. "What do you think?"

She frowned at a knot, working it through with her fingers. "I think he'd take a bullet for me."

"You must be pretty close," I said, ignoring the jealousy that gnawed at me. "How did you meet him?"

She tugged hard at the knot. It felt like a warning.

"Look," I said, trying to catch her eyes in the mirror, "I know who he is."

"You don't know jack, little girl." She pointed the straightening iron at me. "You're going to get him killed."

"I wouldn't do anything to put Reece in danger."

"Wouldn't you?" The accusation cut deep and all the color drained from my reflection. He'd told her. He'd told Gena I'd almost blown his cover at school. Had he told her that we'd kissed each other too?

She set the iron down and leaned over my shoulders, staring down my reflection. "Reece feels protective of you. He likes you." She looked at the pendant. "Maybe more than I realized. Emotions make people do stupid things, and Reece is definitely doing some stupid things. He's like a brother to me. He asked for my help, so I'll give it. But I don't like it. Not one bit. And if you hurt him, I will hunt your skinny ass down and kill you. Are we clear?"

I should have been concerned about the "kill you" part, but the words *like a brother* whispered in my ears like a warm wind. The rest of her admonishment blew out of my mind. I nodded.

Gena resumed her cool composure as she laid out an arsenal of powders, paints, and glosses.

"Take off your glasses," she instructed, dabbing a brush onto a palette.

I held the frames tight to my face.

The *kill-you* expression was back. Gena snatched them off my nose and held the lenses up to her own eyes to examine them before dropping them in my lap.

"You're not wearing these tonight," she said. "Lonny needs to believe Reece would actually date you. You look like a damn librarian."

I ignored the jab and folded my glasses, closing my eyes as she brushed powder on my face. Her hands were warmer, and the smoky taste of her distrust wasn't as strong as it had been when I got there.

"What kinds of girls does he date?" I asked. Were they all brash and shimmer and curves, like Gena? Or like the girl who hung out on Lonny's porch? I tried not to cringe as she painted me, hoping it wouldn't be my mother staring back at me when I opened my eyes.

"The kind that get him in trouble." Before I could look, Gena ushered me to her closet and tossed me a black satin triangle on a string.

"Put this on."

I turned the fabric over a few times until I found the tag and figured out where the stringy parts went. I wiggled my legs into them under the towel, and they awkwardly settled in, but Gena didn't give me time to fidget. I sucked in a breath as she slapped on a strapless push-up bra and fastened the back tight enough to crush my ribs. Before I could exhale, she yanked a stretchy piece of black fabric over my head and smoothed it over my body. With a quick flash of her fingers, she freed the pendant from the front of the halter dress and let it fall back in place between my . . .

Wow . . . I looked down into my cleavage—yes, there was definitely cleavage there. Gena smacked my hands when I tried to pull the dress higher to cover it.

"Leave it. You look great," she said, bending low to rummage in her closet. She tossed a pair of shoes behind her, muttering in Spanish. A pair of clunky high-tops spilled onto the floor. The shoes were much too big to be hers, and the long red laces were a dead giveaway.

The cologne in her bathroom. The shoes in her closet. They belonged to Oleksa.

Oleksa was Gena's boyfriend, and his hatred of Reece suddenly made sense. He was jealous. But did Oleksa know he was dating a narc, or was Gena getting close to Oleksa for the same reasons Reece had gotten close to me?

Gena emerged from the closet with a pair of strappy black heels. I stepped into them and she turned me toward a full-length mirror. I stepped close enough to see, and resisted the urge to touch my own reflection, afraid the slightest movement might ripple the mirage. Not my mother's reflection.

Not Gena's. It was my own, but not a version of myself I'd ever imagined before. I wasn't just a flat, hazy version of myself, I was in full focus; I had definition, an outline. I leaned closer, but a door slammed and I startled.

Reece emerged in the doorway. I turned, lungs failing at the look on his face. I felt his gaze travel hot over the length of my body and climb slowly back to mine.

"Wow," he managed in a throaty whisper. "You look . . . wow . . ." He frowned and turned away. With a shake of his head, his fascination was gone. He scrubbed his face.

"Where's her phone?" he asked Gena.

Gena planted a hand on her hip. "Sweetheart, where the hell do you think she's gonna fit a phone in this dress?"

"There's got to be a pocket somewhere," he growled.

Gena drummed her nails.

"It's okay, don't worry about it," I insisted, sensing an argument brewing. "We left the house in such a hurry, I left the phone on my bed. I don't even have it with me, so there's no point fighting over where to put it."

I glanced at Gena and drew a finger across my neck. I mouthed "Let it go," and she acknowledged me with a slow grin.

"Try to relax tonight." She dragged him to the door and reached up on her toes to kiss his cheek. "And don't do anything stupid."

To me, she pointed and said, "I want all that stuff back."

Then she shuffled us out, slamming the door on Reece's scowling face.

"Let's get out of here," he mumbled, pulling his keys from his pocket. When he got to the bike, he rotated slowly to look at my legs, then at the heels Gena had let me borrow. He shut his eyes and cringed.

"It's okay, I'll manage." I grabbed the helmet and tossed my hair forward, bending at the waist to let the strands fall in. I snapped the neck strap and placed one leg over the bike without Reece's help. The skirt rode up my thigh, but not too much, and the added height of the shoes made it easier to step over. Dress or no dress, I was going with him. "See? It's fine . . . Really."

With a pained expression, he pulled his gaze from my leg. I looked away, humiliated, while he settled into the space between them with an exasperated sigh. He kicked the bike into gear and I tangled my fingers in the folds of his shirt rather than around his waist. All I wanted was to get this night behind us so he could move on with his life and I could forget I'd ever let myself fall for a guy like Reece Whelan.

35

WE PARKED IN A NARROW ALLEY. Brick walls loomed on both sides, cloaking us in shadows. At the mouth of the alley, bodies passed under streetlights, their silhouettes shuffling to a distant beat.

I startled when Reece caught my chin and lifted my head. "Listen." His fingers were ice cold and his anxiety leeched into me, an echo of my own. "I don't want you to eat or drink anything—nothing—no matter who gives it to you. Do you understand?"

I nodded.

"And I never want you out of my sight. Ever. Promise me." I nodded again. Then he took my hand and we followed the sound of the music.

To anyone else, we'd look like a couple. But his grip was too tight, his posture too rigid. A cluster of boys whistled and called out to me. Reece shot them a warning glance, his body inclined slightly ahead and protectively close to mine, but never too close.

We stopped in front of a rusted door. Reece slipped the bouncer some cash and the door slid open. Strobe lights pierced the pavement. The music, barely a heartbeat through the door, roared out. I clamped down on Reece's hand as we stepped into an inferno of color and sound and the steel mouth slammed shut.

He dragged me through a flashing sea of unfocused colors and lights, people dancing on ledges and platforms, and crowding the floor. I scanned the room for Kylie. Reece kept to the perimeter, clear of the mass, and stopped at a bar covered in tiny plastic cups. Our fingers strained to stay clasped as he leaned in to speak with the bartender, a kid I vaguely recognized as the gas pump attendant at the Bui Mart. The kid disappeared into a swale between bodies and I took long steadying breaths while we waited.

Lonny Johnson emerged a moment later. Kylie stood behind him, her hand draped over his shoulder. Her heroin-chic eyes narrowed over my dress and she pressed tighter against him. Lonny jerked his shoulder, dismissing her. I craned my head, anxiously watching as she vanished into the crowd. Reece squeezed my hand, as if reading my thoughts, forbidding me to follow her.

Lonny stepped in close, watching me the way a cat watches a bird through a window.

"Nice. Very . . . very nice," he said over the music, and yet low enough to be a dirty secret in my ear. "I had no idea you had it in you, Boswell. Not bad for a girl from the park. I'm beginning to understand Reece's interest in you." Lonny stroked his goatee and leered. The flashing lights illuminated the hard angles of his face and the tattoos around his neck. I took a step back.

Reece's grip tightened, and he shifted in front of me. I felt his temper flare through our joined hands and swallowed back the coppery tang it left. Without a word, Lonny jerked his head toward a hallway behind him. Reece returned it with a tight nod and he leaned in close to my ear.

"Stay here. Don't move. I'll be back in five minutes." Then he slipped into the crowd.

I stood, the room in rhythmic chaos around me, hundreds of bodies flashing under the strobes. I stood on my toes, searching for Kylie's magenta hair, but the bodies on the dance floor reflected back the color of the changing strobes. The effect was disorienting and I pushed in closer to the dance floor, struggling to find her.

A deejay worked high on a platform in the center of the room. The dancers moved in syncopated rhythms around him. A light caught my eye in a high corner of the room, white and quicker than the strobes. Jeremy stood on a catwalk, snapping pictures. His telescoping lens fanned slowly toward me, found me, and paused. The camera dropped slowly from his face. He stared at me with a pained expression, then turned, shoving people aside until he disappeared from view.

I wanted to follow him. I wanted to explain. But I didn't have a choice. Keeping Reece from going back to jail meant keeping Jeremy in the dark. And keeping Kylie alive meant I had to let him go.

I brought my attention back to the floor, to the wall of moving bodies in front of me. I didn't see Kylie anywhere. I had five minutes to find her before Reece came back. To make sure she was safe.

I drifted closer to the dance floor, careful not to touch anyone. I jumped when a warm hand reached for me, slick with sweat, and tried to pull away as it drew me into the current of bodies.

The touch sent a surge of heat through my veins. Hot and electric and sweet. *I shouldn't be here,* I thought, fighting to hold on to myself. Skin was all around me, touching me, until I was light, floating. I waved my hands in front of my face, watching them paint trails in the air. Someone grabbed me and pulled me close and I absorbed his buzz until I was numb with it.

I was one of them. Somebody. Part of something. Connected and touching. I pushed into them. Against them. Drinking them in. Drenched in their high. Promises drifted to me through the music.

Stay here. Five minutes.

The room was spinning. I giggled, laughter erupting within me until there was only dancing and music and the beat of the room. An arm snaked around me, strong shoulders curling over my back.

"What do we have here?" said a deep voice in my ear. "I had no idea little Nearly Boswell was so hot." I shivered under his breath.

I fought to open my eyes, willing the room to stop spinning. Large hands steadied me as I gave in to the sway. He was tall, his designer shirt closely cut over a muscled chest and rolled at the sleeves. Honey-blond hair fell over his forehead in the most appealing way, and he smiled at me. A small voice in my head whispered warnings, but his hands were warm on my waist. He smelled good, like expensive cologne.

I leaned into him, pulling his head low to my ear. "I know you," I purred, barely recognizing my own voice. "You're dangerous."

Vince growled into my neck, making me laugh. "You have no idea."

He drew me into the sea of dancers, to the very center of the writhing mass.

"Where's your boyfriend?" His face burrowed into my hair, tickling my shoulders. I shook my head and looped my hands around his neck, feeling dizzy.

"I don't have a boyfriend."

His hand slipped under the hem of my dress and worked slowly up my thigh. A delicious shudder rocked through me, sweet like cherry syrup with a burn that licked at my throat. My head rolled back, loose, and Vince nuzzled my collarbone.

"That's too bad. Whelan doesn't know what he's missing."

The name scratched at the edge of a memory, then disappeared in the fog. Someone caught Vince's attention behind me. Vince looked over my shoulder and grinned.

"TJ, I think we owe Leigh an apology," he shouted over the music. "We haven't been very nice. Let's make it up to her. Go get her a drink." Vince winked over my shoulder, his big hands roving higher. Something soured his touch, turning inhibition into something choking and greedy. Promises fluttered at the edge of my consciousness. *I don't want you to eat or drink anything—nothing—no matter who gives it to you.*

"No, I shouldn't . . ." I pushed at his wrists. The room spun and I stumbled into him. His arms circled my waist.

"Leave it alone, Vince." TJ's voice hardened behind me. "I saw Whelan here a few minutes ago."

Vince's face tensed. "I said the lady needs a drink, gimp. You gonna get in the game or sit the bench with your damn brace on all night?"

"Fuck off. I'm not your water boy."

A crowd of glassy eyes turned toward us and away and the moment passed. TJ was gone. My head was heavy and I let it fall against Vince's chest. Through fluttering eyelids, I could just make out a dark-haired boy, coming closer, pushing dancers out of his way.

"Leigh is leaving. Now," said his clipped voice behind me.

It picked at the corners of my mind. I pressed my fingers to my temple and wished the floor would stop moving. He held out his hand.

I reached for it, but Vince dug thick fingers into my shoulder. "I don't think Nearly wants to go anywhere."

I blinked and the room swam.

"She comes with me."

I squinted against the strobes. He stepped toward me, hand outstretched, and I swayed into his arms. His skin sent a chill up my spine and his touch tasted like violence. He grabbed me and the world turned upside down. My head fell, missing the floor as he swung me over his shoulder. Gena's shoes slid off my feet and clattered to the ground.

"Put me down!" I squealed, and pounded his back. My hair grazed the floor and I kicked at the sky. The room spun wildly as I bobbed up and down while he struggled through the crowd and my stomach turned in nauseating circles. I forced my eyes open, tried to focus on a single point. Someone was following us. I reached back and grabbed his wrist for leverage, trying to pull myself up to see his face. His hatred coursed through me, acidic and burning as it climbed up my throat. It was all too much. My heart raced, my stomach lurched, and the room spun faster. Then it all just disappeared.

36

COLD AIR CREPT OVER MY BODY. I woke up in darkness, curled against wet asphalt. Rain pelted my skin and trailed over my legs. I looked down at my dripping hands, sobering as the storm washed away the lingering high and a blinding headache exploded between my eyes.

Reece picked me up under the arms and stood me roughly against the wall. Water pooled at my bare feet. His touch was electric with panic reeking like fear.

"What did you take, Nearly?" He shook me, fingers digging into the bruises on my shoulders and rattling my brain.

"Ow! That hurts!"

"Did you drink something? Did you take something?" He held my face in one hand, forcing my lids open and shining a penlight with the other. I blinked hard against the glare and shoved his chest when he stepped in close to smell my breath.

"I didn't take anything!" I slammed my palm into his shoulder. "Don't touch me!"

Reece reeled back, his face twisting as he squinted against the rain. "What the hell happened to you back there?"

Wet hair clung to my cheeks and I scraped it away. "I don't know! I don't know what happened. I'm sorry."

"Sorry?" he shouted, so close I could feel the heat of his breath. "Sorry is all you've got?" He mopped sheets of water from his face, pacing in short, agitated strides. I flinched as he stepped toward me, bending close. "Do you have any idea how I felt when I came back and you were gone?"

His fists braced the bricks on both sides of my head, caging me in. "And you were . . ." He spun on his heels and paced, threaded his hands behind his head, unable or unwilling to look at me. He kicked the Dumpster and I jumped. "I don't know what the hell you were doing!"

"Well, I do!" My body shook with fine tremors. I wrapped my bare arms around myself, clutching at the guilt and humiliation inside. "Someone had to keep an eye on Kylie! He was there!"

He blinked away water. "What's that supposed to mean?"

"The person who killed Marcia and Posie and Teddy was there! At the rave!" I looked back at the warehouse, trying to make sense of what I remembered, but it was all so fuzzy. I remembered being upside down. I remembered being followed. Someone walked behind me. The one I touched before I passed out. I'd known it when I'd felt him. The killer. He was there. In the warehouse.

I turned toward the opening of the alley. "We have to go back!" My numb feet caught on the pavement and I stumbled, bracing a hand against the wall. Reece stepped in front of me, blocking my way.

"We're not going back! Damnit, Leigh, I thought you were dead!" His face was haunted. "I'm not going back there again. Not with you!"

Not with you. I'd screwed up. The deal was off.

I let my shoulder fall against the wall.

"When are you going to tell me what's really going on? When are you going to start trusting me?" he said.

A tear slid down my cheek. It was all just slipping away. Jeremy, the scholarship, my mother's trust, my friendship with Anh . . . I looked in Reece's eyes. I was losing him too.

"I can find him, Reece!" It roared out of me. Not a whisper. Not a scratch. It clawed its way up and ripped me apart. "I can feel him!"

He shook his head. It rippled with questions. "What do you mean, you can feel him? Feel who?"

I wanted him to understand without having to explain. Without seeing that look on his face. "I can feel you! I can touch you and know exactly how you feel! And I can feel the person who's doing this! I can solve this! I can find him. Without Lonny's list! Without your alibis!" My head thundered. I gripped my temples and doubled over, sick with the pain. I braced myself against the wall, unsteady on my feet.

Reece grabbed my elbow, fearful and confused. "Are you sure you didn't take anything?"

"Don't touch me!" I tore my arm away. I'd just come clean, confessed my deepest secret, and he thought I was high.

He shook his head and turned away. Rain beaded like mercury over his leather coat, fell in rivers down the back of his neck. He pulled out his cell phone and bent low over the screen, shielding it from the downpour.

"What are you doing?" I asked.

"Calling you a cab." He made the call and stuffed the phone back in his pocket with a curse.

I shivered. A steady slap of footsteps and the clicks of heels grew louder as a stampede of wet bodies rushed past the mouth of the alley. Reece watched them, his eyes narrowing.

"Hey!" he shouted. The brick walls on both sides echoed, and a fleeing boy with a drooping Mohawk turned toward us. "What's going on?"

"Someone called the cops. Party's over, man." The kid shrugged and took off running.

Reece swore. "You need to get out of here."

"Why? I've got nothing to hide. I was with you all night."

He scraped the water from his eyes and tipped his head, incredulous. "With me all night? When I came back from my meeting with Lonny you were gone! I've been looking for you for an hour! When I found you lying in the alley I thought you were dead!"

I stared, openmouthed. "What do you mean, you found me in the alley? You carried me out."

A yellow taxi cruised past the alley, stopped, and reversed slowly. Its headlights swung toward us, blinding us and silencing our fight. It parked behind Reece and I shielded my eyes against the glare. Reece's eyes widened and he rushed toward me. His face was frantic as he lifted my hair, turning my cheek toward the light.

"You're bleeding." His hand came away with a red, watery smear. We both watched as it melted away in long pink streaks, pooling in the grooves of the pavement where he'd found me. I touched my neck, my shoulder, my face. No cuts. No breaks. My hair was thick and sticky against my bare shoulders. I pulled my fingers through it and held them up to the taxi's light. They were red and slick. Reece knelt, angling his body out of the light's path. A red stream bubbled along the base of the wall behind the Dumpster. He stepped slowly, arms spread and palms back, holding me behind him as he tracked the source. I followed, watching the river thicken, glossy and almost black where it rounded the Dumpster. The air smelled like wet pennies and I clapped a hand over my mouth.

The Dumpster cast a shadow over a mound beside it. Reece flicked on his penlight and stumbled back. The body lay broken and wet, in a puddle of red. Blood-soaked hair plastered her cheeks, obscuring her face. It was a girl, her wrists and ankles tied together, making a crude triangle of her body. Her skin shone white where the rain smacked against it, except for one forearm, where angry red lines cut deep enough to expose tendons, but no longer bled. She was empty. The last of her life gurgled over the street. Stuck in my hair. I'd been lying in Kylie's blood.

I spun around and clutched my stomach as it reeled. I sucked in shallow breaths and swallowed hard. I couldn't look anymore.

"It's a number cut in her arm, isn't it?" I called over my shoulder. I shut my eyes, waiting.

"Seventy-six," Reece answered, hoarse and shaken.

The taxi leaned on his horn and flashed his lights, oblivious to the gruesome scene we'd discovered. Reece grabbed me by the arm and dragged me toward the cab. Opening the door, he tossed me inside.

Sirens screamed in the distance. Reece dug inside his jacket, dropped my glasses in my lap, and slammed the door. Then he leaned inside the passenger window. He eyed the cabbie as he peeled a bill from a roll of cash.

"This is to take her home."

The cabbie nodded, taking the money.

Then Reece handed over the remaining stack. The cabbie's eyes grew wide as he closed his hand around it. "And this," Reece ordered in a thick, rough voice, "is for not asking questions. You were never here."

He gave me one last look, beat a fist against the roof, and the taxi took off.

37

I FROZE IN THE DOORWAY. Smoke curled from Mona's lips under the harsh fluorescent light. Her elbows perched on the table, an ashtray spilling over between them.

"Why aren't you at work?" I touched the soaked ends of my hair and resisted the urge to check them for blood. I'd stood under the security light in the pouring rain until the water stopped running pink, but I could still feel it.

Rainwater dripped steadily onto the carpet. Mona's eyes drifted over the wrecked dress and rested on my bare feet as she sucked another drag. "Jim hired another new girl. He sent me home early." She'd been coming home earlier, her tip jar lighter on Friday mornings than it used to be. The kitchen light deepened the lines around her eyes and her hands bore new creases like smoke rings. "You never stay out this late."

"How would you know? You never wait up." I listened for sirens, then shut the door and slid the dead bolt in place. I leaned back against the door and looked at her, wishing she weren't here. I wanted to scrub away every drop of Kylie's blood. I wanted to hide under a mountain of blankets with my father's ring.

"Never had a reason to." Mona crushed out the remains

of her cigarette, emptying the last ribbon of smoke from her lungs. Her chair scraped against the floor and she left the room.

I kicked the door with my bare foot. Had I expected anything more from her? She never waited up because she was never here.

A moment later, Mona returned, carrying a stack of clean towels and a hairbrush.

"Sit down." She pulled out a chair and gestured with the brush, filling me with déjà vu. Gena had given me the same command a few hours ago. Now her ruined dress clung cold to my skin, and I'd lost her damn shoes. She was going to kill me. The thought was so absurd I choked on hysterical laughter. Gena wouldn't have a chance to kill me. I'd be behind bars for the rest of my life.

I dropped wearily into the chair. My raw nerves jumped when a towel snapped next to my ear and wrapped around my bare shoulders, followed by the pull of a brush through my hair. She was careful not to touch me. Even so, I tensed, waiting for my mother to scream, to find a long bloody strand, for the towel to turn pink. But the brush kept up its rhythm. It was the same kind of brush she'd used when I was a girl and caught on the tangles with every stroke, but she expertly worked it through. It eased the blistering pain in my head. My heavy lids closed, fatigue consuming me.

Mona worked in silence to the crush of rain against the

roof, to the soft pitter-patter of water dripping from my hem to the linoleum floor. The seconds ticked away. I wasn't sure how many I had left.

"You said Dad had a record. I want to know what it was."

She was quiet, the only sound the rustle of the brush. "Once you know something about a person, you can't unknow it."

"I already know about the fake IDs in his wallet. I know he had phony credit cards and used different names. But I want to know who he was. Not those other people he was pretending to be. I want to know why he left."

The brush paused and I heard the snap of her lighter. The soft suck of air into her lungs. She tapped out her ash and set her cigarette in the tray, careful to push it away from me. "I don't suppose if I tell you, it'll be enough to keep you from making the same mistake I made."

I wasn't sure of the answer. Whose mistakes was I really making? Hers or his? "What was he like?" I asked.

She thought for a moment, and I thought I heard her smile. "We were sixteen when we met. He was sweep-you-off-your-feet handsome. And smooth. Charmed the pants right off me. I'd only known him a month when I followed him right out of my parents' house." She pulled at the memories with deep long strokes. "It was a nice house. Safe," she said. "I don't remember my parents ever locking the door." She sounded younger, softer, the raspy edge almost gone.

"Then why'd you leave?"

I felt her shake her head. Heard the distant, less critical voice of retrospect. Different from the sharp jabs she usually threw at his name. "Don't know what it was about David, except that he could hold your hand and know exactly what you were feeling."

I'd been listening before, but now I prickled under the brush.

"He was always holding me, back then . . . in the beginning. Before we grew up and things got hard."

"What do you mean? How'd things get hard?"

She was quiet for a moment, as if she was giving me time to change my mind. Giving me one last chance not to know. I sat on the edge of my chair, hungry for her answer.

"Your father was charismatic," she finally said. "He had a way with people. He always nailed the interviews, but could never hold a job. Floated from one to another, but he was always grifting. Finding ways to play off people's emotions. It was like he could see right through them. They trusted him. Some days his ability to read people paid off big. Others, well . . . That's what got him in trouble." She brushed while she talked. I felt her shake her head. "I kept telling him he was in over his head, that it was only a matter of time before he took advantage of the wrong people, but he didn't listen. He was hooked on the rush. Drunk on the money. He couldn't see the lives he was destroying.

"One day, the police came to the door with a warrant. He was using some guy's company as a front to launder money. The guy was loaded. Big house on the golf course in Belle Green. David met him at a poker game one night. Said as soon as they shook hands, he knew they'd get along.

"Before I know it, they're thick as thieves . . . organized gambling rings, extortion, laundering. Until they got caught. That was the last time I saw your father. He left me a note, took the car across the state line into the city, and caught the first plane to who-the-hell-knows. Never came home.

"He loved you, though. Oh God, how he loved you," she breathed. "He'd have grifted the moon for you. He used to set you in his lap and hold your little hands for hours, like touching you could fix anything." Her nostalgia trailed off and the trailer was silent except for the rain. "Couldn't get you to stop crying for weeks after he left."

I wasn't sure what to feel. My father had loved me, every bit as much as in my white-washed memories. And he was like me in ways Mona had never understood. But he was a thief. A con man. And he'd left us in a run-down trailer with nothing, just to save his own skin.

The brush moved easily now, but she didn't stop.

"Why didn't you tell me?"

She snorted. "When I was your age, if my mother had told me I would be anything like her, I never would have believed her. I would have laughed if she'd told me I'd be seventeen and pregnant, and that one day even my own daughter would hate me, and I would grow old alone like she did. I wanted to believe I could be different. That the direction of my life would be different." She sighed. "No kid ever wants to believe they'll be like their parents, Nearly. That's something you have to come to accept on your own."

She was worried I'd fall in love with someone like my father and give up my future like she did. But I *was* him. In over my head with the wrong people, too stupid to listen, too selfish to turn myself in before it was too late. So what if I went to jail? I should have gone straight to the police. Should have told them everything. If I had, maybe Kylie wouldn't have bled out behind a Dumpster. Maybe Marcia, Posie, and Teddy would still be alive.

Mona stopped brushing and began working my hair into a tight bun, awakening the pain in my head.

"Nothing can change where we come from, Nearly. But you can change where you're headed," she said quietly. "That boy isn't good enough for you. He'll be gone before you know it."

My chair screeched and crashed to the floor behind me. I ripped out the elastic band and threw it at my mother's feet, unable to look her in the eyes. Unwilling to look in my own.

This wasn't Reece's fault.

It was mine.

• • •

I leaned against my bedroom door. I had the mother of all psychic hangovers, and the smell of Kylie's blood lingered in my throat.

A red light flashed on my bed.

Reece's cell phone.

I shut my eyes, remembering the look on his face when I'd started to tell him . . . He hadn't believed me.

I grabbed the phone and squelched down on my bed, Gena's dress soaking through my sheets.

TXT ME WHEN U GET HOME—from REECE.

I sent a quick reply.

I'M HOME. I'M SORRY.

I'm sorry I broke my promise. I'm sorry four people are dead. I set the phone down on the bed, stripped off the cold dress, and put on my pajamas. I pulled Reece's pendant over my head and held it. It didn't seem right to wear it anymore. We had a deal and I blew it. And that's all it had been . . . a deal.

I stuffed it into the pocket of my hoodie and hung it across the back of my chair. I reached under my mattress for the bag and dumped the contents on my bed. Pushing aside my father's ring, I picked up the train ticket instead. I'd bought it using every penny I'd saved. Some days, when I thought I couldn't stand it here one more day, I'd hold it and dream about running. Never coming back. But then I'd think of my mother. Her broken smile was a cuff around my heart and I couldn't stomach the thought of leaving.

I stuffed everything back in the bag, then curled up under my comforter and switched off the lamp.

The phone vibrated and I sat up, squinting at the screen. Not Reece. A chill pulled up my spine, drawing the skin tight.

1 New Text from Unknown Number.

MISSED U @ THE PARTY.

IT'S JUST A NUMBERS GAME.

STICK AROUND NEXT TIME AND I'LL SPELL IT OUT FOR YOU.

38

I'D LEFT THREE PHONE MESSAGES and way too many texts for Reece. All went unanswered. The next morning, I flipped through the local white pages directory, determined to find him. There was only one listing for Whelan. I tore out the page and took a few dollars from Mona's tip jar and walked to the bus stop at the end of the street. It was early and the air was already brutally hot and too sticky to breathe. When I emerged from the bus in a small neighborhood of run-down townhouses, the streets were empty.

I checked the numbers on the pale green siding, and found the one in the listing. It was missing a shutter and the shades were drawn shut. The tree in front was brown and barren, and looked like it had been left to rot. A security door with heavy black bars prevented me from knocking, so I tapped hard on the window beside it. A dog barked loudly in the unit next door.

I waited and knocked again. A woman peeled back the thin curtain and peered out at me. She cracked the door just enough to poke her face through. "What do you want?"

I forgot myself, taken aback by the woman's features, how they were so like Reece's. She started to shut the door.

"Wait!" I threw my hand in the opening. "I'm looking for Reece Whelan."

Her features turned hard, the way Reece's could turn when he was angry. "No one lives here by that name." She looked pointedly at my fingers where they gripped the door frame.

"Please," I said, hesitantly removing them. "I need to know where I can find your son."

Her eyes glassed over. "My son is dead," she said, and shut the door.

The dead bolt slid home.

I pulled my phone from my pocket and scrolled to the contact list. There was only one other number, and I called the only person who might know where to find him.

• • •

"You shouldn't be here." Reece stood half dressed, holding the door to barricade my way.

"I called. You didn't pick up your phone." I jammed the cell into his stomach, knocking enough wind out of him to make an opening for myself. "I got a text last night," I said as I ducked under his arm.

I looked around his apartment. Sparse but tidy. The warm citrus and sandalwood cologne he wore last night lingered in the compact space.

He raked a hand through his unwashed hair and shut the door, looking weary. His jeans rode too low on his hips and I wondered when he'd last eaten. I looked away as he scrolled through the phone, face drawn and shadowed.

"Who else has the number?" He tossed me the phone.

"Just you."

"Anyone else have access to your locker?"

Jeremy had my combination, but I wouldn't let him get caught up in this. I bit my tongue and lied. "No."

His jaw ticked as he studied my face. "How'd you find me?"

I didn't want to tell him how I'd looked up his address and knocked on his mother's door. Truthfully, I was afraid he might ask me what she'd said. And I could never look him in the eyes and tell him he was dead to her. Instead I looked around the room and skipped that part.

"I called Gena. I told her it was an emergency and then bugged the crap out of her until she gave me your address. What is it with you people and milk crates?" I changed the subject, nudging an overturned crate with my toe, remembering the ones in Gena's apartment. His crooked smile, the one that used to come so easily, hadn't made an appearance and I was surprised that I missed it. He fell into a lumpy sofa with squeaky springs, lacing his fingers behind his head.

"You people? Care to elaborate on that?"

I stood in the middle of the room and did a slow 360 so I wouldn't have to see the suspicion on his face. "Nicholson's people."

He tipped a soda can to his lips and looked at me over a long pull. I could feel him puzzling through me, trying to figure out how I knew and how much I knew.

I glanced around the room, pausing in front of his bedroom door. A pair of faded jeans and boxer shorts were tossed on the floor beside the unmade bed and I wondered if anyone slept there with him. Or if he truly was alone.

"Do you have a roommate? Narcing must not pay you very much."

"Enough for milk crates." His eyes made a lazy pass over the tousled sheets. "And no, I don't have a roommate."

My face warmed and I turned away.

"What do you remember?" he grumbled.

"Everything, I think. I sobered up pretty quickly. The rain helped, but the headache is a killer." The nagging tension lingered behind my eyes and made my glasses feel too heavy. I had to ask the question that had kept me up all night. "Was she . . . ?" I couldn't make myself say the word, even though I'd known she was dead the second I saw the bloodless cuts in her arm.

He nodded.

I sank down onto the sofa beside him. "What happened after I left?"

"I cleared out before the cops came."

"Are they coming for me?"

The pause felt too long. Reece looked down at his lap and picked at the tab of his soda can. "I don't think so. Gena called me this morning and filled me in. The judge denied the cops' request for a warrant."

"Why?" Not that I wasn't grateful and relieved, but I was surprised.

"They don't have enough evidence to charge you with a crime. The most they can do is bring you in for questioning for a few hours with your mother and a lawyer. Gena and I were with you before the rave. Plenty of people saw you inside the warehouse, and an undercover cop claims he saw you before the time of Kylie's murder. He verified that you were inebriated and unconscious, and therefore incapable of any involvement. And as of this morning, we have a statement from a very cooperative taxi driver who says he dropped you off, drunk and barely conscious, at your trailer before midnight."

I raised a finger to interrupt. I'd gotten home at 1:30 a.m. and I was completely conscious.

Reece continued before I could correct him. "Forensics estimated Kylie's time of death at twelve thirty a.m. and you were already at home, in bed, sleeping it off." He leveled me with a hard stare, daring me to argue. "You were accounted for all night. This is a high-profile homicide case involving minors. One of the victim's fathers sits on the town council. The judge isn't going to let anyone screw this up by botching an arrest. She's going to make the DA produce hard evidence beyond reasonable doubt."

The breath I'd been holding rushed out. "So I'm okay? They can't arrest me?"

He thought for a moment, then said softly, "For now."

I massaged my temples. Reece disappeared into the kitchen and returned with a soda and a bottle of aspirin.

He shook his head. "I never would have put you in a situation like that if I'd known you'd get stupid."

I spilled a few pills into my palm and tossed them back.

"Imagine how I feel." I set the bottle down on a crate, my throat squeezing around the pills and forcing them down. "The first guy I ever kiss is a narc who's trying to shut me up, and the first guy to feel me up is Vince DiMorello . . ." I shuddered.

Reece paled. "That was your first kiss? That day in the hall at school?"

I didn't answer.

He dropped his head into his hands and let out a slow breath.

"Don't flatter yourself." I stood up, defensive. "I've kissed other people . . . like Jeremy."

Reece stiffened. "Jeremy?"

"Yes, Jeremy."

He stood up and pulled his hand through his hair, looking at me with a grave expression. "We need to talk. I should probably get dressed first." He backed toward his bedroom. "Wait here. I'll be back in five minutes. I'm serious this time. Five minutes. Don't go anywhere," and he disappeared into his room.

I guess I deserved that.

His muffled voice came through the bathroom door over the sound of running water.

"There's leftover pizza in the kitchen. Help yourself."

We need to talk. So this was it, I told myself. I'd broken our agreement, and the deal was over. The official break-up of a non-existent relationship. I pulled his phone from my pocket, and set it on a small shelf where he kept his key ring and his wallet. Then took off his pendant and laid the thistle beside them, next to a framed photograph. I picked it up. The faded image under the glass was lightly torn around the edges. Two boys stood arm in arm, one a smaller version of the other. Matching grins and blue eyes, their unruly bangs falling into identical sets of dark lashes.

But Reece said he didn't have a family.

There are a lot of things about Whelan you don't know.

I set the frame down. The shower was still running in the next room. I reached for the worn brown leather trifold and opened it. His driver's license was there, bearing his own name and his real photo. A few credit cards, a library card, and a gym membership. When I flipped open the third section, something fluttered out. I bent to pick it off the floor. It was black-and-white and grainy, and folded to fit inside the wallet's crease. A photo of a girl. I held it closer to see her. She had long hair, high cheekbones, and pretty eyes. Her lips looked full and glossy, even without color. I recognized the dress before I recognized her face. It was me. At the rave. Reece must have cut it from a surveillance photo and saved it. But why? And was he disappointed to find out I wasn't really like the girl in the picture at all?

I returned the photo to the wallet and set it on the shelf. Then sank into the couch where Reece had been sitting. It was still warm and made a strange crackling sound under me. I pressed and released my weight, feeling something give beneath the thin cushion. Reaching under it, I withdrew a clump of papers—the torn pages from Reece's textbook. *I need you*, it said, the words opening a fresh wound inside me. I pushed the pages aside, letting the crinkled periodic table drift to the floor.

I glanced to the closed bathroom door, listening to make sure the water was still running. I stuffed my arm back under the cushion and my fingers closed on something heavy. They withdrew a thick file folder and I turned it sideways to read the tab. *Boswell, Nearly*. Bold red letters across the front said *Confidential*.

My profile was printed inside: name, date of birth, nick-name, schools attended, no previous criminal record . . . I paused at my parents' names. Mother, Ramona Stevens Boswell. Father, Donald D. Boswell—I knew David was his middle name from the real driver's license I kept under my bed. A brief note about him followed and I devoured the details even though they made me sick. He had no less than a dozen aliases and was "wanted" for felony charges, missing for five years, and his only known associate, listed merely by case number, was apparently serving time for another three.

I flipped the page. My name, followed by the words *accomplice* and *possible suspect* jumped out everywhere, beginning with the notes from my first "interview" with Lieutenant Nicholson.

Then came pages of reports in Reece's blocky print. I glanced through them, surprised by their brevity. Sparse of detail and sterile in content, several dates and conversations were missing. Nothing about my escape from school the night of the play. Nothing about our conversation under the bleachers. Nothing about my trip to the hospital to see Posie, or our conversation by the airport after we'd fled the museum.

I flipped past them, thumbing through toxicology and autopsy reports. A handwritten note, time-stamped early this morning, confirmed they'd found ketamine residue in Kylie's body last night.

I flipped past the lab reports to a stack of photos. Dozens of them.

I was captured over and over again in grainy black-and-white images. Me, walking to school. Me, at the Bui Mart buying my newspaper and laughing with Bao. Me, getting into Jeremy's car. Me, holding Reece's hand in a dark alley. Me, dancing with Vince DiMorello. Lonny Johnson whispering in my ear. Me again, barefoot and laughing, slung over the shoulder of a dark-haired boy with a close-shaved head. Oleksa. Oleksa had carried me to the alley?

. . . an undercover cop claims he saw you before the time of Kylie's murder, and verified that you were inebriated and unconscious . . .

I dropped the file. The contents sprawled like wreckage across the floor. Bodies lay tangled among them. Naked arms with haunting markings . . . all of them numbers. And—a periodic table.

I stood quietly, the lumpy sofa squeaking with release.

It's personal. I'll put it all on the table for you. That was the clue under the bleachers.

I reached for the periodic table. Reece had circled five elements in blue. The sides of the cube snapped together inside my brain.

Ten, the atomic weight of the element Neon. Abbreviation Ne.

Next had been Marcia Steckler. She'd been 18, Argon. Abbreviation, Ar.

I stopped when I reached Posie Washington, straining to make out the blistering mark in the photo, but I remembered it as clearly as I remembered the smell of her flesh burning. Element number 3. Lithium. Li.

I set Posie down, the photos like headstones laid out in a neat row.

Teddy was marked in stars, element number 5. Boron. B.

And now Kylie. I knew her number. And the fifth element had already been circled on the table. Number 76. Osmium. Abbreviation, Os.

Reece had solved the puzzle. It was so simple. I'd been reading into it too deeply, making it more complicated than it needed to be. Thinking only of the ink message on my chem lab table, and the carved one in physics. Assuming there was some complex hidden meaning in those messages I had missed. I'd never told Reece about the messages on my lab tables at school. When he saw the clue under the bleachers, his mind probably jumped to the only "table" he associated with me. The one we'd been studying together. The periodic table of elements.

Each victim's number represented the atomic weight of an element on the periodic table. And together, in order, the pattern became clear.

Ne + Ar + Li + B + Os = me.

The killer was spelling my name with the bodies of my own students. And he wasn't finished yet.

Are you clever enough to find me in time.

"Did you find the pizza?" I started at the sound of his voice. Reece rubbed a towel through his wet hair, his white T-shirt pink where it stuck to his skin. His eyes followed my guilty glance to the disassembled file on the floor. The towel stopped moving. "What are you doing with these?"

"I was going to ask you the same thing." My voice was shaking. "This is a confidential police file. How did you get it?"

He didn't move. Didn't look at it. "I borrowed it."

"Why?" I already knew the answer. It hung in the silence between us. "You said it yourself, you know it's a set-up. You're concealing evidence. Why?"

His brow pulled down.

"They're going to arrest me, aren't they?" I threw a pointed finger to the pile of loose photos and reports on the floor. Photos of a pretty girl with long legs and wavy hair and a gorgeous boyfriend. A girl who tangled with drug dealers at illegal parties and wore provocative clothes. A girl with too many secrets. And now everything was spelled out so clearly. "This—my name—is all the reasonable doubt they'll need, isn't it?" My knees felt watery and the room wavered.

I lunged for the door. Reece grabbed my hand, his emotions slamming into me. But my own were too jumbled and I couldn't untangle the mess of feelings and scents in my head.

He pulled me toward him, grabbing my face in his hands.

"Don't touch me!"

Reece stepped back, palms held high. I braced against the wall, warning him off with my eyes.

"Give me a reason." He eased forward, speaking in a low voice. "You're always telling me not to touch you. What are you so afraid of?"

"I'm not afraid."

"Bullshit." He inched closer. "You said something in the alley. That you can find the killer because you can feel him. What did you mean?"

I shook my head. "It doesn't matter. You won't believe me anyway."

"I'll believe you. I want to help you."

I turned my face to stop him from coming any closer.

"Explain it. Help me understand. What will happen if I touch you?" He waited, inches away.

I felt naked, completely exposed. I let the truth spill out of me, hoarse and wet and uncertain. Too afraid to look at his face. "When I touch someone, I feel what they feel. I can taste it. I don't know how or why. I just know I can't control it. The only way to stop it is not to touch anyone at all. So I don't. Because it's too hard to be inside someone's heart. And that sucks."

I looked tentatively at Reece. ". . . And I don't know, maybe that's one reason why I read the personals. Because

I was tired of being the girl who would never know what it's like to fall for someone." I took a shuddering breath, waiting for him to laugh or tell me I was crazy. He didn't. "And then these ads started showing up, and it's like they were written for me. I put the pieces together and I knew that something was wrong. So I went to Nicholson and everything backfired." I swallowed, steeling myself for the craziest part. "I felt him at the rave. I touched him and I knew it was *him,* but I never saw his face. It was all too much. All the people and the drugs. I felt it all and every-thing went wrong!

"And that's what will happen if I touch you. I'll feel it all. I'll know how much you hate me, how you think I'm crazy, how you think I—"

"Then do it." I flinched at the urgency in his voice. He stepped in close, until my back pressed against the wall and there wasn't any air between us. He dropped his voice to a whisper. "You think you know how I feel about you? Then touch me." He took my sleeve and drew my hand to his chest. The damp shirt clung hot to his skin. It rose and fell fast with his breath.

Slowly, I slid my hand up over his collar, and spread my fingers over his bare skin. His pulse thrummed hard. My heart raced with his fear and the rush of his desire.

He leaned in slow, lips close but not touching. Waiting, as if I might pull away. I leaned into him. His mouth was soft and yielded to mine. He returned my kiss slowly. I brought my arms up around his neck and drew him into me, drinking in his tenderness and need. His fingers dug into my hips and pulled me close. No guilt. No regret.

"Why are you doing this?" I closed my eyes, afraid of his answer.

He pressed his forehead to mine, a bittersweet sadness spilling into me. His lips parted, hesitated. "Because I might not get another chance."

We both jumped at the bang on the door. Neither of us moved.

"Police. Open the door."

Reece looked to the lineup of crime scene photos on the floor. Another loud bang. He cursed softly and pushed me gently aside before I could register his panic. He kicked out a foot, scattering the pictures into a random patternless mess before he scooped it all up and shoved it into the open file. His other foot found the periodic table and kicked it under the couch.

My eyes flashed to the sofa, and back to Reece.

The police didn't know about the message under the bleachers.

I'll put it all on the table for you. The table. That clue was the Rosetta Stone to the whole case. It was the only clue that could lead the police to the periodic table and spell out my name. But it never made it into the file. Reece never told them. And without Reece's notes, the numbers—the most incriminating pieces of evidence against me—were meaningless. My mind rewound to his phone conversation in the park by the airport, the visitor's log he'd stolen from the hospital, the cabbie he'd paid to give a false statement . . . He'd been systematically destroying evidence. Concealing facts. Covering for me . . . The police weren't here for me. They were here for him.

He took a deep steady breath, surveying the room as he walked to the door. With a last pained look at me, he flipped a lock and the chain stretched taut, snapping against the strip of sunlight that poured in. Blue uniforms appeared in the gap.

"Reece Whelan?" The officer held a slip of paper against the opening. "We have a warrant to search the premises."

Reece shut the door, slid the chain back, and two uniformed officers stepped into the room. He waved to the female officer and gestured coolly to the file on the milk crate. "Hey, Rhonda. No need to search. I'll spare everybody the drama. It's right there."

The other officer crossed the room and inspected the tab. He thumbed through the file, pausing to glance at me over the photos, and then nodded to his partner. She approached Reece and turned him face-forward against the wall. He didn't resist. She smiled apologetically, as if they knew each other.

"Sorry, Reece, but you know the drill. You're under arrest for obstruction of justice." She snapped the first cuff shut and recited the rest of his Miranda in a monotone voice. "Do you understand these rights as they have been read to you?"

Reece nodded, his face turned in profile against the wall as the second cuff clicked shut. He craned his neck, speaking over his shoulder to her as she patted him down. "Do you think you can give us a minute?"

"Make it quick," she said, dropping back a few feet. The blue uniforms stood close to the door, hands on hips, listening to their radios.

Reece spoke in a low voice, careful not to be overheard. "You need to know something. We busted Lonny after the rave. I've been in lock-up all night. We had to make him think I got busted too. I grabbed your file when they released me this morning, and I left the reports from last night's bust on Nicholson's desk. Lonny made a deal and turned over a list of his ketamine buyers," he said so quietly I almost couldn't hear him. "You weren't on it . . . but Jeremy was."

"Jeremy?" I stared at Reece. That just wasn't possible. It had to be a mistake. Jeremy wouldn't buy street drugs, let alone from someone like Lonny.

I took a step back. "No. They've got the wrong Jeremy. There's more than one Jeremy at West River. There has to be someone else I know on that list. Who else did Lonny sell to?"

The officers paused their conversation and turned toward us. Reece spared them a glance and pitched his voice lower. "Vince." He bent to look me in the eye and whispered, "Think about it, Leigh. You know he's not smart enough to pull off something like this."

But Jeremy? Jeremy was smart, and he knew me better than anyone. He knew I read the *Missed Connections*. He had access to my locker. He'd been at every crime scene. And he and Anh . . .

Nicholson's question haunted me. *Do you know the person who wrote these ads, Miss Boswell?*

"What are you saying?"

Reece didn't speak, his thoughts implicit in his silence.

I shook my head. My heart warred with itself. All the clues, all the circumstantial evidence fit. Anyone who didn't know him as well as I did could actually believe he did this.

"Maybe you're wrong," I said, desperate to believe it. "Maybe it isn't the same Jeremy."

Reece put his lips close to my ear and whispered, "Leave town, Leigh. Get out of the state. Get someplace safe until I'm . . ." I felt him pause for a breath. "Just get away until this whole thing blows over."

"I can't!" I whispered back. Where would I go?

The officer cleared her throat in warning. Reece pulled back and raised his voice just enough to satisfy her. "Try. For me. I'll be gone at least two weeks, and that's if things go well." If not, then they'd send him back to juvie. He'd risked everything. His future. His freedom. For mine.

"Take the trash out before you leave." He aimed a meaningful glance toward the sofa. "And try not to do anything stupid while I'm gone." He straightened as the officer laid a hand on his shoulder.

I shook my head. They couldn't take him. This wasn't his fault.

"If you get into trouble, call Gena," Reece said quietly. "I'll find you when I'm out. I promise."

They escorted him to the door. His cuffs rattled and something crumbled inside me. He stopped in the doorway and turned.

"And Leigh? I always knew you were worth it." He smiled weakly as the officers closed the door.

I pulled back the curtain and watched through the window as he ducked into the squad car and the door snapped shut. Reece didn't look back.

39

I KNEW SOMETHING WASN'T RIGHT the minute I stepped off the bus. Sunny View was too quiet. No filthy puddle-jumping kids with shaggy hair pitching gravel in the street, the usual troublemakers nowhere in sight.

I paused beside a neighbor's trailer. I could just make out
the corner of my own a few yards away. A car was parked in
front, but we didn't own a car. The dark blue Crown Victoria
sat catty-corner in the street, its front fender leaning into our
trash cans. There were three antennae on the roof and extra
lights mounted in the rear windows. An unmarked police car.
I couldn't see my porch from where I pressed up tight against
the neighbor's siding, but I heard a persistent knocking on
my door.

I patted my pockets as I backed up the street, retracing my
steps to the bus stop. I'd left the phone in Reece's apartment
and locked the door behind me when I'd left. No way to call
Gena. And nowhere to run.

I jumped at the *snap-clink* of a lighter flipping shut. Lonny
perched on his saggy front porch, elbows on his knees. His
tank top was moist at the neck, tattoos blooming like ghosts
through the thin white cotton. He squinted at me, reaching
slowly behind himself into the waistband of his jeans. He laid
something between his legs. The silver barrel glinted in the
sun. We stared at each other while he lifted the cigarette to
his lips. His exhale felt like a bullet between the eyes.

A screen door slammed on the opposite side of the street.
I turned slowly. TJ stood barefoot on his front step, holding
a trash bag full of empty cans. His uncle was slurring and
swearing through the open door, but TJ didn't seem to hear.
He looked at me with his brows drawn together, and then

to the gun between Lonny's legs. The two locked eyes. TJ set the trash down, but he didn't go back inside. Instead, he watched.

I slipped quickly between the police car and my porch, and stood behind the two plainclothes officers. Lonny'd spent the night in jail because of Reece, and his girlfriend was dead, maybe because of me. He wouldn't think twice about shooting me, but he'd think twice about doing it in front of two cops and a witness.

My mother stood in her robe in the open door. Her hands weren't visible, and the detectives stood at the bottom of the porch, eyeing her cautiously. Sweat trailed over their temples and darkened their collars, their balding heads cooking pink in the sun. My mother kept her eyes square on their faces and said, "Nearly, get inside."

I scrambled past the officers and under her arm.

"Gentlemen," my mother said sharply, "my daughter is a minor. I know her rights. You need my consent to ask her anything or to come inside my home, and I've no intention of giving it to you." They couldn't see her fingers close over the baseball bat she kept behind the door. "You'd best be on your way."

The older one placed a toe on the stoop. "We just want a few words with her . . ."

The bat came off the floor, and my mother's voice dropped low. "We've got nothing to say, unless you've got a warrant."

The man paused, his foot creaking on the drooping wooden step. His eyes flicked to her arm where it disappeared behind the door, and he stepped back, slow and easy. Neither spoke, and when the silence threatened to extend indefinitely, Mona slammed the door. She kept one hand on the bat as she slid the dead bolt home and snapped the chain in place. Then she stood sideways at the window, peering through the curtain slit. She didn't let the fabric fall until a cloud of gravel kicked up, bouncing off our aluminum walls like hail.

Mona paced to the kitchen, snatching her cigarettes off the counter.

"What do the police want with you?" Her voice was eerily calm as she slapped the box hard against her open fist.

I sank slowly into the scratchy vinyl chair. I couldn't explain. I wouldn't know where to start.

"Does this have something to do with that boy?" Mona asked through a mouthful of smoke. "I knew it. I knew he was nothing but trouble." She shook her head, letting her ashtray clatter to the table.

"It's nothing like that, Mom—"

"Don't lie to me, Nearly!" She smacked the table hard enough to rattle me.

I looked at her hand and saw my crinkled trig exam—the one I'd used to wrap her Mother's Day gift—smashed flat under her palm. I'd scored 100%, but I'd missed the bonus question, an impossibly tricky equation that no one in the class had bothered to answer. The bonus question was filled in, complete, in the same messy scrawl my mother used to write our rent checks every month.

"Stop talking to me like I'm an idiot," she said.

I pulled the test toward me, my mind working over the numerals and letters, the logic sinking in. My mother, who climbed a pole for a living and scraped her paychecks from a stage, had finished my trig test.

"What are we doing here?" I whispered.

My lips parted, clearing a path for all the angry words I'd been swallowing for years. But I couldn't squeeze all that bitterness through the knot in my throat. I balled up the test in my fist and shouted, "What are we doing here?"

My mother's eyes were glassy, her lips pressed into a thin line. The cigarette smoldered away between her fingers.

"All this time you could do this?" I shook the test in her face. "And you kept us here?" Years of questions and anger burned to the surface. That test was like a match in my hands. I wasn't supposed to be like her. I was supposed to be like him. The one who'd found a way out. "Why?"

She was crying, her eye makeup dripping in long black streaks down her face. "I never graduated high school!" she shouted, as though that were somehow my fault. "What was I supposed to do? How was I supposed to take care of you? Your father left me nothing!"

I gritted my teeth, holding back the worst of the things

I wanted to say. I wanted to hurl everything I had at her, to throw everything I knew now back in her face, but each word was a boomerang. I couldn't inflict pain without hurting myself.

"You don't get to lecture me on boys, or grades, or school anymore. You don't get to build my future out of your busted, burned-out life! That was your failure. Not mine." I took a last look at the trig exam before tossing it into the trash. "It's too late for extra credit."

I locked myself in my room and collapsed into my bed.

In a matter of hours, I'd probably be arrested for four murders I didn't commit. My mother had kept secrets from me for years. Neither of my parents were who I thought they were, and this trailer—this life that had always been the best she could do for us—was a lie.

I reached under the mattress and withdrew the train ticket from the bag.

Reece was the only one left I could trust. Leave town, he'd said. Run, before everything came crashing down around me. It didn't matter if running made me look guilty. The police thought I was guilty anyway. Get someplace safe, he'd said. Save yourself.

But that wouldn't save *him*.

And if I ran, that would leave Jeremy squarely under the investigators' microscope.

Besides, I only had the ticket, no cash. The ticket was

enough to get out of town, but the only cash in my future was the scholarship I was going to lose anyway.

I shut my eyes. Kylie's bloody face stared back at me. Emily, Marcia, Posie, Teddy, and now Kylie . . . And yet, this whole mess was far from over. Whoever was framing me wasn't finished.

Ne + Ar + Li + B + Os.

My name was still incomplete.

Obviously, whoever was doing this was in no hurry to have me arrested, only giving the police part of the picture. Just the bodies of my students. He was holding back, biding his time, withholding the one piece of evidence that would seal my fate—the clue he'd left for me under the bleachers—but he'd put me in an inescapable box. Made it impossible for me to go to the police without incriminating myself. He was forcing me to play this through, but I was damned either way. In the end, it would be my name spelled in blood. But why? Why me?

I lay there for hours, watching the light shift in my room. By late afternoon, my head was swimming and I was no closer to understanding any of it. I should've been studying for my chemistry final, but there hardly seemed any point in it now.

The front door slammed and I peeked out my window. It was just before dark and Sunny View Drive took small bites of my mother until she was a tiny red speck under the traffic light. I was alone.

I opened my door and headed to the kitchen, hungry, tired, and confused. Mona had fished the trig exam out of the trash and left it for me, smoothed out on the table. Stuck to it was a yellow Post-it note addressed to me.

N— This is for you. I was saving it for your graduation. Use it if you must. Save it if you can. Please stay out of trouble. And be safe. It's yours to waste now.   —M

Mona's note lay on the table beside a fat brown envelope that said *For Nearly*. The handwriting on the envelope looked familiar. Not like Mona's. More like my own.

I picked it up, the paper crackling loud in the silence. I opened it. Turned it upside down over the table. Tight rubber-banded rolls fell out with a series of thuds.

Money.

A lot of money.

But it was the yellowing letter that I reached for first. It peeled open, brittle like the skin of an onion. My eyes burned as I read it.

M—I need to lay low and I can't stay. Hide this. It's all for Nearly. For college. I know how much that means to you. It's not much, but I'll send more through Butch as often as I can. He'll watch out for you. I'm sorry I let you down. I love you both.   —D

I tore off the rubber bands, fanning the cash in my shaking hands, a ripple of loose bills spilling to the floor as I counted. Five thousand dollars. Not as much as the scholarship, but enough.

I scooped the rolls of money into the envelope and clamped it tight over my chest, the names of a thousand distant cities rolling like a bus departure ticker through my mind. A lightness filled me, but it didn't last.

If I weren't so worried about what might happen to Jeremy, I could've run.

40

I SLIPPED INTO CHEMISTRY CLASS at the last possible second. Whispers and stares followed me. They'd grown louder and harder to ignore since Teddy and Posie died, and the connection between the victims became undeniably obvious. Anh acknowledged me with a nervous smile.

I kept my head down, sparing a quick glance at Oleksa's empty chair, and dropped into my own just as the bell rang. Anh sat rigid, her desk cleared of all but two number-two pencils and her calculator. By the bags under her eyes, I guessed she'd been up all night studying—an entire night more than I had. I wanted to tell her to relax. That her victory was a sure thing. Winning the scholarship was no longer an option for me. I hadn't studied. I was short on community service hours. TJ was the one she should be worrying about, and even he was a full percentage point and a half behind her.

Rankin was silent as he passed out the final exams. Whispers spread throughout the room.

"Is there a problem?" Rankin spun around, angrier than I'd ever seen him. A few students glanced nervously at each other, nudging each other in the elbow until Oleksa's lab partner finally spoke up.

"We thought you'd cancel the final today. You know . . . because of what happened to Kylie over the weekend?" I hoped for his sake he hadn't bet money on it.

Rankin's harsh laugh shook the room. "Oh, you did? Frankly, I'm surprised you even know her name." He razed every whisper with a stare. "If a single one of you can look me in the eye and tell me Kylie Rutherford was a friend—that you know anything about her except the color of her hair—you may be excused from my exam. The funeral is on Wednesday and I shall see you there."

No one spoke. I felt a few sets of eyes turn in my direction. I didn't look up from my desk.

"Precisely what I thought," he snapped. "Turn your papers over. You may begin."

I lost myself for the next hour in black-and-white Scantron bubbles and the scratch of lead against paper. TJ was first to put down his pencil and hobble to the front of the room. Anh and I didn't look at each other when we finished at the same time. We turned our papers in facedown and walked out wordlessly.

Jeremy waited in the hall. For Anh, no doubt. He hadn't been picking me up for school and it was the first time I'd seen him since the rave. I plastered on a neutral smile just in case and squashed the seed of suspicion Reece had planted before his arrest. Lonny had to be wrong. It was someone else's Jeremy on that list. Not mine.

I crossed the hall toward him and called out his name, but he didn't seem to notice. He reclined against the wall, one foot propped against it, head back as though he had all day to wait. Eager Jeremy, the one who would have followed me anywhere, was gone. This Jeremy didn't even look up.

"I need to talk to you."

He looked through me, straight to the chem lab door. Then his face came to life and he waved at Anh behind me. Jeremy pushed off the wall, moving around me as if I weren't even there. He'd dropped me. But I wasn't expendable. I threw myself in front of him, tripping him up enough to earn a dark look and taste of his bitterness when I grabbed his hand.

"There's this crazy rumor going around. Someone said you're buying drugs from Lonny Johnson." I held tight, riding out the rush of disbelief, fear, and rage that mirrored the shifting expressions on his face.

He jerked away. "Would you rather I'd bought them from your boyfriend?"

My mouth fell open and I stared at him, dumbfounded.

"I don't understand," I uttered in complete denial. "You're kidding, right?"

He kept walking, but I stood my ground, letting him crash into me, desperate to make him look at my face. I lowered my voice to a frantic whisper. "Lonny is dangerous. The drugs he sells are dangerous. Why are you doing this?" I reached for his hand, but he wouldn't let me touch him. I saw his lip tremble a second before he clenched his teeth. What was he hiding from me? Why was he buying roofies? He couldn't be the one responsible for these crimes. I knew Jeremy. Didn't I? "I don't get it, J. This isn't you."

He laughed through his teeth. "Yeah well, this isn't you either! You put on one hell of a show Friday night." His sneer felt like a mask. I hardly recognized him under all his disdain. "I guess it's true what they say. You really can't take the girl out of the trailer park. You're more like your mother than you give yourself credit for."

"Go to hell." I shoved him hard enough to knock him back. When he righted himself, his arm was wound back. His gray eyes were hard and unapologetic. This wasn't my Jeremy at all.

"Jeremy, stop."

The small voice belonged to Anh. She stepped between us, turning her back to me to look at Jeremy. Did she know what

he was involved in? Had he told her more than he told me?
All this time I'd been trying to protect him by keeping my
distance, but I'd only succeeded in pushing him away.

"It's okay." Jeremy smoothed his shirt where I'd pushed
him. "Our conversation was over."

He reached out to her. She hesitated before slipping her
hand in his and letting him lead her away. She looked back
at me over her shoulder, unspoken apologies on her perfect
guilty face.

The bell rang and I was alone. Just like that, he'd let me go.

41

I WAS INTENTIONALLY LATE to Respite Meadows cemetery.
Sweat trickled over my neck and I peeled off my hoodie,
tying it loosely around my waist. Kylie Rutherford's funeral
had ended hours ago, but the air was still heavy with grief. I
weaved carefully between the angel-topped stones and mau-
soleums, inscriptions obscured by colorful arrangements.
Loving mother. Adored father. Beloved brothers and sons.

The rows narrowed until the perfectly level landscape felt
less like Astroturf and more like the crabgrass that thrived
in Sunny View. It was neatly trimmed, but bare in spots
and smelled of onion weed. I slowed and raised my head
in a grove of less ostentatious memorials. Some only head-

markers, devoid of color and ordered in neat, tight rows. I stopped by a mound of soft brown soil. The small temporary plaque read KYLIE M. RUTHERFORD. 1998–2014.

Damp grass had been crushed into the earth a few brief yards in either direction, bearing footprints of those who'd come to pay respects. I studied them, kicking at the ruts and feeling like an intruder on their grief, because it had been my name etched in her skin. I fought back a deepening sadness, tripping my way backward over shallow stones, regretting my decision to come.

I gasped as I backed into something hard, too tall to be a headstone. A hand clamped down on my shoulder. The fingers were covered in tattoos. I turned slowly and swallowed hard, looking into the dark and shining eyes of Lonny Johnson.

I put two quick steps between us. "What are you doing here?" Wind blew my hair across my face, and I left it there like a curtain, hating the way he looked at me.

He grinned, as though amused by my discomfort. His steel-toed shoes stepped forward until they almost touched mine. He squeezed my shoulder, brushing a thumb over my collarbone until I tasted metal and blood, anger and violence, and the saltwater burn of his grief. Beneath it all was a barely perceptible sting of regret. It hardly felt like enough.

"Came to pay my respects. She was a good girl." He tipped his head. "Like you." His cool smile disintegrated as he took in the fresh dirt on her grave. "This should never have happened."

My face twisted, anger welling up from some dark place inside me. It wasn't fair that I should feel so guilty when Lonny was the one dealing the drugs. He'd sold the ketamine that was at least partly to blame for her death.

"Don't you feel even the least bit responsible?" My hair stuck in the corners of my mouth, muffling my words. I swatted at it, feeling clumsy and childish.

Lonny's face lit with something I could almost mistake for affection, his own sinister brand of warmth. "I like you, Boswell. You've got guts. A lot of people wouldn't talk to me like you do. Even fewer while threatening me with a baseball bat." Lonny lowered his head to mine, brushing back the stubborn wet lock of hair. My flinch didn't faze him as he tucked it behind my ear.

"Because I like you," he said, "I'll tell you a secret." His goatee tickled my cheek when he leaned in close. I shivered, completely aware that we were alone. His confession was a whisper in my ear. "I do feel responsible. And someone's going to pay for that."

Lonny pulled back slowly and reached behind himself. A voice inside me screamed "Run!" but it was too late.

• • •

Lonny retrieved a single black rose from his back pocket and held it delicately poised between his fingers. I fell hard on my knees, legs numb with fear. Lonny strode past me, stopping just short of Kylie's grave.

He tossed the rose onto the clump of dirt, near where her headstone should've been. It could have been mistaken for such a callous gesture, but his shoulders sagged. He paused a moment, lowered his head. His arm moved almost imperceptibly in an up-down-side-to-side motion. Blessing himself, I realized, stunned that he might recognize a power higher than himself.

"Be careful, Boswell," he said, head bent over the grave. "It might have been a game before, but now it's gone too far."

"What do you mean?" Knees still watery, I pulled myself up and followed him through a winding maze of headstones, stubbing my toes on the low plaques that Lonny seemed to float over like a ghost.

"Think about it," he said without slowing. "Steckler? Washington? Marshall? . . . Kylie? . . . They only had one thing in common."

Like I needed to be reminded.

I gritted my teeth and scrambled after him. "I didn't do this."

His laugh rumbled through him. "Don't have to be a genius to have figured that out." He paused beside a gleaming white stone. Slipping his hands in his pockets, he eased back against it, leg stretched out to the side like he was leaning on a barstool. He pushed and pulled the barbell through his lip while he studied me, a catlike curiosity behind his eyes. "You didn't do this, but you know who did. Someone's trying to frame you. It's personal."

"I don't have any enemies. And if I knew who was doing this, I'd have told the cops."

"If I've learned anything, Boswell, it's that you can't trust criminals or cops. You can never be sure whose side they're on." Lonny kicked the headstone with the heel of his boot, drawing my attention down. RYAN WHELAN. BELOVED SON. JULY 13, 1995–MARCH 25, 2013. The stone was crowned with a sagging thistle and said nothing about a beloved brother, though it was large enough for the sentiment. Reece's brother's grave. He'd been telling the truth when he said he didn't have any family . . . not anymore.

"Thistle." Lonny massaged his knuckles, watching my face. "Interesting choice."

I looked again between Lonny and the stone. Lonny knew something about Reece. Something I didn't know. His eyes lit with a crooked smile at the curiosity he must have seen on my face.

"Old legend . . ." Lonny studied his fingernails and looked past me, over the flat expanse of a thousand graves. "Norse soldiers planned a night raid on Scotland. They infiltrated barefoot, which might have worked except one stepped on a thistle and screamed. That one thistle"—Lonny lifted a single finger—"one insignificant thorn in the heel—alerted the Scotts. The Norse were slaughtered."

I touched the thistle's hanging head. "Ryan Whelan was a thistle?"

"Ryan Whelan was a narc. His little brother, Reece, was trying to break himself in as a dealer. Reece was young and full of himself. He never thought his brother would turn him in. A little over a year ago, Ryan blew the whistle on a deal his little brother was involved in, and the police set up a team of undercover cops to make the buy. Reece figured it out and got spooked and blew big brother's cover. The bust became an ambush. Shots were fired, and Ryan took a bullet for some undercover lady cop."

An undercover lady cop? *I think he'd take a bullet for me.* It all made sense. Gena was more than a narc, she was a cop. She said she'd met Reece a year ago, and they both worked for Nicholson. That was why she was so protective of him. Why she treated him like a little brother. Reece's brother had taken a bullet for her.

"Reece's brother saved her life?"

"He died doing it. And Reece got nine months in juvie. He was only supposed to serve six for the drug charges, but rumor has it that the lady cop's boyfriend came after him during the trial, and Reece got an extra three months for assaulting an officer." Lonny's eyes were adrift in a memory. "The thistle doesn't get to win, Boswell. Doesn't matter who steps on him first, he gets crushed." Lonny scratched his chin and shook his head. "A lot like us, you know. Stuck by the roots. Up until a few nights ago, I wasn't sure what side your boy was on. An enemy can make himself look like a friend. A wolf in sheep's clothing."

I kept quiet, determined to hold Reece's secrets close to the vest. He'd been responsible for his own brother's death, lost his family, and now he'd thrown away his future trying to make it right. Trying to balance the equation by protecting me. I didn't care whose side Reece was on. I only knew he was on mine.

"I know who he is, Boswell." Lonny stood up slowly, rolling his shoulders. "It's not hard to figure out. Reece sold his soul to Nicholson to get even with anyone who had anything to do with his brother's death. He wanted revenge. He's setting us up and rubbing his hands together as Nicholson hauls us off to jail. Reece Whelan is my wolf. My thistle. Who's yours?"

Lonny watched me, his brows arching up.

"Don't you get it?" he said. "These murders are a set-up. It's about revenge. Someone's sold his soul to get even with you. Whoever it is, he's close. He's close enough to know you, to watch you. Maybe even someone you trust. He's setting you up for a reason. It's personal." Lonny shook his head while I struggled with his theory.

Lonny handed me a card, empty except for a number. "Call me when you figure it out."

42

THE BELL JANGLED and Bao looked up from the coffee station.

"D-Day, huh?" he said over his shoulder as he dumped out the cold grounds, consolidated the half-empty pots, and set them back on the warmers with a mindless rhythm.

My Twinkies sat beside the register, on top of today's paper.

D-Day. More than any other Friday, today felt like an ambush. The last Friday of the school year. I'd either won the scholarship or I hadn't. There was either an ad in that paper, or there wasn't. It was only the certain knowledge of either that awaited me. And the twisty feeling in my gut told me that I probably didn't want to know the answer to either one.

"You just missed Anh," he grumbled. "Her country club boyfriend just picked her up. She wanted to get to school early and see who won the scholarship. I'll be surprised if she pulled it off with all the time she's spending with that guy. I told her a million times, she needs to focus if she wants to win. Eliminate distractions." He shook his head, wiping loose grounds from the counter. "I've given up too much to make sure she has a good future. If she's not careful, she'll end up squeezing out rich babies and dressing them in twin sets, and serving tea and crumpets to his buddies on the ninth green. She belongs in medical school."

"Med school? She's afraid of blood."

"She needs to get over it."

Bao swiped hard circles over the counter with his rag, then slung it over his shoulder. It had never occured to me that Bao may want something different for Anh than she wanted for herself. "Hey, you going to prom tonight? Maybe we can double with my sister. Then I can keep an eye on Fowler. I don't like the way he looks at her."

"They haven't canceled prom yet? I thought the school canceled all the after-school activities because of the . . . you know . . ." I gesticulated with my hands, unable to say the M word. ". . . funerals and weird stuff going on."

"No, they just moved it. It's going to be in the gymnasium at school instead of some fancy hotel in Old Town. Twice as many chaperones, a few of the city's finest, and no after-party. No way they'd cancel prom. West River not having prom would be like you not eating Twinkies."

Without a word, I swapped out the Twinkies for a box of donut holes. Bao laughed and shook his head. I counted out a few small bills and left them on the counter, told Bao to keep the change, and turned to go.

"Hey, Boswell," he called as I held open the door. "I'd wish you luck, but you and I both know luck has nothing

to do with it." I looked over my shoulder. Bao studied me
over the handle of his mop. He wasn't smiling.

I stepped away from the heavy silence deeply uneasy, and
the bells jarred my nerves when the door pulled itself closed
behind me.

It all boils down to motive.

Of everyone I knew, Anh probably had more motive than
anyone. She wanted this scholarship as badly as I did, and
needed it almost as much. It had been a close race to the end
of the semester. Close enough to put a strain on our friendship. But not close enough to change the fact that she couldn't
stand the sight of blood and would never inflict violence on
another living thing. But Bao . . . I wasn't so sure.

He was fiercely protective of her. And every bit as smart.
Smart enough to manipulate me with these kinds of clues.
He knew I read the personals. He had motive and opportu-
nity. And he'd said himself, luck had nothing to do with it.

But the person behind all this had a darker motive.
Murdering four people just to frame me? Taking his time
and taking pleasure in it, like it was all a big game? No, it
couldn't be Bao.

I walked to the end of the strip mall and with a cautious
glance over my shoulder, turned into the alley. Flipping open
the paper, I thumbed through the sections and tossed everything but the *Missed Connections* in the Dumpster. Squatting
behind it, I spread the pages on the asphalt.

I read the first line of each ad until I found the one I was looking for. It oozed a cold confidence and read like a chilling invitation. A horrifying secret waiting to be revealed.

Some cats don't dance.
Respite in a box, a toxic paradox.
Dead or alive when you find him?

• • •

Congratulations, Anh Bui topped the bulletin board in big red letters. *Nearly Boswell* and *Thomas J. Wiles* had been printed in small black font, tight on her heels at second and third place. Almost, but not quite good enough.

Anh's face glowed with a wide grin she tried to smooth when I walked in the room. But it was like trying to hold down the roller shades in my bedroom. The harder you pulled, the more they wanted to curl right back up. Her eyes squinted wet and shiny, her future bright with possibilities.

"I'm sorry," she said, her apology bouncing off me. I told myself it didn't matter as students lined up to congratulate her. I didn't need a scholarship anymore. The envelope from my father was a reassuring weight inside my backpack. I smiled at Anh and tried to make myself happy for her.

I didn't bother to look for Jeremy after class. The air in the hall was thick, at odds with the pink prom posters that covered the walls. I waded through with my head down. Conversations quieted as I walked by. They should have been talking about the colors of their dresses and how they'd wear their hair. Instead they were talking about me.

I lifted my head just in time to see Emily Reinnert standing in front of her open locker. A surge of hope propelled me toward her, but her face didn't mirror any recognition. She shut her locker and started to walk away.

"Emily, wait!" I called, not caring who stared. She stopped to let me catch up, but wouldn't look at me.

"You're back." I felt foolish for stating the obvious, but I didn't know what else to say. She was here, and alive, the only person who might remember something. I wanted to ask her all the same questions Posie couldn't answer. I glanced at her forearm, curious about the blue number I'd only heard about. The fading remains of a dark mark lingered, visible under her unbuttoned long sleeve. It looked like a bruise. The kind that I'd seen under Jeremy's sleeves. Carefully placed. Easy to conceal. She hugged her arms around herself and took a step back.

"I came back for finals," she said quietly with quick anxious looks around, a changed Emily from the confident cheerleader I'd tutored.

Vince and Emily have been fighting a lot.

Ever since Jeremy showed TJ that picture of Emily and Vince together. Vince was at the game. Vince was at the amusement park. Vince was on the list.

"Emily, what happened to your arm? Who did this to you?"

Her face paled. "I'm not supposed to talk to you."

"Says who?"

"The police." She walked briskly out the front doors, where a flashing blue light caught my attention.

Outside the window, two police cars pulled up. The officers got out and shut their doors. They carried papers. Probably a warrant. I was out of time.

I ran, following the emergency exit signs to a rear door, looked to make sure no one was watching, and then pulled the fire alarm on the wall, using my sleeve to cover my fingers.

Fire alarms blared, and a rush of students poured into the halls, flooding the exits. The chaos would buy me some time. I'd be impossible to find in a swarm of three thousand people.

I pulled my hood over my head and made my way quickly into the trees behind the ball fields, the same path I'd used to escape unseen after I'd found Marcia's body in the pool. It would take administration at least fifteen minutes to locate the source of the false alarm, clear the halls, and get everyone back to class. By then, I'd be long gone.

• • •

I walked under the high dome ceiling of Union Station, clutching my train ticket. I'd listen to Reece and get as far away as possible. The killer wouldn't know I was gone, and if he did follow through on this morning's clue in the *Missed Connections*, then I'd have an alibi, in another state on the other side of the country. It was the only winning move. I'd stay away long enough for the police to figure out who the real killer was and I'd come back for Reece after the dust settled. Problem solved.

Instinct told me to stay near the perimeter, away from all the people, their exposed arms and hands and faces. But I jammed my hands in my pockets and slipped between the crowds, edging my way to the front of the line. I would be first. I wouldn't lose my seat. I wouldn't change my mind this time.

A phone rang behind me, and continued to ring. A man tapped my sleeve. "Miss, I think that's your phone."

"Not mine," I said. "I don't have a phone." I turned back toward the departure gate. The conductor was readying to board and I hefted my pack higher on my shoulder. The phone rang again. Closer this time.

Something shivered through the material, an insistent vibration inside my backpack. I lowered it to the floor, slowly unzipped it, and reached inside. The phone I'd locked in Reece's apartment five days ago buzzed in my hand.

One new text message flashed across the screen.

Found a stray cat.

Think he belongs to you.

Tonight @9. The answer's in the box.

I shut the phone slowly, watched the blue screen fade to black. Someone had access to Reece's apartment and had taken the phone. They'd been close to me. Close enough to put it in my backpack. Close enough that I hadn't even noticed it happening.

It lit up again, alive in my hand.

Gena's name flashed. Shaking, I opened the phone and put it to my ear. Passengers converged toward the gate.

"Hello?" My eyes skimmed the swarm as it pressed in around me.

"Leigh." Her voice was muffled and cut out in brief silences. "Leigh, it's Gena . . ."

Someone knocked into my shoulder.

". . . called to thank you. . . ."

"Thank me? For what?" I turned slowly, searching the overpasses and stairwells. I jammed my finger in my ear and listened hard.

". . . for springing Reece . . . went to see him . . . duty officer said . . . bailed him out last night. . . ."

"Bailed him out?" A woman in front of me turned to stare.

". . . trying to call him . . . all night . . . no answer . . . maybe he was with you. . . ." Boarding instructions echoed from the overhead speakers. Someone stepped into the back of my foot.

". . . any idea where he is? . . ." Gena asked before our connection dropped.

"Gena? Gena?" The line was dead.

The crowd pressed in behind me, muttering as I stood there with the phone to my ear. I replayed the broken bits

and pieces of conversation. Reece was out of jail. Someone
bailed him out using my name. And now he was missing.

Found a stray cat. Think he belongs to you.

Reece. It had to be. He was the only student I had left.

My feet stuck to the floor when I remembered the ad in
today's paper. *Some cats don't dance. Dead or alive when you find
him?*

"Ticket, please."

I looked up at the attendant, holding my ticket close to
my body.

"Your ticket, miss?" he insisted with a hard smile.

I looked at the black-and-white ticket. It should have all
been so clear. My freedom was on the other side of that door.
But the only answer that made any sense—the only thing I
really wanted—wasn't.

I turned headlong into the crowd and bulldozed my way
through. I had to solve the ad before nine o'clock.

A uniformed police officer shifted his weight, fingers resting on his sidearm as I emerged. A sweating mess of panic and
frustration, I lowered my eyes and walked steadily through
the terminal, pausing only to buy a Metro ticket home.

I fingered Lonny's card in my pocket.

It all comes down to motive . . .

Reece's voice buzzed in my ears.

*Who has a reason to kill people you care about? To put you
behind bars? Who would want to ruin your life, Leigh?*

I'd never hurt anyone. Had never taken anything that belonged to anyone else. But my father had.

He couldn't see the lives he was destroying.

Was it possible all this could have something to do with him? I clutched my bag tight, remembering what my mother had told me about my father. What he'd done. How he'd been caught. My father had lied and stolen and left his partner to take the fall. It was a crazy thought, but could I be paying for his crimes because he wasn't here to suffer for them himself?

And suddenly it all began to make a terrible kind of sense.

I knew whose life my father destroyed.

• • •

Dead or alive when you find him? It was as if we'd come full circle. Back to the beginning. It had all started with Schrödinger, the morning I'd found the first ad, and Rankin's voice droning on about the damn cat. The cat was dead. It had to be. He'd said it himself. The cat couldn't be both dead and alive at the same time. Dead, like the cat on my porch. Dead, like Kylie and the others. He was going to kill Reece.

I got off the city bus at West River and took the side streets at a sprint. Crouching in the bushes next to the high school, I watched as deejays carried amps and speakers, and student council members toted the last of the decorations and balloons to the gym. *Some cats don't dance.* No, the killer wasn't luring

me to the prom. He was taking me back to the beginning.
Back to the chemistry lab where we first learned about
Schrödinger's cat. Where he'd left the first message, *Dead or
Alive,* on my desk.

An unmarked police car idled near the main entrance, so I
slipped inside through a back door, sticking to the quiet, dark
passages and emerging at the empty chem lab.

The lights were off and the room reeked of disinfectant.
Muddy chalk swirls were drying on the blackboard. I rotated
slowly, taking in every detail of the room. Late-evening
sun streamed between the plastic slats and stretched over
the neat rows. I grabbed my stool off the table and set
it quietly on the floor. My desk was clean. Nothing. No
clues, no notes.

The answer's in the box.

I ran to the storage closet and flipped on the light, illuminating floor-to-ceiling gunmetal shelves stuffed with cardboard boxes, all of them sorted and labeled by my own hand.
I moved to the far end of the closet where I'd organized the
fourth semester lab materials. We'd covered Schrödinger six
weeks ago. If there was a clue, it was . . .

Here.

A chill raced through me. The box was labeled *Schrödinger's
Cat* in indelible blue ink, fresh fumes still clinging to the air
around it. It was long and wide, big enough to fill the space
below the lowest shelf. Big enough for a body.

Respite in a box . . .

Dead or alive when you find him?

"Reece!" I dragged the box, leveraging my weight and heaving it out from under the shelf until I could reach the seam. Breathless, I grabbed a box cutter from a supply cabinet and dragged it across the tape, ripping the flaps open and plunging my hand inside. I dropped to my knees, dug to the bottom. Crumpled newspaper spilled onto the floor, exposing rows of heavy microscopes underneath.

With an angry shout, I pitched the cutter across the room. I slumped into the pile of news filler and pressed my head into my hands.

The killer wanted me to find Reece, or he wouldn't have led me this far. There had always been a clue. A bread crumb. A message somewhere to point me in the right direction. Why not now? Or had I missed it?

I dragged my sleeve across my forehead, clearing the sweat from my eyes. Then I scooped up an armful of mashed up newspaper and began stuffing it back in the box. One piece of newsprint stuck flat against the floor. I scraped up the only piece that hadn't been crushed into a ball of stuffing. This one was smooth, torn at the taped corners where I'd ripped it from the inside flap in my hurry to open the box. An obituary.

Catherine Schrödinger. Dead of a heart attack at eighty-eight in Alexandria, VA, in 2007. I skimmed the memorial and viewing information. Funeral services had been held at the family mausoleum . . . in Respite Meadows.

That was it. The clue from the ad that morning.

Respite in a box, a toxic paradox.
Dead or alive when you find him?

Reece was at Respite Meadows Cemetery. I stuffed the obituary into my pocket. Then piled the filling back in the box, rotated it so the writing faced the wall, and shoved it under the shelf. If the police managed to get this far from the ad, I didn't need them arresting me before I could find Reece. I turned off the lights and shut the closet door, grabbed my backpack, and righted my stool.

The room was pink with twilight shadows.

Found a stray cat.

Think he belongs to you.

Tonight @9. The answer's in the box.

I checked the clock and pulled out my phone.

Less than one hour to find him.

43

THE SUN DIPPED UNDER THE HORIZON and the headstones glowed white against an indigo sky. In the cemetery directory I thumbed through last names beginning with *S*. The Schrödinger family mausoleum was located in a private section of the grounds, set far back from the highway. I crunched over a gravel trail through sculpture gardens and dark roundabouts until I recognized the grove from the directory map.

I stepped off the gravel path to the first stone structure, checking the nameplate before moving on to the next. Every trace of sunlight was gone. Monuments were lit by upturned bulbs hidden in the landscape, illuminating angels and crosses that cast creeping shadows across the mausoleum gates.

A branch crackled in a grove of trees behind me. I turned, and my heart jumped into my throat.

"What are you doing here?" I breathed as the figure came closer.

Jeremy stood in a low beam of light. It cut across a shimmering blue cummerbund over a crisp tuxedo shirt. His expression was murderous as he swiped twigs from his lapels.

"I followed you," he growled. "I saw you get off the bus outside the gates. But the damn parking lot was roped off." He kicked grass clippings off the toes of his high-gloss shoes.

He wasn't supposed to be here. "Why aren't you at prom?"

"I got stood up!" Jeremy's hands clenched at his sides. "But you already knew that, didn't you? Anh was supposed to meet me at the dance. I waited. She never showed up. I called her brother from a pay phone. He said she got a phone call from you. That she went to meet you! Then you came running out of school and I followed your bus here. So where is she? Why isn't she here? What did you say to her, Leigh?"

My mind raced. Someone called Anh posing as me. And now Anh was missing. I might already be too late . . .

He shook his head, his voice loud and tremulous. "But it doesn't matter anymore. Because I didn't want to go to the dance with Anh. I wanted to go with you!" Jeremy was shouting now, pacing and agitated. "I've been chasing you since eighth grade, Leigh! Chasing you and you didn't even care! You're too busy falling for criminals to notice!" Jeremy turned to me, dropping his voice low and pleading. His face was streaked with tears. "Do I have to kill someone to make you chase after me like you chase after Reece?"

I backed away at the mention of Reece's name. I was running out of time.

"Jeremy, you have to leave. You can't be here . . ."

He stepped toward me. I stumbled, my heel connecting with a low stone bench and my momentum throwing me backward and over it. My elbows dug in the ground, breaking my fall, and I struggled to get my feet under me. I looked up into Jeremy's face as he advanced, one hand outstretched toward me. A shadow passed behind him.

"Jeremy, watch out!"

There was a muffled thud and he crumpled to the ground. Oleksa stood behind him, breathing hard, the butt of his gun turned outward. I scrambled backward, hands and shoes slipping in the mulch.

Oleksa swiped his sleeve across his forehead and rested his hands on his knees, straining to catch his breath. He nudged Jeremy's shoulder with his foot. Jeremy didn't move. Oleksa rotated the gun, righting it in his palm as he straightened to look at me.

"I told you to be careful. Your friends are dangerous."

"You're the one with the gun." Doubt needled me. Lonny's warning rippled through my head. *You can't trust criminals or cops. You can never be sure whose side they're on.* I hadn't called Oleksa. He wasn't supposed to be here. I inched away from him on my elbows and heels.

"Where's Reece?" he said.

"Where's Lonny?" I fisted a handful of dry dirt like Mona and Butch had taught me, but Oleksa was too far and the wind wasn't right. "He doesn't know who you are, does he?"

Oleksa's face screwed up with a confused expression I'd never seen him wear before. His spine straightened, his body stilled, and his eyes grew wide and alert. I heard the soft click as he flipped off the safety.

A gunshot pierced the silence and a jolt ripped through Oleksa.

I screamed and Oleksa dropped to his knees. His head connected with the stone bench as he collapsed facedown in the grass. I scrambled toward him, but a hand wrapped over my mouth and yanked me violently off my feet.

I choked on the bitter smell of latex, pungent and powdery,

sticky against my lips. The rubber grabbed at my cheeks and I struggled to breathe, unable to hear my own screams.

I kicked out and thrashed wildly. Clawed at the arms around my neck, losing my footing as they dragged me out of the dirt. It shouldn't have been so easy. He should have been stumbling. But he pulled me like a rag doll through the shadows, away from Oleksa and Jeremy, toward a gleaming stone mausoleum. Their still bodies grew smaller until they disappeared in the dark.

We stopped moving at a set of iron gates.

In the grass lay an empty leg brace. He turned my head with a painful jerk of my chin, drawing my attention past it. A fresh surge of terror shot through me.

I was too late.

Two bodies stretched across the ground before the gates of the stone crypt. Anh lay crumpled in the grass, her forearm marked in blue ink. Not with a number. There was no element on the table with the abbreviation L, so he'd used the letter instead. But Reece's body lay beside her, the pale skin of his left forearm marked 74. Seventy-four, the atomic weight of Tungsten. The symbol for Tungsten was W.

Ne + Ar + Li + B + Os + W + L

Indelible ink fumes mixed with the smell of latex. I struggled, breath rushing in and out past the hand over my face. Twinkling lights sparkled around the edge of my consciousness.

"No one would hear you," said TJ's voice through the buzzing in my ears. "It won't do you any good to scream." His glove dropped from my mouth to my throat, and I sucked in a deep ragged breath.

The cool kiss of a gun's muzzle pressed against my temple. I shut my eyes.

"Get inside," he commanded.

I planted my feet. Once I stepped through the gate, it was all over. Butch's lessons came back, a flash of a memory. *Never let them take you without a fight.* I made my body rigid, imagined my shoes anchored to the ground.

"Get the note," he growled, not to me.

"I don't want to," came a tearful reply. "I can't do this. Please don't make me do this."

The girl stepped toward me, until her face became clear. Emily Reinnert stood in front of me, fastening an envelope to my shirt with a safety pin. Her fingers trembled over my skin and I knew without a doubt I'd been right. She was terrified and remorseful. She didn't want any part of this.

Her face was streaked with tears. "I'm sorry. No one was supposed to get hurt," she said. "He said the joke under the bleachers was on Vince. That he only wanted to get back at Vince for kissing me. He said if I was sorry and I wanted him to take me back, I'd help. All I had to do was take a roofie and tell the police I didn't know anything. It was supposed to be a prank. No one was supposed to get hurt. I'd get a few weeks off school and we'd get back together, it would be no big deal, right?" She choked on a hysterical laugh. "I didn't know what he was really doing. I had no idea it had anything to do with you, or the scholarship, or anything. I swear. The police wouldn't let me talk to anyone. My parents wouldn't let me take calls or see anyone from school except TJ." She shook her head. "No one told me about the others. When I read about them in the paper, I told him I didn't want any part of this."

"Shut up!"

Emily clutched her bruised arm to her side. "But then he told me I was already part of it. He said it was too late to change my mind, and if I didn't keep quiet, he would kill me too."

"Listen and do what I tell you!" he snapped. Emily cried into her sleeve and nodded tightly.

He held a blue lab marker in one hand, bit off the cap, and spit it onto the ground. He tossed the marker to Emily. "Mark her. Just like we talked about." Emily's hand was shaking as she drew up my sleeve. The point was wet and cold where she marked me with the letter *L*, upside down, as if I'd drawn it myself.

TJ jerked his chin toward Jeremy and Oleksa. "Now go get your car and bring it to the closest lot you can find. I've got to get those other two out of here. Leigh will take care of Whelan and Anh for us."

I sucked in a shocked breath and looked down at their

bodies. They were still alive. And TJ was going to make me kill them.

I struggled against the arm still wrapped around my neck. TJ's breath was hot and ragged against my cheek.

"When they open the box and find you, will you be dead or alive? In the end, you can't be both." He cupped my chin in his gloved hands, bringing my head back hard against his chest and pressing the gun to my temple, his cheek against mine.

His jealousy and hatred surged through me, putrid and thick and choking. There was a gut-turning sweetness to it, a self-satisfied delight as he drew the barrel over my skin.

"It was your father," I said, trying to calm the tremors in my voice. "Your father went to prison because of mine. That's why you moved to Sunny View five years ago, isn't it? My father set him up, let him take the fall. And mine got away with the money. You blame him for what happened to your dad. And to your mom. You think it's his fault that you have to live in Sunny View. That's what this is about, isn't it? Revenge."

TJ dragged the barrel down my cheek. "Do you know why my mother killed herself?"

My tongue felt thick and I swallowed hard. "Why?"

"Because she was afraid. Because she was terrified of being alone. She locked herself in her fucking Saab two weeks after my dad went to prison. Slugged down a fifth and took the easy way out. She was a goddamn quitter." He laughed, cold and low in my ear. "But the game isn't over yet. Not for me."

"So you're going to kill me? Do you seriously think you'll get away with it? That anyone would believe I could do something like this?"

TJ laughed low in his throat. "Couldn't you, though? Mommy's a stripper. Daddy's a felon. Money's tight. Best friend's a head case. Nobody sees you. Nobody cares. And all this time you're giving a leg up to a bunch of losers who can't even count change in the lunch line. Who *wouldn't* believe you could snap? That you'd want the recognition? The attention? The power? Then all these bodies start piling up . . ."

I felt TJ swallow, felt the sweat bead down his cheeks as he went on. "You know the cops are coming for you, so you freak out. Shoot yourself. And it's all so cut-and-dry, who's going to bother looking at anyone else." He plucked the envelope on my chest. "They'll read your suicide note and think you killed Anh for the scholarship. What other options did you have? Community college? Student loans for the next twenty years? Don't tell me you never thought about it. Never wanted to get out so bad you could taste it. Never thought about pushing sweet little Anh under a fucking school bus so you could take that money and run."

"Never."

"Well, I did!" he shouted. "I thought about it every day!

I've *hated* you every day since I moved into that goddamned trailer! My uncle told me to let it go. That it wasn't your fault. That nothing would bring her back. He told me to take it all out on the game, to play hard and focus on my scholarship. That was the only way out. But then I got benched, and by the time I got out of that damn brace, I'd missed my one shot. Even if I come back next fall, I've lost my ranking with the scouts. Recruiters don't care if it's healed. No one's giving a scholarship to a kid with a knee injury." He kicked the back of my knee, making me falter, and dragged me up again by the hair.

"And then a couple months ago, I find out Emily's messing around with my best friend, sneaking around the golf course at night and giving it up in the back of his fifty-thousand-dollar car. And that's when it all sinks in. I've got nothing left. Your family took it from me. That should have been *my* car. *My* girl. *My* life!" he shouted, shaking me. "But your father made me just like you! Every time I look at you, it's like a vial of acid breaking. I refuse to rot in a goddamn box alone!"

His chest heaved. "You made it so easy, Boswell." He laughed, high and nervous. "I watched you read those stupid ads every Friday morning. So pathetic. So I figure, what better way to get your attention than put the bait where I know you'll see it? Then it was just a matter of pointing it all back to you."

"Here's news for you," I said, stiffening against him. "The cops have a new list of suspects, and I'm not on it."

TJ shifted his weight. Adjusted his grip in my hair. "What do you mean? What list?"

I felt him turn toward the shadows where Emily had disappeared.

"A list of buyers who bought ketamine."

TJ's laughter echoed through the graveyard. "Lonny's list? Guess what? I'm not on it either. But I bet Vince is. I stole the ketamine from Vince's locker. He's been buying roofies for months. How else do you think an asshole like Vince gets laid so much? He's got so much shit stashed in his locker, he never noticed anything was missing. The cops can have Vince. They've got nothing on me."

He fidgeted, searching the dark.

"Where's Emily?" I asked.

"Emily does what I tell her." It sounded like a mantra, like if he said it enough, it might be true.

"It was her, wasn't it?" I needled, to keep him talking. "You made her help you. She was the one who called the hospital pretending to be me. The one who bailed Reece out of jail. She was the one who gave him the roofies and stole his apartment key when he passed out. That's how you got into his apartment and took his phone."

"She'll never say a word. She's in too deep. She was the one who put Reece's phone in your backpack this morning at school. She cleared out the girls' bathroom at the amusement park and watched the door while I marked Posie. She signed in to the hospital, pretending to be you. When this is over, the scholarship will be mine. Twenty-five thousand dollars. I can pay Emily back the bail money, and still have twenty grand. Not as much as your dad stole from us, but it's a start. And the bonus is that it gets your boyfriend out of the picture before he can go to the cops."

A knife twisted inside me. Gruesome images of Kylie and Marcia and Posie flashed in my head. "What are you going to do to him?"

"Me? I don't plan to do anything. But you're going to kill him," he laughed. "Anh too."

It was over. My name had been spelled out in symbols from the periodic table. The set-up was in place. Emily would be back any minute and put the next play in motion. I had to do it now, before anyone else got hurt, including her.

"TJ," I said, fighting the quake in my voice. "Emily's probably gone. You saw how freaked out she was. She probably called the cops. She's probably already told them everything. She's scared. They'll know the truth."

I could taste the conflict inside him. The doubt as he looked back in Emily's direction. She wasn't there. The gun dug into my temple.

"You don't have to kill anyone else," I said as steady as I could. "Take my backpack. There's five thousand cash in it.

It's yours. Plus a ticket to California. You can leave. Run before the cops get here." I jerked my backpack off my shoulder, ignoring his faltering hand and unzipping the pouch. I tossed it, green rolls spilling to the ground. The gun wavered.

"You're wrong," TJ said, jerking me hard to make a point. "It's not just about the money. It's about making you pay! My life meant something!"

"So does Anh's," I cried. "So does Reece's. So does mine! You don't get to decide whose life is expendable!"

"Did you forget? I'm not the killer? *You* are." TJ swung his arms around me and locked my wrists in a painful grip. With cautious precision, he forced the gun into my hand, pressing my bare fingers into place. I struggled and kicked his shins as he leveled my arm at Reece. He was too close, too big, and too strong. If he pulled the trigger, everything I'd done to save Reece would be for nothing. I could taste his resolve settling back into place.

"Eventually they'll solve the puzzle," TJ said, his voice barely straining as he took control of the gun. "The indirect proof. They'll put it all together. They'll find Anh and Whelan. Your prints on the gun. They'll find your suicide note."

My vision blurred with hot tears. I stared down the barrel at Reece's body, wondering how long the drugs worked. When he would wake. Would he open his eyes only to see me pull the trigger?

"Now I'll take from you what your father took from me.

Everything." He leaned in close, sighting over my shoulder, straight to Reece's chest. I locked my knees and pushed back against him, straining to raise my arms. My muscles burned and shook, but his aim was dead on. His finger tightened over mine. I turned my head away from Reece, and shut my eyes so I wouldn't have to see him die.

I held my breath.

"Missing something?" A deep voice cut through the darkness. "I know I am."

TJ startled, loosening my finger on the trigger.

"Step away from the girl, drop the gun, and put your hands where I can see them."

My breath rushed out, relief flooding through me. Emily watched, tear-streaked and wide-eyed from a few yards away.

Lonny stood behind her.

He pushed Emily forward under the white mausoleum lights, revealing the tip of the knife at her throat.

TJ tensed, hesitated, his grip uncertain. "What the hell are you doing here?"

"Looks like I'm late to the party, Boswell. I came as soon as I got your message." Lonny's smile was wicked and terrifyingly eager. He teased a trickle of blood down Emily's throat. She whimpered. TJ didn't move.

"Maybe you didn't hear me the first time, Wiles. I said step away from Leigh and drop the gun."

Lonny's smile twisted and Emily cried out.

TJ's hands shook as he released me. My knees gave out, my limbs sagging limply.

He stepped over Reece, steady and sure-footed without his brace. He raised his hand slowly in surrender, the gun still gripped in it. It was over. He couldn't run. He'd have to kill all three of us and that wasn't in his plan. He already had two extra bodies to deal with. His head turned to the rolls of money, uncertain. He bent, eyes fixed cautiously on Lonny while he reached for the cash.

"No." Lonny's sharp command froze TJ where he stood. "Boswell made you a pretty sweet deal, but I have a problem with that. See, I'm still missing something. You owe me, and I'm not feeling so generous." His knuckles whitened around the knife.

TJ drew himself up slowly. "What do you want?"

Lonny yanked Emily's hair back and she sobbed, tears spilling down her face.

A stab of regret unsettled me. I'd called Lonny because he was my last resort. But he hadn't come for me. Lonny was here because my wolf had killed his girlfriend. Lonny was here for revenge.

"You couldn't kill your own girl, but it was easy killing mine, wasn't it?" His voice rumbled deep in his throat. "Was it easier, watching Kylie bleed out in the street after you'd killed the rest of them?" The gun shifted in TJ's hand, his fingers curling and uncurling over the grip.

"Yeah, I get that. See, we're alike that way. I know how it is. How that first one takes you over an edge. Makes you numb to the rest and then it's all, hell, what's one more?" Lonny bared his teeth and jerked Emily's head back hard, blood trickling down her neck. "Now put. The gun. Down."

TJ lowered his arms and Lonny relaxed by a fraction. But I knew something Lonny didn't. TJ didn't care about Emily anymore. She'd become expendable to him the minute he'd seen the photo of her and Vince.

I braced myself. A cold hand slipped under the hem of my jeans and gripped my ankle. A minty calm that wasn't mine poured through me, cooling the instinct to duck or run. Confidence flowed through me and whispered "Trust me."

TJ turned, lightning quick, and leveled the gun at my head. Even twenty feet away, it felt like a solid cold pressure against my skull, but I didn't flinch. I stared down the barrel as he said, "You're right. It does make it easier."

TJ pulled the trigger.

Lonny shouted.

Something rushed at me, stealing my breath.

Pain ripped through my skull.

And my world faded to black.

44

IT'S STRANGE, THE THINGS YOU REMEMBER, but more so the things you forget. I didn't remember the arrival of the police or the ambulances in the cemetery. I didn't remember the handcuffs clicking shut over TJ's and Emily's wrists.

What I did remember was a voice. A frantic and desperate voice, calling my name over and over. A voice I could almost touch with the tip of a finger before the darkness swallowed me whole.

I awoke in an itchy hospital bed. The room was dark, curtains drawn over the window. Electronic monitors beeped near my head. The only clock in the room said it was four. Day or night, I didn't know.

My eyes adjusted, and I saw Mom asleep in a chair at the foot of my bed.

A nurse padded into the room.

"Oh, good. You're awake," she whispered. She wrapped her fingers around my wrist and watched the second hand drift over the clock. Her touch was soothing, like warm herbal tea, and she smelled like baby powder. "How are you feeling?" She checked the monitors and took some notes on a clipboard.

"My head hurts." I prodded a tender line of prickly threads in my hair.

"You've got quite a few stitches back there." The nurse poured water into a foam cup and held the straw while I struggled to sit up. The effort left me nauseated and dizzy. "I'm giving you something intravenously for pain. You probably feel a little fuzzy."

I set my head back against the pillow. The last thing I remembered was TJ's gun. I recalled with sickening clarity the hideous expression on his face when he pulled the trigger. And the peculiar calm before everything exploded.

"Reece!" I sat up too fast. A blinding pain paralyzed me and I breathed slowly through my mouth to keep from being sick. The nurse rushed to settle me.

"Your friends are fine," she coddled, smoothing my panic and straightening my blankets.

"But Reece?"

"They're all fine. You just sleep now." She rested her warm baby powder hand on mine. The pulse monitor slowed, my heart beating steadily. All fine . . . But how?

"Should I wake her?" The nurse inclined her head toward my mother. "She's been here all day. She refused to leave you. I brought her a nicotine patch and a mild sedative to settle her nerves. She finally fell asleep about an hour ago."

I looked at my mother more closely. She wore secondhand sweatpants, her hair in a sloppy ponytail, and my favorite hoodie draped across her like a blanket. Her naked lids were outlined in dark circles and painted with worry. She could have been anyone's mom—a normal, tired, worried-sick mom—but she was mine.

As if she could feel me watching, she stirred and her eyes blinked open.

"I'll leave you two alone," said the nurse, and she quietly padded back out.

My mother sat up and looked at me with an anguished expression. She inched forward in her seat, hesitant and awkward, as if she wanted to touch me, but she wasn't sure how. "When the police came to the house and told me what happened, I thought I'd lost you." She swallowed and took a shaky breath. "It was my fault. I should have told you everything from the beginning. I was just so afraid you'd go looking for him. That you'd leave." She was crying now. Big, heaving sobs that left streaks down her face. "Losing David was terrible, but I managed. But losing you? I could never imagine surviving a loss like that. I told myself I'd never be able to let you go. But it was wrong. I was wrong. You're so smart and so grown-up. I should have trusted you to make your own choices." Her hands shook as she pressed them to her lips, fighting back tears.

I reached for her, held my hand out in the space between us. She looked at it, and then to me. And then she placed her hand in mine. I shut my eyes and felt all the love that had always been there, that I had never let myself feel before. All those things I'd thought my father had taken with him when he left. Everything I needed was here, inside her. "I'm sorry," I said, letting my own tears fall, "if I made you feel like you weren't enough."

She leaned in and placed a delicate kiss on my forehead and a hand over my heart. Her pride—her adoration—was a burst of sweet citrus inside me. "You are, and will always be, your very own person, Nearly. Everything you'll ever need is right in here." She straightened and wiped her eyes. They were red and wet, but creased with smile lines. "I'm going to the cafeteria to find us some junk food. The fat to calorie ratios in this place are seriously disappointing."

We laughed the same laugh. And it felt good.

The door swished shut behind my mom, and then swished open again. The baby powder nurse poked her head in and smiled.

"There's a rather handsome dark-haired gentleman waiting to see you. I told him he couldn't come in until you were feeling up for it. If you want me to ask him to wait . . ."

"No!" I said, louder than I'd intended. "It's fine. He can come in." The nurse helped me elevate the bed and then padded out the door to find my visitor. I wished I had a toothbrush, and I struggled with the IV tubes while I worked my weak fingers through the snarls in my hair, exhausted by the small effort.

The door finally cracked open, and light spilled in from the hall. Every nerve in my body crackled, until Oleksa peeked his head in and surveyed the room. I sunk back into my pillows. He lifted a swollen and bruised brow, as if asking permission to come in. Gena followed, her fingers laced through his, wearing matching badges on lanyards around their necks.

The lanyard rose and fell with Oleksa's chest and my eyes flew open wide, remembering the bullet that ripped through it. How was he still breathing? TJ had shot him in the back right in front of me. I couldn't have imagined it.

"You're alive?"

"Kevlar." He tapped a fist over his chest and winked. "I'm bulletproof." The warmth was completely foreign on the cold face I'd been terrified of for weeks. As was the mysterious disappearance of his heavy Ukrainian accent. Hints of it lingered in his clipped consonants, but his dialect was as relaxed as his smile.

"Leigh Boswell," Gena said, "I'd like you to meet Detective Oleksander Petrenko."

"Call me Alex," Oleksa said casually, as if we were meeting for the first time.

I narrowed my eyes at him. "We've met. I think it was the night *Detective* Petrenko beat up my boyfriend."

An uncomfortable silence shrouded the room as we all interpreted the part I hadn't said aloud. The part I hadn't even admitted to myself until now. I was in love with Reece. Even though it terrified me. I needed him in painful, complicated ways that felt completely illogical and yet one hundred percent right. He was the reason I didn't get on that train—the one person I couldn't leave behind.

Oleksa cleared his throat and lowered his eyes, giving the blood in my cheeks time to settle. "Whelan had that one coming," he said a little defensively.

"As far as I'm concerned, that assault charge is on you, sweetheart." Gena smirked at him. "You threw the first punch. What did you expect him to do?"

"Reece almost got you killed that night. If Ryan Whelan hadn't been there, it would have been you in that grave."

Gena rolled her eyes as if she'd heard the story a thousand times. "That was a long time ago, baby. You're just pissed off because he broke your nose."

Oleksa pinched the small knot at the bridge of his nose and took a long slow breath.

"I knew it." I struggled to sit up. "You're the lady cop. The one Ryan saved."

Gena's glossy smile was bittersweet. "Ryan was a good kid," she said softly.

I looked at their clasped hands, Lonny's story slowly coming back to me through the fog. *He was only supposed to serve six for the drug charges, but rumor has it that the lady cop's boyfriend came after him during the trial, and Reece got an extra three months for assaulting an officer.* "And you're the cop Reece assaulted? And the one who carried me out of the rave." It was Oleksa who'd told the cops I was unconscious in the moments leading up to Kylie's murder, persuading the judge not to grant the warrant.

"Like I said, he had it coming." Oleksa's face grew serious. "Whelan is dangerous. What happened last night doesn't change anything."

"What exactly did happen last night?" I touched the back of my head. "I remember TJ pulling the trigger, and then . . ." The hand on my ankle, the figure that leaped toward me, could only have been one person. "The nurse said Reece is okay?"

"Reece is fine." Gena gave me a reassuring smile. "He was conscious enough to shove you out of the path of the bullet. He knocked you into the mausoleum steps and you hit your head pretty hard. You bled all over and scared him to death. He thought he'd killed you."

"He wasn't hurt?"

"He'll have a pretty sexy scar in his right shoulder." She winked. "But the exit wound was clean. No permanent damage. He's already been discharged."

Gena and Oleksa were quiet while I let that sink in. Reece had taken a bullet . . . for me. Gena had been right about him, though you wouldn't know it from the look on Oleksa's face. I hoped Reece's sacrifice was enough to clear his record, and that the bullet he'd taken was enough to chase away the last of his demons.

Speaking of demons . . .

"And Lonny? He's not in trouble, is he?" For all his ulterior motives, Lonny had been there when I needed him. I shuddered to think what might have happened if he'd shown up a minute later.

"Emily wanted to press charges against him for assault, but we handled it." Gena snickered and cocked a hip. "And she had the nerve to ask for her five thousand dollars of bail money back, but she posted it under your name. There's no way she can prove the money was hers without incriminating herself more than she already has."

Oleksa chimed in. "We're calling Lonny's actions a citizen's arrest. Emily and TJ are both in custody. No charges have been filed against Lonny, for now."

"And it might help smooth over a few bumps on his record if he can stay out of trouble," Gena added.

"Seriously unlikely," Oleksa muttered.

Gena pointed to the chair where my mother had been sleeping. My backpack rested against it, a long-stemmed black rose balanced on top.

"Lonny came by to see you earlier, but you were still sleeping. He said you left your bag at the cemetery. He told me to tell you 'it's all there'—whatever that means—and that he'll collect on the favor when you're feeling better." Gena lifted an eyebrow. She was good at passing silent messages. This one seemed to say: "Don't go there, girlfriend."

I suppressed a smile. I'd be lying if I said Lonny didn't scare me anymore, but I'd come to realize that he wasn't so black-and-white either.

"And Jeremy? He's okay?"

Gena and Oleksa exchanged a quick glance and my heart squeezed.

Oleksa dipped into the pocket of his cargo pants and tossed a plastic pouch onto my lap. "Jeremy's in the room next door. He asked me to bring you these."

I didn't register the Twinkies. Gena was first to speak. "A crisis counselor is with him now."

"Crisis counselor?" I asked through dry lips. "Why does he need a crisis counselor?"

Gena opened her mouth, then shut it again. Oleksa gave her hand a quick squeeze, answering for her. "During our investigation, Lonny informed us that Jeremy bought a fairly large bag of ketamine. Obviously, he never intended to hurt anyone else, but . . . " Oleksa faltered. "We're concerned he may have intended to harm himself."

I dropped my head back against the pillow. Shut my eyes. Listened to the beep of the monitors as the IV feed shot me with another dose, grateful for the woozy blur that smoothed away the worst of the pain. Of all the answered questions, this one tore the largest hole in my heart.

Gena and Oleksa turned to go.

"Get some rest," he said. "Someone from Nicholson's office will be coming soon to take your statement."

• • •

Something warm pressed into my hand. My lids fluttered open at the brush of lips over my forehead. Not soft, like my mother's. Scratchy whiskers tickled my skin. My eyes adjusted to the dim light. Reece's face hovered over me, his tired eyes shadowed under a chaotic mess of hair.

I inhaled deeply, not caring that he wasn't showered or shaved. The smell of his jacket was warm and reassuring. I crushed it between my fingers and it creaked as he settled next to me on the bed.

"Sorry it took me so long to get here. I can't ride my bike, so I'm stuck taking the bus." He shrugged his right shoulder. His jacket hung limp under the empty sleeve. "I would have called, but you keep losing this at very inconvenient times." He tapped my hand where it curled around his phone.

"I'm just glad you're okay." I shut my eyes, the gunshot still echoing in my head.

"It'll heal. I got released this morning, but you were sleeping. I've been at the station all day getting my ass chewed by the lieutenant." He brushed the hair back from my face. "I nearly missed you. They're getting ready to send you home. I came as soon as I could."

"Why?" I asked.

"What do you mean, why? Because I wanted to see you." Reece's shoulders sagged. "And I wanted to give you these." He opened his jacket. His right arm was bound tight to his chest and wrapped in a blue sling. His hand spilled over with purple thistles. "I thought you might like them."

I smiled behind the bouquet. "That's not what I meant. Not, why did you come." I liked to think I knew why he was there. "Why did you get your ass chewed?"

"Oh, that," he said, dismissing it with a wave of his good arm. "I'm in a little hot water for interfering with a homicide case that I shouldn't have been involved in. But I wouldn't have done anything differently, so it doesn't matter."

"Wait, I don't understand. You're in trouble for protecting me?" I sat up, the monitors jumping in response to my heart rate. "That's ridiculous! They told you to follow me, and I wasn't guilty—"

"Calm down, it's okay." He glanced at the monitors and pressed me back to the mattress with a firm hand to my shoulder. Then drew it down to trace a finger over the naked skin where his pendant used to be. His touch was tender and sweet. "Do you remember when you asked me why I was following you?"

I nodded, his finger tracing slow patterns over my heart.

"I never followed you because I had to, or because I thought you did anything wrong. I did it because I care about you."

He shifted, reaching behind his head to unclasp his pendant. When his hand found mine, the silky metal chain, warm from his body, spilled into it. He threaded our fingers together. He felt different. Peaceful.

I leaned forward and let him fasten the thistle around my neck.

"There's something I've been meaning to ask you . . ." His eyes flicked nervously to mine. ". . . About the ads."

"What about them?" I asked, ready to tell him the truth.

"Before this all started . . . before TJ started writing the ads . . . what were you looking for? In the personals, I mean." I'd never heard Reece stammer before, never heard him sound unsure of himself. A twinge of jealousy leeched through our joined hands. He wasn't asking me about my father. My cheeks warmed.

"I'm not sure really," I said, thinking back to the way Friday mornings felt before TJ's first ad. "But I think maybe I've found it."

He leaned in slowly, tilting his head to brush his lips against mine. Every rule, every shred of hesitation I'd felt before, dissolved away. I wanted him, every part of him, and we could mess with outcome later.

Reece grinned and pulled back too quickly. "Oh yeah? And what about the no touching thing?"

I wrapped my arms around his neck and pulled him in. "It was a shitty rule anyway."

His mouth moved to my chin and kissed a slow trail down. "What are you going to do now?" I asked.

"Make out with you." His voice was a deep purr and it tickled my neck.

"That's not what I meant." What I meant to ask was where he would be and when I would see him again, but it was hard to concentrate. The beeping of the monitors picked up speed and the screen flashed with irregular peaks. I tugged his jacket and slid over, making room in the bed.

As if reading my mind, he said, "I can't stay." But his kiss said otherwise. He eased down into the bed, careful of his sling and my tubes, though neither one of us wanted to be careful. "I have to get back to the station. I'm getting transferred."

"Transferred?" I pushed him back so I could see his face, hoping I didn't sound as clingy as I felt. "To where? Summer break already started."

He shrugged carelessly, preoccupied with my lips. "Nicholson's making me go to summer school. Says I've got to make up all the classes I've missed." More kisses. "We sort of made a deal."

"A deal?" I raised an eyebrow and pulled away, leery of any deal Nicholson proposed.

Reece gave my lips another longing glance and sighed. "They expunged the assault and battery charge, but now I've got the whole obstruction of justice thing to worry about. I agreed to stay on as a narc. One year in exchange for dropping the charges."

Summer school, transfers, a whole year apart. He grabbed my chin in his unbound hand and leaned in for one deep lasting kiss. It felt like a good-bye and the pulse monitor beeped erratically.

"Now get some rest," he ordered, planting a final peck on my head as he left.

Not likely, I thought, still prickling with adrenaline and wondering when I'd see him again. He was halfway out of the room and my insides dropped like I was falling.

"Reece!" I called out. He paused at the door. I hardly noticed the differences in the two sides of him anymore. He was whole and I was complete when I was with him. Somehow, we balanced. "In case I don't see you, thanks for . . ." The best kiss of my life, defending my honor, making me feel beautiful for one night of my life, giving me a reason to stay and fight. I settled for ". . . everything."

His wicked smile stretched wide across his face. "Oh, you'll definitely see me again. That's the other part of the deal. Nicholson can make me go to summer school—" He bit his lip, giving me a top-down look that made me warm all over. "But I get to pick my tutor."

Epilogue

THE TRAILER WAS DARK when I woke Friday morning. I took out the photo of my father from under my mattress. I hadn't yet come to terms with the man my father was, or the lives he'd destroyed. But I accepted that he was part of me, and that he'd loved me once. That neither his name nor his gift would ever define me. I was independent of anything my father might have been or had become. Independent of what my mother expected or wanted me to be. I wasn't *nearly*. I was *enough*.

The window air conditioner droned too loudly in the cramped space, like the static thoughts inside my head. Still numb, from my skin to the deep solitary places inside myself, I slumped into a formless secondhand T-shirt and my frayed sneakers, scraped out a few dollars of Mom's cookie cash, and headed out into the glare of an otherwise gray day. It would take time before my world felt sunny and whole again. It would take time before I would feel at all.

Jeremy hadn't called, and I hadn't seen Anh since the cemetery. I'd been out of the hospital almost a week, and there'd been no sign of Reece. Mom had the decency not to say "I told you so." But when I left the house that morning, I knew she was thinking it.

It was a poor substitute for Reece, but ironically, there I was, the bells on the door ringing as I crossed the threshold of the Bui Mart, Mom's tip money clenched in my hand.

I took a deep breath and stepped inside. There was no music, just the hum of the freezers and the churn of the slushie machines. Bao didn't look up, barely acknowledging me with a dip of his head. The counter was empty.

I could forget it, I thought. Leave without my newspaper and never come back. But more than forgetting, I wanted everything to be like it was. Once the details of the case became widely known, Anh's family made it clear that I should have gone to the police from the beginning. That maybe, if I had, Anh never would have been abducted in the first place. They blamed me. For the deaths. For Anh's suffering. For everything. Somehow, even though I *had* gone to the police after the second clue, even though I'd proven my innocence, she'd won the scholarship, and we'd all managed to survive, I was still the bad guy. I'd learned the hard way that sometimes, when people are hurting, they just need someone to blame.

I paid Bao my usual amount. He looked at the bills like I'd scraped them off the floor at Gentleman Jim's. I wanted to tell him to keep the change, but he counted it out precise to the penny, setting the coins on the counter instead of in my hand, his eyes cast down. Never on mine.

When I got home, the trailer was quiet. Mom's breathy snores whispered through the thin walls of her room. I took the newspaper to my bedroom but didn't lock the door.

I wasn't sure what I expected when I thumbed to the *Missed Connections* that morning. I didn't need to know where my father was, or even if he was thinking of me. I knew there'd be no mysterious ads today, and yet I couldn't seem to find peace in Reece's absence, or comfort in the fact that it was all over.

I scanned the ads quickly. One particular ad tugged at me, unexpected, and yet somehow familiar. My heart skipped as I read, and a peculiar feeling fluttered in the pit of my stomach.

Bad element seeks Nearly perfect girl.
I need you. Pick u up at 6.

Acknowledgments

I am grateful for the support of so many people who have guided me through this journey. First and foremost, my extraordinary agent, Sarah Davies, who pulled Nearly from the slush pile and pushed me to make her better. Thank you for believing in me before I believed in myself, for taking my hand and venturing down an uncertain road together.

For my GeNiUS editor, Kathy Dawson, who saw through the almost in Nearly to the everything she could be. I am so, so lucky. And for the entire team at Penguin and Kathy Dawson Books: Claire Evans, Regina Castillo, Greg Stadnyk, Nancy Leo-Kelly, and Penguin's fantastic sales and marketing teams. Thank you all for bringing Nearly to life.

Special thanks to Lydia Kang, for her medical expertise regarding nasty acids and chemical burns.

To my earliest readers, Tessa Elwood and Tamara Ireland Stone, who fell in love with Nearly in her infancy and encouraged me to go on. And my critique partners, without whom this book would still be a mess of sticky notes and red lines on my floor. Ashley Elston, Tessa Elwood, and Megan Miranda—you made me laugh, pulled me off the ledge, and made me a better writer. I've learned so much from each of you.

It takes a village to write a book with young children in tow. Special thanks to Mary Behre, for taking my children out when I needed to write, and for taking me out when I needed a break. And for our Paamul friends, who welcomed our family with open arms, and encouraged and supported me.

To my parents, for building a writing room in a tree house in the jungle, and telling me to "go write a book." I could never have achieved this dream without you.

To my brother, Shannon, for his service to our country, and for sacrificing to protect the freedoms I enjoy.

To Connor, for always believing, and Nicholas, for always asking why. I am stronger and wiser because of you.

To Tony, for supporting every crazy dream I chase, even when I turn our world upside down. I love you.

About the Author

Elle Cosimano grew up in the Washington, DC, suburbs, the daughter of a maximum security prison warden and an elementary school teacher who rode a Harley. She spent summers working on a fishing boat in the Chesapeake Bay, baiting hooks, scrubbing decks, and lugging buckets of chum. A failed student of the hard sciences, she discovered her true calling in social and behavioral studies while majoring in psychology at St. Mary's College of Maryland. Fifteen years later, Elle set aside a successful real estate career to pursue writing. She lives with her husband and two sons in Northern Virginia.

Elle is a member of the Society of Children's Book Writers and Illustrators, Mystery Writers of America, International Thriller Writers, and Sisters in Crime. She was selected for the 2012 Nevada SCBWI Agented & Published Authors' Mentorship Program, where she worked under the guidance of Ellen Hopkins. She annually attends the Writers' Police Academy at Guilford Technical Community College, Department of Public Safety, to conduct hands-on research for her books. You can learn more about Elle at her website: www.ElleCosimano.com.